Trends & Issues
IN MODERN MISSIONS

A Survey of Nine Key Issues
in Contemporary Missions

Don Fanning

Forest, Virginia

First Edition 2011

Published by
Branches Publications
1985 Colby Dr.
Forest, Virginia 24551

© Copyright: Branches Publications
Don Fanning

All rights reserved

All parts of this publications are protected by copyright. Any utilization outside the strict limits of the copyright law, without the permission of the publisher, is forbidden and liable to persecution. This applies in particular to reproductions, translations, microfilming, and storage and processing in electronic retrieval systems.

Contents

Chapter 1	Brief History of Methods and Trends of Missions	5
Chapter 2	Holism: Serving the Whole Person	43
Chapter 3	Tentmaking, Platform Ministries and NGOs	55
Chapter 4	Partnership and Dependency	83
Chapter 5	Short Term Missions	115
Chapter 6	Contextualization	155
Chapter 7	Church Planting Movement	189
Chapter 8	Church-Based Leadership Training	207
Chapter 9	Chronological Bible Storying/Teaching	239

Chapter 1

Brief History of Methods and Trends of Missions
How did we get to where we are today, and
what can we learn from the past?

Although in this short space we can never treat all the trends and paradigm shifts that have occurred throughout the history of the Church this chapter will introduce the major shifts in strategy and methodologies of doing missions since the beginning of the Church.

The major divisions of Church history to be discussed will be:
Ante Nicene: 100-325
Post Nicene: 325-500
Medieval and Renaissance Missions: 500-1792
Great Century of Mission Pioneering: 1792-1910
Century of Technological Missions: 1910-Present

I. Ante-Nicene Mission Efforts 100-325

The Early Church initially spread among only the Jews until after Acts 11:19 or about 20 years after the resurrection, and then the gentiles began to dominate the Christian church becoming more unique and varied than when controlled by early Jewish Christian leaders. As the gospel spread and churches were established throughout Asia Minor, Palestine, North Africa, Greece, Macedonia, Cyprus and Rome. The impact was soon to reach a "critical mass" when persecution was ineffective to stop the growth of the numbers of followers.

Not only do we depend on the writings of the NT, but also the early writings of the Early Church leaders to understand the spread of the gospel. Tradition says Thaddeus went to Edessa, Mark to Alexandria, Peter to Bithynia and Cappadocia, Paul to Spain, and Thomas to India. No one was ordering these men to spread out sharing the gospel. They just took on this responsibility willingly.

"The strength of this witness, however, was uneven. The strongest areas were Syria, Asia Minor, North Africa, and Egypt, with a few other noteworthy cities such as Rome and Lyons. Village people in most areas were largely untouched." (Shelley, 1995, p. 32)

Local churches were small and able to meet in homes, but multiplied rapidly. Presbyters and deacons lead multiples of these small groups, while Bishops were responsible for the multiplication of leaders of these small groups or house churches. Their focus was the writing and training of multiple leaders.

Much of their writings have survived, detailing their apologetic defense of Christianity against heresy and governmental false accusations.

By the end of 1st century, there was an estimated 100 city churches, mostly Greek-speaking, meeting in thousands of homes throughout these major cities. Copies of the OT and NT were few and mostly incomplete until the third or fourth century when the canon was finally complied. Many false books claimed to be part of the Bible, so finally the united church council made the list of recognized inspired book official, condemning any other as false. Meanwhile, the gospel spread throughout this period mostly by oral teachings, probably similar to the Chronological Bible Storying of modern times.

Factors of Growth

The Roman road system gave the ability to walk on pavement throughout the empire and created a mapping system for navigating across countries.

In a wild environment with little law, safety of travel was secured by the *pax romana*, "Roman Peace," through the universal military presence enforcing strict laws against sedition and marauding. Cairns states that freedom of travel would have been difficult for evangelists before Augustus Caesar (27 BC- AD 14), who swept the Mediterranean of pirates, and soldiers protected the roads primarily for commerce, but coincidentally opened the opportunity for spreading the gospel.

As English is the universal language today, so Greek was in the first centuries. Although every region had their own dialect (i.e., there were 19 mentioned in Acts 2 from among the Jews at the Feast of Pentecost who lived in these regions), but the common Greek language gave unity and ability to communicate (even if this were a second language or trade language).

With the Roman conquests local people lost confidence in their gods since they were not able to protect them from the Romans. The Roman gods were little different from the local ineffective gods, but anything associated with Rome was respected.

Pagan mystery religions gave adherences an emotional or mystical experience, which became the chief rival of Christianity. "The worship of Cybele ... goddess of fertility had in its rites ... the drama of the death and resurrection of Cybele's consort, Attis, that seemed to meet the needs of the people." There were similar expressions with Isis, imported from Egypt, Mithraism, from Persia, each with parallel resurrections and saviors (Cairns, 1981, p. 37). These became the chief competitors for the gospel. Mysticism would eventually infiltrate into Christianity and distort it's truth-based foundation.

Greek philosophy provided intellectual concepts that Christianity could use as a bridge for transmitting truth as well as for destroying older religions. Polytheistic religions became rationally unintelligible, but philosophy could not meet the spiritual needs, so one either became a skeptic or sought comfort in the mystery religions of the Roman Empire ... namely Stoicism or Epicureanism (Cairns, 1981, p. 39). Philosophy focused on a subjective individualism for personal truth, by the destruction of their ancient superstitions, while creating a love of new truth, yet revealing the inability of human reason to reach God.

Jewish synagogues were everywhere teaching the values of a sound spiritual monotheism, thanks to the remnant groups from the Jewish captivities, 722 BC of Assyria and the Babylonian captives 606 thru 586 BC. The surviving remnants were called the *diaspora*. They taught that a personal God would hold them accountable for their sins, but that He also wanted a relationship with every people because He provided a way to cover their guilt if people could hear of His promise and trust in His Word. .

The Scriptures were proven again correct that God's perfect timing makes no mistake, "But when the fullness of the time came, God sent forth His Son, born of a woman, born under the Law" (Galatians 4:4)

2nd Century Dynamic Growth

Wherever the roads went the gospel spread along the Roman Road system just as when the British built the train system in 1890s in Argentina. The Christian workers from England planted Plymouth Brethren churches in every town.

In the Early Church the evangelists were Greek speaking, then a few centuries later they were Latin speaking, which appealed to educated and upper class. The main opposition during this period was a growing Gnosticism, which emphasized the spiritual over the material, virtually denying the humanity of Christ and focusing on a higher level of "spiritual" or mystical knowledge.

> "Many Gnostics recognized a kind of proletariat and bourgeoisie of heaven. The lower spiritual class lived by faith and the upper class, the illuminated or the perfect, lived by illuminated knowledge. Still a third group, the spiritually disadvantaged, were not capable of *gnosis* ("knowledge") under any circumstances. Some capricious deity had created them without the capacity to "see" even under the best guru." (Shelley, 1995, p. 52)

Many of the Gnostic influences would find their counterpart in Christianity for centuries. Their appearance of super-spirituality deceived many. Gnosticism was a challenge from without, but also from within a new challenge pushed the Church to formalize the conclusion of God's revelation: Montanism.

Montanus' doctrine of the new age of the Spirit suggested that the Old Testament period was past, and that the Christian period centering in Jesus had ended. The prophet claimed the right to push Christ and the apostolic message into the background. The fresh music of the Spirit could override important notes of the Christian gospel; Christ was no longer central. In the name of the Spirit, Montanus denied that God's decisive and normative revelation had occurred in Jesus Christ (Shelley, 1995, p. 65).

Many of these concepts have infiltrated again into the Church in the twentieth century. The combination of mysticism, Gnosticism and Montanism has brought many to seek for a fresh revelation virtually discarding the value of the inspired text of the Apostles. The popularity of these movements, however, brought many from paganism and secularism into the sphere of the gospel knowledge, albeit with a strong mystical focus.

What a brutal world it was in which the Christian virtues were displayed! It was a world where an emperor's son celebrated his birthday by watching animals tear people apart in the arena; where married life was usually dysfunctional; where promiscuity, temple prostitutes, and homosexual practice were common; where the population decreased for the first three centuries of the Christian Era (simply because the world was too miserable a place to raise children); where many newborn daughters were exposed and left to die that men greatly outnumbered women; where callous enslavement of conquered peoples supported the lifestyle of the elite few. Even their religious practice was abhorrent: Roman deities did not promote morality among their followers but rather lewd, occult rites and costly ceremonies (Blincoe, 2003, p. 100).

There is a hint of the size of the church in Eusebius' letter at AD 251: he lists 46 presbyters; 7 deacons; 7 sub deacons; 42 clerks; 52 exorcists, and readers; 1,500 widows and needy in the church of Rome. Estimates approach 30,000 members (Eusebius 1984:265). If this church could exist in such an environment of fear and corruption then it could survive in any circumstance.

Kenneth LaTourette, church historian, states that Christianity was active in all provinces of Empire before the beginning of the third century.

3rd & 4th Century—Less Dynamic Growth

Emperor Diocletian inherited an Empire in decay and acted decisively to end any type of anarchy. Two years before the end of his 20 year reign he decided suddenly that Christians needed to be purged from the Empire and began the worse persecution in Roman history. Diocletian's Edict of Persecution in AD 303 was continued under Galerius. His tactics became so gross that the population became more sympathetic towards the Christians. Finally Galerius issued an edict of toleration in his last official act in AD 311. It is estimated that 15,000 died as martyrs, and some recanted Christianity under torture, as did the Bishop of Rome.

In the struggle for control of the Empire, Constantine won a decisive battle against Maxentius outside of Rome when he saw, in a dream, "In this sign conquer." He attributed his victory to the God of Christianity, so in AD 312 he issued his Edict of Tolerance for Christianity. Dreams have played an interesting role in the lives of men and women.

The enemies of the Empire usually came from the east or northeast, and now Constantine's new religion was based in the east, so it became natural to move the capital out of corrupt Rome to rebuild it on new principles. With the enormous dislocation of the economic center of the Empire, a political vacuum was left in Rome.

The Edict of Milan AD 313 made Christianity the unofficial state religion (Kane 1975:32). From outlaw to favored child, Christianity suddenly came into power, prestige and respect. All these were for its future. This would change everything from theology to morality of the Church.

In 380 emperor Theodosius made belief in Christianity a matter of imperial command:

> "It is Our Will that all the peoples we rule shall practice that religion which the divine Peter the Apostle transmitted to the Romans. We shall believe in the single Deity of the Father, the Son, and the Holy Spirit, under the concept of equal majesty and of the Holy Trinity.
> We command that those persons who follow this rule shall embrace the name of Catholic Christians. The rest, however, whom We adjudge demented and insane, shall sustain the infamy of heretical dogmas, their meeting places shall not receive the name of churches, and they shall be smitten first by divine vengeance and secondly by the retribution of Our own initiative, which We shall assume in accordance with divine judgment (Shelley, 1995, pp. 96-97).

This occurred in spite of the fact that "the Christians represented not more than 10 percent of the total population" (Kane, 1978, p. 35). As a result of this edict for over a thousand years the Roman Church began to hunt down any dissident "heretic" to torture and kill them.

Now men no longer had the opportunity to study the biblical evidence and allow the Spirit to guide them to trust its promises in faith. Now it was a matter of merely swearing allegiance to the Roman religion, no matter what one really believed, or be expelled or killed. "Evangelism" would mean to conquer forcefully. The declaration of Theodosius would become the legal basis of the Inquisition a thousand years later!

Special characteristics of Early Church: Bishops

"Bishops" continued the itinerate work of the apostles and prophets, among house churches in urban areas. In this period the Bishops "grew up" the work, that is, they did the initial evangelism, training and organization. They were the founders of the Roman Church in a region. As it grew, they grew in power and prestige. Later Bishops would be assigned to a territory where none existed; though there may have been a few Christians. Then they would be expected to develop a metropolitan church in an area that they had been assigned. *Presbyters* would pastor the smaller local church bodies under the Bishop's supervision and authority. Instruction would continue until they could elect their own presbyters and bishops.

Gregory Thaumaturgos was appointed bishop of Pontus (S. coast of Black Sea in N. Turkey) about AD 240. Tradition says that he started with a congregation of 17, and died with only 17 unconverted in the city.

The British Isles was probably won to Christ through Christian soldiers and merchants. The Celtic ascetic monk and reformer, Pelagius (AD 354-440), was a proponent of free will, defined as original sin did not affect human nature, and the human ability to choose to overcome sin without Divine help. He taught that man has full control and thus full responsibility for his own salvation, and/or full responsibility for every sin. Because man does not require God's grace for salvation, Jesus' death did not offer a redemptive quality, but only left us an example to follow. He argued against Augustine of Hippo (AD 354-430) in the deterministic controversy, and represented the Celtic churches in AD 414. Pelagius claimed Augustine was influenced by Manichaeistic beliefs, of which he was a disciple before his conversion, which held to fatalism and predestination that took away all of man's free will. Two extremes of theology were locked in controversy.

Providentially, missionary work among the Goths began with Ulfilas (AD 310-383), bishop, missionary and Bible translator, who brought Arian Christianity[1] to these Germanic tribes just before they overran the Roman Armies. Ulfilas was not only a Bible translator, but he also reduced the Gothic

---

[1] Arianism taught that the Trinity is not one Being, but three. The Son was begotten or created before time began and was in fact the Creator, then the Father working through the Son, created the Holy Spirit who was subservient to both the Father and the Son. This was made famous by Arius (AD 250-336), who taught in Alexandria, Egypt. Eventually the Eastern Church would become Semi-Arian, while the Western Church would maintain the Nicene Creed of the Trinity.

language to writing and giving them the Scriptures in their own language.

When they conquered Rome, just 30 years after Ulfilas' death, they were sympathetic to the Christian church and protected it.

In order to make Christianity more easily acceptable, they substituted celebration feasts for martyrs in place of pagan feasts, which was an accommodation to their former pagan traditions.

Lay Missionaries

Once the Church gained her freedom of expression no longer did they have to keep it a secret. Businessmen carried the gospel on trips; conversations typically included a discussion on Christ, though more often it discussed the Church, especially the Roman Church. Christianity was the topic of the day, since now everyone had to become a Roman Christian, but few knew what it meant beyond baptism. It did not matter. It was the only way to become "civilized."

Roman soldiers and merchants first brought the gospel to Britain until the beginning of the fifth century, when they withdrew to defend the eastern front from invading barbarians. This left the Celtic peoples vulnerable, and most were slaughtered by invasion of the Angles, Saxons, Jutes and Vikings. Those who escaped fled to the western and northern hills of modern day Scotland and Ireland.

Military personnel retired with large estates on the frontier of the Empire, especially in Gaul, to act as a buffer zone, since they were skilled in warfare. Those who were believers opened their estates and homes to Christian meetings. This modified house-church concept often started larger congregational churches, esp. in SW Europe. The wealthier landowners built larger churches and paid the priest.

Missionary Methods

Now that they were free to do so, there was much preaching in public. Those who understood the gospel now faced an extremely difficult task of assuring the genuine conversion of the new multitudes. Every opportunity for conversations about Christ was exploited.

As the new reality set in, many sought opportunities to teach in schools, and develop training schools for presbyters and other church leaders.

Using their homes, without buildings, the congregations divided into cells. This simple methodology was beginning to disappear as soon as the huge Cathedrals became available to the Christians. Soon every church had to model the prestigious Cathedrals.

The gospel spread mostly through oral witnessing, personal testimonies and word-of-mouth sharing of personal faith. Literacy was scarce, especially on the fringe of the Empire.

The Church Fathers utilized their only means of communication: writing literature especially on evangelism, apologies, letters, and polemic discussions of the time. However, this was primarily targeting the elite or educated decision-makers.

Likewise, much time was spent copying Scriptures as the only means of duplicating the texts in Greek, Hebrew and mostly Latin. This process was long, expensive and tedious. Memory was the key means of transmitting the words of the Bible.

There was a public testimony by conduct, trials, or martyrdom of many Christian as well as the leaders before the Edict of Tolerance. After AD 313, there were no public displays of courage or faithfulness, so people looked to the new, popular and prestigious religious leaders instead of to their neighbors on a more public forum. After this date everyone was assumed to be Christians or enemy of the state. Sincerity became difficult to determine.

A notable public testimony was their dedication to show the love of Christ through social service: Harnack lists 10 different ministries from supporting widows and orphans, to helping prisoners and slaves that characterized the early Christians.

Christianity eventually became identified with the Roman Empire, thus to be a Christian, one had to be a Roman, and visa versa. The Christianity that spread throughout the Roman world – Roman-Empire Christianity – only extended to the imperial borders. In order to expand still farther, the gospel message needed to be *de-Romanized*. Not until the faith broke free from its Roman cultural identity would it be able to bless other nations (Blincoe, 2003, p. 101), but this was hard in coming.

II. Missions in Post-Nicene Era (AD 325-500)

The Nicene Council was the first ecumenical conference of bishops, which met to unify the Christian doctrine. If all Romans were obligated to be Christian, then what did Christians believe? It marked a major clarification over the watershed issue (one is either on one side or the other) of the deity of Christ and the nature of the Trinity, as well as the date of Easter. Was Christ God incarnate or a created perfect being, but not eternal?

Constantine presided over the council with the title of *Pontif Maximus*, a title later transferred to the Pope. Arianism would be a conflict for years, but this issue forced the Coptic, Nestorian and Armenian churches to break with Roman Christianity, since they had always been Arian in their beliefs. However, succeeding emperors would seek to reconcile this division with a modified, middle of the road position to unify the empire, especially since many of them were Arian.

The Church experienced great growth within Roman Empire through government involvement and subsidy. Now government tax money paid for huge churches (cathedrals or basilicas) to be built to house the masses. The Roman governorate, the *diocese*, became ruled by a Christian *vicar* (the imperial word for governor).

Approaching pagan tribes presented a challenge that would eventually bring havoc to the Christianity of modern Europe. Meanwhile the isolated pockets in Ireland of an earlier Celtic Christianity in the extreme western part of the Empire would mount missionary ventures back into modern Europe to re-Christianize the newly conquered portions of the Roman Empire.

Constantine identified Christianity with the Empire, thus Christianity became the best way to pacify warlike tribes, so he sponsored the "evangelism" outreaches to the "barbaric" tribes outside the Empire's borders. Eventually this would identify with and become Roman, with becoming a "Christian."

Great preachers in this period made early translations of Scriptures into tribal dialects and benevolent work, which won many to Christianity.

Monasticism and Missions

Monasticism began in the deserts of Egypt probably around AD 318 after Pachomius's model of self-discipline. However, the St. Benedict model became the Roman Catholic model through the Middle Ages. These monasteries so contributed to the religious, economic, educational and governmental life of their day that the years 550 to 1150 can be called the "Benedictine centuries."

The dualistic views of Gnosticism had invaded the Catholic Church teaching as indicated by the emphasis that the flesh is evil and the spirit is good. Thus to crucify the flesh by withdrawal from the world, which was corrupt and sensual, and then to develop the spiritual life by meditation, 18 hours of discipline and ascetic acts every day, were seen as spiritual. The Great Commission often got buried in a self-centered goal of becoming righteous enough to be acceptable to God. Monastic life was a way to earn or merit your salvation. The gospel of God's righteousness as a gift through faith had long been lost in the minds of men and focus of the Church.

> Shortly after the days of the apostles the idea of a lower and a higher morality appeared. ... The New Testament, "The Shepherd" teaches precepts of faith, hope, and love binding upon all. But, it also offers advice for those who aspire to do more than what is required of the ordinary Christian. Soon other Christians sang the praises of self-denial, especially of celibacy -- the renunciation of marriage. Once it was introduced, the practice of penance encouraged acts of

exceptional virtue as a means of removing sin. Thus Tertullian, Origen, Cyprian and other leaders threw their support behind the idea of a higher level of sanctity (Shelley, 1995, p. 118).

However, the purpose of the monasteries was not as much to contribute to culture, as it was to ensure the salvation of its religious members. They took vows to remain in the monastery for life and to be submissive to their superior, because he/she held the place of Christ in the community. They lived a highly regimented life in silence. A monk once confessed to me that he was taught that if he were totally submissive to his Father Superior and accepted by him, then Christ would likewise accept him. Thus there was great fear to be rejected by their religious leader: God would have the same rejection.

Tension eventually arose when some wanted a life of service, while others wanted solitude. Eventually other orders were developed that encouraged interaction with the population. Monasticism became a refuge for those in revolt against the growing decadence of the times.

Too often monasticism merely pandered to spiritual pride as monks became proud of ascetic acts performed to benefit their own souls. As the monasteries became wealthy because of community thrift and ownership, laziness, avarice, and gluttony crept in. Monasticism aided in the rapid development of a hierarchical, centralized organization in the church because the monks were bound in obedience to superiors who in turn owed their allegiance to the pope (Cairns, 1981, p. 155).

Most outstanding evangelist: Patrick of Ireland (AD 389-461)

Patrick began as a lay evangelist, as a captive in war while a teenager. He would later preach to the Irish Chieftains and to crowds in open fields. "He often gave presents of large sums of money to Irish Chieftains in order to obtain their favor. He used great sums of money to buy the freedom of many slaves. (Slavery was so prevalent in Ireland that "one woman" was a monetary unit of measurement)" (Morrison, 2004). Of course, Patrick is famous for explaining the Trinity to the Irish Chieftains with the illustration of the Shamrock with its three-leaf clover. The three are distinct, but not separate.

There were Christians already in Ireland before Patrick, but he organized those already in Ireland and mobilized their outreach by example and emphasis. His organized effort of evangelism and church planting resulted in over 200 churches and converted over 100,000 people (some accounts give 200,000) to Christianity.

It should be noted that Patrick's autobiographical confession was difficult to translate as the grammar was poorly written. In the beginning of his writings he explained how unworthy his writings were, but that he felt compelled to write anyway. The only written language he knew was Latin, which he only marginally knew at best, primarily using it for Catholic rites. Regardless, his efforts are commended as one of the few records of his time. Those with little skill can still change the world.

Following the example of Patrick, the Irish Christians became some of the most daring missionaries and educators in all of history. Leaving their homeland to carry the gospel elsewhere was an important part of the Irish Christian tradition. It should be noted that Patrick was neither Irish nor Catholic. He was a Briton by birth and was part of Celtic Christianity, which in his day was independent from Rome. Later when Celtic Christianity succumbed to Roman Catholicism, but the missionary tradition of the Irish continued through the period of the Catholic Counter-Reformation, over a thousand years later.

Factors of Post-Nicene Expansion

Initially, "conversion" became the Norm—convenience or required for assimilation into the new Empire rather than a bold faith brought about their change. The mass methods of conversion of some these Catholic monks brought mostly nominal Christians into the fold. "If a ruler accepted Christianity, he and his people were baptized whether or not they fully understood the meaning of the act or the implications of Christianity for their lives" (Cairns, 1981, p. 155).

Whatever Constantine's motives for adopting the Christian faith, the result was a decline in Christian commitment. The stalwart believers whom Diocletian killed were replaced by a mixed multitude of half-converted pagans. Once Christians had laid down their lives for the truth; now they slaughtered each other to secure the prizes of the church. Gregory of Nazianzus complained: "The chief seat is gained by evil doing, not by virtue; and the Sees [central government of the Catholic Church] belong, not to the more worthy, but to the more powerful" (Shelley, 1995, p. 118).

Expansion outside the Empire was impeded by Persian Zoroastrianism (in modern Iran), especially when they came to power after AD 228, yet many early Christians reached India, Ceylon, and Arabia. Most of these were the Syrian Christians who were condemned by early councils, thus were eliminated from our "Christian" history, i.e., the Nestorians. These Christians will be discussed later.

The Roman Catholic Church provided an element of stability and security in a disintegrating society. When the Empire divided between East (Constantinople) and West (Rome), most of the leadership left to go to the Eastern Empire. Rome was bankrupt of leaders, so the Bishop of Rome assumed great political and governmental authority over much of modern Italy.

The moral living of Christians showed superiority, but it was not easy to transform. The task of converting these northern peoples was enormous. To bring them to a nominal adherence to Christianity was not so difficult, because they wanted to enter into the grandeur that was Rome. Christianity was, in their eyes, the Roman religion. But to tame, refine, and educate these peoples, to transmit to them the best of the culture of antiquity, to teach them the Christian creed and, above all, to instill in them even a modicum of Christian behavior-- all that was another matter (Shelley, 1995, p. 155).

Zealous missionary activity came especially from the Irish missionaries who re-evangelized Britain after the Saxons destroyed the churches when the Romans left them. Then the Celtic monks continued evangelistic trips to the Continent, again to re-evangelize what was left after the barbarians tribes had brought havoc to the scattered churches and monasteries. The fact that these Celtic missionaries did not recognize the Pope at this time was a disturbing factor in Rome. However, "More than half of the commentaries written between AD 650 and 860 were by Irishmen" (Blincoe, 2003, p. 103).

Demonstrations of the power of the gospel come to us mostly through legends, but were believed and became factors in many conversions. "Many tales circulated about the miraculous powers of the saints. The story was told of two beggars, one lame, and the other blind. They happened to be caught in a procession carrying the relics of St. Martin and were fearful lest they be cured and so deprived of their alms. The one who could see but not walk mounted the shoulders of the one who could walk but not see, and they hurried to get beyond the range of the saint's miraculous powers, but, poor fellows, they failed to make it" (Shelley, 1995, p. 158).

Cairns describes this period of monasticism, which brought admiration by helping the poor and defending the oppressed. Monasticism went through four main stages during the period of its emergence in the Western civilization. "At first, ascetic practices were practiced by many within the Church. Many later withdrew from society to live as anchorites or hermits. Thirdly, a cloister for common exercises or disciplines might be built. And fourthly, organized communal life within a monastery appeared" (Cairns, 1981, p. 152).

Monks, particularly from Britain, became the missionaries of the medieval church. They went out as fearless soldiers of the Cross to found new monasteries, and these became centers from which whole tribes were won to Christianity (Cairns, 1981, p. 155). Most of this was government subsidized for political or territorial reasons.

Neighboring tribes that migrated to the Empire quickly converted in two ways: directly from paganism and indirectly through Arianism, a heresy that denied the eternality of Christ. These tribes liked to think of Christ as a real human and not so eternally divine; He was seen as a glorified warlord. Arian Germans were slow to accept the centralization of religion through Rome.

IV. Medieval and Renaissance Missions (500-1792)

The Roman church became the base of great expansion, but Romanism was in decadence by now. Shelley quotes Pope Gregory around the end of the sixth century as saying,

> "All of Western Europe was in chaos. Serious men ... thought that the end of the world was at hand." [Pope Gregory asks], "What is it that we can at this time delight us in this world? Everywhere we see tribulation, everywhere we hear lamentation. The cities are destroyed, the castles torn down; the fields laid waste, the land made desolate. Villages are empty, few inhabitants remain in the cities, and even these poor remnants of humanity are daily cut down. The scourge of celestial justice does not cease, because no repentance takes place under the scourge. ... If we love such a world, we love not our joys, but our wounds" (Shelley, 1995, p. 166).

Gregory clarified the Catholic message showing that in water baptism God grants forgiving grace freely for Adam's sin without any merit on man's part, but for sins committed after baptism man must make atonement by penance, which is a form of self punishment inflicted by the man on himself. If man punishes himself, then God will withhold His punishment. Forgiveness is seen as three-fold: repentance, confession and meritorious works, which involves personal sacrifice or suffering. The greater our sins the more we must do to make up for them. Sadly, whether one has done enough to atone for his sins cannot know until after death. If insufficient, then the horrible pains of Purgatory await the sinner for a determined sentence of time. With this message the Roman Catholics sought to "evangelize" the world. At least, it is said, if you are baptized, eventually you will make it to heaven. One priest told me, that the appreciation for heaven is proportionate to the length in purgatory!

As the persecution from pagan Rome ceased, in the eastern part of the Empire the Zoroastrian rulers in Persia (Iran) sought to eradicate Christianity in their empire from the middle of the 4th century and continued through the sixth century since any association with Rome was a disadvantage in Persia, China and India.

Nestorius was a Syrian in Antioch who became the patriarch of Constantinople in 428. At that time the rival theological schools of Antioch and Alexandria hotly contested their views concerning the relationship between the humanity and divinity of Christ. The controversy was over the use of the term "Mother of God" to describe the Virgin Mary. Nestorius opposed this term, arguing that it implied Mary was the mother of the whole pre-incarnational Godhead rather than just the human mother of the physical

Jesus. He preferred the term "Mother of Christ".

> The Council of Ephesus, convened in AD 431, was a sad display of petty church politics. It resulted in the excommunication of ... Nestorius ... who went into exile, living out the rest of his life in monastic seclusion until he died. After the verdict of Ephesus, many followers of Nestorius fled to Persia. The Church of the East, struggling to survive in the non-Christian and often hostile Persian Empire ... but they welcomed the Nestorians, not as heretics, but as fellow victims of religious persecution. Eventually the Church of the East officially adopted the Nestorian Christology" (Miller, 2003, p. 112).

Over a thousand years later in the Protestant Reformation, some groups denied the real physical presence of Christ in the communion (transubstantiation) and the communication of attributes between the two natures of Christ, resulting in being e accused of restoring the Nestorian *heresy*.

Providentially, the Persian government gave refuge to the fleeing refugees. Nestorian Christianity reached China by 635, mostly by foot. The Nestorian Stele, set up on 7 January 781 at the capital of Xi'am province, describes the introduction of Christianity to China from Persia. They also reached Mongolia and Korea. In the twelfth century it was one of the widespread religions in the empire of India and China in the time of Marco Polo. Without government subsidy their monasteries were poor and had no political backing or protection.

"For over a millennium, in the centuries between the reign of Constantine and the Protestant Reformation, almost everything in the church that approached the highest, noblest, and truest ideals of the gospel was done either by those who had chosen the monastic way or by those who had been inspired in the Christian life by the monks. ... These monastic movements revived the church and were the source of most missions outreach throughout the 'Dark Ages'" (Blincoe, 2003, p. 103).

However, the missionary gains of the first 500 years were mostly lost to Islam in the Middle East and N. Africa and Buddhism in S.E. Asia.

V. Encounter with Islam (600-1215)

Just after winning over animistic idolatrous tribesmen within the Arabian Peninsula, militant Islam attacked outside Arabia from 630 till 732. During this period most of the Middle East, N. Africa and Spain fell under their control. The options offered to these conquered peoples were to die by the sword, pay a heavy tribute/tax or convert to Islam. The Eastern Church (Constantinople) lost more than the Western Church (Rome), including the loss of Jerusalem. Missionary activity in the East virtually ceased in the defense against the invaders. Nearly all of the Eastern Empire would fall to Islam in the Second Wave of conquest 700 years later, though the Easter Church that spread beyond the Empire to the north and east would survive because it was outside the conquest of Islam.

After sweeping across N. Africa in less than 100 years, in 732 the armies of Charles Martel at the Battle of Tours, in central France, finally stopped the Islamic invasion from Africa from conquering all of Europe through Spain. Charles Martel became the grandfather of Charlemagne who would expand the Frankish (French) realm into an Empire in an attempt to revive the Roman Empire in the West to protect Christianity.

Islam took all of N. Africa in the West to Afghanistan in the East. Islamic rulers imposed the Islamic law (*sharia*), which encompassed all aspects of the lives on their followers, called Muslims ("those who submit" to God's will in the *sharia*). The political control over conquered territory was in the name of the *caliph* (the successor of Muhammad as the supreme earthly leader of Islam). Within a hundred years Muslim conquerors surpassed the achievement of Alexander the Great in a decentralized, but religiously unified empire from Spain to Indonesia. This vast area remains the most unevangelized peoples of the world gripped by fear and hatred toward pagan non-Muslims.

In addition to loosing vast territory to the Muslims, the Eastern Church was enveloped in a series of ongoing controversies within the Catholic Church, namely, which language was sacred for ceremonies (Greek or Latin), were statues or pictures (icons) to be revered in the Iconoclastic Controversy, and which dates were to be sacred days for Easter. The iconoclastic controversy was partly due to the accusations of Islam that Christianity was nothing but idolaters with their statues and images in all the churches.

VI. Christianity mounted a series of Crusades to take back the Holy Lands (1072-1272)

The Roman papacy had enormous authority over the lives of everyone, including kings, in fact, kings derived their powers from the pope!

> The papacy's chief weapon in support of this authority were spiritual penalties. Almost everyone believed in heaven and hell and in the pope's management of the grace to get to one and avoid the other. Thus the pope's first weapon in bringing peasants and princes to their knees was the threat of excommunication. He could pronounce their anathema [*damnation*] and they would be "set apart" from the church, deprived of the grace [rites] essential for salvation. ...
> While under excommunication, persons could not act as judge, juror, witness, or attorney. They could not be guardians, executors, or parties

to contract. After death, they received no Christian burial, and if, by
chance, they were buried in consecrated ground, the church had their
bodies disinterred and destroyed.

The second weapon in the papal arsenal was the "interdict." ... While
excommunication was aimed at individuals, the interdict fell upon
whole nations. It suspended all public worship and, with the exception of baptism and extreme unction, it withdrew the sacraments from
the lands of disobedient rulers (Shelley, 1995, p. 185).

When the Pope promised complete forgiveness and immediate entrance into heaven for anyone killed in the Crusades to retake the Holy Lands from the Muslims, the armies swelled. The passion for a unified Christian Empire included its Holy Lands and the rights to pilgrimages to visit the sites of Jesus' life. "It has been estimated that nearly a million people took part in the activities associated with the First Crusade." (Cairns, 1981, p. 220) There were eight crusades lasting over a period of 200 years, but the results were a failure to accomplish their goals and the Christians were finally expelled from the Holy Lands in 1291.

The Venetian shipping merchants charged exorbitant prices to transport the Crusaders. In order to pay for their travel, occasionally they were ordered to attack several opposition cities, including Constantinople. By their conquest they established a Latin [speaking] Empire of Constantinople in 1204. The defense of the Eastern empire was never the same, and as a result, would fall to the Muslims in 1453 as they crossed over into Europe in a vengeful effort to get even for the atrocities of the Crusades, four hundred years earlier.

The Crusades created a disaster for Christian missions due to cruelties and atrocities committed in the name of Christ by western Christianity that has never been forgotten. This bitterness has not left the region in 900 years and every westerner is blamed today for the slaughters of yesterday.

When Jerusalem was liberated in 1099, the Crusaders, not content
with wiping out the one thousand-man [Muslim] garrison, proceeded
to massacre some seventy thousand Muslims. The surviving Jews
were herded into a synagogue and burned alive. The Crusaders then
repaired the Church of the Holy Sepulcher, where they publicly gave
thanks to Almighty God for a resounding victory (Kane, 1978, p. 54).

In spite of the atrocities of the Crusades, it opened the eyes of Europeans to world travel and more sophisticated and luxurious civilizations than they ever knew existed. The Venetian shipping companies, gaining the Mediterranean trade in silks, spices, sugar, fruits, gems, and perfumes gave rise to enormous business of luxuries that they had seen in the Near East. Nothing in the West ever compared to the luxury of the East.

VII. Reaction and Renewal (1054-1650)

The **Eastern Church** was isolated into pockets and maintained a fortress mentality, defending their views against the Western Catholic Church as well as Muslim accusations. In the East the priests could marry but had to be unshaven. There were differences of opinion on when Easter should be celebrated and especially the iconoclastic controversy. In 730 the emperor removed all images except the cross, in order to refute the Muslim charges of idolatry. To this day there are no statues in the Eastern churches, only icons, or pictures of Christ and the Apostles, which were to be accorded reverence, but not worship. In 1054 the two churches disagreed on the use of unleavened bread in the Eucharist (in the West). The pope issued a decree of excommunication of the Eastern patriarch and his followers, who in turn, at their Synod issued an excommunication to the pope in the West. Missionary work in the East focused toward the north into Bulgaria (864), Russia (955) and much of eastern and central Europe followed the patriarch of Constantinople.

The **Western Church** became the major power, which dominated the political, cultural, economic and religious life of Europe through fear, especially the fear of excommunication. The rise of universities and Scholasticism strengthened the intellectual foundations of papal power, since they controlled it. Monastic reform added to papal power by giving the pope many zealous monks, who were his obedient servants. "It is doubtful whether the papacy has ever exercised such absolute power over all phases of life as it did in medieval Europe during this era. However, it would soon find nationalism in France and England and conciliarism harder to handle." (Cairns, 1981, p. 209)

Such power brought inevitable corruption especially between 1305 and 1517. Coinciding with the unethical practices of fund raising for cathedrals and internal conflicts ("Babylonian captivity"[2] of the papacy and papal schism), the rise of nationalism pulled the loyalties of the people toward their rulers, especially when it concerned the taxes going to Rome. The enforcement of Canon law[3] and submission to a rigid doctrine based on tradition through the cruelties of the Inquisition brought fear, yet rejection and lack of respect from the people.

By the sixteenth century the years of internal battling and bickering, abuses of the masses by the sale of cheap indulgences to raise money for huge

---

2   The Avignon Papacy (1309-1378) when 7 Popes lived in Avignon, (modern) France, where the French kings controlled the Papacy. In 1378 the Papacy returned to Rome, but the French elected their own Pope (called an antipope)
3   Before legislative and judicial concepts of government were developed, the only governing power was the decisions of the rulers. The Roman Catholic Church developed laws ("canons") not only for faith and the Christian life, but for every aspect of life to give order and justice. This, in essence, gave the Pope, as Supreme Pontiff, the totality of legislative, executive, and judicial power in every realm. Pope Gregory IV (1298) is credited with the first collection of canons.

cathedrals and basilicas, and the secularization or sale of religious positions (simony) increased until a reformation movement began—of which, Luther was in the middle.

Roman Catholic Missions

During the age of discovery priests joined the explorers of Spain and Portugal going to the Americas, Africa, Asia and the Far East. The Portuguese focused on Brazil and Africa. One of the most notable was Matteo Ricci's Jesuit mission (1583-1610) to China, which made a revolutionary approach to missions: totally contextualize your life and message. The Roman Church was organized around Religious Orders whose dedicated members were trained and ready for any assignment. Their vows of poverty, obedience and celibacy gave them the most ideal qualities for pioneer missionary work. They had no need to call on or be limited by volunteers.

The priests had fresh images of the Crusades and the Inquisition, which influenced their strategy of applying cruelty and forced conversion techniques on the conquests of the new lands.

Medieval dissidents to Roman Catholic abuses in Europe were suppressed, and documents were destroyed by the **Inquisition**. Forerunners to the Reformation include men like Peter Waldo, John Wycliffe, John Hus, Savonarola and the Brethren of the Common Life. All of whom were severely persecuted as well as were their followers for centuries.

Petrobrusians, Arnoldists, Henricians, Waldensians, Bohemian Brethren, Lollards, Hussites and Taborites all sought biblical authority for faith, and paid dearly for their conviction. "The followers of Wycliffe were suppressed by force in 1401. Thereafter those who held his views went underground and, no doubt, helped to prepare the way for the Lutheran and Calvinistic teachings that invaded Britain about a century later. Bohemians studying at Oxford in Wycliffe's day carried his ideas to their homeland, where they influenced the teachings of John Hus" (Vos). These were brave men willing to suffer to proclaim the Bible truths.

Protestant Reformers (1517-1650)

The Reformation was led by Luther, Zwingli, Calvin and Knox, but all lacked a world vision.
One would naturally expect that the spiritual forces released by the Reformation would have prompted the Protestant churches of Europe to take the gospel to the ends of the earth during the period of world exploration and colonization, which began about 1500. But such was not the case. The Roman Catholic Church between 1500 and 1700

won more converts in the pagan world than it lost to Protestantism in Europe (Kane, 1978, p. 73).

The hermeneutic of the Reformers took Romans 10 and Psalms 19 as the fulfillment of Great Commission. They were consumed with their reforms and personal survival in bitter battles with Rome and among themselves. The Lutherans and Calvinists began battling each other as soon as they split with Rome, instead of uniting against a common enemy. They both thought the other was apostate or heretical. Kane wrote, "The controversy over 'pure doctrine' played a larger role here perhaps than in any other period of church history" (Kane, 1978, p. 74). They were more concerned about maintaining their own territory and their theological distinctives than reaching out to the lost world.

There were Predestinarians, whose preoccupation with the sovereignty of God all but precluded the responsibility of man. If God wills the conversion of the heathen, they will be saved without human instrumentality. If God does not will the salvation of the heathen, it is both foolish and futile for man to intervene. Calvin wrote, "We are taught that the kingdom of Christ is neither to be advanced nor maintained by the industry of men, but this is the work of God alone" (Kane, 1978, p. 74).

The Europeans had limited contact with other religions, so they had little idea of the lostness of the pagan world.

Protestants rejected monasticism, which was the chief strategy of Roman Catholic missionary effort—but no substitute structure similar to the Orders was developed for the first three hundred years after the initiation of the Reformation!

Reformers were very territorial—developed their own state churches to compete with the Roman Catholic churches for control of their populations. They gained political control through city councils. Their armies only protected them within their territories.

Eschatology taught they were in the end times, so long range plans, especially global missionary plans, were not necessary, in fact, it was futile. Wrong thinking cripples the Great Commission time and again.

VIII. Reform and Revival (1650-1792)

Initially Protestantism lacked spiritual depth and had little or no notion of evangelism. Their indifference was partially from their pride as well as from the Protestant version of the Inquisition: no one was ever allowed to dissent or disagree with their teacher's (Luther or Calvin) point of view.

Since this was now the new Protestant state religion, they were content to be right with little or no concern to extend into new territory in the Reformed territories. Everything else was either Catholic or the other Protestant religion anyway.

Pietism sought to renew the spiritual life by small groups, prayer and Bible study, especially in Lutheran churches. "As the Protestant Reformation was a revolt against the false doctrines and corrupt morals of the Church of Rome, so the Pietist movement was a revolt against the barren orthodoxy and dead formalism of the state churches of Protestant Europe." (Kane, 1978, p. 76)

> Pietistic theology can be summed up in a few sentences. There can be no missionary vision without evangelistic zeal; there can be no evangelistic zeal without personal piety; there can be no personal piety without a genuine conversion experience. True religion for the Pietist is a matter of the heart, not the head; hence the emphasis on the cultivation of the spiritual life (Kane, 1978, p. 77).

University of Halle was founded on principles to equip missionaries in godly living and missionary endeavors. The Danish-Halle Mission was the first Protestant mission organization primarily to supply chaplains to minister to the expatriate colonists from their mother country. But the churches mostly criticized the university's efforts and would not support the missionaries.

The most famous graduate of Halle University was Count von Zinzendorf (1700-1760) who gave refuge to the Moravian Church and missions (Anabaptists) on one of his estates. "The Anabaptists were cruelly victimized by both Protestants and Catholics. They were forced to jump to their deaths from tops of haystacks (to land on long spikes) and to be drowned, burned, and hanged" Cairns, 1981, p. 306). This radical movement has become the pioneer of modern evangelical Christianity. The four-fold foundation was:

(1) The principle of Discipleship, which was defined as a relationship with Jesus Christ that goes beyond an inner mystical experience and acceptance of doctrines or creeds. It must involve a daily walk with God in every aspect of life.
(2) The principle of Love, which grew logically out of the first principle. They acted as pacifists, neither going to war nor defending themselves against persecutors, nor acting against the state.
(3) The principle of congregational view of church authority as each believer is voluntarily baptized upon his profession of personal faith in Christ; he immediately becomes a priest to his fellow believers and missionary to unbelievers.
(4) The principle of the separation of church and state. They held that Christians were a "free, unforced, uncompelled people." They insisted that

the church was distinct from society. This became the first group to proclaim a true religious liberty: "the right to join in worship with others of like faith without State support and without State persecution." (Shelley, 1995, p. 185)

Count Von Zinzendorf spent his life and fortune for world missions. His connection with the Danish court and to King Christian VI enabled the embarking of Moravian missionaries on Catholic ships. He personally saw the Moravian church spread throughout Germany, Denmark, Russia, England and America in 1741-42. The village of Herrnhut on his estate, from which hundreds of missionaries were sent, had no money of its own, and Zinzendorf financed this vast missionary effort almost exclusively from his own resources. However, his travels forced him to be careless about managing his personal affairs, which often were not self-sustaining. At times he had to borrow money and in 1750 almost was reduced to bankruptcy. This led the Moravian church to organize a financial board. He continued on for ten more years until his death. His legacy will be eternal! His support primarily provided their travel expenses one-way.

> The Moravian missionaries, beginning in 1734, were purposely sent to the most despised and neglected people. These missionaries were to be self-supporting. That emphasis led to the creation of industries and business concerns which not only supported the work, but brought the missionaries into intimate contact with the people (Beaver, 1999, p. 246).

The Moravian missionaries were the forerunners of the Wesleyan revivals and William Carey's Baptist Missionary Society.

> Moravian missionaries exposed the Wesley's to the gospel message while the latter were on a fruitless missionary journey to the New World and had not yet been converted. Later, another Moravian, Peter Boehler, brought the Wesleys to Christ. Shortly thereafter, John Wesley visited Zinzendorf in Germany and then embarked on his lifework (Vos).

The history of the church has never been the same.

IX. The Great Century (1792-1910)

The term "the Great Century" was coined by Kenneth Scott Latourette in his seven-volume *History of the Expansion of Christianity*, in which he devoted 3 volumes to the 19th century.

The model of the Moravian Church, which would become the motivation for missions for the next 200 years, is reflected in this statement:

> Within twenty years of the commencement of their missionary work, the Moravian Brethren had started more missions than Anglicans and Protestants had started during the two preceding centuries. Their marvelous success was largely due to the fact that from the first they recognized that the evangelization of the world was the most pressing of all the obligations that rested upon the Christian Church, and that the carrying out of this obligation was the "common affair" of the community. Up to the present time the Moravians have sent out nearly 3,000 missionaries, the proportion of missionaries to their communicant members being 1 in 12 (Robinson, 1915, p. 50).

What began in the 18th century as an exception became the norm in the 19th century. For a hundred years (more or less) at least a thousand mission organizations sent out thousands of recruits and most were motivated by the courage and commitment of these early Moravian missionaries to sacrifice their lives for world evangelism. The mentoring influence of courageous servants lived long after their deaths.

European Beginnings (1792-1810)

All though we call William Carey (1761-1834) the "Father of Modern Missions," it is not entirely correct. There were at least three other mission societies dedicated to operate in the American colonies, but only one was cross cultural.

Carey was a tri-vocational Baptist pastor/shoe cobbler/teacher. In his spare time he taught himself 7 languages, world geography and Scriptures, and read everything he could get his hands on. One such book was, "The Last Voyage of Captain Cook," that described the people of India.

In 1792 Carey wrote his 87-page book, *"An Enquiry into the Obligations of Christians to Use Means for the Conversion of the Heathen"* to answer the hyper-Calvinism apathy of his day. Many believe this to be the most convincing missionary appeal ever written.

Yet the Baptist Calvinists of his association of pastors, when he challenged them to discuss the Great Commission responded, "Young man, sit down. When God pleases to convert the heathen, He will do it without your aid or mine."

The whole task seemed so impossible to the Christians that Carey challenged them with this expression: "Attempt great things for God; Expect great things from God," based on Isaiah 54:2-3. When they continued to be filled with uncertainty, Carey takes out a booklet called, "Periodical Account of Moravian

Missions," and said with tears in his eyes, "If you had only read this and knew how these men overcame all obstacles for Christ's sake, you would go forward in faith." They agreed to act and formed *The Particular Baptist Society for Propagating the Gospel among the Heathen.* Nine months later Carey sailed for India. After a five-month trip on a small sailing ship he and his family arrived to begin a 40-year unbroken service to India.

Carey's philosophy of ministry:
1. Widespread preaching
2. Distribution of Bible in the vernacular language
3. Church planting
4. Profound study of non-Christian religions
5. Ministry training

American Involvement (1810-1832)

Initially the American involvement was focused on home missions on the frontier and Indian tribes in the North East. Admittedly these efforts were often a cross-cultural ministry near home.

> By mid-century (1850) half of the American people were west of the Appalachians. ... Only five or ten percent of the American people were church members. In time, however, the crude, turbulent, and godless society of the West was tamed and more than any other single force it was evangelical Christianity that did it (Shelley, 1995, p. 384).

A group of students started a student movement at Andover Seminary in Andover, Massachusetts, and Williams College in Williamstown, Massachusetts. One day in 1806 they met for prayer and discussion. Suddenly, rain drove them under an overhanging haystack to pray. There they came to a conviction, "We can do it if we will," and thus became known as the "Haystack Prayer Group."

Led by Adoniram Judson and Luther Rice, along with four others, the first American missionaries were commissioned under the newly formed the American Board of Commissioners for Foreign Missions (ABCFM) of the Congregational Church in 1810. Judson and Rice were sent to India to work with Carey in 1812. Over the next 30 years Americans would go to India, Ceylon (Sri Lanka), Hawaii, China, Siam, Greece, Cyprus, Turkey, Syria, Persia and Africa.

Unmarried people were not allowed to enter the mission field. The mission provided a list of women that were "missionary-minded" or men that were "young, pious, educated, fit and reasonably good-looking" (Golossanov, 2006), in order to facilitate their acquaintances and from whom to choose a life's mate.

En route to India Judson became convinced about baptism being by immersion and decided to leave the ABCFM, a Congregational mission which sprinkled converts. On another ship, without communicating with Judson, Luther Rice had come to the same conclusion. They were baptized in Serampore, in NE India, resigned from their mission (ABCFM) and Judson offered himself to the Baptists. As a result, they were ordered out of India by the East India Company, so Judson went to Burma (today Myanmar) where he stayed for 38 years, and Rice returned to US to raise support for Judson.

Upon his return, Rice met Richard Furman and formed the first Baptist mission association in America, the General Missionary Convention of the Baptist Denomination (origin of the International Mission Board (IMB) of the Southern Baptist Convention (SBC).

X. Significant Events and Missionaries (1832-1865)

The Second Evangelical Awakening (1800-1830s) among laymen emphasized prayer, renewed personal salvation experienced through revival meetings, discipleship and godly living. The camp meeting revivals had a number of offshoots including the Mormons, Seventh-Day Adventists, the Holiness Movement and *Camp Meetings* in the open air, which would continue for 150 years. These camp meetings were characterized by highly emotional preaching, congregational interaction, little biblical study, rather they preached "as the Spirit led." The emphasis on continued prophecy in the meetings, led some to accept false views thinking they were from God's fresh revelation. These revivals led to resolving social problems (slavery, poverty, women's rights, and led to establishing numerous mission boards and hundreds of missionaries were enthusiastic about evangelizing the world.

The Southern Baptist Convention was formed in 1845 and, also, the Foreign Mission Board (later IMB)—not to defend slavery, but to facilitate a missionary effort by cooperative effort among all the Baptist churches and through volunteer church support.

Meanwhile in England, in 1840 David Livingston went to Malawi, Africa to explore the vast interior of the African continent. No one had any idea there were thousands of tribal groups in the interior of Africa.

In 1854 Hudson Taylor arrived in China and the New York Missionary Conference, organized by Alexander Duff, sought to answer the question, "To what extent are we authorized by the Word of God to expect the conversion of the world to Christ?"

The problems of paternalism and dependency provoked Henry Venn (1796 – 1873), leader of the Church Missionary Society, to set out the ideals of "indigenous churches" that is, they were to be self-governing, self-supporting and self-propagating churches. These later became known as "3-selfs churches."

One of his famous quotes is to encourage the "euthanasia of missions," which meant that missionaries were to be considered temporary workers, and not permanent. He knew the terrible results of dependency upon foreign missionaries with their finances. John Livingston Nevius (1829-1893) followed Venn's concepts in developing the Nevius Plan for indigenous policy in China and Korea.

Golden Age of Colonial Missions (1865-1910)

Colonialism was the extension of a nation's sovereignty over territory beyond its borders through the establishment of either settler colonies or administrative dependencies in which indigenous populations are directly ruled or displaced. These countries were dominated to exploit their resources, cheaper labor and large market potentials, resulting in the obligation to change their social, religious and linguistic structures according to the conquering nation. The term *colonialism* is used interchangeably with *imperialism*. Missionaries are still accused of this malady.

Mission efforts were bound to colonial expansion of the major powers. British missionaries went to British controlled countries, as did Dutch, German, etc., to their respective colonies.

Advantages of Colonialism:
- Brought entry into new fields
- Brought needed political development to often chaotic nations
- Brought education, medicine and technology

Disadvantages of Colonialism:
- "Gunboat-diplomacy" forced commercialism that was inevitably associated with missionaries' country of origin, therefore, by association, with them.
- Exploitive exportation of resources with little national benefit was blamed on all foreigners (i.e., Boxer Rebellion in China turned against all foreigners).
- Generated resentment against Western Christianity since Western society is not seen as distinct from its religious heritage.
- Premature indignation resulted in failures in India
- Resulted in pious paternalism or benevolent imperialism, which taught that a hand-out, begging life-style was effective.
- Missionary strategy is aimed at individual conversion, church planting, social transformation through evangelism, education and medicine, but all ministries were dependent upon foreign subsidy and, generally, could never be assumed by indigenous people.

- Initial "radical discontinuity" declined with the inroads of liberalism and pluralism
- 1860 saw first single women's appointment to a foreign mission.

Faith Missions started

Hudson Taylor founded China Inland Missions (CIM) in 1865 on the principle of faith support and prayer for recruiting missionaries from the working class and single women (a new practice) as well as their financial support. They made no appeal for funds, but depended upon God to move in hearts of people through prayer alone. By the time of the Boxer Rebellion (1900) the anti-imperialist peasant-based movement expelled all foreigners, as well as Christians who were held responsible for the domination of China. Tens of thousands of Chinese Christians were killed.[4]

Their focus was unreached provinces, identifying with the Chinese by dress, pigtails and worshiping in Chinese homes, indigenization by the 3-selfs principles. Recruiting was based on spiritual qualifications, not education or church orientation and headquarters (decision-making) was on the field, not back at home. Revolutionary concepts.

Student Volunteer Movement (SVM) founded in 1886 sought to recruit college and university students in the US to missionary service abroad. D.L. Moody challenged the students with the Princeton Pledge, "I propose, God willing, to become a foreign missionary." The SVM would send 6,000 to China, especially to work with Hudson Taylor. The movement's motto: *The evangelization of the world in this Generation.*

By the turn of the century four types of Missions agencies now functioning: (1) Interdenominational, (2) Denominational, (3) Faith Missions, (4) Specialized Missions

After the 1950 communist takeover of China the CIM of Hudson Taylor relocated their personnel in SE Asia and renamed the mission to OMF (Overseas Missionary Fellowship). This mission continues today with the same passion of its founder.

Outstanding Missionaries of Era

Charlotte "Lottie" Moon (1873) was a pioneer single female missionary to China for 40 years where she became an evangelist and church planter. She died in 1912 as a result of semi-starvation having given everything she had for the Chinese girls in her ministry. The annual SBC missionary offering for missionary support through the International Mission Board (IMB) is given in

---

4   48 Catholic missionaries, 182 Protestant missionaries, 222 Chinese Eastern Orthodox and 500 Chinese Protestants and thousands of Chinese Catholics were killed.

memory of her sacrificial life.

In 1888 the first party of Americans joined the China Inland Mission led by Hudson Taylor.

Amy Carmichael (1867-1951) served in India and was the author of many books. She spent 55 years of service rescuing girls from Temple prostitution in Hindu worship. She heard Hudson Taylor speak about missionary life when she was a teenager and committed her life to reaching people for Christ.

Evaluation of Colonial Missions

William Carey envisioned a global missionary conference, which began with the first all-India Missionary conference in 1872 with 136 participants.

In 1910 it was realized: World Missionary Conference, Edinburgh, Scotland, with 1200 representatives present.

The association with colonial governments (British citizens with British colonial powers) gave foreign missions an imperialistic flavor or reputation especially since financial resources all came from abroad through them. Governmental paternalism was reflected in missionary paternalistic or dependency strategies as well, since the foreign missionaries dominated everything and would not release control to the nationals, except in insignificant areas that had nothing to do with finances.

> By all odds the missionaries of the nineteenth century were a special breed of men and women. Single-handedly and with great courage they attacked the social evils of their time: child marriage, the immolation of widows, temple prostitution, and untouchability in India; footbinding, opium addiction, and the abandoning of babies in China; polygamy, the slave trade and the destruction of twins in Africa. In all parts of the world they opened schools, hospitals, clinics, medical colleges, orphanages, leprosaria. They gave succor and sustenance to the dregs of society cast off by their own communities. At great risk to themselves and their families they fought famines, floods, pestilences, and plagues. They were the first to rescue unwanted babies, educate girls, and liberate women. Above all, they gave to the non-Christian world the most liberating of all messages – the gospel of Christ. They converted savages into saints; and out of this raw material they built the Christian church, which is today the most universal of all institutions. By the end of the century the gospel had literally been taken to the ends of the earth. ... The emissaries of the cross were to be found in all habitable parts of the globe, from the frozen wastes of Greenland to the steaming jungles of Africa. Churches, chapels, schools, and hospitals were scattered with great profusion from Turkey to Tokyo, from Cairo to Cape Town, from

Monterrey to Montevideo, from Polynesia to Indonesia. There were, to be sure, a few areas of the world where there were no resident missionaries, but that was because of government restrictions, not because the church lacked either the will or the power to press forward with the task of world evangelization. Included in the Christian church, for the very first time, were representatives of "every tribe and tongue and people and nation" (Rev 5:9) (Latourette, 1953, p. 469).

XI. Advances in 20th Century

Wars bring havoc and danger to missions. It was one thing to be associated with the abuses of Colonial powers but another when missionaries are associated by nationality with the cruelties of war. The respect for their message inevitably deteriorated: In the period of 1900-1941 there were 24 international wars; later in the period of 1945-1969, there were 100 wars of independence from Colonial powers! With Christians on both sides of the battlefront it was difficult to evangelize.

Optimism was crushed after the holocaust of WWII. The eschatological motivation during the 19th century, which had been a post-millennial hope that evangelism would bring in the kingdom, was shattered. A new and popular eschatology of premillennialism became the passion of the evangelical churches.

After WWII, the major base of global missions shifted to the US since most of the economy, resources, manpower and authority of the European powers were destroyed by the war.

Since 1950 the massive missionary evacuation of China has remained permanent. Only in recent years has the door begun to open ever so slightly for missionaries to be allowed under special work visas to reside in the country under considerable observation.

Nationalism on rise

In an effort to quench any future world war, 51 nations started the United Nations in 1945. Since 2006 there has been 192 member-nations of the UN. A number of countries still do not meet the criteria for membership. Operation World lists 237 of these countries that exist today.

After WWII the influence of colonial power was annulled. The political imperialism ended, but economic imperialism has continued often with the same resentments towards anyone of the dominant powers. Much of this resentment has resulted in rebellions and revolutions, while being willing to accept any other economic system [i.e., communism] in order to not become dependent on the Western foreign power [i.e. European or N. American].

Independent people condemned former colonial masters and often by association, the missionaries from the countries of the same colonial power.

Western education contributed to nationalism because it taught the ability to be independent and self-sufficient. They learned how the West became so prosperous and thought they could do it too, often with worse abuses than the colonial powers.

Religious turbulence with the rising aggressiveness of Islam has brought insecurity in many regions of the world making missionary work risky or almost impossible by foreigners.

Doctrinal Issues

In 1900 the Pentecostal Movement began inauspiciously, but grew exponentially by the end of the century, permanently dividing Evangelicals in a race for world evangelism.

The Protestant Ecumenical Movement began in 1910 in the Edinburgh Missionary Conference with noble goals. Rather than gather missionaries, now it was time to recognize the national leadership, so national church leaders were invited, eventually forming the World Council of Churches (WCC) in 1948 and the National Council of Churches (NCC) in 1950 in most individual countries, which included the moderate to liberal Protestants.

Comity Agreements (refers to legal reciprocity or jurisdiction over other areas), thus the mission fields divided up to eliminate competition among mission agencies, but it did not apply outside of the liberal organizations (WCC and NCC).

The theological and methodological differences (social emphasis especially) led to breakdown of any attempt at unification among mission efforts. In 1932 a move to favor social action rather than conversion became the chief aim these missions. The Liberalism controversy led to denominational splits and new mission organizations in the 1920's thru 1950's, destroying the possibility of any kind of organizational unity in the Ecumenical movement.

1. New Organizations

- WCC—formed in 1948 in Amsterdam: Evangelical doctrine marginalized
- IFMA—formed in 1917 by NA "Faith" interdenominational missions (now called "**CrossGlobal Link**")
- EFMA—formed in 1945 by NA Evangelical denominations and Para-church (IMB joined the EFMA in 1995) Now is called the "**Mission Exchange**"
- FOM—Fundamentalists Missions
- AIMS—formed in 1985 (Assoc. of International Mission Services) formed for charismatic agencies
- Independent Missions
- Many independent missions remain unaffiliated with any association

- ❖ Wycliffe and New Tribes Mission are largest organizations
- ❖ 50% of all missions agencies are not associated with any major grouping
- ❖ Evangelical denominations and mission boards are growing substantially

2. Liberation Theology

Liberation Theology focuses on Jesus Christ not only as Redeemer, but primarily as the Liberator of the oppressed (economically, judicially, and politically). This is a theology that is driven by the concept of human rights activism. This was primarily a Catholic Church based movement, since it was begun by Peruvian priest Gustavo Gutierrez in 1968.

It is sometime called *Christian Socialism,* since it attempts to resolve inequalities by Marxist-style rebellion and socialist restructuring of society. They were especially directed against oppressive dictatorships or insensitive democracies when they formed in the 1990s, especially in Latin America.

The allegorical interpretation of Exodus, "liberating the captives" is interpreted to mean that the poor are the privileged channel of God's grace. Their concepts have been rejected by evangelicals, especially the hermeneutics, as well as the socialist/communist guerrilla connections. With fall of dictatorships, their reason for being has pretty much dissolved, though they continue fighting in a few countries. Recently the Revolutionary Movement has learned how to gain the political power (i.e. Hugo Chavez in Venezuela) in order to bring about their new social order.

Since the missionary effort is associated with North American missions the attitude in these countries toward American foreigners tends to be a distrust and renewed accusations of colonial exploitations as though the missionaries were guilty of such abuses. This has given rise to the new nationalism with increased restrictions on foreign missions.

3. Pentecostal Explosion

Although there were some isolated manifestations of Pentecostal-like experiences earlier, it is generally agreed that the Pentecostal movement began in 1900 in Topeka, Kansas, in the small Bethel Bible Institute. For the first time speaking in tongues by some of the students was directly associated with the baptism of the Spirit. Later in a Houston church, a young African-American pastor, William J. Seymour, heard of the Baptism-tongues doctrine while listening in an adjoining room. He was soon thereafter called to a small mission in Los Angeles called the Azusa Street Mission. There a revival broke out which lasted until 1924. These meetings would change the Christian world scene.

The Pentecostal Church and the Assembly of God church grew out of these meetings. Oral Roberts and the Full Gospel Businessmen's Fellowship in 1951 became the most famous Pentecostal evangelist/healer of the movement.

Though the movement sparked a number of denominations, there was a widespread reluctance to accept this new radical church in Protestant/Evangelical circles. The movement's growth was not sensational until after 1960, when an Anglican priest spoke in tongues showing that you did not have to be Pentecostal to have the same experience, thus giving birth to the Charismatic Movement. The statistics are revealing showing the growth of the Pentecostal/Charismatic Movement:

- 1960 –11 million (14% of Evangelicals)
- 1990—93 million (31% of Evangelicals)
- 2003 – 500 million (65% of Evangelicals)
- Evangelicals have grown at 4.5%, but driving force is the Pentecostal/charismatic growth, which is at 7.4%)
- 70% of all Protestants in Latin America are Pentecostal.

Kane gives these reasons for Growth of the Pentecostal Movement:
1. Generally indigenous from inception.
2. Strong emphasis on every believer being a personal witness, especially testimony.
3. Focus has been the lower classes looking for acceptance, identity, prosperity and hope.
4. Emotional and celebration worship style appeals to their emotional make-up
5. Emphasis on fullness of Spirit that can be felt thus is perceived as being real.
6. Occurrences of healings and miracles draw many and give assurance of God's presence (Kane, 1978, p. 100).

Charismatic experience has penetrated Catholics, Eastern Orthodox, Anglican and Protestant denominations around the world. There is a growing acceptance of the Pentecostal forms of worship (praise choruses, clapping, lifting hands, simultaneous verbal prayer, and popular or rock-type music) even in non-Charismatic and traditional churches. In the majority of the churches around the globe there is little to no difference in the worship style among the churches in 2010. The pressure is enormous for the non-Pentecostal churches to adapt Pentecostal-like styles or loose their members.

Acceptance of worship form has not always led to acceptance of Pentecostal doctrine, though many argue that it will eventually. When no one in the church knows the difference between the two (Pentecostal and non-Pentecostal doctrines) the inevitable shift to the Pentecostal experience takes precedence over doctrinal issues. No one is interested in the biblical views, rather the priority becomes, if it feels good and is popular (what the people like) then it must be the best approach to worship.

Female "liberation" found favor in the Pentecostal movement with many women pastors and tongues-speakers. This trend is likewise filtering into other evangelical churches, regardless of what the Bible may say on the issue. Whoever is popular and the best speaker become the criteria.

Success and popularity of the charismatic movement have led many traditional evangelicals to ignore the criticism and join the movement. The numbers are hard to verify, but clearly a majority of the N. American population is declaring themselves to be Evangelical Christians, and is increasingly so in many Latin American countries, with the majority of this population being Charismatic.

XI. Post WWII Mission Innovations

Faith Missions—following Hudson Taylor and George Mueller's examples – found numerous recruits following the war. Bible Institutes were filled with students wanting to prepare to be foreign missionaries. Most missionaries for decades came from Bible Institutes (esp. Moody Bible Institute).

Some of the largest mission agencies are the Wycliffe Bible Translators (also known as SIL, *Summer Institute of Linguistics*), Campus Crusade for Christ, New Tribes Missions and the IMB.

The utilization of radio, aviation, Bible correspondence, gospel recordings, cassettes, films, Theological Education by Extension (TEE), printing press and other technologies helped expand the opportunities to multiply each missionary many times.

Bible Translation

Cameron Townsend went to Guatemala in 1917 and tried to reach Indians in Spanish by selling Bibles. The text was not their heart language. An Indian asked him, "Why, if your God is so smart, hasn't He learned our language?" This motivated Townsend to found the Wycliffe Bible Translators in 1942. Today they are working in 50 countries. There are 6,528 languages in world, but 4,564 do not have any portion of Bible yet in their language. Although this represents only 6% of world's population they are the bulk of the Unreached People Groups (UPG), which must be reached to fulfill the Great Commission. Wycliffe today has 6,267 missionaries committed to this task committed to the task of reaching the last unreached people group by 2025.

Media

Literature production: Bibles, tracts, booklets, books, literacy methods, correspondence courses, SS materials, newspapers, magazines, music recordings.

Radio broadcasts can reach into homes that could never be visited. The two main Christian broadcast stations are HCJB and Trans World Radio. They transmit in over 120 languages to over 100 countries utilizing shortwave, AM, FM, satellite and the Internet as vehicles for transmitting the message of the gospel.

Films are excellent tools, especially the *Jesus Film* which has been translated into 1,015 languages, with teams operating in 100 nations, which have resulted in 230 million conversions. The original project had a $6 million price tag and was all raised by donations.

Student mission emphasis

The major driving force of the missionary movement has always been the response from college/university students. Though often the decision to be a missionary is made often in the teen years, the college missionary commitment usually seals the decision.

There have been three Student Volunteer Movements that have been responsible for motivating 70% of the missionary force that is on the field until the modern era. The Urbana 2009 saw 16,000 students from hundreds of colleges and universities gathered in St. Louis, MO. to learn about how to become involved in foreign missions. Furthermore, there will be almost 3 million young people going on short-term trips overseas in 2010, which experience typically becomes the foundation for future mission commitments.

Training of Nationals

The major aspect of missions—multiplying leaders—has some limitations. Existing brick-and-mortar buildings can only house and train a limited number of leaders. In 2002 in Brazil alone there are 300,000 church leaders who had had no formal biblical or post-high school training.

Recent innovations seek to move the seminary to the student's home: Theological Education by Extension (TEE) and Church Based Training (CBT) and other similar programs. Although distant educational training apart from a personal mentor and professor is never quite as effective as resident learning, it can be comparable if used with periodic seminars or gatherings of students to meet face-to-face (F2F) with an instructor giving a personalized touch to the training.

Introductory correspondence courses even go to non-Christians (i.e., Muslims). Recent developments in the online education programs in multiple languages could be a significant key to multiplying professionally and biblically trained nationals from all over the world, willing to give their lives to share the gospel to unreached peoples.

The Changing Role of the missionary

In most of the countries of the world national churches have assumed much of missionary work. Some countries have Evangelical churches that number in the thousands and some into the millions.

Missionaries need to learn to be a mentor, coach or trainer of nationals instead of the CEO of a mission organization or pastor.

Dr. John Nevius was a missionary to China with the Presbyterian Church. He published the Nevius Plan to describe the plan for his denominational mission, which included the following basic provisions:
1. Policy of self-support without any mission subsidy except in the early stages.
2. Policy of self-propagation: every believer is to be both a learner and a teacher of someone who knows less.
3. Policy of self-government: every church must follow its own self-chosen leaders and support them when possible.
4. Policy of wide itineration of the missionary, so as to avoid dependency on him.
5. Policy of strict church discipline
6. Policy of benevolence by the national Christians.

Roland Allen was the last of the pioneer advocates of the indigenous church policies in the early 1900s. Some of his principles were:
1. Begin the works in strategic centers of population and influence
2. Do not aim at any particular class of people.
3. Converts were to remain in their occupations and witness where they worked instead of extracting them, which alienated them from the people they could reach the easiest.
4. No church programs should start what could not be supported or done by nationals. There would be no outside subsidy except at the beginning under special circumstances.
5. Gifted nationals were developed for evangelism work.
6. Nationals provided their own buildings without dependence on foreign resources.
7. The missionary was never to do any ministry or use any technology that a national could not do.

Church Growth Movement methodology was begun by Dr. Donald A. McGavran, who was the founder of the School of World Mission and Institute of Church Growth of Fuller Theological Seminary in 1955. The basic foundation of Church Growth is that the goal of missions is church planting and that God wants church growth. These principles help the missionary determine how the church grows and how to discover ripe fields for the harvest. Insight are taken from cultural anthropology, sociology, social psychology in seeking answers to these questions. McGavran's princples continue to dominate much of mission strategy in the 21st century.

Research periodicals that keep missionaries abreast of the latest research in missiology include the *International Review of Missions, Missiology, Evangelical Mission Quarterly, International Bulletin of Missionary Research*

Research Organizations that help the student and mission personnel keep up with the latest developments and statistics include MARC (*Missions Advanced Research and Communications*) Center, US Center for World Missions, Overseas Ministry Study Center (OMSC), Billy Graham Center for World Evangelism at Wheaton and the Research Division of the IMB.

The demographic change of the world that has changed the focus of missions include the world population in 1900 was1.6 billion; in 1995, it was 5.75 billion; in 2000, it was 6.13 billion, and in 2006, the population was 6.3 billion.

Urbanization has been the major change in these population statistics, therefore, in the strategies of mission: in 1900 urban populations were less than 15%; in 2000, it was 53% of the world's population.

The **10/40 Window focus** was coined by Luis Bush in 1990 to refer to the 10° N. latitude to the 40° N. latitude across the eastern hemisphere where there exists the least access to the Christian message and resources on the planet. This area has three key elements that focus our attention: the greatest poverty (82% of the poorest), the lowest quality of life (84% of lowest life expectancy, infant mortality and illiteracy) and the largest number of unevangelized people groups of the world (97%). The population is more than 2+ billion, made up of Chinese, Hindus, Muslims, animist or atheists virtually unreached: the most neglected people in world. Likewise, this area contains many govern- ments that are formally or 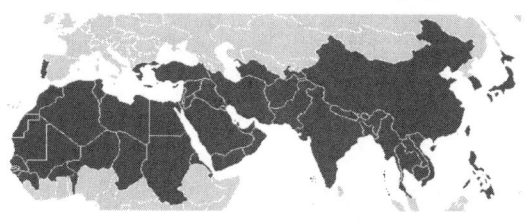 informally opposed to Christian work of any kind within their borders. It takes a lot of creativity to accomplish God's purpose here, thus the term Creative Access Countries (CAC).[5]

View of world as people groups rather than geographical divisions

The shift to understanding the world through the concept of People Groups, especially Unreached People Groups (UPG) stemmed from the Joshua Project. It is where "there is no indigenous community of believing Christians

---

5   Also known as Restricted Access Country (RAC)

with adequate numbers and resources to evangelize this people group." In 1998 these PGs numbered approximately 11,874 ethno-linguistic people groups; with 3,915 UPG's being virtually untouched with the gospel.

IMB Concept

The International Mission Board of the Southern Baptist Convention represents the primary mission arm of over 42,000 churches. They have chosen to primarily target the 4,000 people groups, or 1.6 billion unreached people that are still alive with little or no access to the Gospel. They have approximately 5,184 field personnel and reported 475,072 baptisms in 2006 in 135,252 churches with an active membership of 8.8 million. They started 23,486 new churches in 2006 among 1,170 different people groups.

Since about 1995 the IMB has focused on research and survey of unreached people around the world. Their strategic coordinators have developed a strategy of evangelism and ministry for developing a Church Planting Movement (CPM), especially among UPG's.

In recent years the IMB has had to cut back on their missionary force due to the lack of financial support. Of the 42,000 churches in the SBC only 7,000 actually take an annual offering for the IMB. With the financial crisis in the US in 2009-10 the short-falls have cause the IMB to reduce the number of salaried missionaries.

The missionary is a catalyst to involve many people in different locations and nationalities as they partner together to reach a specific group. Originally these missionaries were called "non-resident missionaries"—those who don't live in access area— and are called "strategic coordinators." The strategies that are being developed now do not call for large financial investments from the US, but are able to bring significant conversions into the kingdom.

Personnel for the Mission Task Unfinished

Multiple options exist today for unique ministries with 4,400 mission agencies (and still growing). The primary task of church planting, which develops into a movement of churches planting churches without foreign intervention, has become the goal of all missionaries on the cutting edge of missiology today.

"Tent-Makers" and "Platform" ministries are designed to gain access and acceptance in Limited Access Countries (also called Restricted Access Countries or Creative Access Countries).

Personnel skilled in TESL (Teaching English as a Second Language), technical, journalist, business professionals, teachers, sports coaches, etc., the list is unlimited. Virtually any area of expertise with missions and intercultural training can find a key part in the global task of reaching the last group of UPG's or help mobilize the churches to reach the masses of unevangelized everywhere. Learning a skill that meets the "felt" needs of people in other lands and cultures in order to have an open door that can develop relationships, trust, and respect, provide a platform for seed planting the gospel truths in the difficult areas yet unreached with the gospel.

As we enter the 21st century the major increase of missionary personnel is now coming from the 2/3rd world (66% of world population and territory). If this statistic continues, then a strategy will need to be developed to mobilize, facilitate, train and support this group of servants that God is raising up in these last days. There were 13,000 internationals in missionary service in 1980; then 36,000 in 1988 working in 2,425 people groups in 11 countries. Today there are over 66,000 international missionaries as opposed to barely 40,000 American and European missionaries! This is a new day for missions.

References

Beaver, R. P. (1999, 07/07/13). "The History of Mission Strategy." In R. a. S. C. H. Winter (Ed.), *Perspectives* (3rd ed., pp. 241-252). Pasadena, CA: William Carey Library.

Blincoe, R. A. (2003, 07/07/13). "As the Waters Cover the Sea: His Glory Expands to the Nations." In Meg Crossman (Ed.), *Worldwide Perspectives* (pp. 99-120). Seattle, WA: YWAM Publishers.

Cairns, E. E. (1981). *Christianity through the Centuries.* Grand Rapids: Zondervan Publishing House.

Golossanov, R. (2006, Spring). "Did you know?" *Christian History & Biography, 90, 3.*

Kane, J. H. (1978, 07/07/13). *A Concise History of the Christian World Mission.* Grand Rapids: Baker Book House.

Latourette, K. S. (1953). *The Great Century in the Americas, Australasia and Africa.* New York: Harper.

Miller, L. (2003, 07/07/13). "The Great Missionary Church of the East." In Meg Crossman (Ed.), *Worldwide Perspectives* (pp. 112-119). Seattle, WA: YWAM Publishers.

Morrison, S. (2004).. Retrieved 7/14/07, from www.biblequery.org/History/ChurchHistory/MiddleChurch.htm.

Robinson, C. H. (1915, 07/07/13). *History of Christian Missions.* New York: Scribners.

Shelley, B. L. (1995). *Church History in Plain Language.* Nashville, TN: Thomas Nelson Publishers.

Vos, H. F. *Exploring Church History.* Nashville, TN: Thomas Nelson Publishers.

Chapter 2

Holism: Serving the Whole Person

Any analysis of the world's population at the beginning of the 21st century reveals the fact that the vast majority of the Unreached People Groups (UPG) are extremely poor, live in difficult circumstances and are located in regions where traditional evangelical missions are not allowed or wanted. Since this segment of the earth's population represents approximately two billion people or nearly 1/3rd of the globe, they cannot be ignored or considered too difficult to reach. Hesselgrave related how his university professor had visited Japan after WWII to find a poverty-stricken and demoralized population. After Hesselgrave gave his proposal for his missionary objectives his professor commented, "You might want to do some more thinking about that. My observation was that the Japanese people want a changed economic picture right now, not a pie in the sky by and by" (Hesselgrave, 2005, p. 117).

The needs of people are varied. Any mission must take into account the whole of human needs: spiritual, social and personal. Holistic mission include both evangelism and church planting as well as development and social transformation. The amount of involvement will depend upon needs in specific environments, the need of the missionary to establish credibility in a community, and skills and resources that can be brought to bear on a local situation.

"To be 'poor' means to be economically impoverished, devoid of the necessities of life, and very often, part of an underclass devoid of the necessities of life, and very often, part of an underclass that is disenfranchised and helpless to do anything to change prevailing circumstances" (Hesselgrave, 2005, p. 118).

Historically Christian missions have been involved in helping the National develop themselves through physical (medical usually), social and educational needs in most regions of the world. Among evangelical churches in the era of church planting focus (especially since 1970) these efforts have been seen as a supporting ministry, definitely not "front-line" missions, and have struggled to receive church support. This is evident in Gaustad's quote, "However much the missionary acts as teacher, doctor, or technical assistant, he remains primarily a missionary, an evangelist" (Gaustad, 1966, p. 349).

The Roman Catholics and Liberals have spearheaded the focus on helping the poor to the point that the poor are seen as the object of God's special love, therefore must be our special love as well. This particular focus began to emerge as the target of Evangelical missions following the 1974 Lausanne International Congress on World Evangelization. At this time, holism began to have a dominant position in mission strategy for a number of reasons. Demographic and statistical studies of people groups and unreached populations have made this target group the major center of missions in the 21st

century. How to train for this ministry, overcome many obstacles and opposition, gain credibility and gain access to individuals within these areas looms as perhaps the major challenge of this century.

Global Context of Missions

The global environment in which missions is to find new avenues of exposure to the gospel include the understanding of the plight of desperate people for survival and the meeting of new social and personal needs radically different from the American culture. Demographic studies by McConnell shows three major demographic changes that need to be considered in any mission strategy. They are (1) migration, (2) the HIV/AIDS pandemic and (3) the plight of children at risk (McConnell, 2005, p. 46).

Migration

During the twentieth century, the human population grew from 1.4 billion to 6.2 billion. Increasing the impact has been the regional disparity of the growth. Economically less developed regions account for 4.6 billion people, and it is projected hat 98 percent of the global population growth will occur in these regions in the next thirty years (Population Issues, 1999).

In the more developed regions of the world, nearly one in ten persons is a migrant. This, in 2002, migrants accounted for 18 percent of the total number of births and two-thirds of the total population growth in the more developed regions (McConnell, 2005, p. 47). It is no wonder that populations seek to migrate since developed nations amount to only 15 percent of the world's population yet contain 60 percent of the world's gross domestic product. McConnell quotes Bryant Myers' study of the challenges of missions saying, "The economic nature of migration is illustrated by the flow of migrants from Mexico to the United States, accounting for 8 percent of global migration" (McConnell, 2005, p. 49).

Not only for economic reasons but also because of political upheavals and rival people group warfare has forced the displacement of huge populations in order to survive. "In 2002, over 40 million--16 million refugees and an estimated 26 million internally displaced persons -- fled their homes because of persecution, war, and human rights abuses" (McConnell, 2005, p. 49). Can this mass of humanity be ignored?

HIV/AIDS

Since its first discovery in 1981, the AIDS disease has become a pandemic, which has made it the deadliest epidemic of our time. "The disease has killed 22 million people, with another 42 million infected. This number continues to rise as 16,000 individuals are infected daily. ... Estimates show that sub-Saharan

Africa, the hardest hit, has 28.1 million cases. The disease is also spreading rapidly through the massive populations of Asia, where it is estimated that 6 million people are infected in India and 1 million in China (McConnell, 2005, pp. 49-50). These mind-numbing statistics bear witness to the claim that HIV/AIDS is the greatest humanitarian crisis in the twenty-first century.

> "Over 13 million children have lost one or more parents (to AIDS), accounting for one-third of all orphans in the world." The ripple effects of this horrible disease include family destabilization, loss of income from infected members, inevitable malnutrition, school drop-outs, inevitable adoptions already burdened, and single-parent and grand-parent families of orphaned children (McConnell, 2005, p. 50).

Major Christian efforts have been organized since the mid-1980s Christian organizations like MAP International and World Vision have attempted to mobilize the Christian population to respond practically to this crisis. UNICEF has documented over 686 Christian or faith-based organizations, most of which started between 1999 and 2003.

The proliferation of initiatives was strongest among Pentecostal groups, accounting for 64 percent of the total. Uganda had the highest number of faith-based organizations (194) and was the only country in which estimates indicate that the total number of orphans will decrease by the year 2010 (McConnell, 2005, p. 61).

As the churches around the world are exposed to such massive needs they are responding with their limited resources in their immediate environments. At the Lausanne II Congress in Manila a Manifesto was issued to underscore the role of the local congregations to "turn itself outward to its local community in evangelistic witness and compassionate service." This manifesto demonstrated the effectiveness and responsibility of the local congregations to respond to the HIV pandemic to demonstrate the biblical principle of how to "love your neighbor as themselves" (Matt 22:39) (Lausanne Committee for World Evangelization, 1989).

Children at Risk

Sadly those who survive and are the most vulnerable to the changing world scene are the children, who had little or nothing to do with their life crisis.

Some of the categories of the risks that are faced by children, which the churches need to take into consideration, include:

- Disabling or bonded child labor
- War and other forms of violence
- Sexual abuse and exploitation

- Disease, drug abuse or disability
- Neglect or loss of family or primary caregiver
- Extreme poverty
- Oppressive institutions (McConnell, 2005, pp. 51-52)

Due to the drop in infant mortality rates between 1960 and 2001 from 141 deaths per 1000 to 63 deaths per 1000 resulted in a population growth from 3 billion in 1960 to 6.1 billion in 2001. As a result, more than half of the populations of most countries are below 15 years of age. Thus children are the most vulnerable and dependent segment of the population. McConnell quotes a statistic from Viva Network showing that 1.5 billion of the world's children face life-threatening risks. Furthermore, 80 percent of the 15-24 year-old youth live in developing countries where education and employment is increasingly scarce. This unemployed segment of the population becomes the major social resource either for building future economic opportunities or to be exploited by destructive political, military, or criminal forces within society (McConnell, 2005, pp. 52-53).

Statistics showing over 10 million children exploited in the sex trade in virtual slavery, sometimes even sold by their parents in order for the adults to survive.

Historically the missionary movement has universally seen the care and education of children as foundational to their mission. McConnell quotes a study by David Barrett and Todd Johnson in 2000 that estimates there are 170,000 Christian primary schools, 50,000 Christian secondary schools, and 1,500 Christian colleges and universities worldwide.

However, among mission agencies targeting the completion of the task of world evangelization, few have included a Christian education component. "It is estimated that 14 percent of the $270 billion of the annual expenditure of organized global Christianity goes specifically toward education." However, ninety-seven percent of the total annual expenditure is on Christians, in spite of the fact that nearly 85% of the decisions for Christ are made between the ages of four and fourteen.

Recent estimates reveal that there are 25,000 projects that are touching the lives of 2 million children through the ministry of 100,000 full-time Christian workers (McConnell, 2005, p. 64). How should the Church respond to these needs? Most prefer to ignore them or

Three views of Holism:
1. Liberationism leading to revolution from any oppressive regime
2. Holism (Stott) seeks an equal priority modeled after the incarnation
3. Conversionism or Prioritism focuses on evangelism of the lost.

1. Radical Liberationism

Living in the 3rd world no one is ignorant of the inequities, corruption and injustices both in the judicial and business environments. The questions constantly are on one's mind: "Do I get involved or leave well-enough alone?" Radical Liberationism is one answer to this question: a radical restructuring of the economic and political environment of a country especially along the Socialist/Marxist view of the class struggles combined with the biblical metaphor of Israel's escape from Egypt and the allegorical application of equating the salvation from sin with the struggle of the poor and exploited for justice.

Roman Catholic priests in Latin America under oppressive and corrupt military dictatorships saw a Marxist revolution in the 50's-70's, which promised a serious correction to society as the only hope for a solution to the corruption in every phase of life. The Marxist thrust motivated revolutionary guerilla warfare in countries like Colombia, Peru, Panama, Costa Rica, Mexico, Guatemala and Nicaragua. Their motivation was to create anarchy in the present environment, which could only be rebuilt on the Marxist principles. Many missionaries felt that if society would not convert to Christ and practice biblical principles, then humanly speaking, the only real solution to society's ills would be a benevolent socialism. Experience would show, however, that corruption often passed on to the next political system as well and the people only suffer more.

2. Two primary types of Holism

Holism has a variety of meanings, but as the name implies, it is a ministry to the whole person or society.

> Depending on who is applying it, "holism" has a variety of denotations and connotations. Some emphasize ministering through word, deed, and sign. Others stress ministering to the whole person--spirit, mind, and body. Sometimes the emphasis is on transforming whole cultures and societies. At other times the emphasis is on transforming the whole world. The holism ... promotes the partnership of social (and, sometimes, political) action with evangelism in ways that supersede traditional theory and practice (Hesselgrave, 2005, p. 120).

Hesselgrave makes a distinction between Revisionist holism and Restrained holism. The former, Revisionist holism, is not as extreme as the radical Liberationism, but does make a full and equal *partnership* of evangelism and social action, which is defined as the balance between loving God and loving your neighbor.

In the Restrained holism there is an attempt to prioritize evangelism, while acknowledging the importance of social action either to help meet a need or give the opportunity to enter an otherwise restricted community. This group sees the ministry of Jesus as the model to follow today. As Jesus' ministry was characterized by actions to "proclaim good news to the poor" (Isa 61:1-2).

3. Traditional prioritism

While recognizing the validity of medical, educational, economic and social needs of a people, *traditional prioritism* maintains that the primary ministry of the church is spiritual transformation, with social transformation taking a secondary role. This position denies a reductionistic view of neglecting social ministries on the one hand, while limiting cross-cultural ministries only to evangelism.

Inadequacies of Holism

Hesselgrave shows that the two foundations of holism are "reason" and "revelation," both of which are essential or the concept will fail. "Unlike Hinduism, Christianity begins with an absolute dichotomy between the Creator and his creation. It proceeds by making very different valuations of body and soul, treasures on earth and treasures in heaven, and this world and the world to come. In fact, these dichotomies and the choices they necessitate attach to the essence of Christianity (Hesselgrave, 2005, p. 123).

Liberationists and holists hold that God has a certain "preference" for the poor, therefore, the focus of the ministry should be toward the poor, because they are convinced God especially listens to the cries of the poor.

As far as revelation is concerned, they view God as a God of love and compassion who cares about the poor and desperate people of the world. Second, the holist is very selective of their foundational passages, especially the definition of the "true and faultless" religion (James 1:27) is concerned with the injustices and conditions of the poor and disadvantaged. Third, the holist appeal to many deliverance passages as models of social concerns (the exodus, the theocracy in Israel, the captivity and deliverance and the announcement of the Messiah and the poor). Fourth, the descriptions of the kingdom (future) are seen as prophetic imperatives of the present ministry as well. Fifth, the commandment to love your neighbor as yourself has practical applications. Sixth, the Great Commission at least implies a concern for the poor and needy by teaching all that Christ commanded. Seventh, the apostles and early churches had a special concern for widows, the poor and the hungry (Hesselgrave, 2005, p. 124).

(a) Incarnationalists

Charles Sheldon wrote a popular novel, *In His Steps*, which presents a pastor's emphasis on the question, "What Would Jesus Do?" (WWJD). His objective was to transform a whole society resulting in a "Christianization" of society. This focus seeks the extension of Christ's kingdom over the whole of life and society by transforming it to a Christian life-style and way of thinking.

Incarnationalists do not think much of priorities of confrontational evangelism, rather they see witnessing in "word, deed and sign" of Jesus as the Transformer of societies and cultures as well as individuals.

Anglo-Catholic John R. W. Stott sees Jesus making His mission *the* model for the church's mission and ours. Jesus is viewed as the great Liberator and Emancipator. Though much of Liberation Theology has died, the basic concept lives on in the "liberation-incarnationalist." John Stott holds that the greatest statement of the Great Commission is John 20:21, "*As the Father has sent me even so* I am sending you." He goes so far as to say that if a church is in a community which socially or physically deteriorates, it is primarily the failure of the local church (Hesselgrave, 2005, p. 147).

(b) Conversionist-incarnationalists

Many of those who maintain clear priorities of proclaiming the gospel, discipling the *ethne*, all peoples, baptizing and instructing them while incorporating them into local reproducing churches reject Liberationism. They focus on a Luke 19:10 passage, "the Son of Man came to seek and to save the lost." They reject Liberationism and are not sure of a holistic emphasis.

Ron Rogers, an outspoken incarnationalist, is convinced that ministry should be modeled after Jesus' ministry rather than the principles of Paul. He would say, "such terms as accommodation, identification, indigenization, and enculturation are often used, it is incarnationalism that 'sets forth the truly biblical model for cross-cultural ministry' and that Christ is the model par excellence of a truly incarnationalist missionary ministry" (Rogers, 2002, p. 44).

(c) Incarnationalist Missions: Modeling modern missions after Jesus

The interlacing of the principles of incarnationalism and evangelical priorities become cloudy and purpose for continuing can become more idealistic than practical. When social change becomes the priority a radical position can be inevitable. It is proposed that the following characteristics of Jesus' ministry should be modeled in contemporary ministries:

- Characterized by humble, self-sacrificial service on behalf of all people
- Willing to renounce His rights and privileges as the Son of God to identify with those He came to serve.
- Became a poor servant to meet the needs of hurting people and the powerless.
- Did not hesitate to engage in a power encounter with the demons to show His power.

- Immersed Himself in the affairs of local culture.
- Communicated, verbally and non-verbally that people could understand.
- Spent most of His time training a few chosen disciples who would carry on His ministry.
- Gave priority to prayer and fellowship with His heavenly Father.
- Did not have a superiority complex, rather assumed a humble attitude in working with people.
- Willing to suffer and die for the people He came to save (Hesselgrave, 2005, p. 149)

Social Component Mandate

Incarnationalists tend to apply evangelism while or after meeting the social needs that the people feel are more urgent than their spiritual needs. When the World Council of Churches (WCC) was dominated by liberals, missions became mostly social especially during the mid 20thcentury. Instead of the *lostness* of people it became the *plight* of people as the major focus. Paradigm shift: 1974 Lausanne Covenant: "We affirm that evangelism and socio-political involvement are both part of our Christian duty." Both are necessary "expressions of our doctrines of God and man, our love for our neighbor and our obedience to Jesus Christ."

Representational Mission: Modeling modern missions after Paul

Incarnationalists and Representationalists see different answers to the basic questions about missionaries:
1. What are today's missionaries to be?
2. What are they to say?
3. What are they to do?

First, are missionaries to be clones of Christ or ambassadors, representatives, disciples of Christ?
Secondly, What is the message of today's missionary? The message that needs proclaiming today is the completed salvation that Jesus accomplished through the incarnation, not the continuation of the incarnation. The Incarnationalists tend to identify the statement "for me to live is Christ" (Phil 1:21) with their justification. However, "in biblical teaching, the truth of the indwelling of Christ through the Holy Spirit is light years removed from the doctrine of the incarnation of Christ. As for maintaining the absolute uniqueness of Christ's incarnation, it must be remembered that the West faces pluralism, syncretism, new ageism, false Christs, and the disintegration of

absolutes" (Hesselgrave, 2005, p. 153).

Teaching the incarnationalism in the East can get confusing since they believe in certain emanations from their gods of the bodhisattvas and *manushi* Buddha's of Mahayana Buddhism, or *kami* of the Shinto's, or cultic saviors of cults. At best, missionaries would only be an inferior model and ineffective savior.

Thirdly, there are certain characteristics of Jesus' ministry that are not repeatable. We should certainly imitate his commitment to obedience, his willingness to give up his glory and comfort, his wisdom how he spoke to different people and his practice of prayer. However, should we cast people out of the church as he did the Temple, raise the dead, or cast demons into pigs. Some charismatic leaders attempt to be a replica of Jesus' ministry or even more dramatic accomplishments, but the comparison is hardly adequate.

All of the models have limitations, even the representational ministry of Paul. Are we apostles? Does every believer have the signs of an apostle? Are we expected to have independent authority as an apostle? Can we speak or write infallibly? Some want to claim this level of comparison.

Five times Paul points to his own life as a model (1 Cor 4:16; 1 Cor 11:1; 1 Cor 9:22; Phil 3:17; 1 Thess 1:6; 2 Thess 3:7-9). Hesselgrave points out ten comparison models as the example of the apostle Paul that are to be emulated.

1. Characterized by humble, self-sacrificial service, giving up his rights to identify with and meet the needs of his target audience
2. Concentrated on centers of learning and commerce, from which the gospel flowed
3. Labored with his own hands to provide for himself and co-workers to give a model to his followers
4. Considered himself an ambassador of Christ and, on Christ's behalf, urged sinners to be reconciled to God
5. Concentrated on raising up indigenous churches that would not be dependent on missionaries or other churches
6. Did not spend a long time in each place, but chose to pick and train a few local leaders who could carry on his work
7. Maintained contact with churches he had established with visits and letters exhorting them to walk worthy of their calling
8. Encouraged believers in the churches to give generously to care for others
9. Accommodated himself to new cultures, becoming "all things to all men" to save some.
10. Maintained his authority as one commissioned by Christ while humbly confessing his unworthiness as a sinner and former persecutor (Hesselgrave, 2005, pp. 157-158).

Redefine or Balance

There are times in the ministry when the primary task of teaching and preaching the gospel can be a full-time occupation. Generally speaking, the people groups where this is still possible are in regions that are already reached with the gospel and a reproducing church. Now it is the unreached people groups (UPG) where freedom to minister is not an option. A secondary role or reason for being is imperative. Some of these areas obligate a social platform to justify presence (i.e. RAC/CAC).

Some opportunities can be integrated with evangelism (i.e. schools, clinics, orphanages), at least on a private basis. In other regions the temptation to avoid evangelism is tremendous in order to be successful or at least continue.

Financial aid, medical, community development programs often become an end to themselves. Depending how you define of the purpose of the ministry: if living a godly life and serving others is seen as the model of Jesus, thus often defined as *presence evangelism*, which minimizes the proclamation aspect of mission work.

As a general rule void such programs that create dependency. The problem with many incarnational ministries is the tendency to do for others what they cannot do for themselves. Paul avoided this weakness by engaging in *temporary programs of evangelisms* that result in *autonomy* and *self-sufficiency*.

Why is the danger so prevalent?

What model of social-evangelistic ministry do you know of in the US?
What business-evangelistic ministry?
What medical-evangelistic ministry?
What Aid-evangelistic ministry?
What engineering-evangelistic ministry?
What sociological, linguistic, anthropological ministry?

With very few, if any, models in our culture, that are effective, the missionary has the foreign task difficult to establish and maintain in prioritism in ministries that he has never seen in favorable environments, much less in resistive regions.

The overwhelming belief is in "Presence" Evangelism – a silent witness, which is ideal in the incarnational ministry, thus their theology tends to be framed to justify their practice.

Some such agencies have economic benefits (i.e., financial support of specific relief or medical ministries) that obligate a minimum of offense (i.e. evangelism or biblical stance on issues).

Summary of Holism

Charles Sheldon, *In His Steps*, helped develop a practical ethic around the question, *"What would Jesus do?"* His objective was the hope that "the application of Christian principles to the ordering of society would lead to the rectification of serious social evils and pave the way for the establishment of the kingdom of God on earth." The results of its popularity and practice was the loss of the real gospel message, for the social gospel.

Once again the Incarnationalist WWJD has surfaced to become a priority in political, social and Charismatic focuses, often to the lack of the true gospel message.

Hesselgrave who understands the often desperate need for holism in many areas yet concludes his analysis of the holism focus of missions with four warning statements:

(1) The gospel is both "true" news and "good" news quite apart from anything that we may do without having to tailor it to special needs or interest groups. (2) The announcement of this good news to the "poor" was primarily referring to a generous salvation offer to a spiritually sinful and needy, regardless of their economic or social status. (3) The focus of the Christian mission has to do with making the "true and good gospel of Christ known to those who are most separated geographically, ethnically, and religiously from centers of gospel knowledge and influence." Though the commands to "love your neighbor" and "do good to all people" (Gal 6:10) and the fact that spiritual and literal poverty often go together they cannot get confused, paralleled or equated. (4) Our task is to seek out individuals and people groups who, "by whatever means," even poverty, have been made open to hear, understand and respond to the gospel of Christ. If economic or social help is to be provided, it should never be seen as a conditioned benefit of having received the spiritual "Bread of Life." Spiritual hope is the primary and best hope to offer anyone (Hesselgrave, 2005, pp. 135-138).

David Hesselgrave quote: "There are strong indications that the 21st century will be marked by major sociopolitical upheavals and a succession of natural disasters. Unless this new – among evangelicals – understanding of mission is successfully challenged, the likelihood of retaining the biblical priority of world evangelization in the face of unprecedented needs of every kind will become increasingly difficult."

References

Gaustad, E. S. (1966, 07/07/24). *A Religious History of America.* New York: Harper and Row.

Hesselgrave, D. J. (2005). *Paradigms in Conflict.* Grand Rapids: Kregel Academic & Professional.

Lausanne Committee for World Evangelization. (1989). *The Manila Manifesto.* Retrieved July 22, 2007, from www.gospelcom.net/lcwe/statements/manila.html.

McConnell, D. (2005, 07/07/24). "Changing Demographics: The Impact of Migration, HIV/AIDS, and Children at Risk." In M. Pocock, Gailyn Van Rheenen and Douglas McConnell (Ed.), *The Changing Face of World Missions* (pp. 45-78). Grand Rapids: Baker Academic.

Population Issues. (1999). *"Demographic Trends by Region."* Retrieved 6/30/07, from http://www.unfpa.org/6billion/populationissues/dempgraphic.htm.

Rogers, R. (2002, Spring). "Why Incarnational Missions Enhances Evangelism Effectiveness." *Journal of Evangelism and Mission, 1,* pp. 43-58.

Chapter 3

Tentmaking, Platform Ministries and NGOs

From the decades of the seventies and eighties there has emerged a large variety of means to go to the nations. Much of this variety has been the result of creative thinking and daring innovations to penetrate areas of the world where traditional missionaries are not welcomed. Christianity is not a social order imposed on different cultures as political structures and economic imperialism was the norm in the nineteenth century. Rather Christianity is driven by the passion to communicate the love of Christ, as His ambassadors, to every people, even if they are resistant and disinterested. This chapter will explore some of the creative ways in which His ambassadors have elected to pour out their lives to gain entrance into difficult regions of the world, build relationships and thus open ears and hearts, and share the greatest story ever told.

In 2003 a sophomore student came to Liberty University to study Bible and nothing else. He had just finished one year at Princeton University where he aced all the general education courses (English, math, history, etc.). His third year he was going to (and did) transfer to a university in Dubai, United Arab Emirates, where he was going to major in petroleum engineering. His goal was to establish his career in one of the Arab republics as a respected professional, to build relationships and make disciples of Christ. He had literally poured out his life to reach others for Christ just as a tribal missionary would do in order to reach an unreached people.

> "In his book, *God's New Envoys*, Ted Yamamori, the president of Food for the Hungry, showed that upwards of 80% of the world population lived in countries which did not permit the unrestricted entry of fully supported traditional missionaries. ... Penetration in restricted countries is hindered by the growth of more militant Islamic states; the hardening of attitudes in China, despite apparent liberalization of economic and political postures and resistance to anything that is perceived as Western and thereby undermining of ethnic identity" (Cox, 1997, p. 111).

For any number of reasons a series of different structures has been developed to enable Evangelicals to enter countries or regions of the world that would normally, but not exclusively, be closed to traditional missionary endeavors. These types of ministries are called Tentmaking, Platform Ministries and NGOs [Non-Governmental Organizations].

The following topics will be discussed:
Tentmaking
Platform Ministries
NGOs

Stephen Bailey became the director of the Alliance Graduate School of Missions after serving as a missionary to refugees and as a tentmaker for seventeen years. He wrote, "If the remaining unevangelized people in our world are to hear the gospel, then Christians will have to enter nations that restrict the access of foreign missionaries. Many of the people who live in these nations are religiously confident with long traditions in Islam, Buddhism and Hinduism. They are generally poor nations. ... They are nations that also often violate international standards in the area of religious freedom and consider the propagating of Christian faith a disruptive Western influence. Some refer to these nations as 'creative access nations' or CANs" (Bailey, 2007, p. 368).

I. Tentmaking

Since the early 70's a concept of ministry called "Tentmaking" has developed for a variety of reasons that is called "tentmaking." This term refers to the activities of someone in the ministry who receives little or no pay for his service through the ministry itself. This person supports him/herself by secular work unrelated directly to mission activity. Not only can a tentmaking ministry become self-supporting, it can also be instrumental in opening doors for a residential ministry in resistive or restrictive regions. This is a "marketplace" ministry on the international scene. Dr. William Danker said that "The most important contribution of the Moravians was their emphasis that every Christian is a missionary who should witness through his daily vocation" (Cox, 1997, p. 112). It was this kind of conviction in the hearts of present day Christians that led to the establishment of the Tentmaker International Exchange (TIE).

The question in today's world of unreached peoples is how can we place credible people into areas where traditional missionaries are not permitted? How can we find, train and send "marketplace Christians" that can carry the gospel into regions where no one else is allowed?

> As teachers and educators, Christians communicate eternal truths of Scriptures through the schools, universities, and training institutes of the world. As workers in nongovernment organizations, they demonstrate the love and mercy of Christ through the relief and community development channels for a world in need. As business people, they trade concepts of discipleship through the commercial

networks of a global economy. They strive to bridge the gap, to connect with those who are isolated from the truth of the gospel. Most focus on least-evangelized peoples. All are part of a vast company of ambassadors, tentmakers, envoys, and kingdom professionals being raised up, trained, and sent out to disciple all peoples on earth. They are creating the future of a church that will not take 'no' for an answer when it comes to global evangelization. They are living out a model of evangelization and church planting that depends on everyday disciples of Christ for witness, teaching, mentoring and community. They are part of today's world of creative-access platforms (Barnett, 2005, pp. 210-211).

The region of the world where tentmaking is going to be practiced will largely determine the nature of the tentmaking ministry. When the Colombian government began to make overtures against American missionaries in the 1970's, I thought it would be wiser to renew my visa as a pilot-mechanic instead of a missionary. We were operating two planes in the province of Amazonas giving life-saving service to remote villages and tribal people. Our thought at that time was to have a non-missionary visa in hopes that the impending restrictions on missionaries would not apply to a technical visa. In our case it did not work, because the restrictions were to be placed against all foreigners living in tribal areas who then had to relocate out of the jungle region.

The renewal of tentmaking in the last two decades of the 20th century is due in part to the focus given in the Lausanne conferences of the 70's and 80's, which turned the attention toward the 10/40 window.[6] The evaluation of this vast unreached portion of the earth's geography which houses most of the unreached people groups left to be evangelized, showed how they are not open to traditional missionary endeavors. Many of them had been dominated by colonial powers for over a hundred years and presently have little interest in welcoming representatives from the West. All the major religions of the world are based in this 10/40 window so there is little interest in allowing evangelistic missionary activities. If the gospel was ever going to penetrate into these restricted areas, high-risk, creative justification for being there had to be developed.

Many readers will be familiar with the Manila Manifesto [Lausanne II Congress] which epitomized a new commitment to World Evangelization. What is less known is the statement issued by the Tentmaker Track. It affirmed the tentmakers are Christians who, in response to God's call,

---

6   A band across N. Africa through the Middle East, India, S. China and S.E. Asia, between 10° North latitude and 40° North latitude, where most of the unreached people groups and most of the poor people of the world are located.

proclaim Christ cross-culturally, witnessing with their whole lives. It affirmed also the vital central position of the established missions movement and drew attention to the need for structures of accountability by tentmaker practitioners to these agencies, as well as to local Christian fellowships and partnerships, and above all to the home churches. It recognized that the tentmaker, especially in his "secular role," was inevitably in the front-line of spiritual warfare[7] (Cox, 1997, p. 114).

This kind of activity is not so strange in the history of missions, but only unique from the way missions have developed in the 20th century through the financial support of Europe and American churches for full-time missions. The notion of living by "faith" and being fully supported by churches and individuals has taken on a spiritual respect that is enviable: to be supported by donors (who supposedly are led by God's Spirit) implies God's special blessing on an individual. To some missionaries anything less than full-time ministry is not quite as "spiritual." Even a denominationally supported missionary is seen as requiring less faith, much less someone earning a salary from a business. However, the faith to establish a business and see it perpetuate is not a lot different than starting a church that endures.

Definition of Tentmaker

What do we mean by the term "tentmaker?" The term originates in the example of the Apostle Paul who made tents in order to support himself and his team in their mission outreach. In Acts 18 and 21 Paul was described as making tents to support himself and his team. He chose not to burden the churches with his support (1 Cor 9) since he had been ordered into the ministry directly by Jesus and had no choice in the matter. What Paul wanted to offer the Lord was a ministry that did not cost the church anything, although,

---

7   The Lausanne Congress statement [Manila Manifesto] identified seven proposals for the church that the future history of tentmaking should prove to be effective for the Lord:
    1) To encourage Christian lay people to seize opportunities for cross-cultural positions to extend God's Kingdom.
    2) To recognize the key position of church congregations in mobilizing and equipping the laity for world evangelization.
    3) To identify and enlist people for cross-cultural witness among unreached people groups.
    4) To produce training materials and programs for tentmakers in the Scriptures, interpersonal relationships and time management.
    5) To involve home churches in assisting in placement and orientation to face culture shock successfully.
    6) To nurture tentmakers through faithful pastoral care to include prayer backing, good communications and visits.
    7) To assist in re-entry culture shock, and to use tentmakers efficiently in challenging and recruiting others.

in this context, his example was not to be taken as the norm, but rather an exception. Even Paul could not do this all the time, since he was itinerating and later spent 6 years imprisoned (Jerusalem to Rome) and thus was forced to depend on others for his support. His intent, however, was to earn his support by making tents, thus the term "tentmaker" as his offering of thanks to his Lord.

John Cox was the International Coordinator of TIE since its inception in Manila in 1989. He traces the historical origins of tentmaking back through the Old Testament; to Abraham as he left the security of home pastures and ventured into new unknown territory; to Joseph as he used his administrative wisdom in the service of the Pharaoh; to Daniel, as he rose high in the diplomatic service of Nebuchadnezzar. "In the New Testament, Jesus himself was best known for a number of years in his secular role as a carpenter before he devoted Himself to His ministry" (Cox, 1997, p. 111).

William Carey, known as the father of modern evangelical missions, was, in fact, a tentmaker missionary in India, who worked as a factory owner, university professor and printer while fulfilling his missional activities. It was four to five months travel each way back to his churches in England whose support could not be relied upon. Thousands of missionaries went to the ends of the earth without any stable or even promised support that they could count upon.

This same conviction was behind the words of William Carey who said, "My business is to witness for Christ. I make shoes to pay my expenses."... What bothered Carey was "why should we enjoy hearing the good news of salvation through the atoning work of grace of our Lord Jesus time and again, when there are still millions in this world who have never had the opportunity of hearing of the love of God even once?" (Cox, 1997, pp. 112-13).

Today a *tentmaker* is a person, who wishes to use his skills (professional, business, or trade skills) to work in a cross cultural situation modeling a Christian work ethic, build relationships, faithful witness, build disciples and hopefully share in the planting of a church in partnership with others.

Why do governments allow tentmakers into their countries when they know there is a dual purpose for our coming? Stephen Bailey, experienced tentmaker, gives several reasons for this flexibility:

1. The governments became convinced that we were worth having in the country. Bailey helped develop a small village silk business that was not cost effective for most business people, but ideal for helping a small community develop an economy through their traditional handicrafts. He states, "The ethic of the Kingdom of God required us to be concerned for our neighbors, risky venture or not. Acting on this Christian impulse taught us a more holistic sense of Christian vocation. We became thoroughly convinced that

our work in the company was an act of worship to God and of witness to the people. Our work with silk farmers was our ministry."
2. The government tolerated our presence because we had partnered with a local group of people whom the government trusted. Bailey reports, "The local partners were not Christians; however, they were sympathetic with our goals for working in the country. Most of them are followers of Jesus today."
3. The government accepted us with a "well, we-will-see" kind of plan. Bailey said, "If we had crossed the line we would not have seen our visas renewed. But what exactly was the line that could not be crossed?" When people began to become Christians the government would give a warning that Bailey was pushing the limits of acceptability. He said, "I always answered in a relaxed and interested way designed to acknowledge their concern, show respect for their authority and assure them that my intentions were for the good of the local people. Sometimes I said something like, 'Yes, my faith is important to me as I am sure your Buddhist faith is important to you' or 'Thank you for bringing this to my attention. We want to always be good guests who show respect for the authorities of the nation'" (Bailey, 2007, pp. 370-71).

Types of Tentmakers

Tentmakers are sometimes viewed as "spare time" Christian workers, since they are forced to work long hours at a secular job then after-hours can be dedicated to reaching people. However, the primary objective of the tentmaking task is to be able to be a witness on-the-job. Jonathan Lewis said,

> "Tentmaking is an opportunity to turn secular work into a vital, strategic ministry for world evangelization. Tentmaker's effectiveness, however, depends largely on their ability to exercise two essential ministry skills -- personal evangelism and discipling activities. Full-time Christian workers, even those who are missionaries, are often so caught up in administrating institutions and programs that they log very little time in personal evangelism and discipling. Their work with Christians often insulates them from everyday opportunities for witness. Tentmakers, however, can dedicate ministry time to these vital activities, particularly in settings which are almost totally unevangelized (Lewis, p. 109).

A common misconception of a tentmaker is that someone else is going to pay him to do mission work. Dave Brown of the Evangelical Alliance Mission

(Wheaton, IL) reported that some of the mission communities still view tentmaking "as a financial ploy of people who don't have the guts to do deputation" (Guthrie, 2000, pp. 120-21). The truth is that many tentmakers do raise their own support when they are affiliated with a non-profit organization and many of their platform ministries receive little or no remuneration.

There is no stereotype of a tentmaker, rather there is a variety of different approaches to tentmaking that are common according to Barnett: (1) Employees whose assignment takes them to a foreign country, not of their choice. This could include Diplomatic Service, education, health, engineering, banking, technology, business, etc., as well as study-abroad opportunities. These can become invaluable opportunities to impact lives internationally. (2) Christian consultants with specific skills can be used to provide expertise, advice, training and stimulus to nationals in their attempt to establish viable businesses, education systems, relief and development programs, and volunteer schemes. (3) Still others may see that this means of gaining inroads, subsisting internationally and develop a platform of respect in antagonistic regions could be the means for them to build disciples internationally, especially where traditional missions are not welcomed or permitted.

> Business delegations traveled to restricted-access nations to find opportunities for entry and access. Intercultural and educational exchange agencies initiated projects in hopes that doors to the restricted-access world would open. Humanitarian relief and community development alliances were formed in hopes of meeting needs and adding value inlands where Western missionaries were unwelcomed but Western aid was well received (Barnett, 2005, p. 213)

David Befus writes a practical guide for international businessmen who want to "apply economic development ... as a tool in evangelism and discipleship" (Befus, 2001, p. 13) entitled *Kingdom Business: The Ministry of Promoting Economic Activity.*

Taking Tentmaking another step, author Tetsunao Yamamori answers the question posed: How do we communicate and demonstrate the gospel to a growing population of globalized people focused "more on finding a job and attaining economic development than on investigating the claims of Christ? His answer is "In a word, the answer is business, or, to be more precise, 'kingdom business'" (Yamamori, 2003, pp. 8-9). Yamamori proposes that tentmakers go beyond securing a paying position in an existing company for contacts to developing their own entrepreneurial business with world evangelism in mind, specifically in restricted-access countries.

Mission Board Relationship

There is no requirement to be a part of a mission board to be a Tentmaker. Often the areas where Tentmaking is recommended in order to have an entrance into the country would not look favorably on a mission board affiliation. This aspect of a mission organization is not going to be a highly published ministry. Most of the stories of people referred to are surnames and places. Security in this kind of work in most parts of the world is high. Foreigners are closely monitored in publications, especially on the Internet. As a result it may take some perseverance to find the information that a future Tentmaker may need.

Some are able to find normal employment openings (i.e., professor in a university) as the best way to initiate their overseas service. Not everyone is mature and flexible enough for the venture of tentmaking. For the majority, a distant relationship with a mission agency is best. They will provide guidance, support and encouragement, but it will be vital that this agency have had experience in this area of the world, already have contacts or networks in-country for vital practical and spiritual support. Most major mission agencies have separate departments for this type of ministry that remain totally independent of the rest of the agency.

Typically these mission agencies will form a separate organization with little or no paper trail to the mother agency primarily for what would be called, a "nonresidential missionary."

> The nonresidential missionary became the prototype for the current role known in some circles as strategy coordinator. Nonresidential missionaries were assigned a specific unreached people group in a restricted-access area and asked to initiate a strategy to reach them. They often established a residence in an "outside" city with a significant population of their people group where natural networks in and out of the restricted-access world existed. Nonresidential missionaries researched their people group, mobilized prayer, developed a strategy, traveled in and out of their unreached region, and facilitated others with access to communicate the gospel and plant churches (Barnett, 2005, p. 214).

As these reports came back to the home office they discovered that many opportunities for long(-er)-term residential personnel was possible among their people group. However, to live in those restricted areas required some sort of a legitimate function or platform from which to help their people. "What had been considered restricted areas simply required some ingenuity on the part of the missionaries. It was not a question of restrictions but of creativity and determination" (Barnett, 2005, p. 214).

Some opportunities for professionals willing to serve short-term do not include a salary, but possibly a small stipend. Personal support would have to be raised or arranged from another source, which would funnel through the Tentmaker department of a mission organization. Many of these opportunities would be serving along side of present traditional missionary personnel in areas of teaching in secular schools (or Christian Day Schools, which are predominantly non-Christian students) or colleges, medical work, sports ministries, ESL/TESL, and business opportunities.

Essential Skill of the Tentmaker

Certainly as much if not more so, the Tentmaker must have a strong personal Bible study skill and experience in leading investigative or Socratic-type Bible study groups for evangelism. Without this experience the best a tentmaker can offer is a nice person working in a foreign country. This is called "presence evangelism," but there has never been anyone won to Christ or a church planted by merely practicing presence evangelism.

Since tentmakers are usually professional people, they will be interacting with other professional people who generally know their religion, values, traditions, beliefs and personal philosophy remarkably well. Persons not as well trained in their distinct Christian beliefs, Bible content and application, worldview, Bible doctrines, and comprehension of the Scriptures will not be respected, even though secularly and professionally they may be very competent. Biblical and cross cultural studies are vital if there is any hope of communicating the gospel to other people groups, because most of them are extremely well trained in their doctrinal beliefs.

Tentmakers need to learn to answer questions, including the difficult philosophical ones such as why there is so much suffering. They also need to know the religion of the people they seek to win. In cross-cultural situations, tentmakers will find new problems and questions seldom encountered in their own culture, such as the worship of ancestors, the spirit world, arranged marriages, polygamy, and many other issues. Sometimes these issues must be resolved before people will believe in Christ. Thus, evangelism is a process of bringing light through the Scriptures (Lewis, p. 130).

Marian McClure, former director of worldwide ministries of the Presbyterian Church (USA) says a public misconception abroad is that Christians want to "foist" their beliefs on others. "On the contrary, most Christians today suffer not from a tendency to foist our faith on anyone, but from a tendency to be excessively private about our faith," she argues. "I have never met a follower of a non-Christian religion who would respect someone who could not and would not express his or her beliefs" (Marquand, 2007).

II. Platform Ministries

Mike Barnett sees platform ministries equally as legitimate as any other spiritual ministry, especially when trained professionally and biblically/spiritually. He said, "Platforms are a product of God's calling, equipping, and gifting. They provide a legitimate reason and right for sharing the faith among the nations. They are not a cover for covert activities but a basis for living among, interacting with, and communicating the gospel to those around us" (Barnett, 2005, p. 211).

In answer to the question, why do we need a platform? Barnett gives the following summary:
1. Accessibility – Reason for entering- If the only way to get someone who is willing to share the gospel into a region is through a non-religious activity, then it must be considered. At the very least, it can become a starting point.
2. Legitimacy – Reason for staying - In order to establish credibility it takes a longer duration than a transient ministry. Permission to enter a region is contingent upon actually providing a service to the people, which validates the foreigner's presence.
3. Identity – Right to be heard - Being identified as a contributor to their society and being observed in a daily work environment gives credibility and genuineness to the Christian witness.
4. Strategic Viability – Basis for relationship - When serving a genuine felt-need of people, inevitably life-long relationships can be built and can become redemptive.
5. Integrity – Witness for discipling - There is nothing like the work environment to reveal the true character of a person. By modeling the lifestyle of a disciple of Jesus a tentmaker demonstrates the sincerity and honesty of a Christian (Barnett, 2005, pp. 235-239).

David Befus' book, *Kingdom Business*, proposes that today's businessmen replace the old paradigm of hospitals and schools with five substitute paradigms of ministry service, endowment, tentmaker support, business incubators, and micro-credit (Befus, 2001, p. 13). His book presents a trend to develop viable platforms that benefits a community and becomes a "bridge" for witness and evangelism.

Today's creative-access platforms generally are used only where the objective or mission cannot be accomplished through official Christian organizations or by those identified as vocational missionaries. Where a missionary visa is unavailable due to prohibitions of governments or cultures, creative-access platforms offer a strategic solution. Though the trend has increased over the past twenty years, creative-access platforms still stand on the leading edge of mission strategies. It is a high-risk, entrepreneurial venture with ample failures to inspire skeptics, but it is a strategic approach to missions with a strong biblical basis and an impressive historical heritage (Barnett, 2005, p. 212).

The term "platform" ministry is used in different ways. It can sometimes mean a generic tentmaking profession or business or it could be a consulting or service ministry that may or may not have a pay structure, i.e. coaching a community volleyball team or TESL (Teaching English as a Second Language). If the individual is receiving his salary from the exterior (mission support, US business salary, etc.), then he is not looking for an income, but rather a justification for being in the country and a means for building relationships that can have a redemptive result.

Platforms seemed to fall into one of two major categories, individual or corporate, depending on strategic objectives, abilities, and inclinations of the mission workers. Individual platforms such as the direct hire teacher, medical worker, nongovernment organization consultant, field worker, or agriculturalist are generally seen as preferable because they did not require significant infrastructure or human and financial resources. ...
In some cases, however, these individual tentmaker platforms were not sufficient for engaging and influencing a people group for Christ. For example, in many 10/40 Window countries, the activities of Westerners were highly restricted. If a direct-hire contract was obtainable, the job was of such intensity and the freedom to interact with locals was so restricted that the platform was ineffective. In these cases, larger-scale corporate platforms were developed that met various felt needs of communities. These generally required significant infrastructure and investment of human and financial resources. At the same time, they often offered a more stable, long-term option for large numbers of mission workers (Barnett, 2005, p. 221).

The most common types of platform ministries, which open most doors for relationship building and witness according to Barnett are (1) becoming a student in a state university studying the language and culture which can open the door to any number of future platform opportunities; (2) tourist with a multi-entre visa, though short-term in nature, allows for residency up to six months to a year in some countries; (3) educators serve the key felt-need of civilization: learning English; (4) sports developer can train in sports that are not common to the country but are common internationally (basketball, volleyball and track) as well as connecting key national players with scholarships, and other sports contacts; and (5) businessperson is perhaps the most effective, but likewise the most difficult to tackle due to different ethics, labor laws, accounting procedures, tax structure, and competition (Barnett, 2005, pp. 240-245).

Challenges to Tentmaker/Platform Ministries

Selling the idea of Tentmaking to the American Christian public is not an easy task. Anytime money comes into the picture or appears to be involved, immediate suspicions arise or the impression is made that someone is making more money than they should. Raising support for this kind of ministry demands a considerably confident relationship of trust.

> "Over the past two hundred years many evangelical missions (and churches) have pushed business ventures to the sidelines. Certainly, the hostilities in the colonial era between missionaries and other business organizations played a role in that. In addition, missionaries and mission agencies were concerned that missionaries making a profit could too easily become profit-focused rather than kingdom-focused and risk being swallowed up with business decisions to the extent that their ministries would suffer" (Moreau, 2007, p. 380)

In 1991, I was asked to start a ministry/business by creating a Christian Day School Textbook Publications. For two years a company was willing to give a subsidy to start the company, after which we were to operate on our own. It was a massive effort and way beyond my business expertise. I had to learn all about the educational system in Latin America, the Educational Reform Acts for Hispanic countries, Latin-American accounting (7-column system), tax structures, employment laws, page-layout computer software, printing and binding techniques for producing the textbooks and then I had to promote the textbook, educational philosophy and get the government approvals. In spite of enormous odds against this project ever being successful, we were able to gain a beachhead in schools, which has now grown to over 600 schools in 14 countries. I have never undertaken a more difficult task. We were able to employ 35 nationals, gain national recognition and commendations by the President of the country.

As an auxiliary area of ministry, we started a "School for Parents" to help parents understand the principles of child-rearing (where else in a secular society is this taught?). The Bible was not mentioned until the fifth lesson when I introduced the fact that all the principles previously taught, which they had already had begun to apply to their families, were actually straight out of the Bible. Their respect for the Bible was established and, thereafter, each week I laid down another foundational principle of the gospel. Soon a number of parents were willing to accept the gospel and come to an evangelical church in a fanatical Roman Catholic country. As the movement has spread over two hundred churches have spun off this Christian "business" in Paraguay alone. Now *Libros Aguila* Publications is supplying textbooks and training to over 900 schools (as of 2007) in 15 countries.

Tentmaking is not a utopia. As with any enterprise there are innumerable difficulties and complications that discourage the faint-hearted. Any one or more of the following have quenched many a tentmaking effort. The way to understand these items is to project yourself into a tentmaking environment, then one of these challenges surfaces. Reflect on how you would/will respond in these conditions:

1. A tentmaker's employer may restrict his witness or freedom to express his faith.
2. Demands on the tentmaker may limit his ability to learn the local language.
3. Terms of overseas employment are often limited to a couple of years.
4. Time demands of the job may limit time for witness and ministry.
5. Some will accuse tentmakers of being missionaries in disguise.
6. Christians back home do not support tentmakers with prayer and member care because they are not seen as missionaries.
7. Expatriate (foreign) workers are often isolated in compounds or are limited to working with only fellow expatriates.
8. Tentmakers may not receive adequate orientation for crossing culture and being effective witnesses or church planters.
9. Tentmakers may lack Christian fellowship and accountability for their mission work (Barnett, 2005, p. 215).

One of the reasons for the creation of Tentmaking ministries is to creatively enter into countries that are antagonistic or restricted and possibly dangerous (esp. from kidnapping or assassination). This is the challenge of independent aid groups and shows the need to protect one other, especially in Muslim lands. This was evident especially in 2007 as we saw that outsiders are more at risk in many parts of Asia, the Middle East, and Africa. "Missionaries and humanitarian groups must coordinate: conduct local assessments, know the unwritten codes, work with locals, and work together as a way to deflect harm that might ensue through rash decisions, they argue" Marquand, 2007).

"Many tentmakers struggle with their identity. Are they business people or are they missionaries? Which should take priority? How should they allocate their time?"

Stephen Bailey gives several responses to this question: he clarifies the concept of a Christian vocation. "Whatever Christians do, they must do to the glory of God. A double-minded person will not only become frustrated in a tentmaking role, but fail the ethical test." The tendency is if they see their business as a platform just for ministry, they will do it half-heartedly, not as for the Lord and in service to the people. Tentmakers must accept that they are Christian business people. "They are in mission because all Christians are to be in mission and to live by the principles of the kingdom that require the disciples of Jesus to care about their neighbors." (Bailey, 2007, p. 371)

Some of the struggles of reality in another country especially for a tentmaker are seen in the following testimonial of one tentmaker:

> Finally, the day of departure arrived. Flight delays made Jose and Maria miss their contact person in the Middle East airport when they arrived, but this inconvenience did not cause them much anxiety. They just stayed in a hotel for a few days. Real stress began to build some six weeks later, when the excitement of the new language, new friends, new sights, new flavors, and new smells gave way to everyday existence. Life was not easy in this new land and city that was to become the Rubios' home. A sense of spiritual oppression was a daily reality, and the lack of fellowship with other believers added to a sense of displacement. The couple began to compensate by deepening their personal relationship with the Lord.
> Meanwhile, Jose was facing the realities of his occupational task. His tentmaking work required him to establish a branch office for his home company that would open a new market for the firm's products. Jose soon discovered that he was not the only qualified person in the city in this field. Even worse, big multinational companies were also breaking into the same market. The ideal job that was to generate Jose's income, provide him with "contacts," and let him share the gospel had to be carried out in an environment of stiff professional and well-funded competition.
> Beyond his secular job, Jose was expected to learn the language so he could communicate the gospel more effectively to Muslims and nurture new disciples. He was also expected to provide leadership to his "church planting team," a group of university-educated, professional Christians who were full of zeal. He would keep the churches back home properly informed about the progress of the ministry. He would measure up to his family responsibilities and would engage in all the time-consuming visits with friendly neighbors (the couple's real target audience). On top of these responsibilities, he would cheerfully provide tours for visiting church members from his home congregation (Lewis, p. 160).

Ethics of Tentmaking

The basic question is whether it is ethical to present yourself to a local government as a businessperson without disclosing your missionary agenda when the government is clearly opposed to the propagation of Christian faith by foreigners. Is it deceitful or untruthful to not tell them that your purpose for being there is both to help and to convert people to Christ? Stephen Bailey answers the question, "Is business as a mission honest?" stating:

> First, it was very clear to the government that I was a Christian and that I worked for a Christian non-government organization (NGO). While they never asked me in an official meeting if I was a Christian, they did ask indirectly. Interestingly they did directly ask if I was working for the CIA. ... I always communicated directly that I was a Christian and that Christian people had sent me to try to contribute to the development of their nation. The government kept tabs on all foreign Christians and occasionally would let us know that we were crossing lines that might threaten the renewal of our visas (Bailey, 2007, pp. 369-70).

When a CAN ("Creative Access Nation") allows tentmakers into their country they do so "with eyes wide open." The idea that these governments are somehow ignorant to the Christian faith of the people they grant business, diplomatic and expert status visas to is nonsense. "In most CANs, governments regularly say things for political (and sometimes geo-political) reasons and then act differently. The practice of looking the other way when something violates policy but benefits the nation is a common occurrence" (Bailey, 2007, p. 370).

Bailey's observation is that these governments throw people out of their countries more often for reasons related to "honor and respect than they do because tentmakers violate their laws. Law plays a different role in these societies than it does in the West. Authority does not rest in the abstract legal system but is directly placed in the hands of real people. These societies remain steeped in a tradition of personal power and are only beginning to adjust to abstract concepts of law" (Bailey, 2007, p. 370).

The whole question about the ethics of a missionary doing business as a sphere of contacts for witnessing and discipling seems out of context. "In the Western church, pastors and ministerial staff members are professional, ordained specialists. We put them on the apostolic pedestal of highest calling. The act of clergy and missionaries returning to the world of the marketplace seems ill conceived and even wrong." (Barnett, 2005, p. 224)

Barnett describes Buddhist priests who hold jobs, Muslim imams that are generally businessmen as well, and Jewish rabbis who are trained for self-support. Only in the Western church is there a culture against clergy holding a secular position as a teacher, farmer or businessman. The vast majority of the pastors around the world are bi-vocational.

One hundred and twenty years ago, England won the bid to build the railroad system in Argentina, and Chile. The Plymouth Brethren church in England saw this as a great missionary opportunity so they recruited church members to migrate to Argentina and Chile with the railroad company and plant churches wherever the railroad went in this resistant Roman Catholic country. They entered as railroad workers but won souls in towns along the new rail system. Today there are over 600 Plymouth Brethren [*Hermanos Libres*] churches throughout Argentina. Was this illegitimate?

> David Barrett and James Reapsome contend that "from the Christian perspective, legality is not an ethical matter, but it is a purely descriptive term describing the secular government's requirements, which may well be arbitrary, harsh, cruel, unjust, ephemeral, inconsistent, unstable, or even impossible to comply with." To put it another way, creative-access missionaries may be illegal, but that does not mean they are unethical. Though Christians normally make every effort to obey the laws of the government, when those laws prohibit them from obeying the Great Commission of Christ to share the gospel with those who have not heard, they may decide to act illegally. After all, time after time the apostle Paul preached, witnessed, taught, or wrote from prison. He did not get there by civil obedience. Strategic questions, not ethical ones, are critical in such cases. Mission workers must ask, Will civil disobedience jeopardize future work in the area? Will we be evicted from the land? Will our platform(s) be vulnerable? Will it threaten the well-being or lives of locals with whom we work? Will our lives be at risk? If so, they must weigh the risks against the potential for accomplishing their objectives, and they must be prepared for the consequences. The question whether to be legal or illegal may be a tough one, but it is not an ethical one (Barnett, 2005, p. 224).

III. Non-Governmental Organizations (NGOs)

Wikipedia defines a Non-Governmental Organization (NGO) as a private institution that is independent of the government although many NGOs, particular in the global South, are funded by Northern governments. Anheier places the number of internationally operating NGOs at 40,000. National numbers are even higher: Russia has 400,000 NGOs. India is estimated to have between 1 and 2 million NGOs (Http://en.Wikipedia.Org/Wki/NGO).

Christ of Galli of Duke University says, "NGOs address a host of issues,

Including, but not limited to, women's rights, environmental protection, human rights, economic development, political rights, or health care. In numerous countries, NGOs have led the way in democratization, in battling diseases and illnesses, in promoting and enforcing human rights, and in increasing standards of living" (Galli, 2007).

> The fall of the Berlin Wall, the 9/11 attacks, and especially the invasion of Iraq, have resulted in more fragmented and weaker states, the rise of guerrilla groups, land and power grabs, and manipulation of ethnic and religious feeling. The environment in places like Iraq, Darfur, Afghanistan, Somalia, Yemen, Haiti and Gaza is a turbulent mix. On the ground is every type of foreigner - undercover intelligence, civil society groups, private security, and state military, doctors, construction teams, mine clearing groups, journalists, humanitarian aid workers, and church people, some of whom do both gospel and aid work.
> Views on missionaries whose chief aim is sharing the gospel in hot spots vary widely among the nongovernmental (NGO) and religious communities. But even those who accept missionaries argue that good intentions, enthusiasm, and bravery must conjoin with a professional approach (Marquand, 2007).

Non-governmental Organizations (NGOs) are an increasingly popular structure for involvement in world affairs without governmental ties. Though they can be political, they are primarily focused on social, economic and humanitarian objectives. The 20th century gave rise to the importance of NGOs. Many problems could not be solved within a nation. International treaties and international organizations such as the World Trade Organization were perceived as being too centered on the interests of capitalist enterprises. Some argued that in an attempt to counterbalance this trend, NGOs have developed to emphasize humanitarian issues, developmental economic and agricultural aid and sustainable development. A prominent example of this is the World Social Forum which is a rival convention to the World Economic Forum held annually in January in Davos, Switzerland. The fifth World Social Forum in Porto Alegre, Brazil, in January 2005 was attended by representatives from more than 1,000 NGOs. Some have argued that in forums like this, NGOs take the place that should belong to popular movements of the poor. Others argue that NGOs are often imperialist in nature and that they fulfill a similar function to that of the missionaries during the high colonial era.

Categories of NGOs

Galli states that it is difficult to categorize NGOs by their specific activities;

many NGOs perform a variety of activities and often shift the balance of the activities they pursue. However, in broader terms, "most NGOs can be classified as operational or campaigning. Operational NGOs achieve small-scale change directly through projects, while campaigning NGOs achieve large-scale change indirectly through influence on the political system" (Galli, 2007).

Nongovernmental organizations are a heterogeneous group. A long list of acronyms has developed around the term 'NGO'. These include:

- INGO stands for international NGO, such as Doctors Without Borders / Médecins Sans Frontières;
- BINGO is short for business-oriented international NGO;
- ENGO, short for environmental NGO, such as Global 2000;
- GONGOs are government-operated NGOs, which may have been set up by governments to look like NGOs in order to qualify for outside aid or promote the interests of the government in question;
- QUANGOs are quasi-autonomous non-governmental organizations, such as the International Organization for Standardization (ISO). (The ISO is actually not purely an NGO, since its membership is by nation, and each nation is represented by what the ISO Council determines to be the 'most broadly representative' standardization body of a nation. That body might itself be a nongovernmental organization; for example, the United States is represented in ISO by the American National Standards Institute, which is independent of the federal government. However, other countries can be represented by national governmental agencies; this is the trend in Europe.)
- TANGO, short for technical assistance NGO.

An idea of how prolific the concept of NGO has grown is evident from a quick search on Google that brought up 41 million hits containing "NGO."

Over the past several decades, NGOs have become major players in the field of international development. Since the mid-1970s, the NGO sector in both developed and developing countries has experienced exponential growth. From 1970 to 1985 total development aid disbursed by international NGOs increased ten-fold. In 1992 international NGOs channeled over $7.6 billion of aid to developing countries. It is now estimated that over 15 percent of total overseas development aid is channeled through NGOs. While statistics about global numbers of NGOs are notoriously incomplete, it is currently estimated that there is somewhere between 6,000 and 30,000 national NGOs in developing countries (Galli, 2007).

Risks with NGOs

The primary areas where NGOs tend to focus are the poorest and most undeveloped areas of a country. Humanitarian efforts are not the only ones interested in these same areas of a country. Often guerrilla groups want to recruit from these segments of the population. Muslim efforts to win these people groups over to their religion often utilize similar projects to aid in their development. From their perspective, NGOs can be seen as competition or threats to minimize the Muslim efforts to do the same thing.

"In the past decade, the number of NGOs [in harm's way] has risen sharply; as have incidents of violence against them," say Larchu of Médecins du Monde and Martin of Mercy Corps. "More than 80 humanitarian workers were killed in 2006 - that's more than U.N. soldiers," says Larchu.(Jerome Larchu, a director of the Paris-based *Médicins du Monde* [Doctors of the World], which has volunteers in 55 countries (Marquand, 2007).

Funding of NGOs

Even in the projects supported by groups like the AIFO *(Associazione Italiana Frantoniani Oleari)*, providing salaries and/or incentives for Governmental personnel is generally not taken in to consideration for reasons of sustainability. For projects managed by NGOs and missionaries, AIFO can provide limited amount of funds towards the costs of personnel. In such cases, AIFO accepts that the salaries provided be at the most similar to those provided by local/national Government in the project areas. The financial costs for salaries in a NGO/missionary managed project should not be more than 35% of the total project costs. Finally, isolated requests like providing a vehicle or buying of equipment are not taken in to consideration by AIFO *Associazione Italiana Amici di Raoul Follereau* (AIFO, 2007).

Effect of Tentmaking and Platform Ministries

It is clear that hundreds of mission workers are effectively engaging people with the gospel through creative-access platforms. The "Mission Handbook" reported 3,200 agency-supported tentmakers in 1999, a growth trend that occurred at the same time the number of "full-time traditional missionaries actually declined" (Barnett, 2005, p. 228).

Actually there are no comprehensive statistics showing how many tentmakers exist, not to mention success or failure rates. Universal agreement on the precise definition of tentmaking is elusive, as each group nurtures its favorite nuances. Nevertheless, interest in tentmaking by US Protestant agencies, although minor when compared to the traditional support-raising missionary, continues to grow. Yamamori, author of the 1993 book on the need for humanitarian tentmakers, "Penetrating Missions' Final Frontiers," says the recent interest in the 10/40 Window "has really accentuated the need for tentmaking." (Guthrie, 2000, p. 120)

When Mike Barnett was asked, "So do creative -access platforms really work?" He responded, "Yes. Where creative-access methods are necessary to achieve the purpose of missions and when platforms are developed to fit that purpose, they work. They may be unnecessary in the midst of a church-planting movement. They may become ineffective when a platform becomes the end more than the means. But they are proving to be pivotal throughout the least-reached world" (Barnett, 2005, p. 228).

Ralph Eckhardt, Director of InterServe, a tentmaking agency, stated, "Certainly, tentmakers are usually not going to build churches and equip other saints for ministry, but that is not necessarily their task in the overall scheme. ... Their responsibility is simply to witness, by word and deed, to people who have never been introduced to the gospel message before" (Guthrie, 2000, p. 121).

Conclusion

A review of history over two thousand years does show that the growth of the church has largely depended on the faithful witness of ordinary men and women, great and insignificant alike, who were going about their daily business (Cox, 1997, p. 112).

It was an American Christian [Ford Maddison] working in Central America as a business man to who is attributed the comment, "In the first Reformation, the people of God were given the Word of God. Now we need a new reformation when the people of God are given the work of God." (Cox, 1997, p. 112)

Unknown to Christian leaders, unknown to the structured church, such people [tentmakers] have gone out in faith to pitch their tents wherever God has led them. In consequence, there are many unsung heroes of the Gospel whose reward will be in Heaven. Very few of their stories will be told. The most significant characteristic of tentmaking is that, in many it has merely been a natural expression of their walk with God who has been the totality of their walk through life (Cox, 1997, p. 113).

Appendix 1

The Tentmaker's Preparation Checklist
Preparation Needed and How to Get It
Retrieved 9/3/07 from **www.globalopps.org**/101/tmprep

The tentmaker's work

1. **Choose a vocation** considering your aptitudes, gifts, interests, what is helpful in a needy world, what skills are marketable and what will support a family.
2. **Vocations needed** most are education (TEFL, math, science, teacher education, curriculum development), science and engineering, computer science, business and finance, health care, agriculture, business development, and operating a business.
3. **Background job research.** Use the Internet to research the kinds of jobs needed related to your vocation, the credentials required, the companies and organizations involved, and how to customize your resume or CV to fit openings. This research can help you determine where you might need additional training and experience.
4. **Degrees needed.** Most positions require at least a bachelor's degree. Many require more. Requirements are rising. Sometimes experience counts more than a degree. The exception is TEFL, which often accepts any native English speaker. As Christians our goal is to genuinely serve people well and bring honor to Christ. A minimal approach is inappropriate.
5. **Experience required.** Besides a few entry-level jobs, you generally need two or more years experience. Employers are also looking for successful cross-cultural experience. You can use work study programs, internships abroad, multinational organizations, Peace Corps, the Mennonite Central Committee, etc.
6. **Terms of employment** usually include round trip travel for the family, good salaries and health insurance, sometimes housing and schooling for the children.
7. **Language learning.** Many positions abroad are in English, yet learning a local language will enhance your cultural adjustment, gain the confidence of local people, and help to sensitively share the gospel.
8. **Finding employment.** Consult your own college department, professional journals, newspapers, magazines, the Internet, and the Global Opportunities web site. Network with people and befriend internationals.
9. **Starting your own business** can demonstrate Christian values and give needy people jobs. But you usually need experience, capital, and far more hours than a salaried position. Red tape and excessive taxation are problems too.

10. **More practical skills** such as cooking, sewing, homemaking, home maintenance and auto repair enhance daily living. Practical skills can help you make friends in another culture and earn the right to talk about the Lord.
11. **Recreational skills.** Sports and hobbies are also valuable bridges for friendship and sharing the good news.

Spiritual preparation to live out & share the gospel.

1. **Relationship with God.** Everything flows from the quality of your relationship with God. How are you doing at being filled and renewed daily through time alone with God in devotional reading and prayer.
2. **Relationship with family.** You will face great stress in a new culture. Work proactively on your family life: read, attend seminars, and seek counsel from sharp, godly couples. How healthy is your marriage and family and how well prepared are you for the stress of cross-cultural work and witness?
3. **Relationship with work.** Work is central to human beings created in the image of God. God is the great worker and we were designed to be co-workers with him and rulers under him to manage and care for the world. Thus legitimate work in itself is meant to be a sacred, God-honoring activity through which we "feel God's pleasure." We are called to honor Christ through our servanthood toward employers, customers, co-workers, and the larger community. Excellence, ethical integrity, genuine caring, Kingdom values, and natural, meaningful witness should mark us as Christians. We should also be engaging and impacting the thought world of our vocation. How well do we understand the areas of honoring Christ in work and how well do we practice them?
4. **Relationships with others.** Team building and conflict resolution skills help work together, overcome disunity, and put common goals first. How much of a team player are you? How well do you do conflict resolution and ongoing cooperation?
5. **Bible knowledge.** How would you summarize the whole Bible in a few sentences? How many books of the Bible can you summarize? What O.T. prophecies about Jesus were fulfilled in the N.T.?
6. **Bible memorization** is a good way to have your sword always ready. Then the Holy Spirit can help you recall them at crucial moments and locate them in your foreign language Bible.
7. **Inductive Bible study skills** observe what the passage really says and interpret what the writer meant with application for today. How effective are you in Bible study, especially in discovering what the writer is doing in a passage?
8. **Leading Bible study discussions inductively**, whether evangelistic or

for discipling and fellowship. Ask questions to help participants discover and draw conclusions from the details. Adapt your leadership to nonbelievers. How effectively can you lead a group to discover the message of a text versus telling them what it says? And how well do you lead a group to respond to and act on the truth?

9. **Evangelism–learn to fish.** Tentmakers answer questions about God from seekers made hungry for God by observing Christians around them—their integrity, quality work, caring relationships and words about God. How effective are you in the workplace? In each of these areas?

10. **Investigative Bible studies for nonbelievers** are discussions of Gospel narratives. Participants answer questions about the text. They discover who Jesus really is and commit themselves to him. How effectively can you lead a group to discover the truth of a passage for themselves without telling them what it says? How effective are you in understanding the author's purpose in a text and in preparing questions to lead people through a text?

11. **Christian doctrine.** Learn the main Christian doctrines as propositions with supporting passages. What would you include in a half-hour talk about God? Or justification by faith? Or the incarnation of Jesus?

12. **Defending the faith** when your Christian beliefs are challenged. How do you answer that there is no God? Or there are 33 million of them? That all religions are basically the same? That the Bible is not true?

13. **Church-planting and other ministries.** Self-reproducing, indigenous churches are the ultimate goal. How ready are you to start one? To lead people to Christ and disciple them in a group and coach them into becoming a church which is led by the local people from the outset? What do you know about baptism, communion, church leadership? Can you preach, teach children, or sing?

14. **Spiritual warfare.** Sin and temptation assault us also through the evil world system and our own sinful vulnerability. We must put on the full armor of God. How prepared are you to maintain your focus and spiritual vitality in an alien culture, with minimal support, and many pressures?

15. **Missions training** including the biblical basis of missions, its history, geography, growth, trends, issues, strategies, mistakes to avoid, current ideas, cross-cultural living and witness.

Where to prepare

1. **Christian institutions** offer science and philosophy, etc., from a Christian viewpoint and a wide variety of Bible, theology and missions courses.

2. **Secular universities/colleges** have better name recognition overseas and offer a whole range of careers. The secular campus is one of the best training grounds in the world. Throw yourself into the campus Christian fellowship and it's training. You are already on your first mission field.

3. **Why not combine schools?** The best academic and spiritual training can occur on a secular campus, supplemented with Christian training courses.
4. **Financing your education.** For ways to avoid being burdened with debts, see our GO Paper, Students and Graduates: Financing an Education.
5. **How long will it take?** All of the pieces mentioned above can be fit into four or five years, if you take advantage of all the learning opportunities

Ruth E. Siemens & Dave English
©2000 Global Opportunities

Appendix 2: Resources for BAM sites

Business as Mission Resource Center **www.businessasmission.com** is part of the YQAM connected family of mission sites. The BAM site has three purposes: (1) promoting BAM as a concept and mission model; (2) connecting those who seek to pursue business as their ministry strategy; (3) train and network likeminded players into a team to multiply business as a mission initiative.

International Coalition of Workplace Ministries (ICWM) is a "fellowship of workplace believres who want to ignite leaders for workplace transformation by modeling Jesus Christ." (see **www.icwm.net**/apps/directories/default.asp?searchid=97). Their list includes over 1,300 organizations listed in five categories (Christian CEO, Business Owner, Self-Employed; Educational Institution, College, University; Workplace Believer; Church; and Non Profit Workplace Ministry)

Urbana Resources (**www.urbana.org**/u2006.ofb.cfm?article=15) which lists papers, BAM companies, organizations, business plan development resources and more.

Holistic Transformation Resource Center (**www.wtrc-tmed.org**) with a focus on the microenterprise development and twenty-one links to microfinance and microenterprise sources and forty-two links to Christian microenterprise organizations.

EC Institute (**www.ec-i.org**) wants to see "business professionals ministering, encouraging and empowering one another to use their business to glorify God, both locally and globally." They provide consultation for global businesses, internships for MBAs.

Global Disciples (**www.globaldisciples.org**), focus on church-based discipleship strategies and a program "to bring together churches, mission agencies, businesses and concerned individuals to find ways for Christians to access restricted areas."

Global Opportunities (**www.globalopps.org**) is "to help the church to understand and engage the biblical model of tentmaking by sending committed, everyday, workplace Christians as mission workers, and to mobilize and equip these Christians to serve abroad as effective tentmakers, primarily to least-reached peoples." This site includes pages that provide links to jobs, short-term opportunities, secure email sources and more. For those who become associates there is the opportunity to become a coach and mentor with other local tentmakers or agency workers.

Integra Ventures' (**www.integrausa.org**) vision is to develop businesses, which will "impact society, change communities and touch lives with the gospel." Integra focus is Eastern Europe, with local independent NGO partners in Bulgaria, Romania, Russia, Serbia and Slovakia.

Oikocredit (**www.oikocredit.org**) is a privately owned cooperative society. Investors can buy shares in the cooperative which typically yield a 2% return rate. The invested money is loaned in various microcredit ventures (especially some local cooperative societies) in developing countries. They presently concentrate on 31 countries across four regions of the world supporting 467 projects.

Regent University Center for Entrepreneurship (**www.regententrepreneur.com**) came out of the Consultation of Holistic Entrepreneurs.

Tentmaker Net provides a short list of Best Practices on BAM (**www.tentmakernet.com**/articles/bestpractice.htm) and YWAM offers an extensive set of guidelines (**www.ywam_connect.com**/ubasicpage.jsp?siteid=29315&pageid=328906) includes definitions, parameters for BAM and YWAM policies and resources.

Newsletter for Tentmakers: **www.globalopps.org**/goworld/index.htm

References

Associazione Italiana Amici di Raoul Follereau (AIFO). (2007). *"Project Support - How to Apply."* Retrieved 9/7/07, from http://www.aifo.it/english/proj/applying.htm.

Bailey, S. (2007, July-September). "Is Business as Mission Honest?" *Evangelical Missions Quarterly*, pp. 368-372.

Barnett, M. (2005). *The Changing Face of World Missions: Engaging Contemporary Trends and Issues* (G. V. R. a. D. M. Mike Pocock, Ed.) (pp. 209-244). Grand Rapids: Baker Academic.

Befus, D. (2001). *Kingdom Business: The Ministry of Promoting Economic Activity.* Latin American Mission.

Cox, J. (1997, July-September). "The Tentmaking Movement in Historical Perspective." *International Journal of Frontier Missions, 14*(3), 111-118.

Galli, C. (2007). "NGO Research Guide." *Duke University Libraries.* Retrieved 9/7/07, from http://library.duke.edu/research/subject/guides/ngo_guide/.

Guthrie, S. (2000, 07/09/15). *Missions in the Third Millennium: 21 Key Trends for the 21st Century.* Waynesboro, GA: Paternoster Press.

. *Wikipedia.* Retrieved 9/7/07, from http://en.wikipedia.org/wki/NGO.

Lewis, J. *Working Your Way to the Nations: A guide to Effective Tentmaking.* Downers Grove, IL: InterVarsity Press.

Marquand, R. (2007, September 1). "Hostage Ordeal Hits Missionary Operations." *CBS News/The Christian Science Monitor.* Retrieved 9/7/07, from http://www.cbsnews.com/stories/2007/08/31/terror/main3224939.shtml?source=RSSattr=World_3224939.

Moreau, A. S. a. M. O. (2007, July). "Business as Mission Resources." *Evangelical Missions Quarterly*, pp. 380-386.

Yamamori, T. a. K. A. E., ed. (2003). *On Kingdom Business: Transforming Missions through Entrepreneurial Strategies.* Wheaton, IL: Crossway Books.

Chapter 4

Partnerships and Dependency

What is the most effective means for accomplishing the task of world evangelism? How does one manage the resources from the First World for accomplishing this "mission impossible" in the Third World? How can you avoid creating dependency (and all the evils contingent to it) while developing a healthy partnership to maximize the resources that God has made available to the churches of the 21st century? Is there a wrong way to manage finances to accomplish a good task?

Sometimes it is hard to harmonize all the biblical principles, practical sense, and expectations of different people into a beneficial strategy for fulfilling a mission. It is not easy to balance, "The love of all evil is the love of money" (1 Tim 6:10) with "Instruct them to do good, to be rich in good works, to be generous and ready to share" (1 Tim 6:18). Later Paul warned that in the last days "men will be lovers of self, lovers of money, ...ungrateful..." (2 Tim 3:2) because godly men or pastors must be "... free from the love of money" (1 Tim 3:3). Those who live in the West, even from the poorest families, have little idea how even a little money can corrupt believers and unbelievers in under developed countries. What seems so normal, big-hearted, generous and giving in our culture can actually generate more harm than good.

A university student in Bogota, Colombia, who attended one of my Bible studies, once told me, "Don, don't trust us, any of us. We will find a way to take all we can from you."

Disillusionment, envy, resentment, and disappointment all breed bitterness and animosity. Perhaps the chief root of this downward spiral is the misuse of money, even when used for good intentions.

My father once told me that the surest way to create your worst enemy out of your best friend is to loan him money. When he is suppose to return the funds, he will likely not be available to do so, and the mere reminder to him will begin a deteriorating relationship that inevitably will end in animosity.

In this chapter we will deal with the following topics:
   The dangers of dependency
   Short-term trips and dependency
   How to avoid dependency
   Four Perspectives for Using Money in Missions

Westerners typically have a difficult time grasping the depth of resentment and jealousy that improper use of funds can create. We are usually clueless about the inevitable envy an American generates, just because he comes from

America, regardless of his economic background. The vast majority of the unreached peoples of the world are living in extreme poverty and depressed conditions that have little hope of improving. Many are willing to clutch at any opportunity afforded them and willing to adapt to any benefactor in order to better their lot in life. This chapter will introduce the inter-cultural student to the difficulties of building relationships in an emotionally charged environment.

I. The dangers of dependency

Robert Reese defines *dependency* as the unhealthy reliance on foreign resources, personnel, and ideas, which stifles local initiative. It may seem relatively harmless but it has far reaching effects. It is expecting someone else to do for you what you could do for yourself. "In mission history, dependency resulted from western missionaries importing foreign forms of worship, church organization, institutions, and theology during the colonial period. Indigenous people could not operate such foreign systems and found they had to depend on outsiders to run them. It is for this reason that some churches in developing nations continue to be weak and ineffective" (Reese, 2007).

Dependency of a church or an individual can be understood as the psychological effect of poverty. Kritzinger's research has revealed that it is "tragic, but true, that poverty breeds a "culture of poverty," which takes away people's dignity and ability to such an extent that they become unable to do anything positive for themselves. The "beggar mentality" causes a person to only sit and wait on other people to do something for them" (Kritzinger, 1996, p. 14). Dependency is certainly one of the most serious diseases a church can contract.

All these, and more could be added, are aspects of the deadly disease called dependency. This syndrome weakens the body (the church) to such an extent that the church, or individual, becomes unable or unwilling to do anything. People, or the church, who are suffering from this disease, are unable to see opportunities or to use them. It is a kind of paralysis, a mentality, that stifles all initiative and causes the sufferer to negate all responsibility.

A dependent person (or church) depends on others to nourish and sustain him or her ... but never receives enough, always complains. The expectation level is always higher than the reality. This mentality stifles all growth and life, and is certainly far from what can be expected from the church.

To make matters worse, dependency is a contagious disease; it catches on. It doesn't take long before all the members are just as dependent on outside help as is the church. "In a country in which the prime human struggle is to climb out of the deep morass of poverty and powerlessness, the church is of no help if it is itself poisoning the people with the virus of not taking responsibility for its own affairs. The church should take the lead with a theology and practice of responsibility and reconstruction" (Kritzinger, 1996, p. 16).

Some evangelicals would like to implement a Marshall Plan for Christ in response to the global economic inequities (Rowell 2006:141-4); short-term mission is one way they can take action directly. They form partnerships with under-funded ministries in the developing countries that they visit. "Eager to solve global problems with American money and technology, they plunge in with solutions before they understand the local situations and forge financial relationships with people they scarcely know. The stage is set for creating massive dependency in the developing world" (Reese, 2007).

Bruce R. Reichenbach commented, "Consistent with their guilt-complex, the Western churches continually search for new ways to infuse financial and material aid into the Third World churches," so creating "money greed" (Reichenbach, 1982, p. 170).

When people come into the Christian faith for the material possessions they get - something goes terribly wrong in the spread of the Gospel. That might be the "single most important reason why the dependency problem so often cripples the Christian movement and why it is so urgent that it be avoided or dealt with where it exists" (Schwartz, 2000, p. 3).

Rick Wood interviewed Steve Saint who reported that the Waodani ["Auca"] Indians of Ecuador had turned from independence in the 1960s to dependence in the 1990s because of short-term mission projects. Saint said that dependency had crept in through two types of well-meaning short-term missions: Bible conferences and constructing church buildings. Those Americans who conducted Bible conferences furnished rice and sugar to create "a big festive occasion." Since the Waodani could not provide the resources for this event, "They figured this is something that the outsiders do. So they never have a Bible conference of their own. Americans who built a church building for the Waodani likewise used material and methods beyond the capability of the local people. Saint noted that the result was that for almost two decades after that project, "the Waodani, to my knowledge, have never built another building to be used for a place of worship" (Wood, 1998).

Well meaning donors gave a portable saw mill to the Waodanis, but how were they to get the fuel to run it, much less get it out to the tribe. It has sat in Shell Mera, nearly the end of the road, for years. Commercial fishermen came to the villages and dug pits to keep and breed fish for their tribe. When I visited the trip several years later the holes are dry because their concept is that men catch fish in the river, thus demonstrate their value to the tribe. A schoolhouse was built and has been repainted ten times, but it is never used for a school since there were no teachers. All of these and more were the foreigner's way of solving jungle problems that wasted a lot of resources and created the expectation that foreigners would do things for the tribe.[8]

When expectations are not met (which they seldom are), disillusionment

---

8   Personal observation from a trip to the Waodanis in the summer of 2006.

and resentment, either with themselves or outsiders result. This either destroys the value of the tribal, or national, identity or creates a thirst for the resources and wealth of others.

II. Short-term trips and dependency

One of the most remarkable phenomena of the later 20th century was the exponential growth of short-term mission trips into every region of the world. Most of these trips were designed to get Americans who were marginally interested in missions at least aware of the immense difference in cultures and living conditions. Most short-termers do not take it much further than a summer substitute for camp.

Richard Slimbach estimated that 450,000 short-term missionaries were sent from North America in 1998, calling this a "short-term avalanche" (Slimbach, 2000, p. 441). According to Scott Moreau, United States mission agencies reported that a total of 346,270 short-term workers (defined as going from two weeks to one year) were sent out in 2001 (Moreau, 2004, p. 13). He adds, "we assume that this still represents only a small fraction of the total U.S. short-term workers, since it does not include those who went under the auspices of local churches or on their own" (Moreau 2004:33). Roger Peterson, Gordon Aeschliman, and R. Wayne Sneed estimate that one million short-term volunteers went out in 2003 (Peterson, 2003, p. 243). One can only guess how many short-term workers are moving from North America around the globe as each year the number increases to a staggering number. The question is what kind of beneficial impact does this movement have for the cause of Christ overseas?

Teams from the United States fan out across the globe to do Christian missions of mercy and evangelism, but they usually know little of the local situations that they encounter. They see things that American ingenuity can fix and having the means to do it, they proceed to solve the problems in the few days they have been in the foreign country and then return home satisfied with a job well done. They may not see, however, the long-term results of their quick-fix solution (Reese, 2007).

Parson describes "one field worker among an unreached people who receives volumes of requests for short-term teams (from the US, Korea, Philippines, Canada, etc.). He could spend so much of his time hosting these teams (sometimes just making sure they don't hinder the on-going work) that he would never get to the work of establishing the church. And very few of these teams ever return to work with him in any on-going partnership (Parson, 1999).

Johnson noted that American materialism and a sense of pity toward citizens of developing nations often combine to produce a dependency on short-term trips. Some people can barely live from one short-term trip to the next one. Visible poverty can create a compassionate reaction in the short-term missionary that combines with a sense of guilt for having so much stuff. This, in turn, can cause rash decisions that produce dependency on the part of the recipient. This may be done through actual donations of money or materials, or simply through making promises to do more that are soon forgotten when the trip is over and the scenes of poverty have faded from memory (Johnson, 2000, p. 44).

Reese asked an African pastor what factors are prolonging dependency after the end of colonialism; he responded that short-term missions are creating dependency on a far larger scale than colonial missions ever did! When asked to explain that statement, he said, "Short-term volunteers are currently supplying pastors in Zimbabwe with all sorts of money and equipment, from computers to cars, without accountability for their use. Church members become amazed that their pastor is driving a new car and has money to send his children to the best schools, or to visit foreign countries, while they remain in poverty" (Reese, 2007)

Because short-term groups often want to solve problems quickly, they can make third-world Christians feel incapable of doing things on their own. Instead of working together with local Christians, many foreign groups come with a "let-the-North-Americans-do-it" attitude that leaves nationals feeling frustrated and unappreciated. Unbeknown short-term missions may unwittingly contribute to a feeling of powerlessness or inadequacy among the very people that they seek to help. This in turn creates more dependency.

Groups are sent to 'fix up' their buildings, do their evangelism, preach in their services, lead vacation Bible schools. Often these churches find that their own efforts fail to bring about the same results as the well-funded foreign campaigns. They can lose their initiative. Some become corrupted, seeking an inside track to foreign groups and the resources they bring. The church may abandon its indigenous efforts and become dependent on the foreign support (Reese, 2007).

III. How to avoid or at least manage dependency

No one should look for quick and easy solutions to the problem of dependency "especially where it has been in place for many years. Old habits are hard to break" more so when changing them means learning a whole new way of getting support for the church ministries.

Those Nationals receiving salary from overseas funds may be reluctant to see the system change. Those responsible for creating dependency in the first place (like missionaries) may hesitate to see it change because they have been getting a good feeling from giving, even if it has created dependency and left others unable to stand on their own two feet (Schwartz, 2000, p. 2). It is like a necessary evil to accomplish a better good. Likewise missionaries are able to accomplish more by paying someone else to work in the church(es), so they look better before their supporters.

On the other hand, Schwartz gives six principles to help avoid dependency while trying to help Nationals establish a ministry.

First, it should be recognized that the healthiest churches are not those in which leaders or members constantly look to outsiders for financial support. If you want to see joy and a sense of satisfaction on the faces and in the hearts of believers, don't expect to see it among those who are dependent on foreign funds. Rather look for it among those who have discovered the joy of giving back to God something of what He has given to them - from whatever resources, which He has put in their hand.

Second, begin to recognize the kind of things, which cause dependency and seek to overcome the temptation to establish or continue such practices. It will take serious determination not to think of solving problems with outside funds and quick fixes. Furthermore, the problem cannot be solved if the concept of stewardship is not first built into the Christian message.

Third, it is important to realize that the need for spiritual renewal is at the root of this problem. Do not expect people who do not know the Lord to joyfully support their own churches. Do not expect believers whose faith has grown cold to be willingly to pay their tithes and offerings to the Lord. True growth in spiritual life must precede an emphasis on stewardship teaching.

Fourth, something else must precede stewardship teaching. This is what I call a feeling of true personal ownership. Without this, people in dependent churches will often look to someone else to build their buildings, pay their pastors, buy their vehicles, or support their development projects. Imagine what could happen, however, if people were to take full personal ownership for their own churches. Things that previously were thought to be impossible would all of a sudden become possible. Resources would be discovered which prior to this no one could see. These would be resources which were close at hand all along. Only when local ownership is fully in place will people begin to discover the joy of supporting their own church and the work of God's kingdom.

Fifth, there is sometimes an initial high price to be paid for transitioning from dependency to self-reliance by God's provision. Some local church leaders may need to say "no, thank you" to the outside funding which has been supporting them and their families. Schwartz described how this happened in East Africa about thirty years ago when local leaders asked the people overseas to stop supporting them financially. They were actually declining the funds used to pay their own salaries. What followed, however, was dramatic. The leaders soon learned that local believers were not only capable of paying their salaries, but also able to pay for their own church buildings and vehicles.

They also planted new churches from their own resources. They started a pension fund for retired pastors, something no one until that time thought could be done with local resources. Then those believers in East Africa heard about homeless children overseas and took a collection in Kenya shillings equal to about US$30,000 to help with that need. All of these things happened after they paid the price to stop the outside funding.

Sixth, one might ask why it is so important to resolve the problem of dependency among mission-established churches. "Think for a moment about how many funds are being raised for evangelism yet are actually being used to support churches where people are already evangelized. Is it right to keep on supporting those who have heard the Gospel many times when there are millions of people elsewhere who are still waiting to hear it for the very first time? In some places, the Gospel has been preached for a hundred years or more and yet the people are still looking to others to support their pastors or build their buildings. For those who have not yet heard the Gospel even once, that is just not fair" (Schwartz, 2000, pp. 3-4).

What steps should be taken to ensure better results? Several steps are obvious. We can classify them in three broad categories: better training, integration of short-term missions with long-term strategy, and a commitment to avoid creating dependency.

Better Training

Evaluation is a major tool for North Americans in most fields of endeavor, so it makes perfect sense to evaluate short-term missions too. As churches and Christian groups gain experience from multiple excursions abroad, hopefully they will begin to have questions about those experiences. What impact has the short-term mission had, not solely on the volunteers who went, but more especially on the people they visited? The impact on the people visited is clearly more difficult to assess, but this only makes the question more crucial, since mission by its very nature seeks to know its impact on those it ministers to. The answer to this question will indicate the direction training must take.

By stressing the target people, cultural issues become prominent. Cross-cultural sensitivity will be the most immediate training need, accompanied by studies of the cultural, linguistic, religious, and historical background of the people visited. What is their worldview and how does it compare to the normal North American worldview? For this important information there is an increasing number of helps (Johnstone, 2001).

Included in the need for better cross-cultural communication is the fundamental principle of putting human relationships ahead of tasks. Generally, North Americans tend to put tasks first. For short-term missions, this is especially true because of time constraints to complete some project that will preferably have visible results. Whereas a particular project may be in the forefront of the volunteers' minds, the people visited will probably rather be fascinated by the visitors themselves. This is because most cultures value relationships over tasks and the people visited probably feel little or no time pressure for the short-term mission project. Good training before going, therefore, will take the emphasis off time and task, and transfer it to building relationships with local people.

This is not just a cultural issue, because people must always take precedence in God's work. If the people visited are not Christians, then interaction with them is crucial for the testimony that the short-term missionaries will leave behind. If the local people are Christians, then fellowship with them in God's work is essential, as they must carry on with whatever work remains after the volunteers depart.

Integration with Long-Term Strategy

Culturally it is important to be people-oriented, which leads logically to the need for long-term strategy. The best short-term missions must become so concerned with the impact that they are having that they will desire to integrate their own short-term goals with long-term planning. This leads naturally to more interaction with career missionaries or local Christian leaders in the places the short-termers want to visit regularly. By asking field missionaries or indigenous leaders how the short-term mission might best fit into long-term goals, the focus will again shift away from the foreigner's needs to the needs of the people on the field.

By focusing on a specific people group in one place for a longer period, the short-term mission will be taking a major step toward developing important relationships. When long-term goals take precedence, this increases the vision and purpose of each trip, which now becomes part of a larger plan. Training becomes more directed. Now the short-term missions can start to take advantage of all the helpfulness of mission history, writings, and field expertise. Even with this advantage, it may not be sufficient to overcome dependency, since many long-term missions also created this problem, but at least it is an essential step.

Avoiding Dependency

Colonial missions, especially of the nineteenth and twentieth century's, created dependency on a large scale by importing foreign institutions, ideas, and funding which indigenous people could not control, but soon could not do without. The amount is not as important as the act of creating dependency.

When short-term missions continue in this fashion, they inadvertently conform to a long established, but flawed mission model. Local people will automatically see the volunteers as an extension of colonialism or colonial practices when missionaries were expected to give and local people to receive. It becomes easy to slide back into comfortable but damaging co-dependent relationships. By co-dependent, I mean that local people are used to asking for and receiving material goods, while the donors receive a good feeling about themselves from helping people in need. Recipients even learn to place donors on a pedestal making them feel special, in return for favors granted.

In the case of a short-term mission, the tendency to create dependency is even greater if long-term contact is not maintained. The short-term aspect creates a lack of accountability that colonial missions had, since the two sides stayed in contact with each other. In the case of short-term missions, neither side may really care about the ultimate outcome as long as the interaction feels good at the time.

The way to avoid dependency is to keep some simple rules, like those of environmental clubs that insist that hikers in the bush leave a minimum of physical traces of their passing presence. By traveling light and having an agenda of learning and sharing on a level of equality, short-term missions will avoid rushing in to help before understanding a situation. The goal is to create no dependency by keeping an eye on the future of the ministry in that place. Reese (2002) concludes his article with four simple rules to avoid dependency:

1. Do nothing for others that they can do for themselves. This eliminates most building projects, because most cultures have been building suitable structures with local materials for countless generations. The only way to justify a building project is if it fits into a long-term plan and can be done under the leadership of local people.
2. Let the local people determine your project. If there are responsible and mature local Christians, becoming their servant will be the most important exercise a short-term missionary could have.
3. Undertake no project that is not sustainable by local people. This eliminates most medical short-term missions. Whereas local people may be grateful for free medical care, there will always be some who fail to receive treatment or whose chronic illnesses will not be helped by short-term engagements. How much better would it be if western Christians actually improved health care year round by training local people in their art? In other words, a better short-term project would be to empower the local people to deal with their own medical or dental problems.
4. Don't create expectations that will burden future short-term missions in that place. By keeping an eye on the future, it will be easier to refuse to create dependency despite the temptations to do so. Most problems of poverty and disease are long-standing and have no simple

solutions, so it is better to do the little that the short-term mission can do without making promises about what will be accomplished. Giving away lots of free materials will not only create dependency but may also set a precedent that future groups will find hard to follow. Charging small fees for services, for example, can actually add dignity to the transaction and make the project more sustainable.

Five ways to create an unhealthy dependency:

Looking at the situation from the opposite perspective, here are five strategies to avoid because they inevitably create a dependency.
1. Make an alliance with a Lone Ranger. "If you're not working with a ministry that has a local board of directors or the equivalent, there's a chance you've been found by a fortune hunter."
2. Send money directly to individuals, especially with no accountability and whom you barely know.
3. Finance pastors and local churches. "It can cause pastors to become preoccupied with raising foreign funds from abroad, and fail to be creative in maximizing local resources. Foreign funding of some pastors and not others creates jealousies, and frees them from accountability to the local Christian community." According to Rickett this is the highest risk of creating an unhealthy dependency.
4. Give resources based only on need. "Needs alone are insatiable." Giving based solely on need creates a pipeline of supply that in turn raises the expectation of future need satisfaction. Money is one form of power, and in international partnerships it has proven to be the most problematic. Rickett wrote, "Unhealthy dependency thrives on the imbalance of power."
5. Hiring local Christians to run Western programs. Hiring local Christians is not a partnership; it is employment. Whenever a Western agency hires local people, at any level, they assume all the responsibilities of an employer: fair and competitive wages, medical insurance, retirement benefits (in Argentina this is 52% of monthly wage paid to the government monthly) direct management of performance, vacation pay and extra-month's salary put in escrow, and compliance with all local labor laws. Lawsuits are common when there is the inevitable non-compliance, often through the ignorance of local labor laws (Rickett, 2003). I knew a missionary who departed from Argentina in the mid-1980s with nineteen lawsuits against him for failure to comply with all the labor laws. He was attempting a "tentmaking" ministry with three businesses that he attempted to manage with an American business philosophy, but this is another chapter.

Beginning with just a few such simple steps may chance short-term missions from being a well-meaning but harmful exercise to one that contributes to world mission in a positive way. It may be helpful to ask the nationals how they would respond to swarms of short-term volunteers from other nations who came to do good in their neighborhood, and then apply the Golden Rule. Certainly, we would appreciate those who treated us and our culture with dignity and respect (Reese, 2007).

IV. Four Perspectives for Using Money in Missions

Financial resources have great potential, but it is very difficult for both the giver and the recipient to resist the temptations of being the corruptor (or manipulator) and the corrupted (who likewise learns the art of manipulation for selfish ends). The following section presents four models of how different ministry philosophies have dealt with this issue.
1. Missionary support model
2. Indigenous model
3. Partnership model
4. Partnership/Indigenous model (Van Rheenen, 2003)

1. Missionary Support Model

A missionary argued that there is no difference between a missionary raising the funds and hiring a national worker to be his associate pastor in the US or overseas. It is common practice to offer a pastor in the US a better salary to lure him from a present ministry to a more lucrative ministry with greater possibility of influence and personal security. Of course whoever pays the bills, pulls the strings. This approach seeks to recruit the best leadership for any ministry. When this philosophy is carried overseas rarely does it work well.

Such programs are varied and wide-ranging. Some claim to be "revolutionizing" world missions through their approach of having western Christians sponsor national missions, churches, evangelists, missionaries and pastors. Claiming to be more efficient and culturally adaptable, such groups appeal to the western desire to be cost and labor effective by claiming that such an approach provides more "bang for the buck." Or alternately, "they bemoan the fact that these poor servants of God have to labour so hard to meet the needs of their families that they have no time to spread the gospel (to which I respond, "Paul didn't seem to have that problem" (Penner, 2007).

Wayne Allen in his 1998 article in the Evangelical Missions Quarterly "When the Mission Pays the Pastor" demonstrated conclusively how churches in Indonesia that numerically through the use of culturally appropriate methods, led and financed by local believers and open to allowing God to direct them. Their growth, however, plateaued or halted when westerners began to subsidize national church workers. Why did the initiation of subsidy coincide with the cessation of growth? Interviews that Allen conducted with village leaders and personal observations suggest the following possible causes:

"First, a loss of lay involvement. When the subsidy began there was less and less reliance on lay leadership and a trend toward dependence on the missionary or "professional" pastor. The lay leadership increasingly came to feel that the work of the church was the responsibility of the paid pastors.

Second, loss of focus. Those receiving the support began to "concentrate more on pleasing the missionary, who paid their salaries than on meeting the needs of their churches. Further, the paid workers lost the vision for evangelism. They increasingly gave their attention to ministering to the needs of the congregation, neglecting to visit the neighboring villages to preach the gospel." Ultimately the paid workers became increasingly aware of how little they were being paid, especially when they discovered how the missionary was claiming the results of the hired worker as his own. This resulted in increased focus on how to increase their level of remuneration, and less attention on the work of the ministry.

Third, loss of devotion. When the churches realized that the missionary was paying the salary of the pastor, paying for the building, etc., they lost their sense of ownership of the ministry. They increasingly came to see the pastor as the missionary's hired worker. They felt "no obligation to give toward the pastor's support. When the pastor saw that the congregation was not concerned with providing for his support and well being, he devoted himself even more to pleasing the missionary who paid his salary. The pastor also increased his efforts to persuade the missionary to increase his salary" (Penner, 2007)

The national leaders learn how to network with various North American partners (often unbeknown to each other) both within and outside of the organization to which they receive their primary support to secure a steady flow of additional funds. Thanks to this foreign money, he drives a car and lives in a house at a significantly higher level than the vast majority of the people in his church. Most of his personal income, along with a major portion of the salaries of his co-workers serving with him in ministry in this country, does not come from the local network of his denominational churches. Rather it comes from sources outside the country. When funds are needed for a building or a new ministry initiative, this leader tends to go to his foreign network to seek the needed funding (Fetherlin, 2005).

Internationally it is very expensive to form and keep a class of professional, well qualified, full-time leaders in the church as is customary in America. "When these leaders have socio-economic needs and expectations above those of the average church member, it becomes virtually impossible for a medium sized church to afford such a minister. Such churches simply cannot afford an old-style ministry. If the "mother church" regards these academic standards as absolutely necessary, it will have to foot the bill!" (Kritzinger, 1996, p. 15).

However, this "benefit" comes with a price to the national. Not only is it damaging to the motivation of an individual, but it is worse to the recipient of the support. "To receive payment from someone in many cultures is not to be viewed as a partner, but as an employee or a client. To be supported by outside (and especially Western) finances is to raise a cloak of suspicion upon the recipient's motivation for serving (or even being a Christian), and his loyalty to the country." The recipient is no longer viewed as "one of us" but "one of them!" This sometimes results in increased persecution or rejection of the gospel, although not necessarily because of Christ but because the "gospel has become wrapped up in dollar bills" (Penner, 2007).

Often local church leaders were converted and discipled by missionaries and now receive their salary from outside support. They have concluded that their people are too poor to support their own churches - and especially their own development projects - so they might as well let the situation continue. Unfortunately, such churches are unlikely to learn the joy of sending out their own missionaries. Some of them feel they cannot support their own pastors, let alone help to plant new churches beyond their borders (Schwartz, 2000, p. 1).

Furthermore, "jealousies between those who do and do not receive support erode Christian community. Many church leaders go through intense **faith dilemmas** when their support is terminated and frequently jump to another religious group or entirely lose their faith" (Van Rheenen, 2003).

Penner gives four suggestions for dealing with personal support in the ministry:
1) Consider other ways that you can assist God's work.
2) Encourage the organization that you are supporting this worker through to change their practices. A more biblical and sustainable approach would be to assist members of local churches with self-generating loans, job training, and stewardship teaching so that the church can become more financially stable, enabling them to support their own workers.
3) Encourage others to not get involved in such programs and to discontinue if they are. There is big money being made through such sponsorship programs. In 2004, the four largest groups in the world who focus on sponsoring national workers distributed over $53,000,000 USD worldwide. This does not include the amount that they kept for administration. That is a lot of money. Many groups have found that sponsoring national workers is a great way to increase donations. I suspect that until such groups realize that it is no longer profitable to engage in dependency creating programs, they will not change their ways.
4) Get behind ministries who are working at creating sustainable ministries

for those who, when they are persecuted, are persecuted for Christ's sake and not because of their financial links with westerners (Penner, 2007).

The personal support model is perhaps the easiest model for the western church to engage in its global program. All they have to do is to write a check, post periodic newsletters somewhere visible and, perhaps, make a visit to the field. However, during such visits the supporters tend to get a glamorized perspective of the work with little of the reality or understanding of what is actually going on between workers and in the community. If this has been the policy of a church it is recommended that they transition to a partnership model in order to keep the accountability factor in the hands of other local Christians of integrity.

2. Indigenous Model

In the 60's and 70's the *indigenous philosophy* made a major difference in the way missionary work was done. Hundreds of foreign supported institutions and ministries were "turned over" to national churches and organizations, many, of which unfortunately, did not survive and innumerable misunderstandings and resentments broke long-standing relationships between missionaries and national associations. Accusations of hording, selfishness, prejudice, discrimination, and corruption were leveled at expatriate missionaries.

"In many cases missionaries hold to perspectives of self-support while national leaders fell that these perspectives are rooted in paternalism and prejudice. ... The issues become so emotional and personal that effective communication is impossible" (Van Rheenen, 2003). As a bitter result, many independent national associations were formed. Great wisdom is required for how finances are utilized internationally. It is much harder to *indigenize* a work than to begin the work following the indigenous model.

Robertson McQuilkin, former president of Columbia International University and executive director of the Evangelical Missiological Society, quoted Bishop Zablon Nthamburi of the Methodist Church of Kenya, when he said, "'The African Church will not grow into maturity if it continues to be fed by Western partners. It will ever remain an infant who has not learned to walk on his or her own feet" (McQuilkin, 1999, p. 58).

Although Bob Finley, chairman of the Christian Aid Mission, Charlottesville, VA, in his article, "Send Dollars and Sense: Why giving is often better than going," basically agrees with the ultimate goal of an indigenous church. He declared that "churches, by their very nature should be self-supporting" and that "the most effective indigenous mission organizations are those independent of foreign control and not affiliated with foreign denominations or missions organizations" (Finley, 1999, pp. 73-75). However, he then declared that "providing financial support to indigenous ministries is effective if a clear distinction is made between directly supporting individual workers ... and ... supporting such workers ... and ... supporting such workers indirectly through indigenous mission boards that give oversight to the handling of funds" (Finley, 1999, p. 74).

Consider the rapid growth of a church in Ethiopia from 1938 to 1943. During this five-year period, membership increased from 100 to 10,000 believers with no missionaries and no outside funding present. The church in China increased from one million to perhaps as many as fifty million believers following 1951 when all missionaries and outside funding were removed (Schwartz, 2000, p. 2).

However, in the indigenous model the missionary strategy is to never involve personal finances, rather only operate on the resources within the Christian community, thus making the ministry self-supporting from the beginning, never letting them taste of the benefits of foreign money, yet never missing it.

Scaffold principle doesn't work

Sometimes missionaries and agencies with great resources begin supporting national pastors, especially in poorer sections of the world, causing inevitable dependency, which hinders maturity. However, this initial support is considered a "scaffold" around a building in construction. Upon completion of the building project the scaffold (foreign support) is removed and the building remains. This metaphor has a number of flaws, though often used to justify foreign involvement. The scaffold never is the building, nor supports or stabilizes the building. It is only a devise for the worker to reach different parts of the building as it grows. When the metaphor is applied to foreign support it fails, because the scaffold is the building itself! When removed, there is nothing left!

Once foreign support is begun or experienced it is very difficult to transition to local support. Van Rheenen states it this way, "Once supported by outsiders, always supported by outsiders."

Indigenous policy is a challenge

At first the work will go slower and require much more person to person involvement with less emphasis on the big rally or congregational meetings, rather more on evangelistic Bible studies or house-churches. In rural areas the churches will develop around families or extended families.

Pastors will not be trained previous to or for the ministry, but rather will be discipled, trained and mentored while in the ministry. Not only is there no dependence on the missionary for economic resources, there is little dependence on him for leadership, if done wisely. The only dependence on the expatriate is for training specifically applied to a given situation. The missionary is always in the background equipping leaders in the making as they lead their people.

Only as these small house groups multiply and require a national leader to continue to train and encourage them will a "full-time" position become necessary. This becomes a decision of the different groups of believers, not a foreign system or an institution imposed on these young believers.

This is usually not an imposing presence for a number of years since it is dependent on the slow building process of national leaders. The more the expatriate needs to justify his ministry with numbers and a show of followers, the higher the temptation to "buy it" with foreign investment. Ironically, the more invested, the less effective this model becomes

3. Partnership Model

The partnership model recognizes the strengths and weaknesses of the first two models, yet recognizes that there are certain circumstances where foreign resources can be utilized to empower mission projects without creating dependency.

The missionary growth in the West is presently something over three percent per year. However, in non-Western countries that same growth rate figure is over 13 percent! ... Non-Western missionary workers now account for as much as 80 percent of all personnel in the various Strategic Partnerships that are operational (Bush, 1999, p. 2).

The greatest obstacle to partnership is that the churches in the West have too much of the money. Though money is only one of many shared elements in a partnership, it wields a disproportionate power, primarily because it is universally seen as the solution to all problems.

The New Testament church grew and multiplied, taught and suffered with little reference to trained leadership, budgets and buildings. Lutz contends that money tends to cloud the issue of equality, since "it too frequently becomes the dominant factor in a partnership."

A mission leader in the West complained, "Since we control almost all the money, they [two-thirds world churches and agencies] almost push us into positions of power because we have it."

On the other hand, a national development leader expressed the quandary of two-thirds world organizations. "If a man has his hand in another man's pocket, he has to move when the other man moves" Lutz, 1990).

When wisely coordinated these international bodies of resources are drawn together into strategic evangelism/church planting partnerships. Anglicans, Southern Baptists, and Presbyterians; YWAMers and Campus Crusaders; church planters, Bible Translators and agricultural developers are intentionally working together to achieve Kingdom objectives.

Definition

Lutz gives this definition of Partnership: An association of two or more autonomous bodies who have formed a trusting relationship and fulfill agreed upon expectations by sharing complementary strengths and resources, to reach their mutual goal (Lutz, 1990).

Collaboration and partnership have been identified as one of the main reasons for the tremendous success that is evident in the initial efforts to reach the great unreached peoples of the world for Christ.

> Mongolia is a case in point. In 1989 there were but a handful of national believers in the country and no church. Just 10 short years later there are now thousands of believers and over 50 Bible-believing churches! Most Mongolian church leaders give much of the credit to the effective witness by expatriate missionaries and emerging national leaders who have been working together in partnership. The breakthrough in Mongolia is not unique. Algeria, Indonesia, Kazakhstan, and other regions are experiencing the powerful witness and blessing that comes when God's people work together (O'Connell, 1999, p. 2).

At great personal sacrifice and cost to their ministry, leaders agree to spend up to six or eight weeks every few years in North America, England or Australia representing their own ministries as well as the US organization. They see for themselves what kind of information churches are asking for, and the questions they want answered.

They also spend time at the mission headquarters and are made to feel special by the service of the mission staff. "They understand for the first time what is involved in keeping up mailing lists, sending out receipts, answering phone queries, and preparing publications. They appreciate having partners who are putting out great effort to reach our mutual goal—the building of the Church around the world" (Lutz, 1990).

Partnerships are not without difficulties

Partnerships are newly planted churches where the people are actively seeking to attach themselves to individuals, churches or mission agencies willing to support them with foreign funds. This is the case in many parts of the former Soviet Union where western Christians are finding small groups of believers and adopting them as their "partners in the Gospel". In some cases, the outsiders visit for as little as two weeks and leave behind a church, which they have "planted". That church may have a pastor dependent on salary from the outsiders, and the building in which they will eventually meet could well be provided through the good intentions of their newfound friends from England or North America.

When this happens, the dependency syndrome is developed within a very short period of time. The westerners who create this kind of dependent church planting have probably never heard about indigenous principles of self-support. Sadly, some do not want to hear about such things because it would spoil the good time they are having planting dependent churches.

Dominance encourages dependency-in children and in ministries. In Africa, a missionary put up a church building for a growing congregation. A few years later, the mission superintendent visited the church and noticed that the roof was leaking badly. He did not say anything, assuming that the elders were making plans to fix it. A year later, he returned again, to find the roof in even worse state of disrepair. The missionary asked the church leaders, "Why don't you fix the roof?"

The rather shocking reply was, "You built it, you fix it."

Some evangelicals would like to implement a Marshall Plan for Christ in response to the global economic inequities; short-term mission is one way they can take action directly. They form partnerships with under-funded ministries in the developing countries that they visit. Eager to solve global problems with American money and technology, they plunge in with solutions before they understand the local situations and forge financial relationships with people they scarcely know. The stage is set for creating massive dependency in the developing world .

Fetherlin quotes Alex Araujo of Interdev, an interdenominational agency focusing on creating healthy partnerships between North American and overseas church partners. These are some questions he asks to keep it sound:

- "Are local believers being prevented from learning to give sacrificially? A healthy indigenous church is able to exist on local resources. It is unhealthy when believers fail to give consistently to sustain the ministry of their local church because they are counting on outsiders to provide funds.
- Is the ministry failing to increase its income level from local/national sources?
  A healthy indigenous ministry will be able to raise at least a significant amount of funds in country. It is unhealthy when an indigenous ministry organization receives inadequate in-country support because national believers assume foreign groups are funding it.
- Is the ministry losing local credibility because of foreign funding?
  It is unhealthy when locals (government, general public, or even other Christians) distrust an indigenous entity because it is perceived as

controlled by outside funders.
- Is the ministry's goal setting and decision-making unduly influenced by foreign funding sources?
  A healthy indigenous ministry knows what its country needs and what should be its goals and objectives. It is unhealthy when a ministry allows foreign donors to shape their goals and objectives in order to preserve the financial help.
- Is foreign funding stunting the development of indigenous para-church structures?
  A healthy national church is one that is able to develop its own para-church organizations to meet specific ministry needs. It is unhealthy when they fail to do so because they have become accustomed to having outside para-churches meeting local needs.
- Is the foreign funding agency assuming moral responsibility for personal care of workers, such as their medical and retirement needs?
  A healthy church looks after the needs of its own people. It is unhealthy when the indigenous church leaves it up to foreign sources to provide health and retirement care for its members and workers.
- Does the ministry leader have exaggerated power and authority because he has access to foreign funds?
  A healthy ministry's leader carries no more power and authority than is appropriate to their role and responsibilities in the local context. It is unhealthy when a ministry leader wields too much power and influence because he gets plenty foreign funds.
- Is worker support level set by outside funding sources rather than by the worker's peers?
  A healthy indigenous ministry sets the support levels of its personnel in accordance with local standards and possibilities. It is unhealthy when outside donors set higher salaries than is appropriate by local standards" (Fetherlin, 2005).

Penner warns the Partnership Movement to always beware of the insipid evil of dependency, "I do not believe that persecution is the greatest threat to the continuing spread of the gospel. I am much more concerned about something that, at first glace, seems benign and even helpful but which I contend is far more insidious. I am referring to the dependency creating practices that ministries are increasingly promoting in the name of "partnership".

Fetherlin describes the following steps to be taken in the development of a partnership agreement:
- At the inception, it is imperative that the district leadership, field directors, and regional directors be involved in the communication

and development of the partnership.
- The partnership must be interdependent! Both partners must benefit.
- It must recognize that every field/missionary team has a limited capacity to facilitate partnerships.
- Prior to the development of the partnership, a vision trip to the partnering field or project is a must! To ensure that the partnership is successful, we suggest that the pastor of the North American church, along with key leadership, be a part of the vision team. This is where the church/district connects with its overseas partner, sees the ministry, and discusses the vision in detail.
- All partnerships must include a *Partnership Agreement* or a *Memorandum of Understanding* (MOU). This agreement should document all of the items agreed upon during the vision trip or in follow-up communications. What did the church/district agree to? What did the field agree to? Be detailed and specific (e.g., if you agreed to send short-term mission teams, when are they going? How many people will be on the teams? What will the teams be doing? Construction, evangelism, prayer walks, etc?)

How to partner:
- Fetherlin suggests that during the partnership period, additional vision trips take place to assure that the partnership is working and that both parties are benefiting.
- The Partnership Agreement or MOU should include a time period. We suggest that the period be no longer than three years; however, a renewal clause should be included in the agreement to allow the partnership to continue as long as both parties agree. We also suggest that the Partnership Agreement (MOU) be signed by the pastor of the North American church and the field director (Fetherlin, 2005).

In addition, a specific exit strategy should be understood and agreed upon before the partnership is initiated. Great effort must be taken to avoid misunderstandings, as well as to fulfill promises.

4. Partnership/Indigenous Model

There is also a combination of the last two models: indigenous and partnership models. In the beginning stages of the partnership, the missionaries will establish the beachhead by planting the first churches, nurturing the church to a functioning level of maturity and disciple-train-mentor national leaders.

If done wisely in the early years, the work is indigenous and self-supporting in the formative stage of the development. Believers come to Christ without clouding their decision with possible personal benefits. At this stage, a partnership is introduced to seek to develop "structures of continuity to nurture existing fellowships and train evangelists to enable this to become a missions-sending movement. In other words, national and missionary leaders collaborate with sending churches and agencies to develop these structures of continuity that will enable the national church to not only stand on its own but cause the movement to expand" (Van Rheenen, 2003).

Final distinctions and guidelines

A distinction should be understood between rural and urban ministries. In the rural areas, there is a greater danger of dependency so the indigenous or indigenous partnership models should be implemented. In the cosmopolitan urban areas, there is less danger of dependency and the partnership model can empower without creating dependency syndrome and the need for external or foreign control.

Rickett gives seven principles that help Westerners manage dependency.
1. Goals and methods of helping are not defined unilaterally. Do not develop a plan then invite non-Westerners to join in at a later stage.
2. Do not base the relationship on a one-way flow of resources. "Complementarity, not assistance, lies at the heart of effective partnerships. ... A partnership moves beyond assistance to complementarity when each partner makes different but crucial contributions to a common goal."
3. Do not allow money to become the most highly valued resource. We tend to put a premium on our own resources rather than on the resources of our non-Western counterparts. In most cases, non-Western partners may rely on Western partners for financial and technological resources, but Western partners are dependent on the human resources, linguistic skills, cultural insight, and relevant lifestyle of their non-Western partners. ... If money becomes the driving force, the golden rule takes hold — the one with the gold rules.
4. Do not fund the entire cost of the project without clear justification. "In the face of enormous economic inequities, there is inherent pressure on Western partners to be the "sugar daddy" or more "needy" partners.
5. Do not interfere in the administration of the partner's organization. It is okay to give advice when asked or to admonish a partner when a serious misconduct occurs.
6. Do not do for others what they can better do for themselves. People, like organizations, become strong and effective only when they make decisions, initiate action, and solve problems. This may lower the level of accomplishment short-term, but will ensure a long-term progress.

7. Do not rely on a "one-size-fits-all" policy, especially with policies. For example, one agency gives only 10% of the total need in any project. This may work well in some circumstances and be detrimental in another.

The key principle today is the interdependency or mutual dependency in the task of world evangelism (Rickett, 2003). The task is simply too big for any one country to have the majority of the leadership and it is growing exponentially. It will take a united effort of the entire Church to accomplish the task. Decisions about money, authority and mission must learn from past errors, glean the wisdom of the sages, gain the trust and confidence of all parties, and commit to one task and then another until the last people group and the masses of unevangelized are within earshot of the gospel message. If we understand the evils of dependency and paternalism, then we can progress in harmony, honoring the reputation of our Lord.

Appendix A

Thesis written on the subject of dependency:

Rowell, John, "To Give or not to Give: Dollars, Dependency, and Doing the Right Thing in Twenty-First Century Missions" Gordon-Conwell Theological Seminary.

Lawal, Julius Baamidele, "Concomitants of economic dependency: A comparative study of institutional pastoral education in Nigeria," Trinity Evangelical Divinity School.

Houghton, Graham, "The development of the Protestant Missionary Church in Madras 1870-1920: the impoverishment of dependency," University of California, Los Angeles.

Fox, Frampton F., "Money as water: a patron-client approach to mission dependency in India," Trinity Evangelical Divinity School.

Appendix B

Xenos Christian Fellowship/ World Team Partnering Agreement

PARTNERSHIP PURPOSE STATEMENT:

The Xenos Christian Fellowship (XCF)/World Team (WT) partnership exists to jointly send and support a church-planting (CP) team(s) to selected, unreached urban centers or people groups so that Christ builds multiplying churches among them.

The partnership will cooperate in selecting, assessing, training, supporting, deploying, coaching and managing the CP team(s).

PARTNERSHIP ROLES:

ISSUES	XENOS CHRISTIAN FELLOWSHIP	WORLD TEAM
POLICY	Accepts and approves WT's policies as governing guidelines for CP activity.	Provides policy to govern the activities of its CP team.
CHOICE OF FIELD	May initiate choice of field. Approves the final selection.	May initiate choice of field. Approves the final choice according to policy governing new CP field selection.
SELECTING TEAM LEADER	Provides insight and recommends an individual to WT. Approves appointed leaders.	Appoints team leader in consultation with XCF.

ISSUES	XENOS CHRISTIAN FELLOWSHIP	WORLD TEAM
SELECTING TEAM MEMBERS	Selects CP candidates for teams according to WT Policy 3.2 *Church Planters Profile*. Presents CP candidates to WT for processing and acceptance. Selects isolated XCF CP's who may be candidates for ministry of pre-existing WT Church-planting teams. Assists WT with assessment process by providing up to two leaders from XCF to serve as assessors at the WT Assessment Center.	Provides XCF with the Profile of a church planter. Channels CP's from other sources to XCF for possible integration into the XCF team. Processes, accepts, and appoints CP's. Provides XCF with appropriate data from screening process to facilitate further training of CP candidate. Assigns isolated XCF CP's to existing WT Cping teams where that is desirable.
COACHING THE TEAM	Supervises CP during pre-field and U. S. Assignment. Participates with WT in caring for the spiritual and emotional needs of the CP while on field assignment. Delegates supervision of CP's field activities to WT. Reviews and approves annual evaluation of CP.	Supervises CP on field assignment. Delegates supervision of CP's U. S. Assignment activities to XCF. Is accountable to XCF for responsible oversight of CP while on field assignment. Provides an annual evaluation of CP to XCF.

ISSUES	XENOS CHRISTIAN FELLOWSHIP	WORLD TEAM
TRAINING	Continues personal development for CP appointee according to the needs revealed in WT's assessment process. Conducts pre-field training of appointee in consultation with WT. Provides meaningful CP internship experience as needed. In consultation with WT, conducts ongoing training of CP while on US assignment. Uses XCF/WT's profile of CP to set standards for training goals.	Provides training in church planting through the WT Institute (Win). (All WT church planters are required to attend Win periodically.) Provide church-planting training modules to XCF as desired by church leadership. Provide the opportunity for two leaders from XCF as desired by church leadership.
FINANCIAL RESPONSIBILITY	Approves annual plans and budget of CP team. Reviews annual reports on CP team field activity. Assists CP in procurement of personal and ministry support as established by WT. Sends support funds to WT for management.	Establishes annual plans and budgets with team. Accepts and approves annual field activity reports. Manages all funds received for CP team personal needs and ministry: salary, medical, retirement, reimbursement of ministry vouchers, etc. Provides annual audit statement of WT financial activity upon request.

BUILDING THE RELATIONSHIP	XCF and WT will each appoint a person as liaison to facilitate communication. The liaison person from XCF and WT will: 1. Meet at least annually; 2. Review team progress toward annual objectives; 3. Address any problems in the XCF/WT relationship and make recommendations to the appropriate entity; 4. Copy each other on pertinent correspondence with the team; 5. Invite appropriate counterpart to accompany them on visits to the field.
CONFLICT RESOLUTION	When disagreements or misunderstanding arise between XCF and WT, the following principles will be followed: 1. The liaisons will discuss the matter and seek resolution; 2. The liaisons will report their solution to the field when parties on the field are involved, restricting those informed to responsible parties only; 3. In the event that a solution is not reached among the liaisons, a Board of Arbitration will be formed consisting of two leaders from XCF and two members from WT USA's Executive Committee or Board to seek resolution of the conflict; 4. In case of dissolution of the Partnership between XCF and WT, all residual account balances and items contributed by XCF will be returned to XCF.

DECISION MAKING	Although WT is responsible for supervision of the CP team's field activities, XCF is encouraged and expected to give input to WT through the project coordinator with regards to the following: 1. Implementation of the philosophy of ministry; 2. Financial management on the field; 3. Emotional, physical, and spiritual care of the CP; 4. Application of biblical values in cultural context; 5. Expansion and extension of field ministries; 6. Redeployment of XCF personnel to new target areas. Although XCF is responsible for supervision of the CP team's activities while on U. S. assignment, WT is encouraged and expected to give input to XCF through the project coordinator with regards to the following: 1. Continued training and education of the CP; 2. The nature of care required before CP may return to the field; 3. The amount of additional funding needed before the CP can return to the field.

CONFLICT RESOLUTION	When disagreements or misunderstanding arise between XCF and WT, the following principles will be followed: 1. The liaisons will discuss the matter and seek resolution; 2. The liaisons will report their solution to the field when parties on the field are involved, restricting those informed to responsible parties only; 3. In the event that a solution is not reached among the liaisons, a Board of Arbitration will be formed consisting of two leaders from XCF and two members from WT USA's Executive Committee or Board to seek resolution of the conflict; 4. In case of dissolution of the Partnership between XCF and WT, all residual account balances and items contributed by XCF will be returned to XCF.
ROLE OF LIAISON PERSON	1. Insure flow of pertinent information to involved parties; 2. Negotiate all terms concerning the Partnership; 3. Act as or procure a training consultant as needed by team and/or church; 4. Develop joint XCF/WT CP profile; 5. Channel annual plans, budgets, reports, and CP evaluations to the appropriate parties; 6. Schedule an annual meeting with his counterpart; 7. Monitor communications between XCF and WT; 8. Recommend any actions that need to be taken to the entities involved; 9. Notify the leadership of XCF/WT in the event of potential conflict and initiate formation of a Board of Arbitration in case of unresolved conflict.

Signed on behalf of the Elders of
XENOS CHRISTIAN FELLOWSHIP

Signed on behalf of the Board of
Directors of WORLD TEAM USA, Inc.

_____

_____

_____

_____

(signature)

(signature)

Date _____

Date _____

References

Bush, L. (1999, 21/1). "The Shape of Partnership." *Interdev.* Retrieved 1/8/07, from http://www.ad2000.org/adoption/Coop/Partner/pidshap.htm.

Edmonds, G. (1999, October). "Strategic Resource Partnerships." *Mission Frontiers.* Retrieved 1/8/07, from http://www.missionfrontiers.org/1999/10/dirset.htm.

Fetherlin, B. (2005). "Signs of Unhealthy Dependency." *The Alliance.* Retrieved 1/8/07, from http://www.cmalliance.org/im/omm/partnerships/dependency.jsp.

Finley, B. (1999, Oct. 4). "Send Dollars and Sense: Why giving is often better than going." *Christianity Today,* pp. 73-75.

Johnson, R. (2000). "Going South of the Border for a Short-Term?" *Mission Frontiers, 22*(3), 40-44.

Johnstone, P., and Jason Madryk. (2001, 07/08/02). *Operation World: 21st Century Edition.* Waynesboro, GA: Paternoster.

Kritzinger, J. J. (1996). "Perspectives on the (expensive) way of being church." *Practical Theology in South Africa, 11*(1), 14-23.

Lutz, L. a. L. B. (1990). *Partnership: The New Direction in world Evangelism.* InterVarsity Press.

McQuilkin, R. (1999, March 1). "Stop Sending Money! Breaking the cycle of missions dependency." *Christianity Today,* pp. 57-59.

Moreau, A. S. (2004). "Putting the Survey in Perspective." In Dotsey Welliver and Minnette Northcutt (Ed.), *Missions Handbook: U.S. and Canadian Christian Ministries Overseas 2004-2006* (19th ed.). Wheaton, IL: Evangelism & Missions Information Service.

O'Connell, B. F. (1999, October). "A New Mission Role for a New Era." *Mission Frontiers.* Retrieved 1/8/07, from http://www.missionfrontiers.org/1999/10/dirset.htm.

Parson, G. H. (1999, October). "Partnership and Unity." *Mission Frontiers.* Retrieved from http://www.missionfrontiers.org/1999/10/dirset.htm.

Penner, G. (2007, June 28). "Why Am I Concerned about Dependency?" *The Voice of the Martyrs.* Retrieved 1/8/07, from http://persecutedchurch.blogspot.com/2007/06/why-am-i-concerned-about-dependency.html.

Peterson, R., Gordon Aeschliman. (2003, 07/08/02). *Maximum Impact Short-Term Mission: The God-Commanded Repetitive Deployment of Swift, Temporary Non-Professional Missionaries.* Minneapolis, MN: STEMPress.

Reese, R. (2007). "Short-term Missions and Dependency." *World Mission Associates.* Retrieved 1/8/07, from http://www.wmausa.org/page.aspx?id=242674.

Reichenbach, B. R. (1982). "The Captivity of the Third World Churches." *Evangelical Missions Quarterly, 18*(3), 166-179.

Rickett, D. (2003). *Building Strategic Relationships: A Practical Guide to Partnering with Non-Western Missions.* Enumclaw, WA: WinePress Publishers.

Rowell, J. (2006). *To Give or Not to Give?: Rethinking Dependency, Restoring Generosity, and Redefining Sustainability.* Tyrone, GA: Authentic Publishers.

Schwartz, G. (2000, July). *"Is There a Cure for Dependency among Mission-Established Churches?"* Retrieved 1/22/07, from World Mission Associates: <http://wmausa.org/page.aspx?id=83812>.

Slimbach, R. (2000). "First, Do No Harm: Short-Term Missions at the Dawn of a New Millennium." *Evangelical Missions Quarterly, 36*(4), 428-441.

Van Rheenen, G. (2003). *"Using Money in Missions: Four Perspectives."* Retrieved 1/20/07, from <http://missiology.org/mmr/mmr15.htm>.

Wood, R. (1998). "Fighting Dependency among the 'Aucas': An Interview with Steve Saint." *Mission Frontiers, 20,* 5-6, 8-15.

Chapter 5

Short Term Missions
A trend that is growing exponentially

The growing phenomenon of allowing American believers the opportunity to experience life and ministry in a foreign culture for a short period of time (from one week to two years) is called Short Term Missions (hence STM). From its beginning in the 60's and 70's in the youth ministries of Operation Mobilization and Youth With A Mission (YWAM) the trend has accelerated exponentially every year and there does not appear to be any peaking of this trend in sight.

Researcher Margaret Lyman of Fuller Theological Seminary reports, "The short-term mission phenomenon has grown from approximately 250,000 to one million per year since 1992 (Lyman, 2004, p. 9). Other estimates go considerably higher.

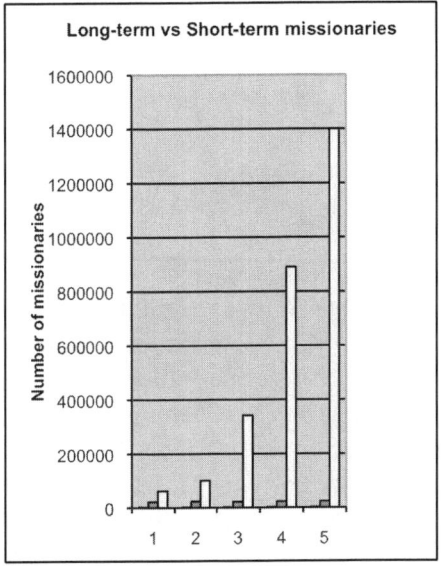

Just how big is short-term missions (STM)? As a grass roots, decentralized movement, its scope is difficult to determine. Yet your own estimate of between 1 million and 4 million North American short-term missionaries every year may well be a conservative estimate. The sociologist Christian Smith, based on national random survey data, reports that 29 percent of all 13- to 17-year-olds in the U.S. have "gone on a religious missions team or religious service project," with

10 percent having gone on such trips three or more times. That is, his data indicates that far more than 2 million 13- to 17-year-olds go on such trips every year (Priest, 2005).

Researchers Robert Priest, Terry Dischinger, Steve Rasmussen and C. M. Brown estimate that the number of annual STMers to be well over a million a year. This is derived from the national survey taken which shows that 2.1% have gone on an STM trip during the past year (2005) and 3.6% claimed to have gone on one when they were a teenager. These numbers indicate more than 1.5 million US Christians annually go on STM trips (Priest, 2006, p. 432).

Movements are usually not planned. Trends start in isolated areas then become generalized as the norm and a movement is born. The consequences are often not planned, but they must be analyzed and dealt with by leadership. In reference to STM, Dr. Sherwood Lingenfelter, dean of Fuller Theological Seminary's School of World Mission said, "It's the biggest change in missions in America." Later he added, "We have declining numbers in career recruits and an increased number of short-termers" (Allen, 2002).

Stan Guthrie describes one of the prime reasons for this phenomenon as a characteristic of this generation: "Baby boomers and busters are less likely to support an enterprise, either financially or personally, without firsthand knowledge of it. Many are interested in projects - the more tangible the better. And that most emphatically includes missions. Putting up a new school or showing the Jesus film to some refugees sounds a lot more doable to them than painstakingly learning the language, religion, and culture of a people" (Guthrie, 2001, p. 86).

As is the case with most trends there are two sides to the story. This chapter will introduce the issues, research and arguments from various points of view. Whatever one concludes, STMs are here to stay unless global transportation costs make it prohibitive for the large numbers of participants. Our conclusions must draw us to wisdom about how to maximize this trend for kingdom purposes that honor our Lord.

> "As the twentieth century closed, a dramatic shift had taken place. Missionary service was no longer restricted to a career option. Mission trips often were short-term experiences. In the midst of this shift, traditional agencies and churches on the mission fields of the world scrambled to integrate the new wave of volunteers. Simultaneously, majority world missionary movements emerged as a significant force for the global spread of the gospel (McConnell, 2005).

STMs have become the chief competitor of domestic summer camp programs. Many youth leaders affirm that their summer missions projects have greater impact than any other single event they schedule (Barns, 2000). "For numerous youth ministry leaders, short-term cross-cultural service trips offer a brief moment for students to experience faith with a new passion and purpose that counters a consumeristic culture's influence" (Linhart, 2006, p. 453).

Testimonies of how STM has affected people's lives are easily found. Warren Day, director of personnel for AIM International, said that he and his wife had three short-term experiences before committing themselves to a career in missionary service. "We had a definite interest in long-term service, but we wanted to know the mission better. We wanted to understand more about the ministry and our ability to effectively function in a cross-cultural setting" (Holzmann, 1988).

Monroe Brewer, mission pastor and has developed a ten-step program for transitioning STM participants into full-time career missionaries (Appendix 3). Brewer declares, "The short-term missionary, the cornerstone-feature of the missions-as-project approach, becomes the single greatest driving force in mobilizing the local church for world missions. At the same time, the short-termers stream becomes the single greatest conduit for flooding the world with field-tested, strategic thinking, and adequately supported long-term missionaries, the hallmark of the missions-as-process approach" (Brewer, 2000).

What we have is a grassroots movement in which, for example, youth pastors as a normal and expected part of their job take their youth groups to Mexico, West Virginia, Guatemala or Haiti on mission trips. Many congregations now routinely organize mission trips for all ages planned to fit around school and work schedules (Priest, 2006, p. 433).

James Engel, one of the most astute watchers of missions trends in the North American church, asserts in his 1989 book *Baby Boomers and the Future of World Missions*, "A short term missionary service program is a must. Organizations not providing this option will face a manpower crisis" (Guthrie, 2001, p. 88).

Objective of STM

What is the purpose or objective of all this incredible activity? Is it to give a "quick fix" to world evangelism? Is it to help the poor under-developed and under-privileged people of the world in a philanthropic or altruistic desire to help improve the world? Is this a calculated recruiting effort to get more full-time missionaries on the field to reach the world for Christ? LAM's appointee coordinator, Kathy Clark reports, "I would say that almost 99% of our applicants today have had some sort of cross-cultural experience (Loobi, 2000). Can we deduce from this last statement that STM experiences are producing more career missionaries?

Who is responsible for evangelizing the world and how does God expect us to accomplish the task? Before the STM trend missionary John Holzmann wrote that "people are expected to arrive automatically at life commitment" with nothing more to urge them in that direction than the testimony of missionaries from some remote location. Holzmann declares that "Short-term missions rectify that situation. They give the needed opportunity for first-hand evaluation."

"People on the inside of the mission industry point out that short-term experiences not only give missionary candidates the opportunity to discover what to expect if they join the agency and team with whom they work, but they allow the agencies and teams to see what kinds of people are applying to work with them" (Holzmann, 1988). This dual objective can be extremely important when the STM is at least several months in duration.

Change in the STMers

Proponents for STMs argue that North American participants change the lives of those they serve by providing needed goods and services and sharing the gospel. In addition, proponents say STMs open North Americans' eyes to needs around the world and make them more faithful long-term supporters of the STM beneficiaries. They also say STMs strengthen participants' faith and act as stepping-stones for young people considering long-term mission careers (Ver Beek, 2006, p. 478).

The ethical hope for many who facilitate STM is that the encounter will raise awareness, foster a deeper faith, improve Godly character, and foster deeper compassion toward others. The problem comes when the "raising of awareness" results in no action and people only "feel" connected to missions, or that they have performed their duty but continue in normal cultural patterns without a nod toward new directions for service and mission (Linhart, 2006, p. 454).

Paul Borthwick, missions professor at Gordon College, writes of his church's reaction to STMs: "God uses short-term, cross-cultural experiences today to transform people's theological world-view. One church explained the effect of short-term missions this way: "We now have a commitment to cross-cultural ministry, which came from our short-term mission experiences. Participants returned with a much larger view of God be-cause they saw Him working through multiple cultures. Our church decided we could no longer be concerned with our church affairs only. Short-term missions made the mandates of Scripture come alive. The Lord of all nations commands our church's involvement across cultures and around the world. Short-term missions helped us take the imperative to 'Declare his glory among the nations' personally (Psalm 96:3)" (Borthwick, 2001).

In the journal *Mission Today*, Bill Taylor gives a ten-fold list of objectives for STMs that become the goals of every short termer. However, sometimes there is a big difference between the "can" and "will" in these statements.

1. They provide hands-on, direct contact with cross-cultural missions.
2. They can stimulate realistic vision for the global task.
3. They can provide an opportunity to see God at work (in one's personal life and on the mission field).
4. They can stimulate significant intercession by driving home the fact that without prayer, little is accomplished.
5. They can offer reality therapy for those who see missions with fuzzy, rose-tinted glasses.
6. They can convert a person into a lifelong intercessor or mission mobilizer back home.
7. They can create within those who go a desire to serve more significantly in their home churches - perhaps using newly acquired skills, and generally with a more global perspective.
8. Short-termers can witness the impact they can make through their example, evangelism, discipleship, or the use or transfer of their specific skills. Through their service they strengthen the on-site, long-term ministry.
9. They can provide the foundation for their own potential long-term commitment to career missionary service.
10. They can bring glory to the Living God through their demonstrated obedience to the Sending Lord (Taylor, 1996).

Amateurization

One explanation for the surge in short-term missionaries is that the definition of "missionary" is being stretched in what one might call the *democratization of missions*. (Ralph Winter of the US Center for World Mission, however, calls it the *amateurization* of missions.) Seth Barnes, executive director of the short-term agency Adventures in Missions, writes, "These changes are forcing a redefinition of our concept of a missionary. No longer is the mission field viewed as the province of an elite few. Increasingly, ordinary lay people are finding that they can be empowered to contribute to the mission enterprise with their time and talent." (Guthrie, 2001, p. 87)

Realistic pre-field training must include serious self-analysis of why do so many want to participate in STMs in the first place. "Lacking the insight into cultural sins that can come from mutual partnerships across cultures, short-term missionaries commit not just errors from lack of training, or mistakes due to inexperience, but sins for which God and their national brothers in Christ must forgive them.

"For America, sins associated with wealth and consumerism comes readily to mind. Wealth puts one on a slippery slope to many sins, including greed, injustice, pride, selfishness, and laziness. These types of sins tend to involve motivations for short-term mission. Americans may draw to short-term mission because it is adventurous, glamorous, exotic, the 'latest and greatest,' that is, something to be consumed, especially if one wants to 'keep up with the Joneses.' Or they may be attracted to it because they are lazy and it seems easy and pleasurable, particularly by contrast with long-term mission, which would require a greater sacrifice. Or they may decide to do short-term mission out of a selfish desire to feel good about helping others, or to become sensitized to poverty and lostness. The list of sinful motives for short-term mission can seem limitless, and the remedy is nothing less than the transformation that comes when we repent of our sins and seek forgiveness (Lyman, 2004, pp. 19-20).

Often this is an unconscious motivation that the short termer is not even aware of, but inevitably surfaces in the pressure of a strange environment. This common experience makes the team leadership critical to the spiritual success of any STM.

Criticism

With such a vast trend that incorporates over a million young people a year there are unavoidable criticisms. Some of them need to be dealt with and some ignored. This section is not meant to be critical or negative, but, hopefully, realistic. Obviously, the criticism leveled against STMs does not come from the immobilizers of the movement, but from two sources: researchers and those on the receiving end.

If we state that the objective of STMs is to see an increase in the number of career missionaries who can plant and nurture new churches to maturity, then we have a significant criteria to measure against. Stan Guthrie, in his concise yet classic *Missions in the Third Millennium*, wrote, "While the number of short-termers has increased the number of career workers has leveled off or declined. Even financial giving to agencies, which one might reasonably expect to grow with the bulging ranks of those who have gone on overseas ministry projects, has remained static" (Guthrie, 2001, p. 88).

Missionary Bill Taylor wrote in *Mission Today*, seven of the short-term mission's short-comings, some of which can be dealt with in pre-trip training and some are inherent in the STM structure and can only be accepted as inevitable.

1. Overstated importance.

2. Self-aggrandizement
3. Ignored national ministries.
4. Too short, too expensive.
5. Exhausted full-timers.
6. Limited results.
7. False impressions (Taylor, 1996).

Why are there some negative experiences on STMs? Glen Schwartz, called the *guru of dependency*[9] gives some possible explanations:

"One is that the anticipation of doing good for someone else is sometimes overplayed. Americans have a penchant for helping 'poor benighted natives' wherever they exist. Sometimes these Americans are seeking to fulfill a felt need for cleanliness or maybe a certain kind of shelter based on their own idea of the same. That felt need is not always shared by those they perceive to be "benighted."
Secondly, the attitude that an "outsider" can do the job better is simply American (or European). This bit of arrogance has been taught to us ever since we can remember. ...
A third reason for the often negative response is that it is assumed that when we as westerners go somewhere, such as a mission field, we must do something. The world has so many needs that we just must help by "doing" (Schwartz, 1986).

It is true that we must help in any way we can with the tremendous needs of a hungry, dying world. What has not struck us is that we must find a way to help that does not leave others feeling that they are too weak, helpless and uninformed to help themselves.

In an article written by Ralph Winters, "The Gravest Danger: The Re-Amateurization of Missions," he notes that popular interest in missions is at an ebb, so "we mission professionals are inclined to accept 'interest' -- warts and all." The short-term phenomenon has had little careful scrutiny. Missions, he concludes, "has become any Christian volunteering to be sent anywhere in the world at any expense to do anything for any time period" (Winter, 1996a, p. 6).

Critics say North American short-term missionaries often lack necessary training and respect for "nationals." They do not speak the local language, often are culturally inappropriate and insensitive, and focus on short-term fixes rather than long-term solutions and meaningful learning experiences (Ver Beek, 2006, p. 478).

Ajith Fernando, national director of Youth for Christ in Sri Lanka,

---

9   From a conversation with Steve Saint who has worked with Glenn Schwartz on a number of mission projects.

comments that many of today's missionaries seem to have an aversion to struggle. "Unfortunately, they don't try to radically identify with the people," he said. "Coming only for short terms, they live as foreigners in Sri Lanka - quite removed from the people and ignorant of their struggles. Often those who join them hope that some of the missionary riches will trickle down. They are taken for a ride by the people who joined with them in the hope of exploiting their wealth. One of the biggest problems in missions today is the `softness' of the missionaries going out from affluent countries" (Guthrie, 2001, pp. 88-89).

Leaders of the STM movement have consistently repeated the claim that STMs adds to the pool of individuals willing to serve as career missionaries and increases people's financial giving in support of career missionaries (Priest, 2006, p. 435). Furthermore, research "indicates that involvement in STMs increases openness to serving as a career missionary" but to prove the increase in giving is more difficult. The majority going on trips are at a stage in life when their income is minimal. After graduation from college their income increases, so naturally there would be a proportionate increase in giving to missions (Priest, 2006, pp. 435-36). The question continues, how long does the openness to becoming a career missionary remain an option in the minds of STM participants?

Others argue that these trips too often become expensive efforts that quench North American Christian's guilt and satisfy their curiosity but do little lasting good. They point out that short-termers for one trip can easily spend $30,000 in travel costs to build a $2,000 house with "less spiritual benefit than if the work were done by local Christians who would follow-up on their efforts." Short-term missions, they argue also "distract full-time missionaries while leaving the local population dependent and misunderstood. The millions (probably billions) of dollars spent could be better invested in long-term efforts" (Ver Beek, 2006, p. 478).

In addition to short-term missions' tendency toward self-focus, short-term trips, even multiple trips, do not necessarily enhance true cross-cultural understanding. Lingerfelter says that a "short-term missionary never goes through what missiologists call a paradigm shift. Thus cross-cultural situations continue to be interpreted through the missionary's own cultural framework, instead of the missionary learning over time to identify with another framework (culture)" (Allen, 2002).

Other critics note that STMers too often constitute "religious tourism" and can be a burden to local missionaries, organizations, and church workers.

> Critics note that many participants lack language skills and the cultural and ministerial training needed for cross-cultural work. ... There is also concern that short-termers may engage in activities that

displace local laborers and professionals. ... and that they may encourage economic and ministerial dependency. ... In addition, there is concern about the cultural imperialist assumptions underlying many short-term projects, and criticism that short-termers (and those who organize and support the missions) tend to be overly goal-focused..., overly confident about the overseas applicability of ministry models used at home ... and unrealistically positive about the effectiveness of their mission. ... As for the supposed transformative effects on participants, while these may appear significant in the short run ..., they tend not to be enduring" (Zehner, 2006, p. 510).

Schwartz reports an incident in Guyana that taught him a significant lesson about how some nationals respond to help given by an STM construction team.

A missionary said in his earlier years (presumably before he knew any better) that he took a large group of young people out to Guyana to build a church building. After three weeks of concentrated effort, the building was completed and presented to the local people. The Americans returned convinced that they had made a solid contribution to needy people. Two years later, the missionary who no longer lived in Guyana got a letter from the church people. It read, "The roof on your church building is leaking. Please come and fix it." (Schwartz, 1986)

When there is perceived benefits from the wealthy American benefactors it does not take long before the nationals know what the visitors want to see. Personal benefit does strange things to people. In an article called "Loving your neighbor while using her," Miriam Adeney reports in *Missiology*, the following truth:

"Tourism threatens peoples' cultural heritages. Those who serve tourists must ask: What parts of our daily life or history are we going to package for alien consumption? How much of our story are we going to tell? How much will we open to public view? How much will outsiders even be able to understand? How authentic will our dances and music be? ... Over time this selectivity can skew the way the culture as a whole is portrayed. Given enough time, the locals themselves may come to believe this skewed picture (Adeney, 2006, p. 466).

For those who are long-term after the visitors depart and know the reality of daily life, the harm that crept into the minds of local nationals to secure a "hand out" is one of the most devastating damage done by foreigners. While only trying to help the local situation, outsiders inadvertently teach residents how to manipulate the visitors to give resources and finances. Once this is learned, dependency is created and self-initiative dies. The ability to unlearn this characteristic is next to impossible and the harm that is done has many more negative ripple effects.

Funding issues

It does not take a genius to calculate the funds that are expended for STMs that come from the available funds that could be available for the work of world evangelism. If the number of STM's per year (2006) was 1 million (all estimates are higher, but for the sake of argument) and the average cost per trip was $1,500 (probably very low estimate today), that total expenditure from God's people was $1,500,000,000. Someone should be asking the hard questions about what are we really getting for our money! Much of this giving was sympathetic giving (family member going on a trip and how could I say "no"), which probably would not have been given to other mission projects.

Just how big is short-term missions (STM)? The above numbers are probably very conservative and underestimated. STM is such a decentralized movement, its scope is difficult to determine. Researchers estimate between 1 million and 4 million North American short-term missionaries every year and this may well be a conservative estimate. "The sociologist Christian Smith, based on national random survey data, reports that 29 percent of all 13- to 17-year-olds in the U.S. have "gone on a religious missions team or religious service project," with 10 percent having gone on such trips three or more times. That is, his data indicates that far more than 2 million 13- to 17-year-olds go on such trips every year" (Priest, 2005).

Two sides to the financial issue: first is the tendency to "help" the poor nationals often creating dependency and the second is to deplete the pool of available funds from wiser long-term projects.

> The more short-termers try to "help" the nationals the more dependency is generated. "Rather than being encouraged toward a self-sustaining mode of existence, the church in many parts of the world was 'helped' by the provision of workers, supplies, and especially money from the Western church. This well intended but misguided short-termers come into this type of situation and say, "Let us 'help' you," problems result. Without mutual partnerships to discern whether and what kinds of help may be needed, short-term mission can dampen initiative and reinforce dependence, thereby weakening, instead of strengthening, the local church" (Lyman, 2004, p. 18).

The second issue of funding is that of the depletion of "available" funds or the "piece of the pie." As evidenced above, this is an enormous pool of funds floating around in the pockets of Christian people above and beyond what is given through their local church tithes and offerings. The question is, how available would those funds be for more worthwhile, long-range, productive financial assistance to the global missionary task?

Guthrie points out that baby boomers and busters are less likely to support an enterprise, either financially or personally, without firsthand knowledge of it. "Many are interested in projects - the more tangible the better. Moreover, that most emphatically includes missions. Putting up a new school or showing the Jesus film to some refugees sounds a lot more doable to them than painstakingly learning the language, religion, and culture of a people" (Guthrie, 2001, p. 86).

Robert Priest raised the financial issue in his article, "Are Short-term Missions Good Stewardship?" He asked the hypothetical question that "if it could be proved that STMs increase the number of individuals willing to serve as career missionaries but does not contribute to a comparable increase in financial support for career service, then the total number of career missionaries is not likely to increase" (Priest, 2006, p. 435). The question remains: has the depletion of available funds for missions by STMs reduced the available funds for supporting career missionaries?

> "What if ... [the] cure for the funding problem faced by career missions — more STM ... is actually a cause of the funding problem, part of the very reason it now takes so much longer for a career missionary to raise support." In any given church the financial support base for missions is fragile. When church groups discovered that they could appeal to this spirit of missions giving for STM, with the innate sympathy of their own young people becoming a "missionary," even if for a week, the motivation to give this discretionary mission giving easily was siphoned off to a STM project, leaving little or none for a long-term career missionary candidate (Priest, 2006, p. 438).

Using a metaphor Priest compares the local churches to prairie grasslands where cattle grazed freely but now has been invaded by sheep (a real problem in the old west). "Just as cows, who formerly had the pasture to themselves, face a competitive disadvantage when rapidly growing numbers of sheep graze the same pasture, so as, would-be career missionaries hoping to graze in pastures filled with flocks of short-termers face a radically different ecological setting than that of missionaries 30 years ago" (Priest, 2006, p. 438).

All of this would not be a problem if the churches could absorb the enormous financial commitment that yearly is increasingly being placed upon her.

Research by various studies has indicated that STM participation "did not appreciably increase their giving. No methologically sound research we have discovered has yet demonstrated a significant average increase in giving by participants caused by STM experience" (Priest, 2006, p. 439).

Research on STM

Any enterprise as large as the STMs should immediately raise questions and force an evaluation on the part of those responsible for the leadership of the churches and the fulfillment of the Great Commission. Are we accomplishing our purpose for being? In the research done by Priest-Dischinger-Rasmussen and Brown of 690 evangelical missions analyzed STMers who were staying for two weeks or more (although 67% of all STMs are less than 14 days) (Priest, 2006, pp. 431-432).

Often global statements are made, especially early in the genesis of a movement that has relatively little statistical data as a foundation, but are "seems-to-me" kind of data. Nancy Bridgeman, director of Student Mission Advance of Hamilton, Ontario, made this early claim that "only two or three out of every 100 who undertake to go to the mission field actually set out, whereas 25 out of every 100 involved in short-term service become life-long missionaries" (Holzmann, 1988).

Effects on Christian Disciplines

Honest evaluations and credible research in the area of STM is limited and is a relatively new field of investigation. What about how STM affects areas of Christian discipline? Randall G. Friesen completed a pioneer investigation of a number of STMs, though limited in scope, pointed out a number of revealing concepts that need to be further validated in different contexts. He compared two groups in his study: first was the group of students who were already committed to a career mission future and those who were merely curious about missions. He stated that in every category studied those interested in full time mission ministry increased in their responses to the areas under investigation, whereas in every area those not interested in full time missionary ministry declined in comparison with their zeal while in the preparation and participation of the short-term mission. The areas under investigation included:

- Interest in full time missions
- Personal worship through music
- Identity in Christ
- Attitude toward family
- Teamwork in ministry
- Evangelism

- Compassion for Human needs
- Concern for Global Issues (Friesen, 2004, pp. 226-230)

Typical response to each of the items under question was the following conclusion to the statistical data collected:

"While both groups experienced positive growth related to this concept [evangelism] during their assignments, those with limited interest in future full time mission work had significantly lower post-follow-up changes scores related to evangelism in the year following their return home. Participants with a limited interest in future full time mission work experienced significant regression in their experience of evangelism, in the year following their return from missions, as compared to those strongly interested in future full time mission work (Friesen, 2004, p. 229).

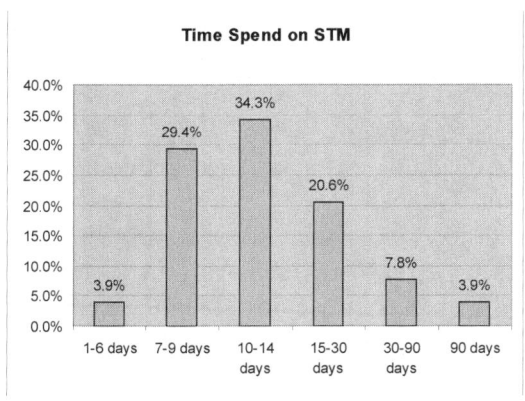

Friesen led over 116 STMs while doing extensive research of all the participants. The STMs ranged from one month to a year over a course of two years which included three stages: pre-trip, post-trip and a follow up stage (one year after they returned from their STM). "First time STM participants experienced the broadest positive change while on assignment, but also the most significant decline in beliefs, attitudes and behaviors a year later. Repeat STM participants were better able to retain their positive changes over a wider number of concepts during the year following their return from missions" (Friesen, 2005, p. 451).

His study concluded with the following implications:
1. Discipleship training before and after STM is critical. Those who lack either the pre- or post- discipleship were far inferior in the results. "The anticipation of an STM experience provides a unique teachable moment in the life of a participant. To miss this discipleship training

window is an irresponsible use of the STM experience.
2. We must do more to debrief and follow up with STM participants.
3. Supportive families and churches can make a significant positive contribution. Mentors for STM participants should be arranged before the young people depart on the STM to be ready to proceed with the positive growth steps that were experienced on missions.
4. Multiple STM experiences are moving young adults deeper into missional life (Friesen, 2005, p. 454).

Benefits of Construction Teams

Kurt Alan Ver Beek, Assistant Professor of Sociology at Calvin College, reported on a house building project in Honduras where STMs joined with a national ministry to build 100 homes. The analysis of the project was whether there was more benefit by the American STM participants as compared to those built by the national Honduran mission groups. The results were (1) there was no difference in the level of spiritual impact on the recipients of the houses, (2) there was no difference in the level of satisfaction of the recipients whether it was built by American STMs or a national Christian group, and (3) There was no other long-term difference, that is there was no difference in the motivation to participate in local Christian ministries (Ver Beek, 2006, pp. 478-79).

When the six national Honduran agencies that worked with STMs were asked whether it would be more beneficial if the Americans stayed home and sent the money they spent on travel expenses for the project (for every 2 homes built they could have built 10), or repeat the project with the American STMs, five out of the six agencies reluctantly said it would be better to have stayed home and sent the funds. This would have resulted in two benefits:
1. More poor people would have been benefited
2. More jobs for Hondurans would have been created. The STMs supplanted the Hondurans in the work (Ver Beek, 2006, p. 482).

It should not be concluded that all building projects will have the same consequences, but this data should certainly be taken into consideration. Usually it is impossible to raise this amount of finances unless we have personal interest in participating in the project. The idea of raising $20,000 and giving it away to an organization overseas is sometimes more difficult than raising the money in the first place.

Giving to Missions

What about the claim that participation in an STM will result in more generous giving to missions? If they do not become a *go-er*, then an STM will produce more generous *senders*, is claimed. Robert Priest, professor of mission and intercultural studies at Trinity Evangelical Divinity School, reports, "In my own survey of 120 Trinity M.Div. students, 56 percent of whom had been on short-term mission trips outside the U.S., the amount of short-term experience was not positively correlated with giving to missions. This result was unexpected and unwanted: It suggested that for these M.Div. students, STM as currently practiced was as likely to lower financial giving as to raise it. ... We probably need to stop making the claim that STM in general leads to greater financial giving." (Priest, 2005)

Career Mission Objective

Another area of investigation helps determine if STM facilitates the increase of future career missionaries in any significant way.

> "A year after they returned from their short-term mission assignment, participants' interest in future full time mission work became more polarized. Participants either became more committed to future full time mission work or less committed to it. With significantly less (ten percent less) indicating an "average" response to future full time mission work. Some 30.3% of participants indicated a stronger interest in future full time missions, while 30.2% indicated a weaker interest in future full time missions. Overall, a year after they had returned from missions, 60.5% of participants indicated that they were interested in future full time missions either to a "greater extent" or a "very great extent." (Friesen, 2004, p. 225)

It appears that the commitment before going on an STM is more important to the long-range results than the trip itself. Once started in a positive direction for serving overseas, the more exposure to such service the deeper the convictions to fulfill it. Friesen proposed the hypothesis that the more often participants served on short-term mission trips would not effect their interest in full time missions; however, the evidence indicated the opposite. "The more the participants served on short-term mission assignments, the more interested they were in future full time mission work (Friesen, 2004, p. 230).

Further more, "the longer the overseas experience (10 months or more) the more positive change in mission concepts became permanent characteristics especially in the values of service in the church, teamwork in ministry, concern for global issues and social justice" (Friesen, 2004, p. 232).

Real Objective of STM

So what, then, is the purpose of a short-term mission? There is an ideal objective, and then there is a real objective. The ideal objective is that genuine evangelism and missionary work can be accomplished on a short trip. However, in nearly all of the descriptions of why STMs are so highly regarded, the real objectives have to do with the changes that take place in the short termer himself. Each of the following quotes from major mobilizers and leaders of STM confirm this objective.

Paul Cull, missionary in Rio de Janeiro, Brazil, wrote, "My belief is that the primary benefit of a short-term trip is to expose the team members to something a little like the reality of the mission field, to give them a taste (albeit, often sugar-laden) of the reality of the call, and to perhaps motivate them for later involvement in world missions" (Cull, 1999).

The positive side of short term Sam Metcalf, CEO of Church Resource Ministries, in his FSTML paper says, "The primary beneficiaries of short-term efforts are those who go on such trips. What such an experience does for participants-clarifying vision, molding character, and providing a context for the Spirit of God to do significant work in lives-usually outweighs any real accomplishments or lasting results in the ministry context. Throwing people into the insecurity and turmoil of another culture does wonders in the process of sanctification (Loobi, 2000).

John Holzmann, Director of Mobilization Media Department for the Caleb Project and former editor of Mission Frontiers, wrote, "Beyond the strategic service they can provide, short terms have long been recognized as great vehicles for the personal growth of those who participate" (Holzmann, 1988). Holzmann added "Short terms reshape participants' lives by, among other things, opening their eyes to a world that's bigger than they ever imagined, exposing them to the needs of that world, and helping them to see that their mono-cultural concept of life and reality is much too narrow" (Holzmann, 1988).

Robert Bland, director of Teen Missions International, is much more blunt about it. "We tell our people who are leading our teams that we're building kids, not buildings," says Bland. "The purpose isn't just what we'll do for these people, but what these people will do for us....There is not a single purpose in missionary work...but to us this is the first purpose." (Allen, 2001)

Edwin Zehner, Ph.D. in anthropology and professor at Central College, Pella, Iowa, and writer, described the major benefit of STM, "In addition to potentially doing practical good, short-term missions are widely thought to transform participants, especially younger ones, by fostering increased cultural sensitivity, spiritual depth, and greater commitment to the cause of world missions" (Zehner, 2006, p. 509).

In David Johnstone's *Missiology* article, "Debriefing and the Short-Term College Mission Trip" he wrote, "Without getting into the conflicting opinions of the value of STMs Johnston "suggest that, while the impact may be varied for those at the receiving end of a short-term mission/service [or even study] trip, the impact is potentially enormous for the student who is traveling and volunteering. ... This fact alone is worth the journey. The educational significance of these experiences is vast. The challenges to their world view, their heightened cultural sensitivity, and increased self-awareness brought about by these trips cannot be easily replicated by other experiences" (Johnstone, 2006, p. 525).

He later adds, "Each trip varies in its accomplishment of ... goals; and in its success and impact on the host community. In spite of these differences, the most significant and enduring impact of each trip is upon the individual team members. For college students, short-term cross-cultural experiences have the potential for being one of the most formative and 'worldview shaping' pedagogical experiences of their college career" (Johnstone, 2006, p. 528).

Marshall Allen, researcher at Fuller Theological Seminary after extensive investigation of STM wrote, "This may be the first missions movement in church history that's largely based on the needs of the missionary" (Allen, 2002). In another article he describes advertisements for STM, "It will change both you and your church," says the Web site for Adventures in Missions, which has taken more than 30,000 youth and adults overseas for short-term mission trips in its 12-year history. "It will deeply enrich your faith and drive home the teachings of Christ" (Allen, 2001). He describes the emphasis many short-termer trip leaders place on the life change of the missionary—"as more important than the effect on the person being ministered to--is a fundamental shift of philosophy that many think is problematic" (Allen, 2002).

Ray Howard, Rocky Mountain regional representative for ACMC, former short-term trainer with Inter-Varsity's Short-Term In Missions (STIM) program, and the current short-term coordinator at South Evangelical Presbyterian Fellowship, Inglewood, Colorado, said his church's concern is "for the short term to be a learning experience for the individual, . . . a reshaping of a life."

The goal of biblical missions is to evangelize the world and build disciples of Christ. But frequently short-term mission projects are billed as tools for personal growth.

In their extensive research on short term trips, Robert Priest, Terry Dischinger, Steve Rasmussen and C. M. Brown concluded, "As currently practiced, STM does not appear to be producing lives of sacrificial stewardship. This is not likely to change unless we become very intentional about the stewardship outcomes we intend, and unless we place the challenge of stewardship at the center of our missiological reflections on STM" (Priest, 2006, p. 441).

> "Like pilgrimages, these trips are rituals of intensification, where one temporarily leaves the ordinary, compulsory, workaday life 'at home' and experience 'away from home' in a limited space where sacred goals are pursued, physical and spiritual tests are faced, normal structures are dissolved, *'communitas'* is experienced and personal

transformation occurs. This transformation ideally produces new selves to be reintegrated back into everyday life 'at home,' new selves which in turn help to spiritually rejuvenate the churches they come from, and inspire new mission vision at home." (Priest, 2006, pp. 433-34)

Representatives from all three of these short-term mission agencies (Teen Missions, TeenMania, Youth With A Mission) said that the life change of the students who go on the trips is a high motivation for taking the trips. Allen concludes,

"But this emphasis on using mission trips to grow and develop the missionary is a drastic divergence from past mission paradigms. Most mission paradigms were based on the Great Commission--the goal being to spread the Gospel to others, not use an overseas experience to grow personally and become better disciples ourselves. Effective discipleship calls for prioritizing culturally appropriate methods of ministry, often requiring long-term missionaries to sacrifice themselves in order to minister within the context of the culture" (Allen, 2002).

Ultimately, each organization and team that takes international short-term mission trips must honestly evaluate their motivation, be honest about their goals, and be culturally informed about the effect of their methodology. While it's true that one of the fruits of a short-term trip is a life change for the missionaries, this should be viewed as a result and not the motivation for the enterprise. The more the motivation for STM is to create a world Christian, a better disciple, an ethically eclectic believer, or even a world prayer warrior, as good as these goals are, they have a major fallacy: they do not produce career missionaries willing to sacrifice their lives, gain the skills and tools necessary to reach a people group long-term. As Hanciles puts it, "If people are going for their own benefit, then why call it missions?" (Allen, 2002)

Recommendations to make STM more effective

The research being done in the area of STM does not lack recommendations for improving and focusing the purpose of STM. As more and more culturally untrained and inexperienced leaders take monocultural American believers into non-Western, animistic or other religious cultural people groups, numerous problems can occur. When the group is led by someone who is honestly not willing himself to give up his lifestyle and go to win a given people group to Christ, it is difficult to imagine how he could challenge his short termers to make such a commitment.

"Short-term mission trip leaders who've never gone through this cultural paradigm shift need to be humble and cautious about their level of cultural understanding, lest they lead trips that are irrelevant to the mission field" (Allen, 2002).

If STMs are merely an effective discipling tool for churches or an exotic substitute for a fun-filled summer camp program (with the same transitory results), then a reevaluation is in order. Many of the recommendations given for STM deal with how to make STMs more of a life-changing discipling experience with focus on personal Christian disciplines and little one ministry skills, cultural understanding and how to learn practical skills and tools for a return to and more effective ministry with the target people group. If a long-term missionary is not the objective of STM, then it will not happen. Since it is not happening, it must not be the objective. "We get what we emphasize" is a true slogan.

Better Discipleship Pre-field and Follow-up

If we are going to target the development of international career missionaries (remember 95% of the world lives outside of the USA), then leaders must be trained in cross cultural understanding, evangelism, and world mission strategies. Randal Friesen said, "Cross-cultural short-term mission assignments have a significant lasting positive impact on participants' value of the global Church when compared to the impact of domestic assignments ... 'World Christians' do no emerge within the North American Church without some level of intentionality focused on discipleship in cross cultural mission" (Friesen, 2004, p. 239). We cannot expect foreign missionaries to erupt from a domestic focus. The world must be seen as the "field," not merely our neighborhood.

Jim Reapsome, former editor-at-large for Evangelical Missions Quarterly and World Pulse newsletter, says in his FSTML paper, "The primary cause of failure often is lack of pre-field preparation. The whole episode becomes a colossal waste of time, and a drain on the missionaries. To this we have to add the high cost of teams junketing off to exotic places. But we have to examine our total investment in light of the returns, as well as the problems we create. One reason for not converting more short termers to career workers is simply that some agencies do not adequately follow up their short-term people" (Loobi, 2000).

Zehner followed up on a number of STM in Africa and came to some conclusions that would help build closer ties to the nationals. Perhaps this is not only a way to leave a deeper impression on the nationals, it likewise might leave an indelible impression on the STMer. During interviews of the local church leaders after a short-term mission trip to Ghana and Rwanda, Zehner found that the American STMs "were good construction workers and that they drew lots of extra attention to local ministries because of their white skin. On the other hand, they felt that the short-termers should not focus on evangelism (due to lack of time to do it well), they wished the short-term missionaries had learned more about the host cultures, and they wished the short-termers would spend more time with the locals rather than just with each other" (Zehner, 2006, p. 511).

Howard Culbertson, renowned professor of missions at Southern Nazarene University, gave the following checklist of what NOT TO DO to help maximize your short-term experience. Please enjoy the sarcasm!

1. Keep narrowly focused on spiritual activities. You want to win that country to Christ. So, focus on your loftiest expectations. Avoid doing such menial work as data entry, loading trucks, or working on buildings. Such things will only distract you from your primary task.
2. To tighten up your schedule, eliminate personal prayer and Bible study. Likely, you will be so rushed that you really won't have time anyway. Besides, can't you get all the spiritual food you need from church services and from group devotions?
3. Stay organized. Set goals before you go. Establish a detailed schedule. Do not deviate from that schedule. Refuse to accept delays, last-time changes, and impromptu visits and invitations. Those things will just keep you from getting things done for God.
4. Help the missionaries by pointing out their mistakes. Bring them up to date on what you've heard are the latest missions trends. Missionaries can sometimes be stubborn. So, you may need to enlist some support among the nationals for your views about how the mission should be running.
5. Get involved romantically with someone. Being away from family and friends make this the perfect time to get involved in a romantic relationship. While it may distract you slightly from the work, you will be able to expose national Christians to America's progressive dating customs.
6. Don't embarrass yourself by trying to pick up the local language. People are always saying that English is spoken all over the world. So, insist that those people use it with you.
7. Immediately begin pointing out your team members' faults. Time is short. It may be difficult for people to make the needed changes in their lives if you don't help them from the start. Especially focus your criticism on team leaders.
8. Make hygiene a top priority. Don't eat any of the local food. To be sure, you may miss some friendly opportunities with "the natives," but you'll avoid all those germs!
9. Keep your distance from team members who couldn't raise their full support. They may try to mooch off you. Don't give in. Letting them

sweat out their finances will build their faith.
10. When you return home, castigate your home church and friends for their lack of commitment, for their weak prayers, and for their inadequate giving to missions. This may be one of the few times you will have their deferential respect; so make the most of it (Culbertson, 2001).

Preparation for Long-Term. Hesselgrave warns STMs to avoid amateurism:

"The Student Volunteer Movement was borne on a wave of enthusiasm and commitment. However, in their enthusiasm, the volunteers tended to ignore the insights of earlier missions workers. They made serious mistakes that resulted in many unnecessary deaths among the missionaries and a demoralization and spiritual decline among national pastors. Their amateurism set missions back instead of propelling the work forward. It took missions educators and institutions forty years to relearn the lessons that had been so quickly forgotten" (Hesselgrave, 2006, p. 204).

Friesen's research showed that "short-term mission participants with extensive pre-trip discipleship training experienced significantly higher change scores during their assignments in their beliefs, attitudes and behaviors related to personal communication with God (prayer), the Bible as a guide for life, the value of Christian community, and relationship with the local church and evangelism, when compared to participants who did not receive extensive pre-trip discipleship training" (Friesen, 2004, p. 237).

Cultural training. Admittedly, it would be extremely difficult to prepare everyone beforehand to fit into a new and complex culture. This can take years of understanding and adaptation. However, the more specific cultural training and general cross cultural skills learned before the trip, the more "hooks" the STMer will have to "hang" his experiences on when they are encountered. Kevin Birth, Associate Professor at Queens College, wrote,
"From my own experience as an ethnographer, I know that training and reading about Trinidadian history, culture and society can only convey the significance of issues of race, class, and religion throughout the country, but not the local manifestation and complex interaction of these issues [voodoo, charismatic extremes, Catholicism, visions, Hinduism]. There is not a former sadhu or a Brother Thomas in every congregation. Instead, every community is slightly different, and every congregation is different (Birth, 2006, p. 501).

Face-to-face with career missionaries. There is nothing like observing a model person to learn a new skill. Ideally, any trip should be centered on the learning experience of watching a mature, experienced missionary minister in another culture. Holzmann observed that "while it is generally conceded that the best short term is one in which you can observe long-term missionaries doing their work, long-term missionaries are not necessarily equipped to meet the special needs that short-termers bring with them" (Holzmann, 1988). For this reason the missionary to be visited and assisted, should be selected with great care that they will have the impact on the STMers that will encourage them to an effective long-term ministry.

More time overseas means greater impact. Friesen point out, "The longer an STM experience, the deeper and more lasting its impact on participants' beliefs, attitudes and behaviors" (Friesen, 2005, p. 450).

Repeated STM to the same area for long-term exposure: Terence Linhart, dean of the School of Religion and Philosophy, Bethel College in Mishawaka, IN, writes, "At best, what a short-term team can accomplish is limited. It takes time to see how local patterns work. What is the right way to plan a schedule? To expend money and account for it? To exercise authority? To take initiative? To settle quarrels? God in Christ took thirty-three years in one place. It takes time to be a friend, to listen and to fall to the ground as a seed, only to find fresh life among brothers and sisters very different from ourselves. Short-term teams do best when they work under long-term missionaries or locals, and when they are part of a multi-year series of exchanges (Linhart, 2006, p. 468).

Writing in the Ask-a-missionary e-mail newsletter, Jim Hogrefe of OMS International, says, "Determine whether or not the short-term trip will stimulate career missionary work or if it is mostly just a one-time project" (Guthrie, 2001, p. 91).

Make the STM a reciprocal encounter. Another model for STM is to make the 'missionaries' as trainee-subordinates to the local church' or local believers instead of the foreigner who has all the answers. Zehner suggest that this would make the primary beneficiary of this focus the STMer who would "be stretched in the following three areas: (a) experiencing God, (b) experiencing the Worldwide Body of Christ, and (c) experiencing Ministry in a different context." It would be designed to "make the sojourner more spiritually minded, less self-sufficient, and less certain of the prospective brought to the field, while perhaps sharing some of the experiential risks faced by the locals. It was hoped that the foreign visitors would thereby develop attitudes that would make better partnering possible, and the process simply required recognizing the local church's ministry leadership even when deploying foreign personnel" (Zehner, 2006, p. 512).

Following in a similar approach, Mike Pocock, of Dallas Theological Seminary, suggest that when an STM is planned in another culture there should be time allocated "simply to listen to local believers tell how God helps them cope with their circumstances." He challenges STMs to let the Nationals be your teachers. "You will learn a great deal bout God and also about the kind of faith it takes to live where they are." He then gives three suggested questions to ask in these settings: (1) How did God convince you to accept and believe the gospel? (2) What have been your greatest trials as a Christian, and how did God help you face them? (3) What are the greatest needs your community and country face? (Pocock, 2005, p. 155)

Don't get involved in "Lone Ranger" mission projects. There is no shortage of needs to be met around the world. Admittedly, existing mission agencies do not cover many areas. Being motivated by compassion many get involved in a one-time project that looks great back home, but often creates disillusionment and frustration on the field, because the STMers have moved on to greater things. Strategic long-term thinking must be part of the plans of STMs. In his chapter on "Amateurization and Professionalization" Hesselgrave gave the following case study:

"Some ten years or so ago, the missions-minded First Evangelical Free Church in St. Louis, Missouri, decided to "jump-start" a church-planting movement in Tatarstan, Russia. Their strategy was both simple and bold. They would send missionary teams on two-week mission strips to assist a national church planter by witnessing and presenting the gospel in a variety of ways. Over time, converts would be organized into small groups for fellowship and Bible study. Out of these groups, one church, or perhaps several, would be organized.
Over a two-year period, the church sent more than one hundred short-termers (mostly laypersons) to Tatarstan with disappointing results. Providentially, a seminary mission student from another church by the name of Carl Brown was in Tatarstan on a two-month assignment at the time. Aware of the arrangement and its lack of progress, he informed his seminary mentors of the situation. Meanwhile, back in St. Louis, Christians made two decisions. First, they decided to pray that the Lord would raise up a church-planting career missionary with whom they could work. Second, they decided to suspend the short-term program in Russia until the Lord supplied such a missionary" (Hesselgrave, 2006, pp. 203-204).

Don't go overseas with the notion that American success means international success. Zehner points out successful American ministries are often assured that they know exactly why they have grown and can transmit their success formula into another culture and economic structure. He comments "In cross-cultural leadership training seminars taught overseas by American church leaders often did not take into consideration the long-term effects on local churches. ... They were also offended by the assumption of many trainers that recently successful American churches had the best, most trend-setting models for the church world-wide, when there were actually larger churches elsewhere with successful alternative models" (Zehner, 2006, p. 510).

Make it difficult. In striving for the goal of culturally relevant short-term missions with long-term impact, Sherwood Lingenfelter, Dean of the School of World Mission at Fuller Theological Seminary, has a radical suggestion: "The best thing to do would be to make it more difficult for people to go," he says. "Instead of trying to get everybody to go, lay out a challenge and see who'll commit to a longer time of prayer and preparation to go."

Lingenfelter points to a short-term trip he led to Chad. When he initially announced the trip, 45 students showed interest. He invited the group to come pray with him weekly for a semester. By the end of the semester, eight kids remained. Lingenfelter says "a small group is better because he can train them beforehand and coach them throughout the trip." In addition, because Lingenfelter's team worked in partnership with the local church in Chad, the trip has had a long-term impact (Allen, 2002).

Friesen's evidence agrees with Lingenfelter when he showed the need for "longer and deeper" assignments in order to produce a paradigm shift on the part of the missionaries in their relationship to the host culture. "Without a paradigm shift, short-term missionaries interpret cross-cultural situation through the missionary's own cultural framework rather than learning to identify with the framework of the host culture. The keys to a paradigm shift include learning the local language and living with the local people." (Friesen, 2004, p. 239)

Debriefing and Follow-up on STM

The experiences on the field can be varied and multiple, smooth and rough, flawless or chaotic, exotic or urban, comfortable or uncomfortable, exhilarating or frustrating, but it really doesn't matter that much as far as lasting desired effects. "An STM provides a fertile setting for Christians to reflect on such things as witness, service, community, sacrifice, spirituality, poverty, materialism, suffering, hedonism, self-denial, justice, racism, ethnocentrism, inter-ethnic relations, globalization, stewardship, and vocation. The context is valuable, even if STM leaders do not foster these reflections among participants" (Priest, 2005). People need to be lead through these experiences to consciously understand the meaning and impact on their lives.

"The data indicates that approximately fifty percent of the short-term mission alumni in the study became *more interested* [italics mine] in future full time mission work during the year following their return from missions. Discovering and following up with those short-term mission alumni, who were moving toward stronger interest in future full time mission work, would be a critical task for mission agencies and local churches" (Friesen, 2004, p. 243).

The less importance that the leaders place on the interpretation of the data gleaned while on this trip, the less importance the STMers will as well. They will remember the fun and adventure like a trip to Disneyworld, but not the pathos of a dying world without Christ. "While good preparation is essential, for a trip of this nature to have lasting impact, there must be an opportunity for the student to reflect and internalize the situations they have encountered. This reflection must be intentional and facilitated for it to have any enduring significance" (Johnstone, 2006, p. 524).

Friesen reports from Tuttle study that the impact of short-term missions on faith and maturity growth in college students identified "the quality of pre-trip and post-trip discipleship training as the most significant factor in the faith development of short-term missions participants" (Friesen, 2004, p. 237).

> To use your vivid image, if one bends a sapling for two weeks, then releases it, one can measure a change in its position. But three months later it may be back to where it started. That is, when these high school students return to the settings that originally shaped their ethnocentrism and negative attitudes towards Mexicans, they may eventually revert to the original pattern (Priest, 2005).

Studies show that STMs "tend to produce temporary changes only" in ethnocentrism, except when STMs were "accompanied by cultural orientation and field-based culture-learning exercises, there was a marked drop in rates of ethnocentrism." Some of these training topics included the culture they will be working with and God's perspective on race. Simply the exposure to another culture may or may not change the ethnocentrism of an individual, but when the "immersion experience is connected with the right sorts of orientation and coaching, significant change is possible" (Priest, 2006, p. 444).

> "Short-term mission participants require a new understanding of the challenges they face following their return from missions. They need a new awareness of the dangers of re-entry culture stress, temptation and loss of spiritual vitality. They need to be prepared for a new level of isolation and lack of accountability once they return home. They need to see the benefits of a life coach who can help them navigate some of the potential re-entry minefields" (Friesen, 2004, p. 262).

Seth Barns, youth writer, has proposed that to reap the dividends of a changed lifestyle on an STM, youth groups must carry forward the momentum which a summer project can generate. "In order for the principles of sharing Christ's love and helping others selflessly to become a foundational part of students' lives," they must be reinforced through a regular long-range program of ministry back home. As Faith Bible's Missel notes, "We're selling our students short if we don't give them continuity. For us this takes the form of evangelism training, evangelism outreach to students, and support of local projects" (Barns, 2000).

The naive are unwilling to seriously face the issues of STMs because the fun and positive feedback from participants blind the leadership ("Success always blinds"), but the career missionary knows the difference. These become the major areas that need to be clarified during and especially following the STM experience. Holzmann identifies several challenges or problems for STM trips:

- Exposure to Need but not to God's Call.
- Exposure to Physical rather than Spiritual Needs
- Exposure to Reached rather than Unreached People
- Exposure on the Part of the Individual and Not His Congregation (in fact, few are interested in their experiences)
- Event Rather than Process Orientation. When it comes to short-term missions, most people focus exclusively on the experience of being overseas, of being in another culture. Yet as natural as this focus may seem, if a person is not adequately prepared for and debriefed from the experience, he's in for trouble.

The leadership is the key for the solution to these issues. How they are interpreted and what significance is derived from these circumstances must be brought out in open discussions. "The short-term experience is a very unnatural, critical event in the life of the person, his family, and the life of the whole church," said Hawthorne. "Too often it is shrugged off as of little significance. But there has to be facilitation (mentoring) before, during, and after the field experience" (Holzmann, 1988).

Warren Day notes that Adventures in Missions (AIM) brings out a number of key issues that apply to all STMs.

- We can't go simply to make ourselves feel good, or in order to say, "Now we've done our part, we've fulfilled our obligation"
- Agencies and churches may be deluding themselves when they think short-term programs increase the likelihood of short-termers becoming long-term missionaries

Numbers of STMers that become career missionaries and testimonies of missionaries are often inserted in publications or web pages that lack serious statistics. It is often wishful thinking or emotional "wanta be..." responses that are never followed up on, "I want to be a full-time missionary." It is fashionable to point out the supposed high percentage of short-termers who end up as career missionaries. Brent Lindquist (executive director of LINK Care Center, a missionary counseling center in Fresno, California) wasn't about to question those figures. He did point out, however, that "we don't know how many of those who went on a short term and later became long-term missionaries were already convinced they should become long-termers before they went" (Holzmann, 1988).

> The encouraging thing is that we know how to make these commitments last. It's not about how good the orientation is before they go, and it's only somewhat about the experience itself. The key to long-lasting change is having structures in place to help us stay motivated and excited about our goals. What we need to keep us on track in meeting our goals—to do devotions daily or exercise four times a week—is accountability and encouragement. Monthly meetings with our groups after returning to the U.S., newsletters about the progress and needs of the people we visited, and Bible studies on the country or theme of our trip are just a few of the ideas that can translate a one-week experience into life-lasting changes in prayer, giving, and lifestyle. Sadly, very few STM experiences are currently emphasizing this sort of follow up. This is where I believe we should begin experimenting and see how STM participants are changed (Priest, 2005)

The study by Borthwick of the nature and value of the debriefing was confirmed by Friesen where there was an immediate team debriefing "where participants share their experiences, reflect on the application of lessons learned to their home community, and a verbal report for the youth group and church. Their longer term follow-up program includes a mission reading program, weekly discipleship groups focused on reaching out, regular exposure to visiting missionaries, prayer for the people they got to know on their mission assignments, and a reunion six months after returning to further reflect and share how their lives have changed since returning" (Friesen, 2004, p. 261).

Recruiting

A positive response to an STM is the goal of every organizer of such trips. The unwritten dream of every STM leader is to hear a testimony like this: "We felt a call first, and that's why we pursued missions, including short-term missions, as part of our preparation time. However, it did influence how we ended up with LAM [Latin American Mission] and in Latin America. We were so totally impressed with absolutely every LAMer we met during our short-term experience, that we decided, 'that's the kind of Mission we want to work with,'" said Paul and Nancy Mauger, LAM missionaries in Costa Rica (Loobi, 2000).

Ralph Winter, founder of the US Center for World Mission, is concerned that contemporary mission candidates tend to be steered in one of two directions. "First they go over prepared, or second, they go with little preparation at all. Either situation places them and their ministries at a decided disadvantage."

- The first situation results from the idea that if a little education is a good thing, more education must be better. ... Today, many candidates' ministries have had "sixteen to twenty years of education" with the unavoidable accumulation of debt to be paid off before acceptance with a mission agency. This typically results in candidates in their mid-thirties, too old to master either the language or the culture very well.

  In the second situation, to avoid the debt-cycle and get to the field as quickly as possible, the candidates seek to avoid college and seminary (including the study of missiology). They may get to the field young enough to learn the language, if they knew how, but their lack of serious education makes them ineffective and limited (Winter, 1996b, p. 6).

STMers that show any interest in pursuing a career in international ministries should seriously be encouraged to get all the cross cultural training, specialized tools (TESL, Chronological Bible teaching, Bible training, language learning skills, world religions and history and methods courses from experienced missionaries before attempting to "reinvent the wheel" by having to learn these skills and others on their own.

For the most effective long range results Friesen recommends that short term alumni be encouraged to continue serving in "longer assignments and to continue serving with greater responsibility. ... Repeat participants are also more interested in future full time mission work" (Friesen, 2004, p. 249). Opportunities to share in the leadership of future trips or mission strategy teams in their local churches can be extremely beneficial.

One of the most interesting suggestions was made by Ralph Winter who suggested an "earlier candidacy (perhaps even before the end of college) and earlier training in language and other needed tools. Deficiencies would have to be met through continuing educational opportunities after candidates are on the field" (Winter, 1996b, p. 6).

Today it is hard to image anyone seriously considering a career in missions without first getting some exposure to a potential or similar culture to which they would be willing to dedicate their lives. "Diving into the deep end of world missions without putting at least a toe in the water is unthinkable to most boomers, however. Gone are the days when a missionary speaker would make an appeal from a pulpit and his hearers would jump up and volunteer for 'the field'" (Guthrie, 2001, p. 86).

Scott Olson, Director of Mobilization, Wesleyan World Mission, said "I'm convinced that if we want long-term missionaries, we have to be totally committed to a short-term program. That has been proven by the fact that fields who have an aggressive short-term program are the ones getting career missionaries right now. We have to look at short-term experiences as part of the "funnel" that intentionally directs people to the needs of the world and what they can do to make a difference" (Olson, 2000).

> "Larry D. Reesor founded Global Focus [a ministry that trains local churches to structure an effective international ministry] on March 27, 1995. Larry served as an evangelist, pastor and missions agency executive for many years. After studying the scriptures, church history and the mission movement, combined with years of practical experience, Larry became convinced of two things which comprise the cornerstones of the ministry. He believes that the local church is God's primary instrument to evangelize the world. He also believes that the pastor and church leaders are the ones whom God has ordained to lead the local church to gain a vision for the world and develop a personalized, prioritized, integrated and strategic involvement in global evangelization.
> As we help churches to emulate the New Testament church, we believe the byproduct will be that the local church will impact the world for Christ" (Reesor, 2007).

Short-term work, whether two weeks or two years, can indeed be effective and pleasing to God. Yes, it can cost a lot of money, disrupt nationals and missionaries, encourage short-term thinking, and inoculate some against career missions involvement. But done well, it can open participants' eyes to the sometimes gritty realities of the world, make them aware of their own ethno-centrism and the gifts and courage of non-Western believers, and spark a lifelong commitment to missions. In the best cases, some real kingdom work gets done, too (Guthrie, 2001, p. 89).

May presents the following rules if STM is to be effective:
1. Short-term missions are great if volunteers remember that the career missionary knows the field better than they ever will.
2. Short-term missions are great if participants remember that their

primary responsibility is to be servants to the missionaries and national partners.
3. Short-term missions are great if they increase the mission's spirit in the church back home.
4. Short-term missions are great if they call people into career service.
5. Short-term missions are great if volunteers remember to give God all the glory and the missionary the credit for the planning, preparation, and labor that made their trip a success.
6. Short-term missions are great if they are never viewed as substitutes for career missions (May, 2000).

Appendix 1

In a *Christianity Today* article, "Agencies Announce Short-Term Missions Standards," by Ken Walker, the announcement is set forth of an attempt to set some guidelines for the 40,000 churches, agencies and schools that are sending more than a million Short-Term missionaries.

1. God-Centeredness
   An excellent short-term mission seeks first God's glory and his kingdom, and is expressed through our:
1.1 Purpose - Centering on God's glory and his ends throughout our entire STM process
1.2 Lives - Sound biblical doctrine, persistent prayer, and godliness in all our thoughts, words, and deeds
1.3 Methods - Wise, biblical, and culturally-appropriate methods which bear spiritual fruit
2. Empowering Partnerships
   An excellent short-term mission establishes healthy, interdependent, on-going relationships between sending and receiving partners, and is expressed by:
2.1 Primary focus on intended receptors
2.2 Plans which benefit all participants
2.3 Mutual trust and accountability
3. Mutual Design
   An excellent short-term mission collaboratively plans each specific outreach for the benefit of all participants, and is expressed by:
3.1 On-field methods and activities aligned to long-term strategies of the partnership
3.2 Go-er-guests' ability to implement their part of the plan
3.3 Host receivers' ability to implement their part of the plan
4. Comprehensive Administration
   An excellent short-term mission exhibits integrity through reliable set-up and thorough administration for all participants, and is expressed by:
4.1 Truthfulness in promotion, finances, and reporting results
4.2 Appropriate risk management
4.3 Quality program delivery and support logistics
5. Qualified Leadership
   An excellent short-term mission screens, trains, and develops capable leadership for all participants, and is expressed by:
5.1 Character - Spiritually mature servant leadership
5.2 Skills - Prepared, competent, organized and accountable leadership
5.3 Values - Empowering and equipping leadership
6. Appropriate Training

An excellent short-term mission prepares and equips all participants for the mutually designed outreach, and is expressed by:
6.1 Biblical, appropriate, and timely training
6.2 On-going training and equipping (pre-field, on-field, post-field)
6.3 Qualified trainers
7. Thorough Follow-Up
An excellent short-term mission assures debriefing and appropriate follow-up for all participants, and is expressed by:
7.1 Comprehensive debriefing (pre-field, on-field, post-field)
7.2 On-field re-entry preparation
7.3 Post-field follow-up and evaluation (Walker, 2003)

Appendix 2

The principles of Global Focus that are keys to the mobilization of a local church are the following:

"Christ's command to Go into all the world and make disciples of all nations is the defining call and commission He gave to the Church. Yet, in order for this mission to be completed, we believe the local church must understand and fulfill its God-given role as His primary instrument. So how do you mobilize the local church for the Great Commission? How do you motivate and equip pastors and church leaders to lead their churches to reach the world both locally and globally with the message of Christ? We believe there are eight key principles and paradigms that must be embraced and implemented in order for the local church to maximize its global impact."

1. Worship must be the primary motivation for missions.
2. The local church must be seen as God's primary instrument to fulfill the Great Commission
3. The pastor must be the key influencer for the cause of global missions and must work in cooperation with church leaders to mobilize the local church.
4. The church must intentionally develop a corporate purpose, strategy and personality related to God's global cause.
5. The church must understand that mobilization is a process, not a "quick fix."
6. Global missions must be approached from appropriate generational perspectives.
7. Personalization must be seen as the key principle that will unleash the local church for global missions.
8. The "partnership paradigm" must be an essential element in mission strategy linking the local church with missionaries, nationals and other Great Commission people and organizations." (Reesor, 2007)

Appendix 3

Monroe Brewer, Director for the Center for Church Based Training in Dallas, Texas, has developed a strategy that "synthesizes" the benefits of both approaches to missions. "This strategy makes the short-termers (one who serves for one to two years) the cornerstone of its "game plan," satisfying the missions-as-project crowd, while at the same time having as its most obvious long-term feature the placement of career workers (those who serve for two to four terms) in the most strategic overseas assignments, satisfying the missions-as-process crowd" (Brewer, 2000)

Ten steps to implement the eclectic approach to missions:

1. Make the short-term experience the centerpiece of your church's missions program.
2. Establish a clear vision statement and work out a strategic and tactical plan for your church's missions program.
3. Infuse your missions budget (whether it is "faith promise" or "unified") with a onetime cash allocation. (It only needs to be large enough to fully support at least one missionary unit for one year).
4. Set up a candidate training program that begins to sort your potential candidates into your "class of '98," your "class of '99," and so on.
5. In sending out your first short-termers, (assuming he/she is fully prepared for the assignment), pick up everything that that missionary unit lacks in support to get to the field. The figure could be 30 percent, 60, or even 100 percent of the total support needed.
6. Send your short-termer to an area that is at least compatible with your long-term strategic plan or even a direct extension of it. Try to send him to the place and with the organization he might go with long-term. That way, whether your short-termers go long-term or not, they still will be forwarding key ministries that your church feels very strongly about.
7. When your short-termers return home, use their experiences to assess their call to the ministry, their personal vision, ministry skills, theological depth, language-learning aptitudes, organizational compatibility, and cross-cultural adjustments. Only a short-term experience can provide you with that kind of assessment. Vision trips and summer ministries don't allow the participants to experience culture shock--they don't have to set up house, learn a language, shop, renew visas--like short-termers do, since the shock doesn't hit until 6 months to 18 months into the experience.
8. Some short-termers will not go back to the field as long-term missionaries. Put their annual budget allocation back into next year's budget. Others will want to go back, but not immediately. They first may need to get more schooling,

pay off debts, get married, or get more ministry experience or training.

9. Those short-termers who desire to return long-term immediately (within the next six months) now have fire in their belly. They can speak articulately and with passion. They have the war stories and the video footage. They now don't mind so much raising support, and others view them as returning veterans, not untried rookies. They can now go to other churches to raise support and can raise it relatively easily. Your church can now reduce the monthly allotment you were giving them, since other support is coming in. Put the unneeded funds back into your "starter fund" for next year's short-termers.

10. About half of your short-termers will not go back long-term; about a fourth will go back long-term, but not immediately; and about a fourth will go back long-term immediately. You will be able to use most of the funds from last year's short-term account to send out new candidates next year. You may need to add $5,000 or $10,000 more each year, but not much (this could be viewed as your budget's inflation-adjusted 5% annual increase). Every year those same funds are there to keep your church's missions vision expanding and maturing (Brewer, 2000).

Appendix 4   ---Sánctified Sarcasm---

Seven Reasons Why You Should Never Go on a Short-Term Mission Trip

David Armstrong was a missionary and short-term mission coordinator at OC International [One Challenge] and is now the Director of Agency Services at Mission Data International.

1. It will distort your perception of the world! Seeing it through the plastic lenses of our society is sufficient. They may be distorted, but you are used to them! Don't needlessly mess yourself up.
2. You could get sick or robbed! It's dangerous out there! Some places have a crime rate almost as high as our inner cities.
3. It will make you harder to live with! The way you view life and even your likes and dislikes are liable to change. Your friends and family probably won't understand or appreciate your sudden changes.
4. Afterwards you will feel awkward at some of the jokes and comments you currently enjoy. They will not seem as funny when you have seen life from the other side.
5. You will experience sadness you haven't felt before. After you see real suffering, you won't pay much attention to your complaining about how hard you've got it. You are even liable to feel guilty and uncomfortable about the nice things in your house and the food on your table. Stay home and stay comfortable!
6. You might lead someone to the Lord. I know that is a laudable goal, but it tends to cause excitement and further interest in Christian Service.
7. You could feel a pull towards going overseas again—for the adventure, of course. The problem is that you could slowly, subtly get sucked into thinking about being a missionary!

My advice? Stay home and stay comfortable!

It is too late for me (Armstrong)

References

Adeney, M. (2006, October). "Loving Your Neighbor While Using Her." *Missiology, XXXIV*(4), 463-476.

Allen, M. (2001, October). "Mission Tourism?" *Faithworks.* Retrieved 8/17/07, from http://www.faithworks.com/archives/mission_tourism.htm.

Allen, M. (2002). "International Short-Term Missions." *Youth Specialties.* Retrieved 8/17/07, from http://www.youthspecialties.com/articles/topics/missions/international.php.

Armstrong, D. "Seven Reasons Why You Should Never Go on a Short-term Mission Trip." *ShortTerm Missions.com.* Retrieved 8/17/07, from http://www.shorttermmissions.com/articles/seven_reasons.

Barns, S. (2000, January). "Ten Emerging Trends in Short-Term Missions." *Missions Frontiers Bulletin.* Retrieved 8/17/07, from http://www.missionfrontiers.org/2000/01/tentrend.htm.

Birth, K. (2006, October). "What is your mission here?" *Missiology, XXXIV*(4), 497-508.

Borthwick, P. (2001). "Reaching the World Short-Term." *Moody Magazine.* Retrieved 8/19/07, from http://www.moodymagazine.com/articles.php?action=view_article&id=153.

Brewer, M. (2000, January). "Short Termers and the Future of American Missions." *Missions Frontiers Bulletin.* Retrieved 8/17/07, from http://www.missionfrontiers.org/2000/01/brewer.htm.

Culbertson, H. (2001, Jan 1). "10 Ways to Ruin a Short-term Mission Trip." *The Network for Strategic Missions.* Retrieved 8/18/07, from http://www.strategicnetwork.org/index.php?loc=kb&view=v&id=7711.

Cull, P. (1999, Jan 1). "Ten Commandments for Short Term Missions." *The Network for Strategic Missions.* Retrieved 8/18/07, from http://www.strategicnetwork.org/index.php?loc=kb&view=v&id=286.

Friesen, R. G. (2004, 07/08/17). *"The Long-term Impact of Short-term Missions on the beliefs, attitudes and behaviours of Young Adults.".* Unpublished doctoral dissertation, University of South Africa, Missiology.

Friesen, R. (2005, October). "The Long-term Impact of Short-term Missions." *Evangelical Missions Quarterly, 41*(4), 448-457.

Guthrie, S. (2001, 07/08/17). *Missions in the Third Millennium.* Waynesboro, GA: Paternoster Publishing.

Hesselgrave, D. J. (2006, 07/08/13). *Paradigms in Conflict: 10 Key Questions in Christian Missions Today.* Grand Rapids: Kregel Publications.

Holzmann, J. (1988, March). "Short Terms." *Missions Frontiers Bulletin.* Retrieved 8/17/07, from http://www.strategicnetwork.org/index.php?loc=kb&view=v&id=4507.

Johnstone, D. M. (2006, October). "Closing the Loop: Debriefing and the

Short-Term College Mission Team." *Missiology, XXXIV*(4), 523-527.

Linhart, T. D. (2006, October). "They were so alive!: The Spectacle Self and Youth Group Short-Term Mission Trips." *Missiology, XXXIV*(4), 451-462.

Loobi, S. G. (2000, January 20). "Short-Term Missions." *LAM News Service.* Retrieved 8/17/07, from http://www.lam.org/news/service.php.

Lyman, J. M. (2004, 07/08/21). *"Examining Short-Term Mission from a Globalization Perspective: Factors in the Emergence of Today's Mission Boom and Validity Issues for a Global Church.* Unpublished doctoral dissertation, Fuller Theological Seminary.

May, S. (2000, October). "Short-Term Mission Trips are Great, IF." *Evangelical Missions Quarterly.* Retrieved 8/1/07, from <https://bgc.gospelcom.net/emqonline/emq_article_read_pv.php?ArticleID=612>(accessed by subscription).

McConnell, D. (2005). "Working Together: Beyond Individual Efforts to Networks of Collaboraton." In M. Pocock, Gailyn Van Rheenen and Douglas McConnell (Ed.), *The Changing Face of World Missions: Engaging Contemporary Issues and Trends* (pp. 247-278).

Olson, S. (2000, January). "Mobilizing Workers for the 21st Century." *Missions Frontiers Bulletin.* Retrieved 8/17/07, from http://www.missionfrontiers.org/2000/01/wesleyan.htm.

Pocock, M. (2005). "The Disappearing Center: From Christendom to Global Christianity." In M. Pocock, Gailyn Van Rheenen and Douglas McConnell (Ed.), *The Changing Face of World Missions: Engaging Contemporary Issues and Trends* (pp. 131-159).

Priest, R. J. a. K. V. B. (2005, July). "Do Short-term Missions Change Anyone?" *Christianity Today.* Retrieved 8/22/07, from http://www.ctlibrary.com/34557.

Priest, R. J. (2005, July). "Are Short-Term Missions Good Stewardship?" *Christianity Today.* Retrieved 8/17/07, from http://www.ctlibrary.com/ct/2005/julyweb-only/22.0.html.

Priest, R. J. (2006, October). "Introduction to Theme Issue on Short-Term Missions." *Missiology, XXXIV*(4), 431-450.

Reesor, L. (2007). . *Global Focus.* Retrieved 8/17/07, from http://globalfocus.info/gfsite/default.php?main_id=1&sub_id=1.

Schwartz, G. (1986, June 1). "Missionary Forays: An Analysis of Short Term Missions." *World Mission Associates.* Retrieved 8/20/07, from http://www.wmausa.org/page.aspx?id=98600.

Taylor, B. (1996). "The Place of Short-Term Missions." *Mission Today*, Berry Publishing Services.

Ver Beek, K. A. (2006, October). "The Impact of Short-Term Missions." *Missiology, XXXIV*(4), 477-496.

Walker, K. (2003, Oct 1). "Agencies Announce Short-Term Missions Standards"

[Electronic version]. *Christianity Today.*

Winter, R. D. (1996a, March -April). "The Greatest Danger. The Re-Amateurization of Missions." *Missions Frontiers Bulletin,* p. 5.

Winter, R. D. (1996b, May-August). "I Have to Eat Humble Pie." *Missions Frontiers Bulletin,* p. 6.

Zehner, E. (2006, October). "Short-Term Missions: Toward a More Field-Oriented Model." *Missiology, XXXIV*(4), 509-522.

Chapter 6

Contextualization

Contemporary evangelism is taking seriously the task of evangelizing Muslims, Hindus, Buddhists and other religions/cultures with the good news of Jesus Christ. One of the most difficult religions to penetrate has been the Muslims. "The unprecedented trickles-and, in a few cases, floods-of Muslims who have chosen to follow Christ in previously evangelistically arid lands undoubtedly constitute the "best of times." In the late 1960s, there was a major turning to Christ among the Javanese in Indonesia, following a conflict between Muslims and communists. We have seen similar movements in North Africa and South Asia, along with smaller ones elsewhere." (Woodberry, 2007, pp. 80-81)

A number of cultural and religious practices and concepts make effective communication in these cultures difficult to communicate and difficult for the hearers to understand. The questions is how much should the message and the messenger change or adapt to make the meaning of the message understood and more acceptable without compromise? This chapter will attempt to introduce us to this complex and slippery topic. "Slippery" because there is the ever-present danger of going too far in the effort to make the message meaningful, with the result that it becomes meaningless. Our task is to relate a foreign truth to an alien culture. "Culture... is generally seen as a society's folkways, mores, language, art and architecture, and political and economic structures; it is the expression of the society's worldview. Worldview has been described as the way a people looks upon itself and the universe, or the way it sees itself in relationship to all else" (Guthrie, 2000, p. 103)

Three similar concepts to contextualization

Pocock distinguishes between contextualization and three similar but distinct terms: Indigenization, enculturation and transformation. The first term, **indigenization**, refers to the "translatability" of the universal Christian faith into the forms and symbols of any culture. This is similar to contextualization's focus but does not go as far as contextualization to include social, political and economic factors as well. The basis of the indigenous concept is self-propagation, self-governance, and self-financing, which is build on the independence or individualization concepts of Western philosophy, thus has come under some criticism.

The second, concept is **enculturation**, which likewise parallels contextualization, which is the reciprocal and critical interaction and assimilation between two cultures. Enculturation refers to "the correct way of living and sharing one's Christian faith in a particular context or culture."

The third similar concept is **transformationism**, which focus on the changes of a society into one that more "adequately reflects the kingdom of God." As individuals come to Christ they are encouraged to "transform their social networks" and eventually the whole of society. Others seek to transform society through legal and mass persuasion techniques, to demonstrate God's kingdom values in a needy world (Pocock, 2005, pp. 327-29).

The definition of contextualization

A professor in seminary asked the class, "What did God inspire: the words or the meaning?" As we wrestled with this critical issue, debating semantics and philosophy, it became clear that God does everything He can (by how He has limited His actions for the maturing of His image bearers) to allow man's free will under the presence and work of the Spirit to understand Him and His will. We came to the conclusion that God inspired both the words and the meaning; in fact, the words became the vehicles for communicating the meaning He intended to convey to us. Without meaning words become merely noise. As we saw this principle of communication then, it would later become even clearer as I learned different languages in an attempt to communicate truth-meaning through different thought structures and word concepts.

In general "contextualize" means to communicate the gospel in understandable terms appropriate to the audience. All Christian communication is contextualized to some extent. Graded curriculum is created for each different age group by adapting the language, illustrations, metaphors, applications and assumed understanding. When attempting to communicate cross culturally it is even more important to understand their age appropriate language, expressions, cultural and religious implications of terms, worldview, and needs of our target audience.

> "Contextualization" is a derivative of the word "context" which has its roots in *contextus* (Latin) meaning "weaving together." In literary pursuits, context is that which comes before and after a word, phrase, or statement, helping to fix its meaning or the circumstances in which an event occurs. Contextualization can be defined as making concepts and methods relevant to a historical situation. ... Missiological contextualization can be viewed as enabling the message of God's redeeming love in Jesus Christ to become alive as it addresses the vital issues of a sociocultural context and transforms its worldview, its values, and its goals (Terry, 1998, p. 318).

Hesselgrave wrote, "Anthropologists make much of how a culture uses linguistic symbols and assigns meaning and function to them. They believe that this tells them much about culture in general and specific cultures in particular. For example, how words function in ritual has something to say about world view" (Hesselgrave, 2005, p. 244). The key to contextualization is "What is meaningful to the receptor audience?" It is ours to discover how they think, then to explain truth in their way of thinking so that truth has meaning.

Missiologist Darrell Whiteman defines contextualization as more than just communicating the message in a new worldview context, but then how it becomes a part of their culture: "Attempts to communicate the Gospel in word and deed and to establish the church in ways that make sense to people within their local cultural context, presenting Christianity in such a way that it meets people's deepest needs and penetrates their worldview, thus allowing them to follow Christ and remain within their own culture" (Whiteman, 1997, p. 2).

To define contextualization is not an easy task since it describes a broad scale of meaning and adaptation from little adaptation to whole scale conformity to another culture and religion making it barely appear distinct from what they already believe (shades of syncretism). Stan Guthrie defines contextualization in this manner:

> Contextualization simply means finding points of contact within other people's contexts and removing things from one's own context that might block communication in order to gain a hearing for the gospel. It can be done verbally and nonverbally. ... Contextualization has been a hallmark of the modern missionary movement, too, from William Carey's translations of Hindu classics in India, to Hudson Taylor's decision to "go native" in China, to Bruce Olson's determination to become a member of the Motilone Indian tribe. It will continue to be a vital cross-cultural missionary approach in the 21st century, because continuing cultural differences in language, belief systems, and worldview will demand it (Guthrie, 2000, p. 102).

Perhaps no other topic has generated more recent interest and explosive encounters among missionaries than contextualizing the Christian faith in Islamic settings. It is one thing to discuss the translation of linguistic meanings into dynamic equivalents,[10] but another to agree on how much to contextualize the lifestyle in order to not become a personal obstacle to the communication of the gospel. Missionary say, "Let the cross be the offense, not my lifestyle." Scott Moreau (Wheaton Graduate School) and Mike O'Rear (Global Mapping

---

10   A dynamic equivalent conveys the same meaning but uses different terminology: "white as snow" (in a desert or jungle culture snow is unknown) can become "white as ___" (anything that conveys the meaning of whiteness).

International) in an article "Contextualizing Ministry among Muslims" said,

There has been strong debate over how far we can go in contextualizing ministry among Muslims before it becomes syncretism. Much of that debate has played out in journal articles of the major evangelical mission periodicals. The journal that has presented the greatest volume of material is the International Journal of Frontier Missions, which has had no less than five entire issues focused on Muslim evangelism—as well as numerous articles in other issues (Moreau, 2005).

What do some contextualized ministries to Muslims look like? Phil Parshall, SIM missionary to Muslims in the Philippines, describes a Javan ministry with the following characteristics:

- Leaders are called "imams"
- Festivals similar to that of Islam were observed
- They collect a *zakat* (offerings)
- Church buildings were called mosques. No crosses were displayed.
- They used a drum to call people to worship as did the Muslims.
- Cows were prayed over at the time of their slaughter in Islamic fashion.
- The following creed was recited in their churches: "I believe that god is one. There is no God but God. Jesus Christ is the Spirit of god, whose power is over everything. There is no God but God. Jesus Christ is the Spirit of God." This was chanted in a *dhikr* (recitation) style with intense emotion, which was purported to lead to some sort of mystical union between God and devotee.
- Believers called themselves "Christians." (Parshall, 2004, p. 289)

Later you'll be able to identify this description as one of six contextualization levels that are practiced today by different ministries in Muslim countries and comparable contextual levels in Hindu cultures. Controversies abound concerning the legitimacy of contextualized lifestyle practices.

The objective of contextualization

H. L. Richard is an independent researcher specializing in Hindu studies writes, "The fundamental stumbling block for most Hindus when facing Christianity remains that Christianity is a foreign religion, and all the evidence shows that this Hindu perception is true. Clearer thinking about Hinduism should lead to a deeper commitment to radically incarnational (contextual) approaches to the Hindu world, so that Hindus might see and feel that Christ and His good news are vitally relevant within their civilizational heritage. Without such shifts of paradigm and approach, there is little reason to hope that present and future Hindus will heed the biblical message any more than their forefathers have" (Richard, 2003, p. 8).

Although contextualization can apply to any attempt to adapt the message of God to all cultures and worldviews, the theme has been especially focused on the Muslim and Hindu worlds. The same concepts have been applied to the Roman Catholic evangelism, Buddhist, Animist, and other religious contexts where conversion to biblical Christianity is the focus. The main emphasis is relevant communication and continued influence of converts on the community in which they were born. This was much the same problem that the early church faced with the conversion of gentiles into a very Jewish-Christian church.

The inspired revelation from God, and of God, was delivered to man within a context of culture and language with full meaning and significance. It is our task to discover first that meaning and significance without changing its author's intended purpose to his hearers in that culture and time, then discern its meaning/application in our culture, language and time, finally make choices for how to communicate this truth-meaning/application for different cultures, worldviews and within the structure/meaning of different languages without losing its original meaning and intent. Quite a task!

Should the Muslim Background Believers (hence MBB) remain in the Mosque or separate to be with Christians? The pro camp points to early Christians continuing to worship in the synagogue. [Scott] Wood writes [in the 2003 EMQ 39(2):188-95]:

> Paul came ... to preach Jesus ... to the synagogue members. Most C5ers[11] come into the mosque and line up in the *shalat* line. They are perceived as Muslims. They have no distinguishing mark that says they are followers of Isa. Even if they pray to Isa, the perception is that they are Muslims. Paul was clearly received (at times) within the Jewish setting but acknowledged as a follower of the risen Messiah. Is this the same with our C5 [fifth level of contextualization] MBBs (Parshall, 2004, p. 291)?

There is general agreement that MBBs should remain in the mosque for a relatively short period of time following a personal conversion, if possible. The question is for how long? To what extent? How secret should he be?

Three areas of contextualization

Contextualization has three different areas of adaptation that are separate but interconnected: communication, conversion adaptation, and messenger

---

11 C1 – C6 are different levels of Contextualization to be explained later. A C5 is a Muslim-looking Christian.

adaptation. The latter two create the most conflict among different participants in the process. How to blend the mandates to "become all things to all men" with "Come out from among them" is the core of the issue that may never be resolved, only wrestled with till Jesus returns.

Communication adaptation

Early attempts at contextualizing came out of discussions or consultations concerning theologies and methodologies especially in Africa and Latin America. Many of these issues stemmed from the emphasis of the meaning of the biblical text over the words of the text. This came out of a method of allegorical interpretation or spiritualizing of the text to arrive at a "deeper" meaning, then a more contextual meaning, which could freely depart some distance from the original intent. This led to the acceptance of ideas, which occurred to leaders in these new cultures which was totally apart from the previously revealed Word of God. Attempts to harmonize the spiritualized meanings of the Bible with the regional expressions often led to syncretistic notions creating a new (African or Latin) theology, church structure and patterns of ministry. Somewhere along this slippery slope, contextualization changed to syncretism.[12]

In spite of the risk, the message must be made relevant to the different people groups of the world. According to Guthrie, the cross-cultural contexualizer faces the process of declaring the truth, which involves a "thorough understanding of one's own culture, the biblical context in which God's word was given, and the culture of those one is evangelizing. The message must be tailored or contextualized in such a way as to remain faithful to the biblical text while understandable in and relevant to the receptor's context" (Guthrie, 2000, p. 104). Missiologist Hesselgrave describes the process as transmitting a neutral message without cultural overtones by dissecting one's own culture from the communication process.

> Decontextualization has to do with freeing a message (e.g., the gospel) as much as possible from elements of the contextualizer's culture, so that the intended meaning comes through with a minimum of interference. Contextualization and decontextualization are ... intimately connected in the translation, interpretation, exposition, and application of Scripture ... [They are] aspects of all four of these operations in communicating God's special revelation" (Hesselgrave, 2005, p. 246)

Contextualization is a scale of transition rather than a clear yes/no, or

---

12 Syncretism ("union of communities") blends different points of view into a mixture of beliefs by ignoring distinctives and contradictions. Some religions encourage syncretism (Hinduism and Buddhism), while most oppose it.

black/white issue. One is always blind to how one's own cultural aspects, since the terminology, thought patterns, values, prejudices, beliefs and communicating process all seem so right, logical and obvious, but all of these elements are different among cultures.

> At Lausanne (1979), contextualization was initially perceived in two ways: as formal correspondence translation and as dynamic equivalence. Kato's paper (which called for contextualization of external forms, e.g., liturgy, dress, language) represents the first view. The report of the respondent group (which called for a deeper level of contextualization, e.g., of thought patterns, worldview) represents the second view. There was a third group, composed of Conn, Padilla and Escobar, however, who felt that it was necessary to go beyond the Willowbank Report and strive for an even deeper involvement with the cultural context (Terry, 1998, p. 326).

This third perspective becomes radical to some perspectives, as it requires considerable acceptance of different perspectives and forms of lifestyle.

Convert Adaptation

How much do new converts have to become like us before they are accepted as genuine converts, not syncretistic nominal followers? Or should they remain as Muslim as possible, for as long as possible, with the hopes that they can spread sufficient curiosity and gospel awareness among their acquaintances before they inevitably separate or are ostracized. One of the issues at this level is how to interpret 1 Corinthians 7:20 where Paul wrote that "Each one should remain in the situation which he was in when God called him." Does this mean that a MBB should remain a Muslim?

Scott Woods comments on the use of 1 Cor 7 to justify the practice of Muslim converts who seek to remain Muslim:

> "The context in 1 Corinthians 7 is addressing the issues of marriage and singleness: believers married to unbelievers; circumcision and uncircumcision and finally slaves and free. This passage has nothing to do with dictating that people from a false religion should remain in their false religion so as not to upset the apple cart. C5 proponents could be accused of isogesis here .This passage makes provision for believers remaining in their familial and social status where they were prior to knowing Christ, but it is not giving an allowance for believers to continue in their former religion." [Woods 2003 EMQ 39(2):188-95].

Does the MBB continue to bear the name Muslim without any qualifier?

Parshall described an interview with Ramsay Harris, a long-term missionary among Arabs: "Most of those I have led to Christ do NOT identify themselves as Muslims anymore, but some do. I do not push them either way. ... For most people the word Muslim means 'an adherent of the religion of Muhammad' ... But there is one principle which must be universal: one must always identify himself with the person of Jesus Christ (Mt 10:33 and 1 Peter 4:16)" (Parshall, 2004, p. 290).

Should the MBB remain in the Mosque? The pro camp points to early Christians continuing to worship in the synagogue. Scott Wood writes: Paul came ... to preach Jesus ... to the synagogue members. Most C5ers come into the mosque and line up in the "*shalat*" line. They are perceived as Muslims. They have no distinguishing mark that says they are followers of Isa. Even if they pray to Isa, the perception is that they are Muslims. Paul was clearly received (at times) within the Jewish setting but acknowledged as a follower of the risen Messiah. Is this the same with our C5 MBBs?

What about the recitation of the Islamic Creed? Can the MBB continue to recite this foundation upon which all of Islam rests? It not only affirms the oneness of Allah, but also the centrality of Muhammad as a prophet or messenger of God. Parshall quotes a C5 missionary who said:

> "I believe that an MBB can repeat the creed with conviction and integrity, without compromising or syncretizing his faith in Jesus ... the recognition of Muhammad would be in his prophetic mission as a messenger proclaiming one god and submission to his will in the context of idolatrous seventh century Arabia, or, in the pagan pre-Islamic setting of any given people who have subsequently accepted Islam. Although Muhammad's mission was chronologically A.D., we should not allow this to cloud the fact that the spiritual milieu to which he spoke was substantially B.C. ... In a Jesus movement in Islam, Muhammad would be understood as an Old Testament-style messenger. For those Christians who may stumble at certain aspects of Muhammad's lifestyle, I urge them to study more objectively the lives of the Old Testament prophets where both holy war, in a form more violent than Islam calls for (genocide in the book of Joshua), and polygamy were quite common" (Parshall, 2004, p. 291).

Parshall takes disagreement with this C5er by showing that by affirming the prophet means affirming his prophecy and the Qur'an as the word of God. Also the deceit of pretending to be a Muslim implies a theology that is assumed by Muslim observers that, in fact, is not true.

The transformation of a MBBer to one that fully walks in the light is seldom ideal. The hurdles of culture, religion, mysticism, fear, ostracism, reason, and emotional responses are no dissolved in a moment. One view of this process is seen in Parshall's comments:

> Conversions out of Islam are usually a process through any number of different beliefs in Islam (once a questioning spirit is begun) then into acceptance of various Christian views until a more orthodox view is understood and claimed. One missionary comments, "If we are so unfortunate to be the mission that plants a heresy, are those that adhere to it any worse off than before?" It is his view that such a "heresy" could be a future stepping-stone for those Muslims to come to full-blown faith in Christ (Parshall, 2004, p. 293).

The solutions are not easy, nor universal. Each situation must be given the liberty to transform into Christ's image as the Holy Spirit convicts and leads through exposure to good exegesis of the biblical texts. Massey describes this process as follows:

> Many C4 MBBs spend years going back and forth between Christian and Muslim communities like a sociological chameleon, trying to maintain acceptance in two different worlds. C4 identity (being neither Christian nor Muslim) is a very difficult position for MBBs to maintain. The more they behave like Gentile Christians, the more they will be trusted by C1-3 believers but distrusted by Muslims. Unfortunately, the more they retain their Muslim culture (e.g., diet, dress, beard, language, liturgy, etc.), the more suspect they tend to be in Christian communities. Theoretically, C4 MBBs should not have to enter C1-3 communities at all. Practically, however, their paths tend to cross more often than C4 advocates would prefer, and so begins the process of Christianization which inevitably pulls Muslims "out" of their community and "into" some form of Christianity (Massey, 2004, p. 301).

Messenger Adaptation

In order to communicate effectively, how much does a Western missionary have to adapt to the new culture? Does the messenger need to become a Muslim in order to win Muslims, if not in religion, then in culture, if they can be separated?

Guthrie reports that at the 1974 Lausanne Congress on World Evangelization, Ralph Winter argued that 2.7 billion people cannot be won to Christ by "near-neighbor evangelism since they have no Christian neighbors." Winter called on evangelists to "cross cultural, language, and geographical barriers, learn the languages and cultures of these unreached peoples, present the gospel to them, and plant culturally relevant churches among them."

Winter's emphasis on crossing cultural boundaries to reach other cultural groups laid the foundation for the Unreached Peoples Group (UPG) movement and the AD2000 and Beyond Movement. It also gave a powerful boost to contextualization as a missionary method (Guthrie, 2000, p. 104).

Being a credible witness is, of course, a precondition for even being able to enter into meaningful discussion about spiritual things. Christian background workers and Muslim converts involved in C4 (pre-) evangelism will need to maintain some essential outward identification with the culture while contributing socially in biblical ways.

- Maintain healthy respect for civil and religious authorities
- Practice generosity and compassion in dealings with the less fortunate
- Maintain dietary habits consistent with Muslim neighbors, including the fast
- Participate fully in neighborhood activities
- Present one's self as a spiritually active and mature member of the community (Leffel, p. 8)

Guthrie describes this adaptation from an interview with Steve Cochraine where Cochraine defended the use of C5 contextualization saying that they were replicating the method of the 17th-cntury Jesuit priest Robert de Nobili,[13] who donned Hindu garb to win converts. Likewise a Youth With A Mission [YWAM] team in North India is working with an Indian Christian. The man wears traditional robes befitting a *sadhu*, or holy man (a Hindu monk). He and the team organize pilgrimages to Hindu religious sites for pilgrims. Along the way, he and the missionaries explain the gospel "in a totally contextualized way. As far as the pilgrims are concerned, he is a Hindu. He's a Brahmin *sadhu* (Guthrie, 2000, pp. 106-07).

Richard calls on the Christian messenger to make significant adaptations to a Hindu culture when he says, "The fundamental stumbling block for most Hindus when facing Christianity remains that Christianity is a foreign religion, and all the evidence shows that this Hindu perception is true. Clearer thinking about Hinduism should lead to a deeper commitment to radically incarnational (contextual) approaches to the Hindu world, so that Hindus might see and feel that Christ and His good news are vitally relevant within their civilizational heritage. Without such shifts of paradigm and approach, there is little reason to hope that present and future Hindus will heed the biblical message any more than their forefathers have" Richard, 2003, p. 8).

Recent surveys of individuals who have moved out of Islam to Christianity gave some of the following reasons for what most influenced

---

13 Nobili was a Jesuit missionary to southern India who pioneered the concepts of "enculturation" adapting the Brahmin customs, which he judged as not contrary to Christianity in order to gain a hearing. He wore the saffron robes and carried a *kamadalu* (a water jug) like Brahmin monks.

wrath and eternity in hell, no matter what the term means. In other words, the main problem with this term is not theological, as so many Christians suppose, and it is not simply a semantic difference, but rather it is an affective and cultural phenomenon: it is an utterly taboo term. The reason is that in most Muslim cultures, people are indoctrinated from childhood, on the basis of At-Tawba 9:30 in the Qur'an that God will damn and destroy anyone who says that Jesus is *ibnullah* ("a son of God"), regardless of what they mean by it. The Qur'an (Maryam 19:88-92) says this term is so insulting to the majesty of God that asserting it could cause the heavens to burst and the earth to split and the mountains to collapse! What the Muslim most fears ... is that his or her own soul will be damned to hell forever" (Brown, 2007, p. 424).

Not every Muslim will react the same way. "A nominal Muslim might entertain such an idea, but pious Muslims are unwilling to doubt the eternal risk posed by this term until they have been born again through faith in Jesus Christ and have come to view the Qur'an in the light of the Bible" (Brown, 2007, p. 424). Brown has seen three reactions of Muslims who are exposed to this "son of God" terminology: (1) Suspicious Muslims are concerned about the taboo term but are cautiously receptive of the scriptural message since they are usually nominal Muslims already doubting the claims of the Qur'an. (2) Alienated Muslims are alarmed by the taboo term and are suspicious of the explanations, but continue to learn out of curiosity or politeness but from a distance. (3) Terrified Muslims[14] resent being "trapped" or surprised by being exposed to the term which could mean their damnation and either determine never to be exposed again or react violently to show God their hatred toward the term and its user, as they suppose is His hatred toward the same. They hope that this reaction will convince God that they were tricked into seeing, hearing, reading or uttering this taboo term, and that God will forgive them (Brown, 2007, pp. 424-25).

It is important to note that the taboo is against asserting that someone is a "son of God;" however, there is no proscription against talking about the term. After all, Muslim missionaries, teachers and imams often talk about the term when they are criticizing Christianity. So Muslims feel free to read or discuss the meaning of the taboo term, as long as they do not read it being asserted or consent to hearing it asserted of someone. That is why Muslims are willing to read or hear an explanation of the taboo term in a footnote or glossary, even

---

14 Brown attempts to explain this affective connotation by a comparison in Christian concepts. Suppose "you were worried that God is displeased with you and wants to send you to hell and then someone asks you to blaspheme the Holy Spirit (Mark 3:29) or to say 'Jesus is accursed' (1 Cor 12:3). That is the kind of fear that Muslims have when asked to say that God has children." (Brown, 2007, p. 429)

though they are reticent to read it or hear it asserted in the text itself (Brown, 2007, p. 427).

The new translation is being promoted in a number of languages throughout the Islamic world. Early feedback from Muslims and MBBs is positive. This offense of the word "son" is gone. Jesus as Messiah is retained and highlighted. The meaning of "Messiah" can be explained. This dynamic equivalent translation defense is that certain NT passages place Son of God and messiah together, thus proving the term's interchangeability (see Luke 4:41; Matt 16:16; and Matt 26:63-64) (Parshall, 2004, p. 292).

"Allah"

The second term that becomes controversial, especially among missionaries, but not so much among Muslims, is the use of *Allah* to represent the title for God. "This debate doesn't exist for Arab Christians, who have continually translated *elohim* and *theos* (the primary terms for God in biblical Hebrew and Greek) as "Allah" from the earliest know Arabic Bible translations in the eighth century till today" (Massey, 2004, p. 284).

Joshua Massey, linguist, cultural anthropologist and missiologists, shows that those who argue for the use of Allah as a reference to God see the origins of the term in a common Semitic language. Most scholars agree that "Allah" is the Arabic cognate of the biblical Aramaic *elah* and Hebrew *eloah*, which is the singular of *elohim*, a generic word for God used throughout the Old Testament. He makes a good point that Allah is never used to refer to a false god or idol in Islamic thought. In fact, "it is nearly impossible for linguists to determine which of these three terms appeared first in the Ancient Near East, or if they all derived from a hypothesized proto-Semitic language" (Massey, 2004, p. 284). It can only be used to refer to the true God of Abraham, Isaac and Jacob.

Recently I was in a N. African country to interview a potential adjunct for our Arabic studies program. I asked this highly qualified professor how he came to Christ and what his perspective was over the issue of the use of *Allah* as a reference to God. He commented that at first he did not know there was a conflict, but was taught not to use *Allah* for God by an Arab missionary. After a few years this became so cumbersome, and no one in his country saw any conflict with the use of the term, that he has now found the use of *Allah* not a stumbling block to true gospel understanding.

Massey's analysis of the term led him to investigate the translations for "God" in other languages and he makes these comments:

> It is ... easy to gloss over the sordid history of many non-Arabic terms Christians use for God. The English word "God," for example, comes from the pagan Germanic *Gott*, a proper name for the chief Teutonic

deity *Odin*, who lives on top of the world-tree and created the first humans with his wife Freya, a blond, blue-eyed goddess of love, fertility and beauty.

Should English speakers therefore discontinue addressing the Most High as "God"? In spite of its pagan origin and present use for both false deities and the Most High "God" (when capitalized) is generally understood by English-speakers as the God of the Bible ... "*Allah*," in contrast, shares the same Semitic roots as biblical Hebrew and Aramaic, is not presently used for false deities, and is clearly understood by all Arab Christians and Muslims as the God of the Bible. "*Allah*" is therefore an acceptable term for Arabic-speaking Christians and Muslims (Massey, 2004, p. 285).

Christian advocates for using *Allah* amongst Muslims in non-Arabic-speaking lands counter that introducing foreign terms for God will create immense communication hurdles, perhaps even guaranteeing that a truly indigenous church planting movement will never occur. The task, they say, is not to discard such easily redeemable terms, but to fill them with biblical meaning. The more a Muslim's understanding of *Allah* is informed by the Scriptures, the more biblical his or her theology of God will become (Massey, 2004, p. 285).

Comprehensive Contextualization

Scott Moreau, chairman of the Inter Cultural Studies Department at Wheaton College, describes the seven-fold dimensions for grasping the scope of contextualization, drawn from Ninian Smart's model for understanding religions, which include (1) doctrinal, (2) mystical, (3) ethical, (4) social, (5) ritual, (6) supernatural experience, and (7) artistic or material elements (Moreau, 2007).

1. The doctrinal dimension refers to beliefs expressed in religious form. It is the attempt to answer questions such as, "How did the world come to exist?" and "What powers rule the world?" These beliefs are found in the Bible, and can be organized in a way that makes sense to a particular audience, whether through books, hymns, sermons, Bible studies and so on. This approach can be focused on a particular goal (liberation theologies) or around a particular set of practices (Pentecostal theologies). It may have a subset in mind (black theologies, feminist theologies) or try to be universal (Western systematic theologies).
2. The second dimension is the mythic. In the broadest sense, myth refers to the stories of a culture that reflect how it thinks about the world. The way we are using the term should not be confused with the more popular idea of myths as stories that are untrue. Rather, myth

in this sense is the power of the stories of a people to embody the things they cherish and value (as well as showing why some things are not valued). Typically, a society's myths express that society's ideals about several themes, including sacrifice, love, honor, power, wisdom and heroism.
3. While the doctrinal dimension focuses on what is true, the ethical dimension focuses on how people should live. This includes how we are to interact with other people and with the rest of God's creation, and how society regulates behavior to prevent or stop people from behaving inappropriately.
4. The social dimension is seen in the ways Christians organize themselves in light of scripture and local cultural values. It includes the sense of "togetherness" that comes from participating in Christian rituals together (e.g., communion) but also includes all of the institutions within the Church and how they are organized and run. For example it includes such obvious things as church governance. However, it goes beyond this to include:
    - All forms of church association (formal and informal, from children's clubs to women's guilds to denominations)
    - The means they have to exchange goods and services (voluntary labor, offerings, church dinners)
    - The enforcement of their ethical standards (church or denominational discipline) * how knowledge is passed on from generation to generation (from formal education to informal conversations with a youth leader).
5. The ritual includes not just what we formally think of as ritual, but any repeated symbolic actions done in relation to Christian faith. This can range from formal Christian rituals such as baptism, communion, marriages and funerals to non-formal ritualistic activities, such as sermons, committee meetings, evangelistic outreaches and prayer meetings.
6. The dimension of supernatural experience takes into account the fact that in every society people encounter the supernatural, whether through dreams, visions, miraculous experiences, signs and wonders or other means. While many in the Western Church have followed the lead of Western culture and dismissed such encounters, the Majority World Church pays careful attention to them and acknowledges them as real and needing to be addressed. This is a difficult area to contextualize, since they are less amenable to "control" than doctrine or rituals. Contextualization of this dimension should include at least three components:
    - Local Christians must study the scriptures and develop biblically-based perspectives on them.

- Christians can then consider developing biblically-founded rituals that enable encounters with God through Christ (e.g., prayer services) as well as rituals that will help people who struggle with negative experiences (e.g., demonic expulsion).
- Those who follow Christ need to be given the freedom—and the language—to talk about their experiences and find Bible-centered and culturally-sensitive ways to handle them.

7. Christians around the world express their values and ideals through artistic and material means. From church architecture that values the sermon (seen by the elevated pulpit facing the congregation) to sculptures that portray Christ's sacrifice on our behalf to clothing that indicates status and authority, Christians regularly create and use imaginative ways to express thoughts, feelings and attitudes about their faith. A comprehensive approach to contextualization recognizes this as an essential element of the faith of a local body of believers and finds ways to enable them to express their artistic giftedness in Christ-honoring ways (Moreau, 2007).

C-1 to C-6 Scope of Contextualism

Many of the principles of contextualization are applied to Muslim evangelism, but similar applications can be made to Hindu contextualization as well. Obviously the length of this chapter will not permit this thorough analysis. However, a comparison chart is included in the Appendix called the H-1 to H-7 chart.

John Travis, professor of World Missions and Indian Studies at Gordon-Conwell Theological Seminary, in 1988 published his perspective of the spectrum of MBBs found in the Islamic world. The "C" stands for Christ-centered communities. The number identification refer to comparison in three areas: language of worship, culture/religious forms used in public and worship lifestyle, and self-identity as a 'Muslim' or a 'Christian.' The scope ranges from C-1 which is a traditional gentile-looking Christian church to a C-6 MBB, often in a hostile environment while participating in a secrete or underground community, which may have little similitude to recognizable Christians. There is universal agreement that this level of contextualization is regrettable though an existing reality, which hopefully will disintegrate when freedom of expression is allowed. Travis states, "What is called "low" contextualization (C-1) may, in fact, not be contextualization at all, but an expression of ethnocentric extractionism. Further, what is called "high" contextualization may not be contextualization at all, but an expression of syncretism" (Tennent, 2006, p. 103).

To grasp the challenge of how to guide the contextualized effort Leffel gives an interesting insight. In some contexts C3 strategy may directly subvert the goal of birthing an indigenous people movement because,

> "Each convert extracted from his own cultural situation reinforces in the minds of Hindus and Muslims the misunderstanding that Christians are opposed to their cultural traditions. In this sense, one could defend the thesis that each convert won from these faiths at present actually represents a setback to winning large numbers from these communities (Leffel, p. 5).

The following description of the different scope of Contextualization applies specifically to the Muslim context. See Appendix C for the H-scale of contextualization in the Hindu context of evangelism. In any culture the continued challenge for the expatriate missionary is: how can a fellowship of biblical believers grow and witness for Jesus yet remain authentic, active members of their secular or non-Christian culture? Something must be done in this regard because the overall historic failure of Christian witness among the Hindus and Muslims must indicate that some form of contextualization is needed as a strategic imperative. The following are the common definitions of the C-1 to C-6 scale of suggested contextualized ministries:

C1 Model: Traditional church using non-indigenous language
- Christian churches in Muslim countries that exist as islands, removed from the culture.
- Christians exist as an ethnic/religious minority.

C2 Model: Traditional church using indigenous language.
- Church uses indigenous language, but in all its cultural forms is far removed from the broader Islamic culture.

C3 Model: Contextualized Christ-centered communities using Muslim's language and non-religiously indigenous cultural forms
- Their style of worship, dress, etc. are loosely from the indigenous culture. Local rituals and traditions, if used, are purged of religious elements.
- They may meet in a church or more religiously neutral location. Majority of congregation is of Muslim background and call themselves Christians.

C4 Model: Contextualized Christ-centered communities using Muslim's language and biblically permissible cultural and Islamic forms.
- Similar to C3 except believers worship looks like Muslim worship, they keep the fast, avoid pork and alcohol, use Islamic terms and dress.
- Community is almost entirely of Muslim background. Though highly contextualized, believers are not seen as Muslims by the Muslim community.

- Believers call themselves "followers of *Isa Al-Misah*," [Jesus the Messiah]

C5 Model: Christ-centered communities of "Messianic Muslims" who have accepted Jesus as Lord and Savior.
- Believers remain legally and socially within Islamic community.[15]
- Aspects of Islam incompatible with the Bible are rejected or if possible, reinterpreted.
- Believers may remain active in the mosque. Unsaved Muslims may view C5 believers as deviant and may expel them from the Islamic community.
- If sufficient numbers permit, a C5 "Messianic mosque" may be established.

C6 Model: Small Christ-centered communities of secret/underground believers isolated by extreme hostility, usually individual believers but sometimes in small groups.
- Believers typically do not attempt to share their faith, others suffer imprisonment or martyrdom (Leffel, p. 3).

Leffel gives a broader explanation of the differences with some opinions about how effective each model ministry might be. C1 and C2 models represent little or no accommodation to Muslim culture, other than the C2 use of indigenous language. These appear much like the traditional Western culture in the Muslim context. This includes Western-style buildings, denominational affiliation openly on signs, and worship. "While we must respect the courage of the few Muslim converts to these churches, we consider the models inadequate for two reasons. **First**, imposing unnecessary cultural forms to the non-Western context inhibits long term efforts to found a truly indigenous people movement from taking root. The church will always be seen as a cultural outsider. **Second**, the distance from Islamic culture to these churches is an unbiblical constraint on conversion and Christian discipleship. In effect, it erects extra-biblical cultural roadblocks to the Gospel" (Leffel, p. 5).

C3 contextualization begins to accommodate some non-religious aspects of the indigenous culture. At the same time, there is a conscious attempt to break from all visible elements of Islam, such as observing Ramadan, dietary laws, association with the mosque and so forth. "This moderately contextualized model assumes that Islamic cultural forms cannot be purged of their religious meaning, and should be abandoned to avoid fostering syncretism. C3 is a form of contextualization that most Westerners are comfortable supporting

---

15 Phil Parshall, *The Cross and the Crescent* (Wheaton, IL: Tyndale House, 1989), p. 77, Contends that because of the theology associated with the Muslim prayer, he strongly contends that remaining active in the mosque is either "compromise or deceit." (See also *Beyond the Mosque* (Grand Rapids: Baker Books, 1985), p. 184.

because it sharply contrasts Islam and Christianity. Conversion means parting from Islamic identity[16] and coming into a new one" (Leffel, p. 5).

> In some contexts C3 strategy may directly subvert the goal of birthing an indigenous people movement because, "[e]ach convert extracted from his own cultural situation reinforces in the minds of Hindus and Muslims the misunderstanding that Christians are opposed to their cultural traditions. In this sense, one could defend the thesis that each convert won from these faiths at present actually represents a setback to winning large numbers from these communities (Leffel, p. 5)

The move from C3 to C4/5 models involves incorporating traditional Islamic religious forms into biblical faith and Christian community. However, significant qualitative differences also exist between C4 and C5 models... Converts from Islam are encouraged to express their new faith almost completely within the Muslim social and religious fold. They do not view themselves as Christians, since in context that refers to traitors against the community, Western materialism and other counterproductive baggage. Converts are encouraged to see themselves as "Muslim followers of Isa," or "completed Muslims," or "messianic Muslims." (Leffel, p. 6)

C6 is more of a survival strategy than a contextualization model. These believers are forced to choose between rejection from the community or martyrdom and complete anonymity. While it may be best in the short term for a convert to remain in a C6 position, it is certainly no long term plan. Building an indigenous church or igniting an indigenous people movement is virtually impossible under these conditions. This strategy may be necessary in some countries where conversion to biblical faith is illegal and an underground church is still in the making. (Leffel, p. 5)

Leffel declares that a number of things need to be carefully considered. It seems that the key essentials for salvation are present: "Jesus gave his life for me" and "Jesus is the only way of salvation." This is fantastic! Yet, the questions are somewhat ambiguous. What does "Jesus gave his life for me" mean? There is no survey data on belief in Jesus' crucifixion and bodily resurrection, necessary for biblical saving faith (1 Cor. 1:23; Rom. 10:9). "In light of the Muslim rejection of the doctrine of Christ's crucifixion and bodily resurrection, this would be vital information to have in formulating our conclusions. The high regard for the Koran, repetition of Koranic verses, and rejection of the trinity are also problematic. After 12 years we still see crucial aspects of syncretism and this, apparently, among the crucial players in the C5 movement" (Leffel, p. 7).

---

16 See H. L. Richard, "Is extraction evangelism still the way to go?" reprinted in Mission Frontiers Bulletin, September-October, 1996, p. 15.

The danger of syncretism

There has been strong debate over how far we can go in contextualizing ministry among Muslims before it becomes syncretism. Much of that debate has played out in journal articles of the major evangelical mission periodicals. "The journal that has presented the greatest volume of material is the International Journal of Frontier Missions, which has had no less than five entire issues focused on Muslim evangelism—as well as numerous articles in other issues" (Moreau, 2005).

"What's the rule-of-thumb definition for the difference between contextualization and syncretism? Simple: it's contextualization when I do it, but syncretism when you do it!" Corwin, 2004, p. 282) Where is the line? If we say that syncretism is adapting any ideas or practices from another culture, then the church and almost everything known today as Christianity is syncretistic.

> Syncretism, or the unbiblical blending of true religion with false, is an ever-present risk for the contextualizer. The key is to keep biblical elements that are non-negotiable and to discard unbiblical cultural or religious elements. Catholic missions in past centuries, in their zeal to bring masses of pagans into the church, sometimes failed this test, as the old gods were simply given new Christian names. In supposedly Catholic bastions from Mexico to the Philippines to Haiti to Brazil, animistic practices survive under a Christian veneer (Guthrie, 2000, p. 105).

The issue of syncretism has surfaced today over a strong debate of how far we can go in contextualizing ministry among Muslims before it becomes syncretism. Much of that debate has played out in journal articles of the major evangelical mission periodicals. The journal that has presented the greatest volume of material is the International Journal of Frontier Missions, which has had no less than five entire issues focused on Muslim evangelism—as well as numerous articles in other issues (Moreau, 2005).

Some critics have questioned the effectiveness of popular evangelism tools such as Evangelism Explosion when used apart from an adequate understanding of the culture and contextualization. Steffen argues that before the "Jesus" film is shown, the audience's worldview must be known, the presenters must earn the right to be heard, the film must be seen first by the community's information gatekeepers, the presenters must grasp how the community makes decisions and must know how to incorporate converts into healthy churches, and the audience must have a significant foundation for the gospel. Not to have these cultural prerequisites in place, he and others argue, is to invite nominalism or syncretism (Guthrie, 2000, p. 105).

Pocock quotes Moreau who gives the following guidelines to guard against syncretism:
Because of the convoluted nature of culture, the declaration of syncretism in a particular setting cannot be simply left in the hands of expatriate missionaries. The local community must be empowered to biblically evaluate their own practices and teachings. Missionaries must learn to trust that indigenous peoples are able to discern God's leading and trust God to develop and maintain biblically founded and culturally relevant faith and praxis in each local context. Finally, Christians of every culture must engage in genuine partnership with Christians of other cultures, since often the outsider's help is needed to enable local believers, blinded by culture and familiarity, to see that which contravenes scriptural adherence to the first commandment. (Pocock, 2005, pp. 331-32).

In principle, Hinduism incorporates all forms of belief and worship without necessitating the selection or elimination of any. The Hindu is inclined to revere the divine in every manifestation, whatever it may be, and is doctrinally tolerant, leaving others" including both Hindus and non-Hindus "whatever creed and worship practices suit them best.

A Hindu may embrace a non-Hindu religion without ceasing to be a Hindu, and the Hindu is disposed to think synthetically and to regard other forms of worship, strange Gods, and divergent doctrines as inadequate rather than objectionable. He tends to believe that the highest powers complement each other for the well-being of the world and mankind. Few religious ideas are considered to be finally irreconcilable. The core religion does not even depend on the existence or non-existence of God or on whether there is one God or many. Since religious truth is said to transcend all verbal definition, it is not conceived in dogmatic terms. Hinduism is, then, both a civilization and conglomerate of religions, with neither a beginning, a founder, nor a central authority, hierarchy, or organization (Richard, 2003, pp. 4-5).

Some hold the theory that syncretism is a temporary or transitory state that many churches or individuals pass through, but eventually mature and come to the knowledge of the truth. Missiologists Ralph Winter states that perhaps a third of the 6,000 churches linked with the African Independent Church movement are messianic, meaning they have someone among their members known as a divine person. Winter believes the Spirit and the Word, without Western intervention, will lead many of these churches into orthodoxy. Guthrie considers this highly debatable (Guthrie, 1998, p. 222). Most hold that once a false doctrine is accepted as divine, it becomes very difficult to ever change it.

> Pocock quotes Moreau who gives the following guidelines to guard against syncretism:
> Because of the convoluted nature of culture, the declaration of syncretism in a particular setting cannot be simply left in the hands of expatriate missionaries. The local community must be empowered to biblically evaluate their own practices and teachings. Missionaries must learn to trust that indigenous peoples are able to discern God's leading and trust God to develop and maintain biblically founded and culturally relevant faith and praxis in each local context. Finally, Christians of every culture must engage in genuine partnership with Christians of other cultures, since often the outsider's help is needed to enable local believers, blinded by culture and familiarity, to see that which contravenes scriptural adherence to the first commandment. (Pocock, 2005, pp. 331-32).

The contemporary trends

It is interesting to note that Jesus never asked any Gentile or Samaritan to convert to Judaism, rather just believe in Him and worship God in spirit and truth. Massey writes, "Christ-centeredness has less to do with religion, and everything to do with Jesus."

> Advocates of C5 *insider* movements are equally concerned about the dangers of syncretism and lazy tolerance, but they are also more concerned about true Christ-centeredness than with conformity to Gentile Christian traditions and doctrinal codifications developed centuries after the apostolic era (Massey, 2004, p. 300).

It must be clear that salvation is a process in conversion. Evangelists need to emphasize what is required for an authentic decision resulting in salvation from a longer process of teaching and discipleship that transforms saving faith into biblical maturity. We expect complete understanding of biblical orthodoxy for salvation, this not supported by scriptural examples in conversion (Acts 8, 10, 16, 17). There are several truths that must be understood and accepted for salvation. These truths are alien to the Qur'an and require a shift from Islamic belief to a biblical faith.

At the 1974 Lausanne Congress on world Evangelization, Ralph Winter argued that 2.7 billion people cannot be won to Christ by near-neighbor evangelism since they have no Christian neighbors. Winter called on evangelists to cross cultural, language, and geographical barriers, learn the languages and cultures of these unreached peoples, present the gospel to them, and plant culturally relevant churches among them. Winter's emphasis on crossing cultural boundaries to reach other cultural groups laid the foundation for the Unreached People Group (UPG) movement and the AD2000 and Beyond Movement. It also gave a powerful boost to contextualization as a missionary method (Guthrie, 2000, p. 104).

A new contextualization trend among missionaries is the use of indigenous music rather than imported Western words and styles. Drawing from the insights of ethnomusicology, missionaries are using local music forms to both strengthen new Christians in their faith and to reach out to unbelievers. The Summer Institute of Linguistics offers summer courses, an annual conference, and a library on the subject (Guthrie, 2000, p. 105).

Ethnomusicology is more than merely designing worship music within the cultural style, instruments and language. It is, by itself, a means of communicating doctrine, applications, bible stories and life stories with a purpose, and becomes a significant teaching methodology in other cultures. It is used this way in English, but we are often not aware of how and what it is really communicating in our culture. This is the primary means of remembering stories, history and legends within most cultures. Why has it taken so long for it to be used as a primary tool within our culture by Christians?

Moreau concludes the concept of contextualization with this comprehensive definition, "The ultimate goal of contextualization is to make the entirety of the Christian faith, including both the message and the way Christians live their faith out in local settings, enfleshed in a way that is understandable (and, insofar as it is possible, commendable) to the non-Christian people among whom that faith is lived out" (Moreau, 2007).

Appendix A

This topic is a hot theme that is polemic especially between the field missionary and the "theoretical theologian" who usually has never planted a church in a hard-core foreign culture. This is not a simple concept that will go away. Every missionary will live with the tension of contextualization throughout his ministry, as long as he/she is working with people of a radically different culture. The following will give you some basic web sites that can be helpful for your personal research.

General Resources
- MisLinks (**www.mislinks.org**/topics/contxtheo.htm). These are divided into general resources and resources by continent.
- The Association of Professors of Mission (**www.asmweb.org**/apm/syllabi/theology.htm) which give a number of syllabi on contextualization from a variety of schools.
- Annotated Contextualization Bibliography (ACB) (**www.wheaton.edu**/intr/Moreau/courses/532/biblio/biblio.htm). This bibliography is split by topics and area of contextualization and geographic regions.

Repositories
- LookSmart (**www.looksmart.com** – go to "articles" tab) holds 3.5 million articles from more than 700 publications. A search for "contextualization" yields 200 hits.
- Network for Strategic Missions KnowledgeBase (NSMKB) (**www.strategicnetwork.org**/index.php?loc=kb&mode=b&sf=Y&fto=322) with 190 articles and 8 sub-topics.
- Questia.com (**www.questia.com**) a subscription-based Internet library service with 1,643 hits on "contextualization." This site is not exclusively Christian so it needs to be limited like *contextualized theology*.

Journal articles
- Bulletin for Contextual Theology (**www.hs.unp.ac.za**/theology/bct.htm - which focuses on African theologies)
- Direction (**www.directionjournal.org**/index/art-subject.html?Mission/International+Church) This is a Mennonite Brethren sponsored journal.
- EMQ (Evangelical Missions Quarterly)(**www.billygrahamcenter.org**/emis/archives.htm).
- International Journal of Frontier Missions (www.ijfm.org/archives.htm) which is a Frontier Mission focus.
- Journal of Asian Mission (**www.apts.edu**/jam/)
- Mission Frontiers Magazine (**www.missionfrontiers.org**/archive.htm)
- To All Men All Thngs (**www.leppc.net**/kearns/TAMAT.htm) with a Hindu focus

Appendix B

H. L. Richard gives these 10 keys to evangelizing Hindus. Friendship evangelism is usually easy to initiate with Hindus. Most Hindus esteem religion in general and are free and open to speak about it. A sincere, non-judgmental interest in all aspects of Indian life will provide a good basis for friendship. Personal interaction with Hindus will lead to a more certain grasp of the essence of Hinduism than reading many books.

A consistently Christ-like life is the most important factor in sharing the gospel with Hindus. The suggestions that follow should help to break down misunderstandings and help to build a positive witness for Christ. However, learning and applying these points can never be a substitute for a transparent life of peace and joy in discipleship to Jesus Christ.

1. **Do not criticize or condemn Hinduism.** There is much that is good and much that is bad in the practice of both Christianity and Hinduism. Pointing out the worst aspects of Hinduism is hardly the way to win friends or show love. Criticizing Hinduism can make us feel we have won an argument; it will not win Hindus to Jesus Christ.
2. **Avoid everything that hints of triumphalism and pride.** We are not the greatest people with the greatest religion, but some Hindus are taught that we think of ourselves in this way. We do not have all knowledge of all truth; in fact we know very little (1Corinthians 8.1,2).
3. **Never allow a suggestion that separation from family and/or culture is necessary in becoming a disciple of Christ.** To insist or even subtly encourage a Hindu to leave his home and way of life to join the 'Christian' way of life in terms of diet and culture, etc., is a denial of biblical teaching (1Corinthians 7.17-24).
4. **Do not speak quickly on hell, or on the fact that Jesus is the only way for salvation.** Hindus hear these things as triumphalism and are offended unnecessarily. Speak of hell only with tears of compassion. Point to Jesus so that it is obvious he is the only way, but leave the Hindu to see and conclude this for himself.
5. **Never hurry.** Any pushing for a decision or conversion will do great harm. God must work, and the Holy Spirit should be given freedom to move at his own pace. Even after a profession of Christ is made, do not force quick changes regarding pictures of gods, charms, etc. Be patient and let a person come to understanding and conviction themselves before taking action.
6. **Work traditional Hindu (and biblical) values into your life, like simplicity,** renunciation, spirituality and humility, against which there is no law.
A life reflecting the reality of 'a still and quiet soul' (Psalm 131) will never be despised by Hindus.

7. **Know Hinduism, and each Hindu.** It will take some study to get a grasp of Hinduism and patient listening will be required to understand where in the spectrum each Hindu stands. Both philosophical and devotional Hinduism should be studied with the aim of understanding what appeals to the Hindu heart.
   Those who move seriously into work among Hindus need to become more knowledgeable in Hinduism than Hindus themselves are. Some study of the Sanskrit language will prove invaluable. Remember the biblical pattern from Acts 17 of introducing truth to the Hindu from his own tradition, and only secondarily from the Bible. For example, the biblical teaching on sin is repulsive to many modern Hindus, but their own Scriptures give an abundance of similar testimony. Bridge from Hindu Scripture to the Bible and Christ.
8. **Be quick to acknowledge failure.** Defending wrong practices in the church and Western Christianity only indicates we are more concerned for our religion than we are for truth.
9. **Share your testimony, describing your personal experience of lostness and God's gracious forgiveness and peace.** Don't claim to know God in his majesty and fullness, but share what you know in your life and experience. This is the supreme approach in presenting Christ to the Hindu, but care must be taken that our sharing is appropriate. To shout on a street corner, or share at every seeming opportunity is offensive. What God does in our lives is holy and private, only to be shared in intimacy to those who will respect the things of God and his work in our lives.
10. **Focus on Christ.** He alone can win their hearts' total loyalty to himself. In your life and speech so centre on him that all see in your life that God alone is worth living for. Hinduism is often called 'God intoxicated', and the Hindu who lives at all in this frame of mind is put off by Christian emphases on so many details to the neglect of the 'one thing that is needed' (Luke 10.42). A Hindu who professes faith in Christ must be helped as far as possible to work out the meaning of that commitment in his own cultural context. Often a new follower of Christ is ready to adopt any and every practice of Western Christians, and needs to be taught what is essential and what is secondary in Christian life and worship. A new believer should be warned against making an abrupt announcement to his or her family, since that inflicts great pain and inevitably produces deep misunderstanding. Ideally, a Hindu will share each step of the pilgrimage to Christ with his or her family, so that there is no surprise at the end. An early stage of the communication, to be reaffirmed continually, would be the honest esteem for Indian/Hindu traditions in general that the disciple of Christ can and does maintain (Richard, 2001).

Appendix C

Hindu Contextual Scale

H1 Traditional Christianity separates from everything "Hindu," including diet, dress, name, caste, ceremonies, etc.
- Does it exist? Many Indian churches and missions have followed and continue this patter, leading Hindus to consider Christianity a foreign religion.

H2 Christians renounce Hinduism but are open to non-religious Hindu cultural practices.
- Name and diet are not necessarily changed, although believers often alter diet even if it is not deemed essential for following Christ.
- Caste is renounced with other religious and seeming-religious practices, i.e., a woman wearing a red dot on her forehead.
- Some music is drawn from indigenous traditions, but most is of foreign origin or adapted from foreign sources.
- Cultural aspects of a few Hindu festivals might be celebrated.
- Often not concerned with receiving foreign funding for Christian work even though many Hindus consider it scandalous.
- Future leaders are training in Western-style seminaries and Bible colleges -- most have courses/discussions on contextualizing expressions of faith, but actions speak louder than words. These institutions are strongholds of Westernized Christianity in India.
- Does it exist? Most Indian churches are comfortable in H2, which has not affected the Hindu understanding of Christianity as a foreign religion.

H3 Hinduism is renounced in favor of Christianity, but with efforts to adapt Hindu religious and cultural practices into biblical faith and practice.
- Efforts to develop contextual Indian Christian theology--willingness to use terminologies from Hinduism that traditional Christians avoid.
- Women wearing red forehead dot is not problematic.
- Vegetarianism is often practiced
- Caste is recognized at least to a limited extent.
- Musical styles from Indian traditions are adopted but Western music is also used.
- Hindu festivals are sometimes celebrated (in varying degrees, often modified).
- Hindu temples are studiously avoided.
- Commitment to indigenous financing is due to the stigma of foreign funding of Christian work.
- Does it exist? No historic Christian movements in India have effectively arrived at H3. The Christian "ashram" (spiritual retreat center) movement

beginning in the 1920s was an attempt. Many individual Hindus converts experimented on these lines while within H1 or H2 churches.

H4 Hindus who come to Christ maintain sociological identity as Hindus within their birth community.
- Do not identify as "Christian."
- Do not develop contextual expressions of faith and discipleship.
- name, caste, diet and dress (including red dot) are not changed because they are aspects of community life.
- Positive adaption of Christ into Hindu values and methods is not attempted.
- Occasional study and fellowship gatherings are culturally neutral, appearing neither "Christian" nor "Hindu."
- Hindu festivals are celebrated.
- Hindu temples are visited for family-related ceremonies.
- Full-time workers funded from abroad are not involved.
- Does it exist? At least one fledging effort to develop ministry in H4.

H5 Hindus who come to Christ maintain sociological identity as Hindus within birth-community.
- Seek to develop Hindu patterns of discipleship in personal devotion, corporate worship, evangelism, etc., and to define their faith in contextual terms (contextual Indian theology).
- Often identify themselves as *"bhaktas"* (devotees) of Christ or *Jesus-bhaktas*-- Christian in India is a sociological term more than a theological tag.
- Initially viewed with skepticism by Hindus, due to traditional associations of Christ with radical cultural and community change.
- Minimal music from existing Christian traditions, perhaps except Christian music in traditional Indian styles.
- Corporate expressions of discipleship are often rare or non-existent due to practical considerations; but desire to follow biblical patterns of a corporate faith expression.
- Corporate development may be mono-caste for a time, but for practical rather than ideological reasons.
- Socially acceptable means of inter-cast fellowship will be developed. (No know current or historic case of Christ-followers has upheld total cast exclusiveness in teaching or practice).
- Hindu festivals are celebrated, sometimes modified.
- Hindu temples are sometimes reluctantly visited for family-related ceremonies.
- Indigenous funding is deemed essential.
- Does it exist? Small stirrings toward H5.

H6 Hindus in Christ remain in birth communities as Hindus.
- Individualized discipleship to Jesus is without corporate expression,

except perhaps attendance at occasional traditional Christian gatherings.
- Not secret, but known as Jesus-followers in their Hindu social circles.
- Hindu festivals are celebrated.
- Hindu temples are visited.
- The 'churchless Christians' -- a misnomer since they are not 'Christians' but Hindu disciples of Christ.
- Does it exist? A significant number in Tamil Nadu in South India. Smaller numbers elsewhere in India.

H7 Hindus in Christ remain in birth communities.
- Keep devotion to Jesus secret.
- Appear to participate fully in Hindu religious activity, but address all prayers to Christ or God through Christ.
- Does it exist? Some such people have always existed, but they are hard to identify and harder still to quantify (Richard, 2004, pp. 317-320).

Appendix D

Excerpts from Todd Johnson's article on "Contextualization: a New-Old Idea" where he describes the pioneering and often radical views of Jesuit missionary Roberto de Nobili.

Unfortunately, the Reformation had little impact in the realm of missions; only a handful of Protestant missionaries went out in the 250 years following Luther's courageous act. The famous Baptist historian, Kenneth Scott Latourette, summarized the situation succinctly: "Between 1500 and 1750 the geographic spread of Christianity was mainly through Roman Catholics" (1953:924). This expansion was greatly facilitated through the founding of the Jesuits in 1534. In fact, the English word "mission," which is technically used today to mean foreign missions, actually originated from the fourth vow of the Jesuits (Johnson, 1987, p. 2).

From the inception of the Jesuits, cross-cultural outreach had a special place in the lives of its members. The next 200 years of mission history was to a large degree written by them. Bishop Stephen Neill writes, "Within the next hundred years Jesuits were to lay their bones in almost every country of the known world and on the shores of almost every sea" (1964:148). The great missionaries of the Church before Carey, Judson and Taylor were Jesuits like Xavier, Valignano, Ricci and Nobili. These early Jesuits often possessed amazing cross-cultural sensitivities, and this was especially true of Roberto de Nobili (Johnson, 1987, p. 2).

In a few weeks discovered the shocking truth: the Hindus had been watching the foreigners carefully to determine what caste they were from, and after repeatedly observing them eat meat and associate with low-caste people had labeled them "*Parangi*" or "those who have horses and guns," a term referring to low caste. The Portuguese, including the Jesuits, were happy to wear this label since they believed it to merely be a Tamil translation of the word "Portuguese." The Jesuits had made a further mistake by referring to their religion as that of the "*Parangi*." To the average Hindu this could mean only one thing: to become a Christian you had to renounce caste and eat meat. For this reason there were no caste Hindu converts in Madurai (Johnson, 1987, p. 2).

Nobili also noticed that several groups of Hindu men lived austere and harsh lives in devotion to their gods. They were from all castes but were highly respected by everyone because they had renounced their lives and practiced simplicity. These were called the *sannyasis*. After some time, Nobili decided to seek to become a *sannyasi* to reach all who could not bring themselves to forsake caste (Johnson, 1987, p. 3).

Nobili's innate courtesy and kindliness made them feel at home. He spoke well, without any mixture of Portuguese, and he said things worth hearing.

He listened too with close interest to what they had to say. When they narrated to him their *Puranic* stories he would never brush them aside with a contemptuous "Nonsense." ... He was struck by their deep sense of religion. With them religion was not a cloak which they only occasionally put on. It was ingrained in their very life, in their thoughts, in their words and in every action (Johnson, 1987, p. 3).

Nobili's royal Italian heritage allowed him to present himself as a Roman "raja," a member of a ruling caste that Indians could understand. ... Nobili was no longer associated in Indian minds with a polluting *Parangi*. He continued scrupulously to observe the rules of the Raja caste. For a time nothing happened. Then men of the three highest castes--the best educated Madurai--began to come and speak to Nobili: at first only one or two, at rare intervals, then in groups. ... Thus Nobili entered a whole new perspective from which he began to see India from the inside out. He soon became aware of the fact that his raja status separated him from the Brahmins whom he most wanted to reach. Another step would be necessary for him to get close to the Brahmins, and for this he had to seek the advice of Hindus. He returned to his desire to live the life of a *sannyasi*. He remembered that the *sannyasis* he admired were respected by all castes. Even as a raja, if Nobili forsook all and became a *sannyasi*, he would be able to share truth with Brahmins. ... He therefore put on the garb of a Hindu *sannyasi*, the ocher-colored robe, the wooden slippers, the sandalwood paste on his forehead, in hand the staff and water jug customary among Hindu ascetics. He built a little hut for himself and lived there in utter seclusion, avoiding the company of Fernandes, the Feringhee missionary, and refusing to have anything to do with his Christians. He avoided eating meat and drinking alcohol, and secured the services of a Brahmin servant and cook. This fact made it clear to those who watched him that he was not an outcaste or pariah but a man of superior caste (Johnson, 1987, pp. 3-4).

As a *sannyasi* Nobili was expected to study hard and teach others the ways to the truth. Since he deeply desired to know the Hindu religion, this was precisely the break Nobili was looking for, and his disciplined study began to bear fruit.

The Father speaks the purest Tamil and pronounces it so well that even the most fastidious Brahmin scholars cannot improve on his diction. He has already read many books, and learned by heart the essential passages of their laws as well as many verses of their most famous poets, who are held among them in great honor. Many are the hymns he has learned by heart, and he sings them with such perfection and grace that all listen to him with pleasure and unconcealed admiration

A formidable obstacle still prevented Nobili from really understanding the Hindu mind. Most of the ancient texts were in Sanskrit, and it was forbidden for any non-Brahmin to study Sanskrit. Even as a *sannyasi*, Nobili was barred from possessing the key that would unlock the Hindu scriptures. By providence, Nobili found a scholar who would teach him Sanskrit, and even at the risk of his life this scholar gave Nobili a copy of the Vedas (Johnson, 1987, p. 4).

The more Nobili learned from the Vedas, the more he debated with Hindus, often using the very strengths of Hinduism to lead them to the cross. He also adapted the teachings of the church fathers and Western philosophers to give Hindus keys to some foundational propositions on which Christianity stood. And yet for all the debates he held and all the booklets he wrote, it was primarily his love and gentle spirit that touched the hearts of his hearers.

He was committed to spreading the Catholic faith, not a system of European philosophy. Nevertheless, to preserve the faith intact, it would be necessary to retain certain basic apprehensions (for example about the nature of divine love and of the soul) not normally perceived in India and, indeed, to communicate them. They comparatively easy task of becoming in all ways India was not open to Nobili. He must communicate those basic apprehensions not only, or even chiefly, by verbal arguments, but, under God, by a good life, for Indians expected of a guru not so much information as transformation of character. Grace in him must act out the truth of his apprehensions. Between Rome and Madurai he himself must become a bridge of love (Johnson, 1987, p. 5).

Nobili contextualized the gospel in three major ways:
1. He took on an identity that was genuine and one which the Indians could understand and respect. He placed himself within the caste system where he could gain a hearing.
2. He studied the religion of the people he was trying to reach and used his understanding of Hinduism to enhance his presentation of the gospel.
3. He did not alienate his converts from the church at large. He never spoke evil of the *Parangis* but rather allowed his converts to worship in the way that was natural to them and then made them understand that the *Parangis* were their brothers and sisters (Johnson, 1987, p. 8).

Nobili was by no means perfect in his contextualization. He used Latin for his first Easter mass, and some of his services differed little from those he had experienced in his native Italy. On the other hand, Nobili always seemed to be looking for a way in which Hindus, especially those from high castes, would be comfortable with the gospel and able to express their Christianity in the context of their culture. By devoting his life to this pursuit, this Italian Jesuit brought more advances to the Catholic church's understanding of what the indigenous church in India should look like than any other before or perhaps after him. He was indeed an incarnational missionary in the fullest sense (Johnson, 1987, p. 9).

References

Brown, R. (2007, October). "Why Muslims are Repelled by the term 'Son of God'." *Evangelical Missions Quarterly*, pp. pp. 422-429.

Corwin, G. (2004, July). "Telling the Difference." *Evangelical Missions Quarterly, 40*(3), 282-283.

Guthrie, S. (1998, April). "Just saying No." *Evangelical Missions Quarterly.*

Guthrie, S. (2000). *Missions in the Thrid Millennium: 21 Key Trends for the 21st Century.* Waynesboro, GA: Paternoster Publicating.

Hesselgrave, D. J. (2005). *Paradigms in Conflict.* Grand Rapids: Kregel Academic & Professional.

Johnson, T. M. (1987). "Contextualization: A New-Old Idea." *The International Journal of Frontier Missions, 40*(1-4).

Leffel, J. "Contextualization: Building Bridges to the Muslim Commuicty."

Massey, J. (2004, July). "Misunderstanding C5: His Ways are not Our Orthodoxy." *Evangelical Missions Quarterly*, pp. 296-304.

Moreau, A. S. a. M. O. (2005, October). "Contextualizing Ministry among Muslims." *Evangelical Missions Quarterly.* Retrieved 9/20/07, from https://bgc.gospelcom.net/emqonline/emq_article_read.php?ArticleID=3535.

Moreau, A. S. (2007, April). "Contextualization that is Comprehensive." *Lausanne World Pulse.* Retrieved 9/20/07, from http://www.lausanneworldpulse.com/perspectives/673.

Parshall, P. (2004, July). "Lifting the Fatwa." *Evangelical Missions Quarterly.*

Pocock, M., Gailyn Van Rheenen and Douglas McConnell. (2005, 07/09/14). *The Changing Face of World Missions: Engaging Contemporary Issues and Trends.* Grand Rapids: Baker Publishing Group.

Richard, H. L. (2001, January). "Ten Tips for Reaching Hindus." *Mission Frontiers Special Edition.*

Richard, H. L. (2003). "New Paradigms for Understanding Hinduism and Contextualization." *Voice of Bhakti, 2*(2).

Richard, H. L. (2004, July). "H-Scale for Hindu Contextualization." *Evangelical Missions Quarterly, 40*(3), pp. 316-320.

Tennent, T. C. (2006, Fall). "Followers of Jesus (Isa) in Islamic Mosques: A Closer Examination of C-5 "High Spectrum" Contextualization." *International Journal of Frontier Missions, 23*(3), pp. 101-115.

Terry, J. M., Ebbie Smith and Justice Anderson. (1998, 07/09/25). *Missiology: An Introduction to the foundations, History, and Strategies of World Missions.* Nashville, TN: Broadman & Holman Publishers.

Whiteman, D. L. (1997, January). "Contextualization: The Theory, the Gap, the Challenge." *International Bulletin of Missionary Research, 2.*

Woodberry, J. D., Russel G. Shubin and G. Marks. (2007, October). "Why Muslims Follow Jesus." *Christianity Today, 51:10*, pp. 80-85.

Chapter 7

Church Planting Movements

How was it that the Early Church spread so rapidly throughout the hostile Roman Empire in the first century of its existence? It was not just evangelism of winning individuals to Christ but also the bonding of every individual believer into local groups that committed themselves to follow Jesus' commands and share their new found freedom of forgiveness and acceptance through Jesus Christ.

Garrison declares that today a Church Planting Movement (henceforth, CPM) is much more than evangelism. Most missionaries have never experienced a CPM where thousands of unreached people begin to turn to Christ and bond together in small churches.

> A Church Planting Movement is not "evangelism that results in churches." Evangelism that results in churches is a part of a Church Planting Movement, but the "end-vision" is less extensive. A church planter might satisfy himself with the goal of planting a single church or even a handful of churches, but fail to see that it will take a movement of churches planting churches to reach an entire nation of people (Garrison, 2003, p. 228).

This chapter will discuss the relatively recent development of the CPM strategy for building His Church throughout the world. Something was needed to break through into an exponential growth pattern if we were ever to reach the world. Dayton showed that "Although the number of Christians in the world is growing, the percentage of Christians to non-Christians has remained more or less constant for the past fifty years." (Dayton, 2003, p. 161)

The transition in mission strategy from its early beginnings was fitting for that time, but as better understanding of the biblical concept of the church, evangelism, and the role of the missionary, new strategies developed to spread the gospel.

Mission Compound or Mission Station Strategy

In the early years of the missionary movement (1800-1914) the standard practice was to build a Missionary Compound or Mission Station. Land was purchased and buildings/houses were erected to facilitate all the mission activities within a secure area. This might include a school, clinic and church, as well as housing for the missionaries and some workers. It was all financed by foreign funds, managed by foreign missionaries and left little possibility for the area Nationals to ever be more than employees of the missionaries, which could be difficult at times.

The primary model of missions up to this time was the Roman Catholic monastery approach, which was modified for Protestant missionaries, but there were a lot of similarities. Dependency was created from the beginning: if you wanted health, education or a job you had to depend on the foreigner. Thus the missionaries were seen as rich and powerful people that could never be imitated. Likewise, during this period often the missionary was of the same country as the dominating country of the Colonial era, so he could easily have had political connections.

The "Golden Rule" of power was fully on the side of the missionary: "He who has the gold, rules." No matter how benevolent, whenever foreigners are ruling or have power, resentment, envy, and disillusionment are inevitable. During most of this period there was little or no attempt to give the nationals any of this power, and certainly none of the "gold."

But great accomplishments were made: medical aid, translation of the Scriptures, literacy, printing establishments, orphanages, abhorrent practices changed (i.e., burning of the living wife in the funeral pyre of the deceased husband, or murdering female babies or twins). Many highly trained national leaders were left to manage. The missionaries demonstrated the Christian Life principles as best they could in the new environment.

When the political world scene changed at the end of WWII, when all of the countries of the world demanded their independence from their European lords, many of the missionaries were expelled. When their liberation from Colonial powers did not come through negotiations, revolutions shook the world scene. Since the only world power that was not obligated to the European Colonial powers was Russia, many of the revolutions sought help from the Soviets and were amply supplied. The missionary cause was devastated in many of these countries, especially in Africa.

In many countries the nationalistic reaction to their new liberation was to obligate that every official entity or organization have nationals as either a majority or in key leadership roles. This forced the missionary to rethink the strategy for the future.

Indigenous Church Strategy

The indigenous policy began in the mid-nineteenth century when Henry Venn and Rufus Anderson developed the Three-Self formula. "They believed that young churches should be self-propagating, self-supporting, and self-governing from their inception." If the missionaries spoon-fed the nationals, they would create "rice Christians"-- people who converted only for the benefits they received. The more that was given to the nationals the more was expected, but the quicker "results" could be tabulated for supporters. Sadly when persecution came, the "rice Christians" vanished.

This movement came to a head in China during the Mao Cultural Revolution in 1948-49 with the expulsion of all American missionaries from China. Any ministry that was mature enough to survive on it own continued. The few who were grounded enough went underground. From this point missionaries began to rethink their heavy financial support of all their institutional ministries (Institutes, schools, clinics, hospitals, etc.).

Most agencies came to the conclusion that they did not want to go through what happened in China, so throughout the 1960's missions began to divest or turn over their institutions to national church organizations. This was often in a gradual reduction of subsidy over a decade, but usually the burden was too great for the association of churches to bear. Many of the former institutions folded or were greatly reduced.

The transition from heavy subsidy to fully indigenous support was more than difficult; it was agonizing and full of suspicion. "What are the rich Americans doing with all the money that was coming to us?" It was only worse when the subsidy came directly from individual missionaries: "You are withholding money that should be coming to us," or "You are getting richer with our money." Once money comes into the picture it can get pretty ugly when it is withdrawn.

The indigenous policy "emphasized the need for true conversion, which was reflected by the willingness of local Christians to support the work of the church. The foreign mission, they said, is like scaffolding. When the construction is finished, the scaffolding is removed. In many mission settings, however, what was built was unable to stand without the support of the scaffolding." (Pocock, 2005, p. 285)

Hodges' definition of an indigenous church is "a native church, ... which shares the life of the country in which it is planted and finds itself ready to govern itself, support itself, and reproduce itself." The church, according to Hodges, must be like a banana plant in Central America -- so indigenous to its environment that it requires no special attention to thrive. Banana plants grow in this climate wherever there is adequate water: A banana plant in Canada, however, cannot survive without special care. Before winter it must be dug up and transported indoors, and it seldom, if ever, is able to bear fruit (Hodges, 1957, pp. 7-8).

During the decades of the '60-'70s, major shifts in church planting strategies began to take place, giving the measure of success not to the size of the missionary led church, but to the ability to transition from missionary control to national led ministries.

The skill of developing national leaders was not taught in the missionary's training nor observed in his home church experience. Most pastors in the US have never discipled a single person. They have no motivation to prepare someone to take their place. To make matters worse, most missionaries have had little or no missiological training. They naively go to the field thinking that everything will work similarly to how it worked in churches back home. With this background it is no wonder that missionaries go to the field ill-equipped, and easily get frustrated. The idea of constantly "working themselves out of a job" gives them little visible credit for *their* accomplishments.

As missionaries were trying to figure out how to implement the "indigenous" policy that their mission agencies were demanding, Donald McGavran began to gain fame for his Church Growth Principles.

Church Growth Movement

Donald McGavran was dean emeritus and former senior professor of missions, church growth and South Asian studies at the School of World Missions, Fuller Theological Seminary in Pasadena, California. He was raised in a missionary family in India but came under the influence of the Student Volunteer Movement and became a third generation missionary as well. His passion was to overcome the social barriers to Christian conversion, especially in India with its caste system limiting the spread of the gospel. His research into how the Church grows resulted in his classic texts, *Bridges of God* and *Understanding Church Growth*. His findings were a key element in changing the methods that missionaries use to focus their ministry on specific people groups and sparked the Church Growth Movement.

McGavran rejected the popular view that missions was primarily education, evangelism, medicine, famine relief, world friendship, etc., but rather he believed that the goal of the Church should always be to disciple the peoples of the world. His passion for the Great Commission and the application of research, including statistical methods to derive the best methodology for a given people group inspired thousands to travel to Pasadena to study under his tutelage.

One of the major tenants of the Church Growth movement is seeking the objective of a People Movement Approach, in stead of individual decisions. McGavran shows how that group decisions or people movements is the natural way of growth throughout most of history around the world. Admittedly this pattern is often unfamiliar to Western missionaries who come from an individualistic society, unique in the world. Around the world most converts often are non-literate and under educated so that decisions are made by the group, not the individual.

McGavran postulates five great advantages to understanding and applying church growth principles:
1. Permanent churches deeply rooted in the soil of the culture, which

are independent of Western support. Thus the new churches are freed from bonds to another culture and have the spiritual authority and motivation to multiply themselves. Since it is their church, not that of the foreigner, they are willing to endure persecution.
2. Churches are naturally indigenous being immersed in their own culture so they can easily clothe all their activities in their cultural ways. Being excited about their own kind of Christianity, they become vibrantly evangelistic.
3. "Spontaneous expansion of churches" is natural because it is linked with growth points among indigenous people, which are not broken when they become Christians. Only moderate assistance from outside is needed usually in the area of training.
4. A People Movement may be created in nearby cultures through cultural bridges that may exist to other communities. As communities are convinced about Christ, bridging to another community may produce another people movement where multitudes turn to Christ together.
5. A People Movement provides a sound pattern of becoming Christian because biases are gone and changes in the lives of Christians can be demonstrable and infinitely reproducible (McGavran, 2003, p. 184).

People become Christian as a wave of decisions for Christ sweeps through the group's minds, involving many individual decisions, but being far more than merely the sum of individual commitments. "This may be called a chain reaction. Each decision sets off others and, the sum total powerfully affects every individual. When conditions are right, not merely each subgroup, but the entire group concerned decides together" (McGavran, 2003, p. 178).

McGavran had considerable criticism of evangelistic methods that focused on getting "decisions," yet little or no fruit ever resulted. Ray Comfort, likewise, has documented the same lack of results in his study of American evangelistic efforts (which are part of the "baggage" that American missionaries take with them to the field.

> At a 1990 crusade in the United States, 600 "decisions for Christ" were obtained. No doubt, there was much rejoicing. However, ninety days later, follow-up workers could not find even one who was continuing in his or her faith. That crusade created 600 backsliders -- or, to be more scriptural, false converts. ...
> Charles E. Hackett, the division of home missions national director for the Assemblies of God in the United States, said, "A soul at the altar does not generate much excitement in some circles because we realize that approximately ninety-five out of every hundred will not become integrated into the church. In fact, most of them will not return for a second visit." ...

A pastor in Boulder, Colorado, sent a team to Russia in 1991 and obtained 2,500 decisions. The next year, the team found only thirty continuing in their faith. That's a retention rate of 1.2 percent.

Pastor Elma Murdock stated, "Chuck Colson's concern was ours. He states that for every 100 people making decisions for Christ, only two may return for follow-up a few days later. George Barna says that the majority of people (51% minimum) making decisions, leave the church within 6-8 weeks." ...

A mass crusade reported 18,000 decisions -- yet, according to "Church Growth" magazine, 94 percent failed to become incorporated into a local church.

In Sacramento, California, a combined crusade yielded more than 2,000 commitments. One church followed up on fifty-two of those decisions and couldn't find one true convert.

A leading U.S. denomination reported that during 1995 thy secured 384,057 decisions, but retained only 22,983 in fellowship. They couldn't account for 361,074 supposed conversions. That's a 94 percent fall-away rate (Comfort, 2006, pp. 97-98).

McGavran's answer would be to not simply preach for "decisions" but to make obedient disciples. Only disciples produce a church that multiplies itself spontaneously within a culture. ... Repentance goes deeper than a decision; it is a permanent change wrought by God's Spirit. We are born all over again. Few purely intellectual decisions in any culture lead to permanent, obedient discipleship (McGavran, 2003, p. 184). He helped stem the tide toward the social concern priority back to a confrontational evangelism and aggressive disciple-making focus.

The application of the Church Growth data can be seen in John Slack's research with the congregations of the Southern Baptist Convention. Here were his conclusions:
1. New units grow faster than established churches.
2. Aging within a church almost inevitably ushers in a "come-oriented" ministry in contrast to a "go-centered" ministry.
3. Older churches do not start as many new churches as do younger churches.
4. Churches and church planting drift upward on the economic scale.
5. The longer a church is in a community, the less like that community the church becomes.
6. Existing, established churches have normal plateau and ministry limits.
7. Only as a church effectively expands its discipleship base will it sustain infinitely reproducible church growth and church planting.
8. More baptisms and greater membership growth occurs in zones or areas that are farther from the existing church and its come-oriented activities.

9. The difference between so-called "responsive" and "non-responsive" peoples is not in the average number of baptisms per church but in the number of new units -- churches -- that are started.
10. Churches in resistant cultures tend to begin as or soon become cosmopolitan rather than community. In resistant cultures, community churches have far greater influence on the culture than do cosmopolitan churches.
11. As beginning models of church planting, training, and materials are repeated and age, they become hallowed -- and almost "unchangeable" -- patterns even when and if they are no longer relevant.
12. If a lost person or people group is illiterate and poor, the chance of their being evangelized decreases proportionately to the heights of their illiteracy and the depths of their poverty.
13. Training in most theological programs has become more academic than functional.
14. Bible teaching, including the Sunday School and other forms of discipleship, to be effective, must be done in the context of evangelism (Slack, 1998, p. 504).

Though these results apply specifically to the SBC USA, the missionaries going overseas come from this type of church and easily carry these same practices with them. We become like our teacher (generally).

Criticism of this movement stems from the foundations being primarily based on statistics and social behavior rather than theology, and also the principle of more numerical growth being equated to evidence of correct analysis.

The principles of the Church Growth Movement laid the groundwork for the Seeker Movement, which produced some of America's largest mega churches reaching over 20,000 weekend attendees. The three most notable church leaders who followed this strategy are Robert Schuller (Self-Esteem Reformation), Bill Hybel (Seeker driven church) and Rick Warren (Purpose Driven or Seeker-sensitive church).

By the 1980's the Church Growth and Seeker movement would be overwhelmed by the Signs and Wonders Movement, Power Evangelism and Strategic Level Warfare, World Prayer movement and the new Apostolic Reformation churches (but this is another trend to be discussed in a later chapter). However, many of the same principles laid the groundwork for these movements as well.

Church Planting Strategy

There are many models for planting a new church, some are preferred or required by different mission boards, but in general, everyone should be contributing directly or indirectly to the planting of indigenous churches, whatever his assignment, platform or task may be, so a good understanding is vital. Basically, a "church planter" and his family moves into a new location to start a church with little or no believers. The *CPer* (Church Planter) has very little connection with or pre-existing support in the target area. They are "pioneering" new territory.

Generally, an existing church or mission agency plays the role of "Mother," providing the initial leadership and resources to get the new church ("daughter church") started. Whether this is a church in the US starting another church in the US or overseas the daughter church usually is a reflection of the Mother church. Usually it is more difficult to get resources for the international daughter church than the US based church. The "bragging rights" syndrome among pastors in the US carries over to the foreign field. Missionaries closely tied to US pastors want to speak their language: attendance, souls saved, baptisms, etc. To maintain their status the effort is made to gain the numbers to keep in the conversation and be respected by their US cohorts in the ministry. With enough resources, this can happen for a while, but the long-range effects are more negative than positive.

When *giants* go to the mission field (as the nationals see us usually), it is hard to take a secondary role and build up the national's ministry as a priority. To hinge success and reputation on a national pastor, to many, is a scary process.

Furthermore, the inequality of resources and income between missionary and national, and the inevitable reduction or elimination of foreign resources when the missionary passes the leadership off to a national, (the tendency of the congregation to respect the foreign missionary more than the national pastor), puts enormous pressure on the national pastor to attempt to "measure up" to the *giant* who preceded him. This is the beginning of the formula for failure.

In the view of contemporary churches "Church planting" is such an all-inclusive and critical "button" that everyone must prove their involvement in a church-planting ministry in order to raise any support, even if they don't participate directly. Nurses, school teachers, accountants, etc., must use the claim to be "church planters" in order to raise their support. Ministries not related to church planting typically find considerable less sympathy in US churches.

Partnership Strategies

Pocock reports, "During the 1990s, a significant transition occurred in the use of money in missions. In 1996, U.S. mission agencies reported that they employed 30,000 national missionaries of other countries and just under 40,000 American missionaries. By 1999, these same agencies were still supporting just under 40,000 U. S. missionaries, but the number of national missionaries they reportedly employed had grown to 71,000. " Pocock reports that over 130 agencies in Canada and the US, "advocate and assist indigenous missions." A trend is evident that there is a modern move from indigenous self-support to international partnerships (Pocock, 2005, p. 290).

Church Planting Movement Strategy

How can a limited missionary pool spread the gospel to millions of people? In greater Osaka, Japan there are 22 million people with only 0.26% attending a church of an average size of 39 attendees. In order to someday reach just 1/3 of this city it would take 100,000 new churches. The old way of doing church would take forever. A new strategy had to be developed to quickly motivate new believers to plant new churches from the beginning of their Christian lives.

Light at the end of the tunnel began to shine when IMB Strategic Coordinator David Watson went to NE India to a highly resistant people group, the Bhojpuri people, the tribal group of Mahatmagndi. Watson pioneered a strategy that now has spread around the world as the primary methodology for reaching resistant people groups.

> When missionaries Jan and David Watson were sent to work with an unreached people group in 1989, less than 30 churches existed for more than 90 million mostly illiterate and impoverished people who speak the Bhojpuri language -- a number that had remained stagnant for more than four decades.
> The task appeared to be nearly impossible -- except for the fact that the Watson's believed in a God who specializes in the impossible. But their early efforts seemed to confirm the dismal outlook. Six evangelists sent by the Watson's to Bhojpuri villages were brutally murdered within one year of each other. Although David wanted to leave, God wouldn't release him to return home.
> That time of soul-searching and turmoil led the couple to adopt a brand-new strategy that focused on simply finding a person of peace, discipling him into the Christian faith, and making him the pastor of a new church.
> The results came almost immediately. In 1993 the number of churches among the people group had jumped from 28 to 36. The next year, there were 78 churches. Then there were 220 in 1995. Finally, Watson could no longer continue counting the instances of exploding growth. In 1998, he cautiously estimated the number of Bhojpuri speakers who had committed their life to Christ in the previous seven years to be more than 55,000. By 2000, the safe estimates were more than 3,200 churches, 250,000 believers, and more than 10,000 new church starts. Today, Bhojpuri believers number nearly 1 million (Perry, 2005).

Headquarters in Richmond was skeptical. "This can't be," they said. "Either you've misunderstood the question or you're not telling us the truth." The words stung, but David held his tongue. "Come and see," he said.

Later that year, a survey team headed by Watson's supervisor arrived in India to investigate. Together they visited Lucknow, Patna, Delhi, Varanasi, and numerous smaller Indian towns and villages David had listed in his report. The supervisor later commented, "I personally went in very doubtful, but we were wrong. Everywhere we went it was exactly as Watson had reported. God was doing something amazing there." (Garrison, 2004, p. 2)

Within a year reports began to filter into different mission circles of similar CPMs that were following a similar pattern. In East Asia, a missionary reported: "I launched my three-year plan in November, 2000. My vision was to see 200 new churches started among my people group over the next three years. But four months later, we had already reached that goal. After only six months, we had already seen 360 churches planted and more than 10,000 new believers baptized! Now I'm asking God to enlarge my vision." (Garrison, 2004, p. 3) The IMB reports, "The Southern Baptist International Mission Board ... is currently seeing more than half a million baptisms each year, the great majority of them resulting form Church Planting Movements. At present, the IMB is monitoring more than fifty locations around the world where variations of CPM can be seen." (Garrison, 2004, p. 3)

Common Characteristics

After considerable analysis and study of numerous CPMs, a list of ten common factors in CPMs has been compiled for future missionaries:

1. **Worship in the heart language**, where people can intuitively express their deepest emotions to a God who cares for them.
2. **Evangelism has communal implications** (as opposed to Western individualism and personal commitment) relying on family and social connections or webs.
3. **Rapid incorporation of new converts** into the life and ministry of the church, especially expected to become witnesses immediately. As they are witnessed to and discipled, so they immediately begin to do the same to others.
4. **Passion and fearlessness due to a sense of urgency** of the importance of salvation and conversion. "A spirit of timidity or fear quenches a CPM. Boldness may invite persecution, but it fuels a CPM."
5. **A price to pay to become a Christian**. CPMs are typically emerging in an environment of persecution and resistance. "Persecution tends to screen out the uncommitted and ensures a highly dedicated membership."

6. **Perceived leadership crisis or spiritual vacuum in society**, especially "during war, a natural disaster or displacement may be a ripe environment for a CPM."
7. **On-the-job training for church leadership** is a critical element to keep the movement growing. If leaders must leave their churches for training, there could be a negative impact on their ministries. Typically these are "short-term training modules that do not impede the primary tasks of evangelism, church planting and pastoral leadership."
8. **Leadership authority is decentralized** for ease of decision-making in a dynamic movement. "It is important that every cell or house church leaders has all the authority required to do whatever needs to be done in terms of evangelism, ministry and new church planting without seeking approval from a church hierarchy."
9. **Outsiders keep a low profile**, in order to "minimize foreignness and encourage indigeneity."
10. **Missionaries suffer persecution**: "the disproportionate degree of suffering by missionaries engages in CPM is noteworthy (Garrison, 2002, p. ch.4). This is especially true in Muslim lands.

David Watson, now an international Church Planting Movement consultant for hundreds of missions around the world, adds a few more distinctives that are essential in order to see the CPMs become successful:

1. **Prayer**: "An emphasis is given in the CPM strategy to know the mind of God and join Him in His work." Sadly, many missionaries have become virtual secularists in spiritual matters, depending on programs, events and technology and little utter dependence upon God's power.
2. **Scripture**: Often strategies take precedence over Scripture, which is often related to a confirming of cultural values, instead of a blueprint to mold a Christian culture.
3. **Household or family focus**, instead of an individual focus. Since families become the major persecutors of new believers, the objective is to win the family together.
4. **Disciples**: In traditional missions every effort is made to bring people to a "decision" to accept Christ, but the efforts are slim to bring them to maturity as true disciples ("learners") of Christ for life. Since few missionaries have ever been discipled, nor have many ever seen what discipleship looks like, this is a major philosophical shift in their thinking.
5. **Teach Obedience**: The objective of teaching is obedience, not just understanding or knowledge. The Great Commission says to "teach them to obey all things..." (Matt 20:20). Watson emphasizes three questions: a) What does the passage say? b) What does it mean for me? c) If it is the teaching of

God, what must I do to obey it? Watson teaches that knowledge-based ministries kill church planting. Only obedience orientated ministries motivate rapid reproduction of churches. In the explosion of multiplying churches there must be great dependence on the Holy Spirit to keep people in line with the Scriptures, (1 John 2:27) and the discovery process which leads to obedience will bring committed believers to live out His will.

6. **Access Ministries**: The "ministry" in a CPM is basically an unpaid ministry, so creative ways are developed for church planters to gain access to the villages that they target for ministry. After making a study of the needs of a specific people group, a church planter moves in to meet that need: store, school, teacher, medical or dental, etc. As the church planter serves the people well, confidence is built and access to the hearts of the people and the right to speak into their lives is granted.
7. **Plan**: Distractions, especially for "tent-maker" church planters, are inevitable, so a plan must be priority: win disciples and gather families into units to study and obey His Word together.
8. **Person of Peace – Discovery Bible Study method**. When Jesus sent out the 70, He told them to seek out a "person of peace." Find someone who would be willing to discover the meanings in the Bible, who often becomes the leader of the first Bible study. Teaching begins as soon as a relationship is built, not waiting until he has decided to follow Christ. Faith must be exercised to believe that God is at work preparing people to hear His Word.
9. **Community of believers** (a simple church): Early groups are "practice groups" (committed to practicing what they learn) where they carry on the essentials of a local assembly. If left alone in most environments, few if any believers can survive in an isolated environment.
10. **Reaching out** (missions): If they have encountered the truth, yet they know that none of their friends has any idea of how to know God, they immediately have a burden to share their new faith.
11. **Reproducing**: Church reproduction is expected in all levels of the CPM process. Everyone is expected to reproduce other believers and corporately to reproduce other fellowships in other areas. It becomes the DNA of the movement.
12. **Inside Leaders**: Instead of depending on leaders for local assemblies from the outside, they become reproducible because the leaders are in every group from the beginning.
13. **Authority and the Holy Spirit**: Dependence is upon the Word and the Holy Spirit to work as the authority for individuals and the corporate group. There is a great expectation for God to work miracles in drawing people to Christ and keeping them sensitive to His will.
14. **Persecution**: Especially in Muslim environments, persecution is the norm.

Watson declares that wherever he witnessed torture or assassinations, a church was born.
15. **Training/Mentoring**: Mentoring is continual training for effective ministry. Those with more experience lead those with less experience and eventually hand off the new ministry into the hands of the maturing leader.
16. **Outside Leaders**: A non-resident leader guides from a distance. His task is to model, to equip, to watch and to leave at the appropriate time. His leaving is not to abandon, but to entrust the young leaders to carry on the task begun.
17. **Self-supporting**: Local leaders maintain all the work. Muslims around the world are never paid for their work as spiritual leader. Believers take up the task of meeting needs in villages, becoming good citizens, and leading the young church, while maintaining a work ethic in order to keep their family needs met. This eliminates the major obstacle to planting multiple churches: money. It is not essential any longer. Only those who are uniquely gifted and mature enough to have an expanding influence will become supported in a full-time sense.[17]

Definitions

Garrison gives this definition of a CPM: "a rapid and multiplicative increase of indigenous churches planting churches within a given people group or population segment." A CPM is more than "evangelism that results in churches." It is a movement where churches birth of other churches is a norm of their existence.

A church planter might satisfy himself with the goal of planting a single church or even a handful of churches, but fail to see that it will take a movement of churches planting churches to reach an entire nation of people. It goes back to what is our objective: plant a church or reach a people group?

A CPM is more than a revival of pre-existing churches. Revivals are highly desirable, but they're not CPM's. Evangelistic crusades and witnessing programs may lead thousands to Christ, and that's wonderful, but it isn't the same as a CPM.

A CPM is not simply an increase in the number of churches, even though this also is positive. A CPM occurs when the vision of churches planting churches spreads from the missionary and professional church planter into the churches themselves, so that by their very nature they are winning the lost and reproducing themselves (Garrison, 2002, p. ch.1).

Garrison reports that other CPM's are surfacing every few months: 30,000 believers in a SE Asia country. 100,000 believers swelling 800 new churches in eastern India; 20,000 coming to Christ over a four-year period in one Chinese

---
17 Watson, David. Church Planting Movements Seminar, Level One.

province; church starts doubling in six months in one Western European country; 383 churches starting in a single state in Brazil (Garrison, 2002, p. ch.2).

This has long been the dream of missionaries, but they have insisted on such a movement happening the way they wanted it to happen. Patterson declares, "I hope it takes you less time than it took me to learn that formal pulpit preaching is ineffective (often illegal) in many of today's remaining unreached fields." (Patterson, 2003, p. 216)

Some tough and often uncomfortable decisions have to be made or the work gets stymied or blocked again. It is essential that everything be evaluated on the basis of whether it is reproducible. "Authentic Church Planting Movements always take on the appearance of their context. If villages are made of bamboo, then church buildings are made of bamboo. In urban areas, cell or house churches emulate family structures instead of a congregational structure that requires expensive buildings used exclusively for worship meetings. CPM practitioners evaluate every aspect of each church start with the question: "Can this be reproduced by these believers?" If the answer is "no," then the foreign element is discarded." (Garrison, 2002, p. ch.7)

A Few Key Principles

Garrison sees the CPM as a "sovereign act of God, but in His sovereign grace and mercy He has chosen to partner with us. There are some practical things that missionaries can do to help initiate or nurture a CPM." The following steps are not meant to be sequential, nor particularly given in a priority of importance, rather each situation must determine which principles are used and how to apply them:

1. **Pursue a CPM orientation** from the beginning. "Missionaries who want to start a CPM must begin by 'modeling a CPM-type church' complete with evangelism, discipleship and multiplication training within a cell-group setting."
2. **Evaluate everything to achieve the end-vision.** "The effective strategy coordinator is ruthless in evaluating all he or she does in light of the end-vision -- A CPM-- discarding those things that do not or will not lead to it."
3. **Gather them, and then win them**. It is most effective to "gather a group of lost seekers into evangelistic worship and Bible study groups. These 'not-yet Christians' are brought into the vision for a CPM even as they are brought into the family of faith."
4. Try a **POUCH methodology**. POUCH church "utilizes Participative Bible study and worship groups, affirms Obedience to the Bible as the sole measure of success, uses Unpaid and non-hierarchical leadership and meets in Cell groups or House churches."
5. **Develop multiple leaders** within each cell church. "Avoid the trap of inadequate leadership required to meet growth needs by sharing the

work with multiple leaders."
6. **Model, Assist, Watch & Leave (MAWL)**. "Missionaries who are competent church planters face as much challenge from themselves as they do from the people group they are trying to reach. There is always a temptation to 'do it myself' rather than turn the work over to the emerging local leadership. This transfer of responsibilities is complicated by the fact that many, if not most, missionaries enjoy pastoring and ministering to people." If the missionary from the beginning wisely shares the leadership responsibilities with nationals, there will be little to transfer. This shared leadership becomes the model for the national leadership as well, thus assuring a "passionate renewal of indigenous church planting" and a movement is born. "Only when the missionary has actually stepped away from the work is the cycle of MAWL completed." (Garrison, 2002, p. ch.5)

Case Study of the Cambodian Church Planting Movement

The 20th century has seen more than its share of wars, dictators, and genocide, but few surpass the tragic modern history of Cambodia. Buffeted by the Vietnam conflict for more than two decades, Cambodia emerged from that war with Maoist dictator Pol Pot driving the country into ruin. During his five-year reign from 1975-1979, Pol Pot's Khmer Rouge engineered the murder, disappearance, or starvation of up to 3.3 million of the country's 8 million citizens.

This reign of terror left Cambodia's infrastructure in shambles, its adult male population decimated, and its youth illiterate. The subsequent rule by a Vietnam-installed government ended the genocide, but could not undo the damage done to Cambodian society.

The societal upheaval set the stage for changes which were to come. Centuries of Buddhist influence were undermined by communist ideology; the Khmer Rouge because of perceived foreign ties specifically targeted Roman Catholicism. Earlier in the century, missionaries from the Christian and Missionary Alliance and Overseas Missionary Fellowship introduced Protestantism, but their numbers never exceeded 5,000. During the Pol Pot's rule, the Khmer Rouge dealt them a severe blow, expelling missionaries and murdering many of the scattered flock. By 1990, Cambodia's evangelical population had dwindled to no more than 600 believers.

According to a senior missionary who served in Cambodia for decades with OMF, the turning point for Christianity in the country began in the 1990s. By 1999, the number of Protestant believers had risen from 600 to more than 60,000. The primary catalyst for change came in December 1989, when a Strategy Coordinator (SC) was assigned to the Khmer people. By 1991, he completed language study and had begun to implement a strategy for reaching the Khmer.

Instead of planting a church himself, he began mentoring a Cambodian layman. Within a year, he had drawn six Cambodian church planters into the mentoring circle. Over the next few months, he developed a church-planting manual in the Khmer language and taught the Khmer church planters doctrine, evangelism, and church-planting skills using resources such as the Jesus film, Chronological Bible Storying, and simple house-church development. He also instilled in them a vision and passion for reaching their entire country with a CPM.

In 1993, the number of churches in this movement grew from six to ten. The following year, the number doubled to 20. In 1995, when the number of churches reached 43, the Cambodian church leaders formed an association of like-minded churches. The following year, the number of churches climbed to 78. In 1997, there were 123 churches scattered across 53 of the country's 117 districts. By the spring of 1999, there were more than 200 churches and 10,000 members.

Few of these churches met in dedicated buildings. The vast majority met in homes in the countryside that could accommodate 50 or more individuals.

The SC departed the assignment in 1996, leaving behind the small team of cross-cultural workers and a network of vital church planting churches scattered across much of the country. The work has continued to grow and strengthen (Garrison, 2003, pp. 231-232).

Although Garrison acknowledges that some people might be concerned about the relatively short amount of time between accepting Christ and being thrust into leadership in these particular movements, he counters by stressing the importance of ongoing theological education. But a CPM will usually add a twist to traditional models of theological education. Instead of ministers-in-training being pulled out of their sphere of influence to go to seminary for a few years, in CPMs new leaders get training as they need it, without having to leave their family and ministry.

"This is really one of the turning points in the history of the church," Garrison said. "Church-planting movements are happening whether we like it or not. Some people are a little threatened by this, but they shouldn't be, because these movements are taking us back to our New Testament roots. That can be a little unsettling, but if God is doing this, that's what matters most. The question for us is, are we going to participate?" (Perry, 2005)

Appendix 1 Resource sites on Church Planting Movements:

The Bible league: **www.BibleLeague.org**
YWAM Church Planting Coaches: cpcoaches.pngusa.net
Train and Multiply: **www.trainandmultiply.com**
email: pwr@telus.net
"Church Growth" at Southern Nazarene University: **snu.edu**/~hculbert.fs/chgrowth
Christian Associates: **www.christianassociates.org**
World Team: **www.churchplanting.net**
The Alliance for Saturation Church Planting offering the Omega Course at **www.alliancescp.org**/html/omegacourse.html
"Church Planting Movements," (available on-line, produced by the International Mission Board), **www.imb.org**/GlobalVision/NewDirections
Prepare: **www.prepareint.org** or write prepareint@hotmail.com

Church Planting Resources:
genesis.acu.edu/cplant/resources.html
www.fcpt.org
www.nextchurch.org
members.optushome.com.au/churchplanting
www.plantingministries.org
UIM International: **www.uim.org**
Antioch Network: **www.antiochnetwork.org**
Global Missions Fellowship: **www.gmf.org**

Church-Planting Handbooks

"Getting Started - A Church Planting Handbook for Laypeople" by Brad Boyston. (You can also download the complete handbook in text format: 184KB) From the introduction: This handbook was written specifically for people who are interested in or involved in helping to start Evangelical Covenant Churches. Christians from other groups will find transferable information but should recognize that the organizational procedures in other denominations will be slightly different.

"Handbook for House Churches" (130KB) and *"Planting House Churches in Networks - A Manual from the Perspective of a Church Planting Team"* (520KB) by Dick Scoggins.

Jim Allen's Church Planting Manual. (158K) (Jim Allen is a "home missionary" of the Assemblies of God in the USA.)

Bill Easum's *Church Planting Workbook*

A strategic guide to church planting from the perspective of the church growth movement is the *Church Planter's Toolkit* by Bob Logan and Steve Ogne.

References

Comfort, R. (2006). *The Way of the Master.* Orlando, FL: Bridge-Logos.

Dayton, E. (2003). "The Spontaneous Multiplication of churches." In M. Crossman (Ed.), *Worldwide Perspectives* (pp. 161-172). Seattle, WA.: YWAM Publications.

Garrison, D. (2002/1999, 07/06/30). *Church Planting Movements.* Richmond, VA: International Mission Board.

Garrison, D. (2003). "Church Planting Movements." In M. Crossman (Ed.), *Worldwide Perspectives* (pp. 228-233). Seattle, WA.: YWAM Publications.

Garrison, D. (2004, Fall). "Church Planting Movements: The Next Wave?" *21, 3.* Retrieved 7/7/07, from www.ijfm.org/PDFs_UFM/21_3_PDFs/118_Garrison.pdf.

Hodges, M. L. (1957, 07/07/08). *On the Mission Field: The Indigenous Church.* Chicago: Moody Press.

McGavran, D. A. (2003). "A Church in Every People." In M. Crossman (Ed.), *Worldwide Perspectives* (pp. 224-227). Seattle, WA.: YWAM Publications.

Patterson, G. (2003). "The Spontaneous Multiplication of churches." In M. Crossman (Ed.), *Worldwide Perspectives* (pp. 213-223). Seattle, WA.: YWAM Publications.

Perry, T. (2005). *"Catch the church planting movement wave!"* Retrieved July 13, 2007, from Pastors.com: http://www.pastors.com/RWMT/article.asp?ID=196&ArtID=8013.

Pocock, M., Van Rheenen. (2005). *The Changing Face of World Missions.* Grand Rapids, MI: Baker Academic.

Slack, James B. (1998). "Strategies for Church Planting." *Missiology*. Ed. Terry, John Mark, Ebbie Smith and Justin Anderson. Nashville, TN.: Broadman and Holms Publishers.

Chapter 8

Church-Based Leadership Training

The concept of developing leaders within the local church for some ministries is not a novel concept, nor does it meet with any significant opposition. For years churches have trained Sunday School teachers, assistant youth workers, visitation and evangelism teams and specific skills for assisting in the ministry of the churches. However, the questions arise when we attempt to train leaders of daughter churches, or full-time church leaders. Will anyone believe that they are adequately trained?

Typically, when someone is hired for a full-time church position the search begins credentialed degreed persons in other churches (to find experienced, proven and talented personnel) or seminaries. The American way assumes a large pool around the country from which to recruit seminary-trained personnel who often are looking for a better opportunity to serve the Lord.

For a growing number of churches one of the weaknesses of the traditional system of depending on recent university/seminary-trained leaders is the inevitable lack of experience. These men graduate with an abundance of head-knowledge in theology, perhaps of the original languages, and preaching theory, but with little practice and wisdom, scant Bible awareness and usually with a fair amount of debt. It is not unusual for graduates to have seldom preached in a church, led a person to Christ, discipled a new believer, counseled a dysfunctional family, managed a church problem, led a deacon/elder board meeting, or created a vision-ministry plan for a local church.

The old adage, "Success blinds," is true in America. "If it ain't broke, don't fix it." To question the status quo is always controversial, but the facts are that we could be much further advanced towards our task of reaching the world with the Gospel if we were open to evaluation and occasionally "out-of-the-box" ideas.

In this chapter we will look at a brief overview of the development of the Western, especially North American, theological models, some of the problems this paradigm has created internationally, a review of the biblical pattern of leadership development, finally, some solutions that are currently being developed.

The beginnings of church leadership training

In 1644 all ministerial candidates were required to read Greek and Hebrew. Was this an arbitrary decision? No! The form of training was determined by the function for which the trainee was being prepared. The Anglicans were under attack by Roman Catholic scholars who were well-versed in the biblical languages. The American colonies (during the first half of the eighteenth century) customarily sent young men back to England for training. However, several things made this an unacceptable arrangement. (1) It was expensive to go abroad. (2) There was no certainty that the students would return. (3) And, even if they did, it was difficult for them to readjust to frontier life.

Dr. Kenneth Mulholland, Dean and professor at Columbia International University, has written extensively on the historical development of the American theological training model. He describes the traditional pattern of leadership development around the world that is modeled after the American pastoral training and Bible Institute movement.

> Generally speaking, that pattern consisted of extracting young, unproven, single, usually male volunteers from their home environment to train them in a centrally located institution, where they resided for about three years. There they were taught the classic theological subjects, mostly by rote, by predominantly missionary professors and a sprinkling of part-time nationals. Academic training was supplemented by practical work assignments in local churches with various degrees of supervision. After three years these young people were declared pastoral material if they had successfully passed the required exams, had expounded no heresy, and had not strayed beyond the bounds of morally acceptable behavior as defined by the sponsoring institution and/or denomination (Mulholland, 1976, p. 169).

When this system is imposed on young start-up churches often scattered throughout a country in generally poor sections of towns or rural regions, just as it is done in America, the problems are legend. Not the least of these problems is the typical scenario in a young church with limited leadership finding a capable young leader in the young people or young couples who has a heart for the ministry. The first response is to send him off to the area Bible Institute for 3-4 years. The percentage of Bible Institute graduates who return to their home church is abysmally small. Some other church or ministry will benefit by the potential leader that was given to the first church.

Did God give them to a local church (Eph 4:11) or should all churches give up their leadership by sending them away for training never to return, then, when they need leadership, they will recruit from other churches? Does this make sense? It is the American way!

As long as the system continues to be underwritten and led by foreign missionaries it appears to work, but the limitations imposed on the churches and the damaged done to the prospective church leader should cause a serious re-evaluation of leadership training programs.

Where did this system come from?

Originally three models of theological education were developed in the United States, namely, the apprenticeship among the Puritans and

Congregationalists, an in-service training among the Methodists, and the "tent-making" ministry among the Baptists.

Puritans, Reform and Congregationalist's plan

The Puritan churches tended to demand an educated clergy throughout the colonial period because of their professional membership; however, they did not make academic accomplishments the only requirement for ordination. The Dutch Reformed Church at Long Island, New York started the first theological seminary in America in 1774. And, after the colonies gained their independence, the forming of special schools for training ministers became common. Seventeen such institutions were established during the early part of the nineteenth century. Typically after the pastoral candidate has completed his formal training he has to prove himself.

"Upon graduation from college, where he received a liberal education supplemented with biblical and theological studies, the candidate had to present himself before the duly appointed church officials in order to be licensed to preach. Once licensed, he sought a congregation which would call him as their pastor. Once called to a particular congregation he was ordained and took up his duties among the congregation which had called him, probably to remain there for life" (Mulholland, 1976, p. 170).

Even with the degree, the prospective pastor would have to be licensed or ordained before he could take a salaried pastoral position. The licensing examination was not a casual approval. Once the licensure was secured then the placement in a local church hurdle was faced.

In addition to presenting his college degree, the candidate was expected to present several written sermons to the examining body and to be able to defend not only his sermons, but his entire theological system to the satisfaction of the group. For this reason few presented themselves for licensure immediately upon graduation from college. Most spent one to three years more in residence at the college under a tutor, at home on the farm, as a schoolteacher, or as an assistant to a pastor, all the while seeking to master the content of the Bible and a system of divinity as well as to write sermons in the fashion of theological dissertations (Mulholland, 1976, p. 170).

Methodist plan

The Methodist church in America followed the plan of John Wesley's circuit riders, mostly laymen, who traveled the countryside on horseback to preach the Gospel in every hamlet, village, and town. Methodism became the fastest growing denomination by the mid-1800s with over 4,000 circuit riders in 1844.

Virtually no town, however small, was without a Methodist group or "class."

The system of ministerial training, that was employed by the Methodists, licensed men of very limited formal education provided that they displayed the requisite spiritual fervor. In the United States a century ago the most common path of specifically ministerial preparation among the Methodists was not primarily a matter of formal education.

Mulholland writes, "Methodist theological education was in-service training. Despite the extensive traveling required to cover their circuits, Methodist preachers were expected to study five hours each day and were provided with a list of specified theological works of high quality to be read. In many cases reports and examinations were required" (Mulholland, 1976, p. 172).

Ralph Winter, former missionary and head of the Center for World Missions, writes positively about the Methodist model: "A candidate for the Methodist ministry, in regard to the learning that comes from books, was not required nor as yet expected to spend three years in a post-graduate seminary. The ecclesiastical structure -- the conference -- had courses of study with prescribed texts, and the student was expected to study mainly on his own and pass comprehensive examinations" (Winter, p. 409). Colonial America was largely evangelized by these courageous preachers.

"Methodist circuit riders served while they studied and studied while they served. Each one was in reality a little bishop over the congregations of his circuit, each of which was under the direction of a resident lay leader who was part and parcel of the community in which he lived" (Mulholland, 1976, p. 172). The key concept of the Methodists was the training IN the ministry rather than FOR the ministry.

Baptist plan

The early Baptists, particularly those in the South, had neither the apprenticeship system of the Puritans nor the in-service training program of the Methodists. Mulholland writes, "Like the Mennonites...the local congregation simply selected from among themselves the most gifted person to service as pastor. ... The pastor continued to earn all or part of his living from his secular vocation unless the congregation grew to such proportions as to demand his services on a full-time basis... it is sometimes termed a tent-making ministry" (Mulholland 1976:172-73)

John Dillenberger and Claude Welch, in *Protestant Christianity Interpreted through Its Development* wrote,

> "...the influence of the churches was weak on the frontier. Frontier towns were small and isolated. It was impossible to provide either clergy or churches for all the communities. Congregationalists and Presbyterians, who insisted upon an educated clergy, were particularly

hard pressed... Methodists were generally more successful, since they organized small groups in 'classes' with a lay leader in charge, just as Wesley had done. 'Classes' and Methodist communities were then visited by a Methodist minister who traveled an extensive circuit of such groups. But the Baptists were generally in the best position. In addition to having fought for political and religious freedom, they did not have the burden of a highly educated ministry. A Baptist preacher was one who felt the call. Once the decision had been made, preaching could begin. Moreover, such preachers were of the same social class of the people to whom they preached" (Mulholland 1976:173).

As time passed the apprentice system became more frequently the norm. "... close examination shows that the Colonial colleges were more like elementary or junior-high-level boarding schools and that specific training for the ministry took place after the period of full time training in 'college,' in a kind of apprenticeship: graduates went to live in a minister's home..." (Winter:386).

Mulholland adds, "The predominant pattern at one time was training in ministry rather than training for ministry. Furthermore, it was precisely those denominations which recognized, set apart, and equipped the natural leaders of the common people for the work of ministry which were best able to respond to the turbulence, the mobility, and the poverty of the American frontier. In time it was the Methodists and Southern Baptists, with their flexible and culturally relevant patterns of ministerial selection and training, rather than the Congregationalists and Presbyterians, which became the predominant religious bodies of the North American continent" (Mulholland 1976:173).

Eventually the apprenticeship model reached its limitations. Inevitably some pastors were preferred over others to be their mentors. Students tended to gravitate to where they could get the best training and have the highest prestige by association with a highly respected mentor. Out of this grouping by choice came the schools and seminaries. The question will always be, which method is the best: apprenticeship, in-service training, extension or distance learning, or resident seminary training? Is the best procedure a blend or combination?

No one can deny that the third-world churches need to have first-rate theologians who can formulate an indigenous expression of the Christian faith for their own people. But it must be remembered that the desperate need of younger churches is training that functions in their present situation and that satisfies their contemporary needs. Therefore, it is unwise to impose on them the recently acquired North American forms of training.

Contemporary challenges

It is becoming increasingly clear just how unwise to export Bible-school forms of training from N. America to foreign countries really is. Many problems are created. Frustrations result. And, in the end, the cause of Christ is often hindered instead of being helped.

Applicants to these schools were often little more than functionally literate. Few of them had any secondary education (Jencks, Riesman, 1968, p. 28). Even after much academic upgrading, over 40 per cent of the ministers in 1926 (among the seventeen largest Protestant denominations in America) had attended neither a college nor a seminary (Niebuhr, Williams, 1956, p. 274, 275).

Mulholland make a accurate observation when he wrote, "The tendency of North American theological educators is to seek to impose those models of theological education which are most current in North Atlantic countries upon the developing nations rather than explore models which were viable in those same countries when they historically faced some of the same problems which the Third World nations now confront" (Mulholland, 1976, p. 173).

The problem becomes a serious issue on the mission field where the American system is creating a major obstacle to multiplying churches exponentially. There are few "seminaries" as we know it, that is, a post-graduate program. Few, if any, Third World pastors have graduated from any university program overseas. At best they may have graduated from a Bible Institute (often a 3-year program). What is often referred to as a "seminary" overseas often is not a post-university graduate program; rather it means a Bible Institute program typically for high school graduates, which includes some studies of the original languages (at least Greek). This is an advanced Bible Institute program.

A few genuine Seminaries have developed in Latin America such as SETECA in Guatemala and other institutions for advanced studies around the world. One wonders how these higher studies are facilitating the church planting movements and targeting the unreached people groups where prestigious degrees are of little benefit.

The world has changed drastically in the past decade, and phenomenally in the past century. The shifts from modern to postmodern, from critical to post-critical, from industrial to technological and from the enlightenment to post-enlightenment world. There are massive shifts in populations as well. By 2050, 1 of every 5 people in N. America will be Hispanic. In 1900 there were an estimated 50,000 evangelical Hispanic believers in South America, but today there are over 100 million. Africa grew from 10 million Protestants in 1900 to 360 million in 2000. Asia is exploding with spontaneous expansion of the gospel. Large-scale conversions are reported in India and China. A major organization predicts hundreds of thousands of new churches over the next few decades. Our successes have created a leadership crisis.

New Paradigms for Church Leadership is needed

Winter saw this coming a long time ago and raised the issue when he wrote, "...there is a minimum of 150,000 with pastoral gifts, probably 90% of which seriously lack further training. But if only 100,000 of them need ministerial training this is a massive, urgent challenge. To meet this challenge there are sixty seminaries with a total enrolment of one thousand plus 300 Bible Institutes with a total enrollment of 12,000. Even assuming these students were all to become pastors, or better still were mainly men in the group of 100,000 who are already on the job, we would still be back-logged for fifteen years in meeting the need by conventional methods" (Winter, 1967, p. 241).

Winter's analysis mentions the fact that in reality most Bible institutes are largely devoted to training Christian youth who are not necessarily pastoral material. To make matters worse, each year approximately 5,000 new congregations are brought into existence in the area where Winter was studying. "This means that the leadership gap instead of narrowing is actually widening... there is simply not enough being done even quantitatively and that the traditional system has proven itself inadequate to meet the need and is unable to expand sufficiently to offer any hope of doing so in the near future, particularly given the present worldwide economic crisis" (Winter, 1967, p. 241). Since then the problem has only become much worse.

It is increasingly apparent that large numbers of potential pastors and/or tent-making ministers cannot be trained by traditional methods of theological education. " Private study and apprenticeship schemes on the one hand tend to be haphazard and atomized affairs. To take, on the other hand, any quantity of mature men through the normal three to five-year residence course in a theological school and to support their families would be a luxury that most churches in the world could not afford. A traditional residence course has other disadvantages" (Hopewell, 1966, p. 333). These conditions would lead many leaders to ideas of distance learning and TEE.[18]

A New Paradigm

A paradigm is "an entire constellation of beliefs, techniques, and so on shared by members of a given community." The Western church leadership paradigm depends on too many features that are not available or affordable around the globe: ease of finances, large salaries, technologies in music, computation, radio-TV, sound-equipment, musical instruments, recording devices, internet, etc. North America has the ability to reproduce the style of highly trained professional church leadership and have generated a high expectation

---

18 Theological Education by Extension

on the part of congregations for super leaders to compete with mega-churches and tele-evangelists.

Formal theological education is likewise a paradigm. All theological schools have highly trained professors, technically-equipped campuses, buildings and classrooms, sophisticated assessment techniques, degrees, online capabilities, etc. What if none of this was available? How would leaders be trained?

Can you imagine this typical situation: the bank loans are only short-term (max. 3 years) at 48% or higher per year interest rates, and social security payments are 40-52% of the salary. Importation rates are 100-200% on most foreign items. Since there is no individual tax system a "value added tax" or sales tax of 15% - 22% is added to every purchase. All items including autos and real estate are purchased with cash only. This economic condition is typical in many countries, which make any American system of education very complicated.

Mulholland proposes a possible solution when he wrote,

"The issue must be faced: Is it not better that many churches have some modestly trained leadership than that a few churches have highly trained leadership and the rest have no trained leadership at all?... Is it possible at this moment in history and in the context of the current situation in Latin America, that heavy dependence upon traditional theological education is not the answer to the leadership training needs of the Latin American Protestant community? Is it possible that once-useful, but now discarded patterns of ministerial training in the developed nations may provide important insights, clues, and even models upon which to construct relevant theological education for the growing churches in the developing nations...?" Mulholland, 1976, p. 174).

When I became a Christian in the independent Baptist movement in the South (1960's), it was common for every church to get a weekly newspaper called the "Sword of the Lord." It contained a sermon (or more), teaching lessons, and articles of importance for the pastor and lay leaders. Many pastors would take those sermons, tweak them and then preach them with little other preparation. Many of these pastors had little college training and few had any seminary experience, but they planted new churches, saw hundreds of thousands of new converts and, at the time, were the fastest growing and largest churches in America. The pastor of my former home church began preaching when he was 13 and started pasturing at 17. Today he pastors a church of 1,300, yet he never finished college nor ever attended any Bible School.

The churches have developed much since those days, but for fifty years the churches in such movements as these had many comparisons to the Third World churches. Perhaps the development of training aids, sermon notes, ministry training by interactive online programs could facilitate their development. By far, however, the reproduction of apprentice/mentor skills and relationships on the local church level must be the major key for the future.

The dependence on expatriate seminary trained professors must end, and church leaders be equipped to train their own leaders. The ministry must cease to be seen as a job opportunity or means of gaining prestige and return to mean self-sacrifice, education and ministry to win people to Christ and equip them for their ministry.

International challenges

On the mission fields led by Western missionaries, often with the Western model, though on a reduced scale, the churches face major bottle-necks of insufficient resources and trained leadership for exploding churches. The dependency on training institutions, which become more academic with each passing generation is becoming irrelevant as they tend towards increasing intellectualism, nominalism, and social focus. Following the traditional model, millions upon millions will need to be raised to house the increasingly larger institutional buildings and to pay the needed salaries in order to keep up. Such funds could be better invested.

We need a new paradigm – church-based theological education – a paradigm based on the way Christ and His apostles developed leaders, which was very different from our institutional model.

Mulholland quotes from Rolland Allen's book, *The Case for Voluntary Clergy*, in which he defends an ordained "tent-making" ministry:

"My contention in this book is that the traditions which we hold, forbidding the ordination of men engaged in earning their own livelihood by what we call secular occupations, makes void the word of Christ and is opposed to His mind when He instituted the sacraments for His people. It is also opposed to the conception of the Church which the apostles received from Him and to the practice by which St. Paul, of whose work God has given us the fullest account, established the churches. The stipendiary system grew up in settled churches and is suitable for settled churches at some periods; for expansion, for the establishment of new churches it is the greatest possible hindrance. It binds the church in chains and has compelled us to adopt practices which contradict the very idea of the Church (Mulholland, 1976, p. 175).

Mulholland gives an illustration from his experiences in Honduras which illustrates the developmental principle of church leadership from among the Assemblies of God. "They asked a new congregation to choose a pastor from among themselves or from another congregation. This person is then licensed to perform the sacraments as well as preach the Word and is subsequently equipped to do so effectively by attending a Bible institute during four months each year over a period of six years. The congregation promises to support the pastor and his family to the best of their ability. While the ideal remains that of a full-time, paid pastor, the group normally cannot undertake his full support. Thus, he continues in his secular work full or part-time until they can provide fully for his needs. The Pentecostals see voluntary clergy and/or a tent-making ministry as a necessary, though ideally not permanent, step in the direction of the full-time pastorate" (Mulholland, 1976, p. 179).

Is the growth of the Church going to make a difference?

Mulholland quotes Thomas J. Liggett (*Where Tomorrow Struggles to Be Born*) in regard to the statistical growth of Latin American Protestantism:
In the early twentieth century the evangelical movement began to gather strength, and by 1916 the Protestant community had reached an estimated total constituency of 122,000. In 1937 the evangelical community had 1,250,000 and by 1961 it numbered an estimated 10 million. In a recent study of church growth in Latin America, careful statistics in 17 countries showed the total number of communicants to be 4,915,477. The same study estimated that the total evangelical community would be at least 14 million by 1970 (Mulholland, 1976, p. 180). Today's statistics for Latin America are over 100 million! The explosion of growth has created mega-churches and multiple-house churches throughout the hemisphere. One has to ask the question, where is the leadership coming from?

The reality of the Third World Leadership

World Vision sponsored a leadership training seminar for various denominations from Colombia, Panama, Venezuela, and Ecuador. Surveys of over 400 church leaders found the following statistics: "31% had no schooling whatsoever, 33% had some primary schooling, 32% had finished primary school (6 grades), 26% had some secondary school, and only 6% had completed high school. Some of this latter group also had studied at the university, and a tiny minority of these had completed their university training" (Mulholland, 1976, p. 181).

Solutions must respond to real life problems. The following eight problems are a glimpse into the situations faced around the world. Whatever technique developed for training leaders these must be addressed with reasonable solutions.

The problem of selection of whom to train

The administration of a centrally located institute is very limited in its ability to select the right students who are leaders or potential leaders in their churches. "Therefore, the general opinion is that since there is such a great need, anyone who desires to train for the Lord's work should be sent to the school. The school will then take the recommendations of the pastor and the church concerning the character of the prospective student. The school is basically dependent upon the references it receives as to the quality of the prospective student's life and potential as a leader. On the other hand, once a student arrives at school and begins to demonstrate his ability or lack of it, it is sometimes difficult to recognize him on the basis of his recommendations. People are often unwilling to give an objective evaluation for fear of saying something against an individual who claims that he has been called by God" (Rowen, 1967, p. 12).

To further complicate the issue of whom to train, the motives for coming to the Institute are often not the best. With the majority of the students not having completed secondary schooling (only through 9th grade has recently become mandatory in Latin America), many realize that they need some schooling to have any hope of a good job. In most schools 70 percent have less than a 9th grade education. The Bible Institute offers either (1) the possibility of a full-time position in a Christian ministry or church, (2) or the credentials that could be used to show tertiary training, even though secondary training was not complete.[19]

These expectations of future benefits are frequently high on the motivation for the student, which, if not met for whatever reason, can result in resentment and bitterness and the abandonment of any service for the Lord.

The Problem of cultural dislocation

In North America the difference between the rural and urban mentality is minimal, but in Latin America the gap is immense. It is hard for the American to realize that to urbanize someone often makes him incapable of readjusting to back to his former rural village life. Rowen observes:

"The campus... must be located geographically. If the campus is in the rural section, then those from the urban centers find it socially degrading to receive their training in a rural setting. Likewise, if the campus is located in the urban center those from the rural districts are confronted with a radically different way of life...

While it is often very difficult at first for the rural students to adjust to urban life, after a few years it is even more difficult for them to readjust to the primitive conditions of rural life. Once having tasted the affluence and financial opportunities of the city, it is a real temptation for them not to return

---

19 Often Bible Institutes provide equivalency training to allow the student to gain a secondary certificate as well.

to the community from which they originally came" (Rowen, 1967, p. 9)

In most cultures the rural lifestyle is considered unsophisticated and backward. To move from the rural to the city is the quest of most young people. When this is successful through work or education, there is a tendency to join in the general attitude of despising the rural life and people, even one's former family. To overcome this new negative attitude is difficult. Even if relocated back into the rural setting, the superior attitude of the big city inevitable generates a condescending attitude toward his former culture, which cripples his ministry potential.

The problem of professionalism

> The theological student enters school as a layman and leaves as a clergy-man. Often he fancies himself as a professional, for there is great prestige in being a professional in Latin America. And being a "professional," he therefore expects better standards of living and educational opportunities which can be met only by a church accustomed to professional leadership. "This syndrome produces a student who sees the ministry as a doorway to middle-class affluence, seeking the pastorate of a city congregation or leaving the pastoral ministry for the world of commerce for which in many ways his seminary training has well prepared him" (Mulholland, 1976, p. 186).

As the professional paradigm began to take shape, several attributes could be found in almost every model:
- Residential education became the accepted standard for students and churches.
- Schleiermacher's four-fold theological encyclopedia[20] framed seminary curriculum
- Mastery of academic disciplines became the goal, replacing the acquisition of sapient learning.
- Pastors as mentors were replaced by professors and scholars.
- The degree system became the accepted standard of measuring preparedness for ministry (Reed, 1992, pp. 244-245).

Rowen comments: "After an individual has attained some formal training in a given area, there is often the tendency to develop an attitude of superiority. Once having learned the blessing and advantages of training it is often difficult for the individual to revert to the simplicity he once knew. Therefore, there is the tendency to elevate oneself above the people surrounding him" Rowen, 1967, p. 9).

In missiological terms, this is called "Lift," moving up the social class

---

20 The standard four-fold pattern of exegetical, historical, systematic and practical theology (*Thomas Albert Howard, Theologia between Science and the State*, p. 311).

ladder. The down side of helping to facilitate this development is the student's unwillingness to throw it away and revert back to the "simple" lifestyle of the country villages. He tends to absorb society's condescending view of country people, even his own family.

The problem of placement after graduation

Even with the shortage of trained leadership in Latin America the placement of graduates has a number of innate problems:

1. Since the church or institution required that the student leave his home and job, and then after graduation he must find a livelihood of some kind, it is only natural that the student expect the church or institution provide that job. When thrust out on his own with no support from either, bitterness and rebellion are not uncommon.
2. The student grows accustomed to dependency either upon his church support or the subsidy of the Institution which covers not only tuition, but travel, medicine, room, board and perhaps study materials, books and clothing. There may be a fee involved, but work scholarships are provided to subsidize the costs. "It is hard to break this pattern of total dependence, especially when it is combined with a professional mentality which conditions him to expect that the church [or institution] simply must make provision for him."
3. "During his theological education his set of values have been altered, such that now he considers it his right to satisfy some of the desires awakened in him through the luxuries he has seen both in the city and the middle-class standard of living enjoyed by the missionaries" (Mulholland, 1976, pp. 186-187) and other national leadership.

To save face in this situation, some will accept menial tasks with the institution or in the city until something better hopefully develops, so as to not return home after graduation practically no better off than when he left.

The problem of dependency

The attitude of dependency is often molded into the character of the student by the system of his training where he is subject to, controlled by and cared for by the institution, its director and often a missionary supervisor. The astute student learns how to manipulate the system of dependency to his advantage. However, his ministry initiative is quenched while he continues to wait on the missionary or institution to direct his ministry activity. His dependency on them restricts him from doing anything outside of what they want. To further this denigrating relationship, a spiritual value is ascribed to this submissive relationship to "authority." This financial and ministry dependency is hard to break after 3 years of control.

"Placing the student in an institution where he is completely dependent on others is not generally the best way to prepare persons who are later expected to be genuinely capable of exercising independent leadership" (Mulholland, 1976, p. 187).

Inefficient teaching methods

The traditional residence programs utilize a passive learning -- a dependency upon the lecture system for imparting instruction, which is generally a repetition of material already in an assigned textbook or class notes. Often grades are given for the ability to accurately transcribe the lectures in a notebook. Discussions, problem solving, case studies are seldom introduced, thus most learning is irrelevant to real life. One is expected to learn what he is told and not to think beyond this boundary.

Furthermore, "the notion of squeezing all the education necessary for a life of ministry into three years of intense study is naive. A program of life-long-learning is much more realistic. But that kind of education, which teaches men to wrest truth not only for the printed page, but from all of life's experiences is not overly stimulated by the passive teaching methodology so common in traditional theological education" (Mulholland, 1976, p. 189).

Problem of dropouts

The dropout rate in the ministry among men trained in traditional theological institutions is high. In a Bible Institute in which I was the Academic Dean, a survey of graduates at least five years out of school revealed that barely 3% could be identified as active in a church ministry!

Furthermore, because of the high investment in each student and the embarrassing situation of sending home a student who claims to be called of God, once a student has begun his course of study "there is a tendency to try to see him through his schooling regardless of whether or not he is a good student or has potential as a leader in the Church. There exists the tendency to perpetuate the training of the unqualified for face-saving reasons" (Mulholland, 1976, p. 189).

In all my years in the ministry and working with Institutes and Universities, I have never heard of a student being counseled positively not to continue his theological studies because he did not have the leadership gifts, speaking gifts or spiritual maturity to be effective. Generally, the only ones discouraged are those with early manifestations of moral or rebellious problems which result in expulsion. He would be better off supporting a ministry from a secular profession. There continues to be the naïve opinion that by studying at a certain institute, if one is spiritual, then a leadership role is waiting for anyone who graduates.

Problem of economic costs

Most training institutions are started by foreign funds and run by highly trained and financed foreign [expatriate] missionaries. As long as these subsidies are continued the program continues smoothly. Of course, whoever is managing these funds is the maximum authority in the institute and whoever is the beneficiary of these funds must demonstrate his submission if they are to continue.

If all costs are considered, the cost to train one resident student per year in most countries would exceed $6,000 to $10,000 per year if there are more than 100 students. In three years, this means that it will cost between $18,000 and $30,000 to train one student, depending on the country. These numbers assume expatriate professors have their own salaries and national professors and administrators are paid a small salary. Maximum tuitions charged range from $150 to $350 per month typically for 10 months, depending on the country. Thus the tuition is not nearly enough to meet the expenses. Programs must be created to subsidize the institution (camps, retreats, etc)

The annual cost of a reasonable size Bible Institute could easily reach $1 million a year. To "indigenize" these expenses, forcing the national church to progressively assume these costs, is extremely problematic and, at best, requires a considerable readjustment downward of the expenditures.

"Residence education is costly in current expenses and capital investment, and more so when there is a markedly low student-faculty ratio. Thus, full-time personnel who could easily serve more students simply do not have those students on their campus. Receipts from student fees are negligible and offerings from churches minimal, and the investment per [for each] student is extremely high" (Mulholland, 1976, p. 189).

Conclusion

Mulholland concludes his article asking, "Is 'the way we've always done it' the best approach? Does the traditional residence pattern we have so eagerly exported really fit the needs of Third World churches? Is that pattern genuinely biblical? Can traditional residence institutions possibly train the vast number of leaders required by a rapidly growing church? And can they produce the kind of quality leaders who are authentic representatives of their own people rather than pale shadows of their missionary teachers? These are serious questions every theological educator, every missionary, every pastor and laymen interested in the church's worldwide mission needs to struggle with and draw his own conclusions" (Mulholland, 1976, p. 189)

A BIBLICAL PERSPECTIVE

The Pauline Cycle[21]

In the study of the four evangelistic journeys of the Apostle Paul in the book of Acts a pattern becomes evident. Paul would go to strategic areas or cities where he had some contacts or open doors for ministry. Once a new group of believers were converted, they were immediately gathered into a bond of fellowship as a local church. Daily he was teaching and equipping the members to become leaders as God gifted them. Soon he entrusted the ministry to those who proved faithful, often in a matter of months. Paul did not waste time with those he suspected to be unfaithful, vacillating or unwilling to do whatever it took to establish a ministry (as with Mark).

Later he maintained contact with these leaders personally through letters, and Paul sent his trusted team members to visit and to establish them firmly in "the teaching," in order that they would be strong and not deceived by false teaching. Once established in the faith, these believers were given the responsibility for leading the believers and amplifying the evangelistic outreach of their local church while training others as they were trained (this is a major key that cannot be replicated in the traditional training pattern).

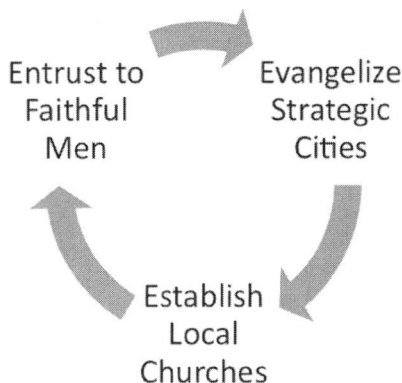

Paul's Letters as Tools
for Establishing the Churches

The Early Church devoted itself to the "Apostle's teachings" (Acts 2:42), which was referred to as "the faith," "the deposit," and "sound doctrine," which they were to master and cling to without wavering, then pass it along. There is no clear "doctrinal statement" as we have developed in the Western church, but rather elements of the doctrine are weaved throughout the epistles coming out of real life situations, that now need to be understood in their ancient context, deriving principles that can be fit into other similar circumstances of contemporary life. Doctrine today is seen as cold, boring and useless because

---

21 Modeled after the BILD (Biblical Institute of Leadership Development) model of church-based training in Ames, Iowa.

most of these doctrinal conclusions were derived out of old controversy, systematized into outlines, rather than being derived out of practical cultural applications.

The biblical model of the Pauline cycle – the training of leaders – is evident by Paul's development of leaders in his ministry. There seemed to be two areas of this leadership development: (1) local leaders or elders and deacons, which was based on age, respect, character, family and sound doctrine; and (2) ministers of the gospel (Timothy and Titus-types) who moved throughout the churches, strengthening and establishing them. Timothy worked closely with Paul as a sort-of apprentice, for a number of years (10-15 years) until he was commended to the leadership of a church.

Paul and Timothy Model (2 Tim 2:2)

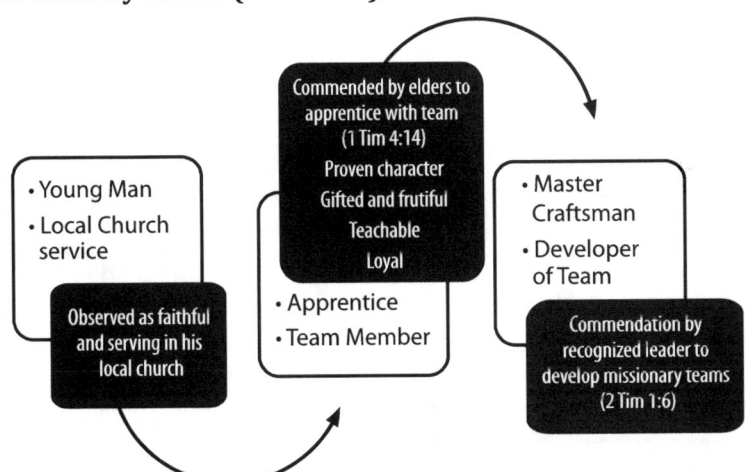

The model that consistently appears in Scriptures is one of local church focus and training *in* the ministry, rather than *for* the ministry. The Western or Greek model of learning centers and official schools would eventually take over the responsibility of the training for the local churches with negative results.

Biblical reasons for CBT

In the Book of Acts the focus on starting churches and raising up leaders from within each local church as the key strategy for spreading the gospel message in Paul's repeatable and multiplying movement (Acts 14:21-23). The churches became the main training center (Acts 13:1) and sending agency (14:26-27) for further expansion beyond their immediate region. Nine of Paul's letters were addressed directly to a local church or churches in a region. Paul did not have any alternatives sources from which to recruit leaders, such as Bible Institutes, so he trained leaders in the Jewish tradition through mentors (as he had been trained "at the feet of Gamaliel," Acts 22:3). He did not do his teaching at a formal training institution, and therefore the respect by his peers was due to his relationship to his mentor. The transference of knowledge, respect, skills and ministry philosophy are the keys to mentoring leaders in the church ministry.

2 Timothy 2:2 [NET], "And entrust what you heard me say in the presence of many others as witnesses to faithful people who will be competent to teach others as well." Timothy was present when Paul taught many disciples in the founding of local churches. When Paul wrote 2 Timothy, Timothy was serving the church in Ephesus. He taught Timothy some of the aspects of church life (1 Tim 5:19-22; 2 Tim 4:2-5) as Timothy was applying them in his ministry. The "faithful people" (*anthropos* is generic to mean men and women) were *reliable* or *dependable* in the daily/weekly functions of the church. That is to say, those who are not functioning in a local church were not yet proven faithful enough to be trained. Titus, likewise, received special instruction in his epistle by Paul concerning his church ministries as an on-going, on-the-job training (Titus 1:5-9).

Another key verse for CBT is Ephesians 4:11-13 where Paul declares that Christ gave various leaders to the church (4:11), with emphasis on the "he" in the original text. Without entering into a debate on the nature of the five categories of leaders[22], their united purpose is clearly stated: "to equip the saints for the work of ministry" ([NET]4:12). The entire church membership is gifted by the Spirit, and now must be trained by the leadership, to "serve" [diaconia, "aid, support, minister"]. There is an obligation of every church leader of every church to train all the members in at least the basic four-areas of ministry[23] and then the special service that God has uniquely gifted each of them to fulfill. This duty or responsibility cannot be delegated outside the church because the "ministry" and "edifying" are related to the local "body of Christ."

Furthermore, the objective is "until we all attain to the unity of the faith" in a practical bonding of individuals in a local church setting, and in "the knowledge of the Son of God," resulting in a "mature person" who is like his Master. Even when Paul taught in a teaching center for two years (Acts 19:9-10) his goal was the establishing of believers in a local church (Acts 20:17-38). They, in turn, went to all of Asia with the Word of God reproducing churches.

Aquila and Priscilla are an excellent example of a teaching couple ministering to others.[24] While helping in the church at Ephesus, they took a gifted

---

22 The author holds that the first two, apostles and prophets, were given to the Church to deliver the special revelation and inspired text of the "foundation" of the church (Eph 2:20 and Acts 2:42). Whereas the evangelists, pastors and teachers were to teach, exhort, preach and expound on the basis of this foundational, infallible text given in the beginning of the Church to be used to edify and equip all the believers for their ministries (4:12).
23 Evangelism, Discipleship, Mentoring and Basic Counseling.
24 They are mentioned six times by name in the NT (Acts 18:2, 18, 26; Rom 16:3; 1 Cor 16:19 and 2 Tim 4:19), and always mentioned together in their ministry!

and knowledgeable teacher of Scriptures, Apollos, and "invited him to their home and explained to him the way of God more adequately" (Acts 18:26NIV). More than likely the church in Ephesus met in the home of Aquila and Priscilla (1 Cor 16:8, 19). They provide a direct example of training that occurs in the context of a local church.

Development of CBT

The church-based leadership training movement is a result of a number of other precursor movements that led to CBT. In 1963 at the Evangelical Presbyterian Seminary of Guatemala, teachers were struggling with the problem of how to prepare seminarians of a diverse ethnic and educational background. The residential seminaries were producing pastors who were well-trained academically, but the graduates who had been subsidized by Western donations would only continue in the pastorate if the subsidy continued. When this did not materialize as expected enrollment declined.

Emilio Castro adds other factors which need to be considered. 1) The residential model encourages "professionalism," understood as a "competitive desire to climb the promotional ladder," something which should not be a part of the Christian community. 2) The residential/professional model is very difficult to sustain among a people who are already living in poverty, therefore the economic viability is called into question. 3) Extraction from the cultural milieu of the student makes it difficult for him to return to his former lifestyle. Barriers are raised that make it almost impossible for him to relate to his own people" (Castro, 1983, p. x).

The traditional missionary model failed to capitalize on the natural leaders of a community, preferring to do it themselves to keep control or their authority, or to send young ambitious men who were unproven and unaccepted as leaders at that time to be trained at a distant site.

The result is that the serious men of the church, the natural leaders of the village life, and the natural leaders of the church are all silenced. The "system" has cut them out of the leadership role. "The church is not led and administered by the people to whom all would naturally turn, but either by a foreigner, or by a young man who has come with a foreign education" (Allen, 1962, p. 106).

The leaders of the Guatemala seminary became convinced that the Seminary would need to go to the student, especially to the natural leaders in the communities, instead of expecting the student to come to the seminary. Since the most respected leaders were already married and established in a profession (rather than young unproven men just out of high school), it would make sense to devise a way to train them without the need of uprooting them to another location. They developed a program of study during the week followed by a visit on the weekend by a professor to a gathering of students in a given area.

TEE

Theological Education by Extension is a pioneer approach to take the seminary to the student. The students studied specially prepared (self-instructional) lessons during the week. The teacher would come once-a-week (or once every-other-week) for a couple of hours to help the trainees apply to their lives the truths they have learned. However, there are two requirements: (1) the students must faithfully prepare their lessons for each class and (2) they must teach what they have learned to their congregations during the following week. In other words, leadership training by extension is an in-service program, which matures the *whole* church.

The procedure is unique. The instructor must not dominate his classes. He must not lecture (or preach a sermon). The "palm tree meetings" must focus on leading the students to *experience* (that is, relate to their daily lives) what they have studied and discovered. The teacher is there to clarify and amplify the information. He should lead the trainees to live what they have learned. The emphasis is on both knowing and doing.

This rising demand to take the seminary to the churches and the need for more theological training, especially on the international scene, resulted in the TEE movement. TEE was an attempt to train the leadership of churches that could not come to an Institute, primarily because of distance, family or workloads. The courses were the same as taught in the resident course, but these were written in self-teaching, programmed instruction modules, which were difficult to write and had to be designed for each age group, culture or educational level to be effective. Periodically the specialist, a Bible teacher from the institute or the missionary, would visit the different regional centers for a face-to-face encounter between professor and student(s) to answer questions and clarify issues. This meant for the missionary a considerable itineration and often inconsistencies due to their other obligations.

The student is NOT working for a diploma. Instead, a graduate is a trainee who teaches others to convert the lost, plant a church, and nurture that congregation to the point where it will establish other churches. Then (and only then) will a student be considered a trained leader. This is measurable. And it is biblical.

Lester Hirst describes a typical program of Theological Education by Extension and how it meets the needs of the church. He lists these objectives: 1) Training is programmed for every level of local church leadership; 2) Training takes into consideration the aspects considered to be important for leadership development. They are knowledge, skills, and character; 3)

Courses are taught not only by outsiders, but local leaders are incorporated as teachers; 4) Flexibility is allowed and encouraged; 5) The training program is linked integrally to the local church (Hirst, 1986, pp. 420-424).

Programmed instruction is a teaching method utilizing a sequence of modules or paragraphs, followed by an immediate question, case study, or some form of responding to the information in the module. This response, once written, is immediately corrected somewhere nearby usually on the same page. The answers can be written upside down on the bottom of the page, on the next page, or along a column to one side of the paragraph. Usually this answer would be just below the question area so it can be easily covered until the student has made his response. This principle of "reaffirmation" (or correction) is a key to the learning technique of programmed instruction, the pedagogical methodology of TEE. The student's response is either affirmed or corrected.

Jeff Reed[25] points out the significant changes in attitudes and practice that is evident in the churches by noting the increasing emphasis on the local church as the context of theological education, and spirituality and godliness as the desired results of the study of theology. "This can be seen in the TEE movement (Theological Education by Extension), in the extension and satellite school programs inaugurated by virtually all seminaries, in the creating of the DMin degree, in the emergence of various non-formal theological education programs worldwide, and in the emergence of a significant body of literature critiquing our current paradigm" (Reed, 1992, p. 245).

However, by the mid-80s it was generally assumed that TEE was on the decline and in many places, rather than becoming the best of both worlds by supplying organized theological study in an in-service context, it actually became the worst of both worlds, marked by undisciplined and unaccountable study and poor mentoring of educational experiences (Reed, 1992, p. 241). Having said that, some institutions continue to use TEE, since they have not heard of a tool that is any better for the remote churches.

CBT

The Church-Based Training of leaders has taken a number of turns. Multiple new approaches are attempts to replicate the Institute/Seminary classroom training via cassette, video, DVD or programmed instructions, each with its inherent educational problems. Another option is a new pedagogy which takes advantage of the small group discussion/discovery techniques of Socratic discussions following a guided independent reading and study program. Jeff Reed proposed a new educational paradigm for training leaders:

"It is my belief that most theological education renewal in the last few

25 Founder of BILD, Biblical Institute for Leadership Development, a sequel to TEE programs.

decades has centered around the adaptation and adjustment of an old paradigm, a paradigm which is likely to significantly impede the creation of radical new forms of the emerging needs of the twenty-first century... I am not calling for us to abandon the concept of seminary... Nor am I calling for elevating one form of education - informal - over the other two identifiable forms: formal and informal.... But the form they take, the paradigm in which they reside, is another matter altogether... I am convinced that our twentieth-century, institutional seminary model reflects the paradigm of the educational institution of contemporary culture, and are carriers of their values and often their diseases" (Reed, 1992, pp. 241-242).

Change is never easy and the leaders of the CBT are proposing a significant change in the ministry philosophy of the local church. Reed later comments, "It simply is not enough to slightly rearrange Schleiermacher's fourfold curriculum design, polishing it with contemporary titles. Nor is it enough to extend our classrooms into the evening or into the four walls of a church. Often these discussions are driven more by financial than philosophical concerns".

Advantages and Practicality of CBT

Church-Based Training differs from TEE in a number of areas. TEE was limited to the set curriculum of the program, and to the content of the interactive responses. The learning objectives were fixed and measured by the precise expected responses of the student. Little was to be learned outside of the programmed content area. The difficulty was writing a long series of interactive questions that excluded "copy framing," that is, merely copying the answers from the paragraph/module into the answer blank. To design questions that could measure the integration of the module into the thinking of the student to use in problem solving made programmed writing a difficult task. Asking questions that merely repeated some factual or historical fact to a specific question designed to measure the memory or retention of the student becomes a low level assessment tool, regardless of the affirmation or correction. The same may be said of classical lecture-based Institute training programs.

Another major difference is the equipping of local leaders to do the training in their church, instead of master teachers from outside the church, who may be more respected in some ways than their pastors. The objective is to build up the church leaders so the congregation does not need to look outside its own constituency for respected leaders to train them.

Reed points out that the main philosophical reason for a radical shift from "parsonage seminaries" to institutional seminaries are that the formalization of training would:
- give a sufficient length of time to study

- provide access to a good library
- promote the ability to specialize in an area of study
- allow greater devotion of all available time for study and teaching
- allow student to profit from other ministerial candidates, forming friendships that could promote harmony in the church
- promote unity and one-mindedness in the church by having ministerial students taught sound doctrine in one institution (Reed, 1992, pp. 243-44).

The view of theology shifted from the disposition and orientation of the soul for the purpose of acquiring wisdom, which all men needed for useful service of God in whatever capacity in society, to the mastery of academic disciplines--knowledge and information--as preparation for a professional ministerial service or teaching in theological institutions (Reed, 1992, p. 244).

Borrowing from Edward Farley's *Theologia: The Unity and Fragmentation of Theological Education*, Reed summarizes his concepts: "The change involved far more than just a change to an institutional form. The orientation of theological study changed from that of laying a foundation for the lifelong pursuit of wisdom to an intense mastery of academic disciplines. Theology lost its soul, and the pursuit of knowledge replaced the pursuit of wisdom (Reed, 1992, p. 245)

Some of the main reasons for these shifts are:
- the enormous cost of doing theological education in our Western institutional seminary
- Graduates of formal institutions are often ill-equipped or lack the gifts and abilities to truly lead
- the inability of formal structures to meet the needs of the rapidly expanding Two-Thirds World church
- the discipleship and church renewal movements, with their accompanying literature, which are calling the church back to its roots of New Testament form and function; significantly altering the way the church perceived and practices theological education.
- the emergence of the technological society where knowledge and information can no longer be contained and centralized, but are rapidly disseminated across geographical boundaries through computer and laser technology (Reed, 1992, p. 245).

A New Paradigm is surfacing

A new paradigm is emerging around the world and in many N. American churches as well. Western, evangelical seminaries will be challenged to shift to a new paradigm if they expect to be relevant in the twenty-first century. Many will make this shift through Distance Learning Programs (DLP) or remote seminary locations. Already many larger churches are training their staff from within. Seminary students should learn their courses well enough to teach them to others. Seminaries need courses that can and should be taught in churches.

Our Western institutions are generally regarded as ineffective and inappropriate for the Two-Thirds World especially with their dependence on expatriate professors. Some of the recommendations from the CBTers are the following:

- a shift from traditional, academic-based accrediting systems to church-based assessment procedures which accommodate formal, non-formal, and informal forms of theological preparation (Collins, 1979)
- a shift in emphasis from residential, for-service model to a church-based, in-service model of ministry preparation
- a shift of the foundational training back to local churches, with seminaries assuming a resource role to the churches
- a shift of the primary ministry context of professors back to local churches, becoming resource scholars and mentors for training proven and gifted leaders in churches
- a shift from centralized to a decentralized staff, moving them back into strategic local churches around the country
- a shift from a fragmented curriculum based on Schleiermacher's fourfold model, to a model consistent with the unfolding agenda of the Scriptures and the current needs of the churches (Farley, 1983)
- specifically, a shift from a curriculum-based on systematic theology to a curriculum based on biblical theology and theology in culture, relevant to the belief framework of a given culture (Conn, 1984)
- a shift from an academic-testing course design to a wisdom and problem-posing course design model (Freire, 1984)
- a shift away from costly institutional overhead by selling unnecessary properties related to large in-residence programs and focusing on serving as a resource center to area churches (Reed, 1992, pp. 246-247).

These are not easy recommendations to attempt to implement, but they can be much easier if attempted in new ministries, especially overseas, which could begin with these concepts as integral to the ministry philosophy. A slow start can be expected, but once the leaders begin to multiply and train other leaders the growth can become exponential.

A careful distinction must be made

There is a distinction between the seminary moving its classes within the walls of the church as a form of "church-housed" and the new paradigm of "church-based" training. There are a number of key principles involved. In a church-based program the leaders of the training program are primarily from the church itself. The design is to reaffirm the value and quality of the local church leaders. Any outside initial training is to equip these church leaders to train up other leaders within their church. The protection and defense of the local church leadership is a priority, and for this reason the current church leadership must be committed to the philosophy and practice of discipling, training and mentoring of others in their church for their ministry.

The ideals of the core principles found in the letters to the first churches (especially Ephesians) and to church leaders (Timothy and Titus) point to the biblical nature of leadership training being church-based:
- training took place in the context of the ministry
- training was viewed as an entrusting of the ministry to faithful men, by faithful men who were doing the work of the ministry
- confirming of those trained was fundamentally the responsibility of leaders at the local church level
- training of leaders was not viewed as an end in itself or as an entity separate from the church, but was always understood to be a matter of establishing churches

The conclusion then is that leadership development in the early churches was church-based at its core. "The church-based training of the early church as clearly understood as a flexible leadership development strategy rooted in the life and ministry of local churches, in which 'gifted men' (Eph 4:11; 2 Tim 2:2) entrusted more and more of the ministry to other faithful men while they themselves remained deeply involved in the process of establishing churches. This type of paradigm we are calling church-based. The extension of the formal theological seminary into the four walls of a church building through various forms of extension would more accurately be referred to as church-housed" (Reed, 1992, p. 248).

BILD approach to the CBT movement

This new paradigm is not an easy transition to make, but Jeff Reed makes the following suggestions for developing a network of leaders and churches to facilitate the continuity and perpetuity of sound leadership training yet maintain the centrality of the local church in the process.
- Regional resource hubs...which are capable of housing extensive resources, hosting conferences, and maintaining an on-line computer center.
- Teams of church-based, gifted leaders who share a common vision and understanding of the plan and purpose of God for the Church, supported by their churches to participate in the resource network. They will conduct on-site seminars, assist in establishing churches and training leaders, and oversee the academic development of exceptional leaders seeking to

become part of this professor network.
- A core curriculum designed to facilitate ordered learning at the foundational level, conducted by church leaders, taught in a flexible, "problem posing" style in the context of the local church ministry. Churches in each culture would be challenged to develop specialized courses addressing the issues and needs of the church and its outreach in its own culture.
- A prudent stewardship strategy for sharing the costs associated with necessary travel, seminars, and regional resource and computer centers.
- A publishing house which publishes works that emerge from local churches that are deep in truth and sound doctrine, and resources, journals, and books that emerge from writing guilds sponsored by the network.
- A church-based assessment and recognition system that assesses the level of preparedness that has been achieved through the network and its participating churches (Reed, 1992, p. 249).

To get an idea of how to build up a comprehensive program for the local church to train its leaders the basic outline below can indicate how vast the program can become for the benefit of thousands beginning in a single church. BILD - International has developed such a Church-Based Leadership Training Program whose core ingredients are as follows:
- A 10-year church-based strategy guide for churches
- A 30-course core curriculum and lifelong-learning update system
- A comprehensive seminar training network
- A comprehensive church-based assessment strategy built around a life-development portfolio, with a minimum of seven years ministry experience built into the assessment
- An online computerized resource center
- A publishing and translation network
- An international network of resource scholars
- An international network of individual churches and associations of churches
- An interface strategy with theological seminaries, graduate schools and Bible colleges and other training organizations
- The cultivation of church-based regional resource centers, a new generation of seminaries
- An international network of such resource centers for the purpose of writing, holding councils, and sharing resources (Reed, 1992, p. 250).

Conclusion

Paul defined the major function of the church leadership to that of "equipping the saints for the work of the ministry" (Eph 4:12), yet few church leaders (pastors or elders) ever spend time or effort in this priority task. The delegation of the task to Bible Institutes, Christian Universities and Seminaries fails to erase the ultimate holder of the responsibility of multiplying trained leaders for the expansion of the Church. The one thing that cannot be delegated is responsibility, especially a responsibility that was specifically placed on the shoulders of the church leadership, not the leadership of a parachurch organization.

I have asked many pastors who, or if, they have ever discipled in their walk with God on a mutually accountable plan or mentored the leaders in their church to be equipped for their personal ministry and continual training responsibility for other leaders. I have never met a pastor who has answered in the affirmative. To be fair, I have known a number associated with CBT (both BILD and CCBT – Center for Church-Based Training in Dallas, Texas) who were experts and practitioners in training leaders. They have been my models for how this vital ministry is to function.

I conclude with this picture. Can you relate the relevance of this picture to our topic? If you can, then you can see the vision of what CBT can accomplish.

Appendix A

Web sites for CBT:

ACCESS-ible Education: http://www.bild.org/news/Article.htm?key=200603ACCESS

BILD, Biblical Institute for Leadership Development: http://www.bild.org/Home.htm;jsessionid=6F5E8AC607B8B2F51421B6859AA82C7C

Center for Church Based Training: http://www.ccbt.org/

Complete course description of Joe Wright in English and German at www.bao.at

More intensive training on a faster track can be found at Evangelical Academy (http://www.evak.at). These courses can be applied to a Master of Arts degree through Columbia International University.

The Church-Based Training International (CBTI) is a Church of Christ application of the CBT principles. There are a number of helpful articles worth reading that are collected from a number of sources including non-Church of Christ authors. See http://cbti.faithsite.com/content.asp?CID=3962

Worldwide Leadership Training: Retrieved 1/20/07 from http://www.whatgodintended.com/leader-training.asp

Appendix B
Some Limitation of Formal Education

As in any human endeavor there are limitations in the best of circumstances, especially in the area of formal education. A great deal of investigation is being done today on how to teach more people while maintaining a quality and excellence in higher education. The following paragraphs will list a number of weaknesses in the formal education system that is common today in the public and private arena.

1. **Inflexibility**: There is often a significant difference between what is discussed in the classroom and what happens in real life. This difference is mostly because schools are not able to adapt to the reality outside of their institution, or they are not aware that there is a difference. Most steps taken in the typical institution are mandatory by some accrediting association whether they facilitate more teaching or not.
2. **Ineffectiveness**: Because of growing demands there may be many inadequacies to meet the needs. Often there is little that can be done in a classroom setting where listening to lectures makes a difference in the student's increased knowledge. For economic effectiveness larger classrooms become practical in spite of the fact that the ineffective lecture method becomes the only pedagogy possible.
3. **No direct causal evidence**: many key competencies for success have been show to acquire without formal schools. Variations in the schooling techniques in classrooms show little difference in acquired learning, whereas activities outside of the classroom are more effective in learning skills and traits that continue.
4. **Western Industrialized education**: Raw materials in this side produces specific product on the other side. Teachers must produce as many students as possible to be economically viable instead of being a tutor. Standardized materials, minimal curricula, time limitations, competition

with other activities, and end product certification, instead of learning a skill become the wrong objectives.

5. **Elitism**: The screening process of who graduates with the highest grade point makes for special people, regardless of their personal qualities. This process determines which people will play the highest roles and given the best opportunities whether they are gifted or not. Attitude toward non-formally trained personnel ranges from doubt to rejection.
6. **Authoritarianism**: Authoritative roles are determined by the certification process of formal education, regardless of other qualities that might limit them.
7. **Costliness**: Formal training is a highly labor intensive industry and has inflationary bias built into the production quotas. Teacher salaries can makeup 50% to 75% of the operating budget of formal schooling. With debt availability, schools can charge whatever and the students must borrow what they cannot pay to acquire what they absolutely must have in life: a degree.
8. **Inefficient wastage**: Great expenditures are exhausted on students who do not graduate, or do not work in the area of their studies.
9. **Exclusivism**: Thousands are not able to acquire the schooling that they need to advance. Fifty thousand students in Guadalajara, Mexico and unable to enter into the university system every year. Classes are that are offered during the day hours eliminate those who work or have a family. Many schools have little or nothing for adult training.
10. **Equating schooling with training**: For many church leadership positions in N. America there is no need to apply without advanced degrees, regardless of other attributes.
11. **Indirect rewards**: The question is usually asked: where did you go to school and that says it all. The higher the prestige of a school, the more the "school word" is used to communicate an assumed knowledge. With informal training, the rewards are determined on what specifically you are able to do.
12. **Irrelevance**: Subject matter is often unrelated to the community or real life. Concepts that make learning relevant are "work study," "internship," "on-site experiential learning," etc. Instead of receiving practical training after formal training, it should be built into the program before graduation.
13. **Isolationism**: "Life in the bubble," isolated from the real world for years at a time can not help the maturation process. Spiritual leaders become different from the laity and unaccustomed to them.
14. **Asks the wrong questions**: Educators ask how to focus on the few who show promise instead of how to adapt the program for the needs and variety of ministry possibilities.
15. **Inappropriateness of curricula**: In the Two-Thirds World most

curriculum is imported from foreign countries to prepare foreign-type leaders. One suggestion is to not consider learning by courses offered, but rather in terms of the experiences that will be needed. Abandon metaphors of the Industrialized approach, the trampoline mentality and the formula techniques for success.

16. **A dysfunctional system**: Most international education depends on rote learning, which leads to certification mentality. There is little thinking skills, analysis or discernment qualities. Facts may be memorized, but what do you do with them?
17. **Failure's negative impact**: Many in formal schools are programmed to fail. In some universities it is necessary to fail 50% each year because of the lack of facilities. Does this failure scar the student for life and is it avoidable? When the school is designed to train the elite the have-nots are crippled for life. Educational leaders who feel proud about this failure rate are cruel and little benefit to society.
18. **Conformity**: Breaking out of the mold to teach topic not taught elsewhere runs into opposition. The first point of acceptance of new courses is that the subject is taught in other accredited institutions. Deviations from the approved path are considered spurious. Rewards are given to those who conform, both students and educators.
19. **Bureaucracy**: The qualities of creativity, spontaneity, and freedom are impeded by the process of administrative hierarchy and obligatory bureaucracy. In order to keep "control" and assure accreditation, processes are set up to assure outside agencies that we can govern ourselves as an institution. Obstinate individuals, unlimited paperwork and multi-layered procedures cripple initiatives for improvement. The higher the level of trust and shared vision the smoother bureaucracy, but this can be rare to encounter.
20. **Urban-metropolitan mindset**: Most schools are in the cities, but globally, a majority of the students come from small towns or rural areas. The more these students are trained in this mindset, the less effective, and less interested they become, in reaching the very communities they came from.
21. **Cultural dislocation**: The effects of changing his cultural setting for the most formidable time of his life, results in changes that make the student a foreigner to his own community when he returns after 3 or 4 years. These cultural changes can be obstacles to an effective ministry.
22. **Professionalism**: The attendance at a formal school can fulfill the dream of a student to become a professional or middle class, and/or the status of a professional spiritual person who should be paid for his services for life. This sense of "job-security" can distort the motivation for ministry. When this is combined with the patron system of leadership, the prophet-centered communities of Africa or the Indian guru's authority, these ethnic

tendencies can magnify the Western model moving the biblical leadership further toward the horizon.

23. **Traditionalism**: When missionaries exalted the dominant leadership in the church, even when they pulled out, the national leadership eagerly wanted to have the same authority and prestige. The missionary – professor who prides himself in his knowledge in the academic realm tends to reproduce the same attitude in students. He is what he is because of his education. This attitude only becomes exaggerated in students, especially in the Two-Thirds world.

This is not to say that formal education is bad or unnecessary, but it does point out that there are pitfalls to understand and avoid. Non-formal education may have its own set of limitations, but it represents a vast area to be developed. Mentor-protégé and tutor-student methodologies need to be developed as an integral part of the ministry. Few pastors in N. America have ever been discipled, much less mentored in the ministry. What hope is there that their followers going to the mission field will have a clue as to what to do to develop leaders within their own ministry, without depending on any outside institution?

In the Two-Thirds world formal schooling has created too great a disparity between the many who function as church leaders without formal theological training and the few leaders who have obtained the necessary academic degrees but know little of people ministries. The traditional ministerial preparation and inevitable middle-class upward mobility attached to the superficial elitist role that has been earned feeds on the pride of accomplishment and the lust for power instead of the sacrifice of humility in giving one's self to care for and nourish others in their growth path and walk with the Lord. Maybe prestige and titles are all they claim to be.

References

Allen, R. (1962). *Missionary Methods: St. Paul's or Ours*. Grand Rapids: Eerdmans.
Bagley, B. (2005, October). "Keys to an Effective Non-Formal training Event." *Evangelical Missions Quarterly*, 41(4), pp. 506-512.
Brainerd, E. (1974). "The 'Myth' of Programmed Texts." *Evangelical Missions Quarterly*, 10(3), 219-223.
Castro, E. (1983). *Ministry by the People: Theological Education by Extension* (F. Ross Kinsler, Ed.). New York: Orbis Books.
Covell, Ralph and C. Peter Wagner. (1971). *An Extension Seminary Primer* (South Pasadena, California: William Carey Library.
Emery, James H. (1963). "The Preparation of Leaders in a Ladino-Indian Church," *Practical Anthropology*, vol. 10, no. 3.
Forman, R., Jeff Jones and Bruce Miller. (2004, 07/11/04). *The Leadership Baton*. Grand Rapids: Zondervan.
Foulkes, I. W. (1984, October). "From the Third World: A New Approach to Theological Education." *Evangelical Review of Theology*, 8(2).

Getz, G. (2007). Center for Church Based Training.

Hirst, L. (1986, October). "Making TEE Serve the Needs of the Churches." *Evangelical Missions Quarterly*, 22(4), 420-424.

Hopewell, James F. (1969). "Training a Tent-Making Ministry in Latin America," *Theological Education by Extension*, edited by Ralph D. Winter (South Pasadena, California: William Carey Library.

Jencks, Christopher and David Riesman, (1968). *The Academic Revolution*. New York: Doubleday and Company, Inc.

Kinsler, F. R. (1981). *The Extension Movement in Theological Education: A Call to the Renewal of the Ministry*. Pasadena: William Carey Library.

Kuligin, V. (2007, July). "Going the Distance: Adapting Full-time Residential Curricula into Distance Format." *Evangelical Missions Quarterly*, 42(3), 298-305.

Mulholland, K. B. (1976). *The Way We've Always Done It*. Presbyterian and Reformed Publishing Company.

Niebuhr, Richard H. and Daniel D. Williams. (1956). *The Ministry in Historical Perspective*. New York: Harper and Row.

Reed, J. (Executive Director, BILD International). (1992). "Church-Based Theological Education: Creating a New Paradigm." *North American Professors of Christian Education* (NAPCE).

Rowen, S. F. (1967). *The Resident Extension Seminary: A Seminary Program for the Dominican Republic*. Miami: West Indies Mission.

Winter, R. D. "An Extension Seminary Manual." *In Theological Education by Extension*.

_____. (1966). "This Seminary Goes to the Students," World Vision Magazine, July-August,

_____ (1969). "New Winds Blowing," *Church Growth Bulletin*, edited by Donald A. McGavran (South Pasadena, California: William Carey Library,), vols. J-V.

Wright, J. (2007, July). "Training Leaders: A functioning model for missionaries." *Evangelical Missions Quarterly*, 42(3), 288-295.

SUGGESTED READINGS

Covell, Ralph, and Wagner, C. Peter. *An Extension Seminary Primer*. South Pasadena, California: William Carey Library, 1971.

Emery, James H. "The Preparation of Leaders in a Ladino-Indian Church." *Practical Anthropology*. vol. 10, no. 3, 1963, pp. 127-134.

Hopewell, James F. "Training a Tent-Making Ministry in Latin America." *Theological Education By Extension*. Edited by Ralph D. Winter. South Pasadena, California: William Carey Library, 1969.

Jenks, Christopher, and Riesman, David. *The Academic Revolution*. New York: Doubleday and Company, Inc., 1968.

Kaller, Donald W. "TEE: Brazil's Success Story." *Christianity Today* (February 13, 1976) pp. 13, 14.

Kelly, Robert. *Theological Education In America*. New York: George H. Doran Company, 1924.

Kornfield, William J. "The Challenge to Make Extension Education Culturally Relevant." *Evangelical Missions Quarterly*. vol. 12, no. 1, January 1976, pp. 13-22.

Latourette, Kenneth Scott. *A History of the Expansion of Christianity*. New York: Harper Brothers Publishers, 1970.

Niebuhr, Richard H., and Williams, Daniel D. *The Ministry in Historical Perspective*. New York: Harper and Row, 1956.

Winter, Ralph D. "This Seminary Goes to the Students." *World Vision Magazine* (July-August 1966) pp. 10-12.

Winter, Ralph D. "New Winds Blowin2." *Church Growth Bulletin*. Edited by Donald A. McGarvan. South Pasadena, California: William Carey Library, 1969. Volumes I-V.

Chapter 9

Chronological Bible Storying/Teaching

We had to start early in the morning, about 3:30 AM, to load the canoe and get to the rapids by dawn. The Caquetá River stretches across the middle of the state of Amazonas in Colombia, SA. At a couple of places the river narrows and tumbles over rapids making travel impossible. After two hours of portaging fuel barrels, equipment, trading goods, and outboard motors we pulled the 35 ft. canoe up the churning white-water rapids to a calm spot on the bank where all our goods had been carried. By dawn we were loaded up and began the 30-hour trip to the main Miraña village for my first contact with this bi-lingual tribe.

Since I was one of the first missionaries to every travel in the state of Amazonas, Colombia, I decided to dedicate the first term to reaching as many as possible with an itinerating evangelistic Cessna floatplane ministry to as many Colombian villages as possible on the Putumayo River. I began to discover along the Caquetá River that most of the villages were bilingual tribal people groups (Miraña tribe). The further north I explored along the Miriti River (Yucuna, Tanimuca and Lutuamas tribes) and the Apaporis River the less bilingual the tribes became.

On my first trip to the Mirañas in the early 70's on this lengthy canoe trip I began to ponder, how do I begin the gospel story? I had not been trained in this phase of tribal work. I knew they had little or no Christian exposure except an occasional visit by a Roman Catholic Jesuit priest who merely forced everyone to the river's edge and sprinkled water on them saying something in Latin, and then he would traveled on up river to another settlement. I wondered who he was trying to impress.

Should I begin with the birth of Jesus? Did they need to know about their sinfulness and need of the "good news" of forgiveness? As I pondered the alternatives, only 30 minutes before arriving at the first village, it just made more sense to start at creation and walk through the Bible. I would not have to cover everything, since I would be coming back periodically from then on.

Over the next few months I would return with the Cessna landing on the sandbar in front of the villages while continuing to work on two short airstrips by their villages. As I soon discovered, this trip had an ancient tradition that a Being created the world only to abandon it to the spirit world. They had a hope that someone would come to tell them of who He was. When I started talking of the Creator they hung on every word. Over the next few years many of the Mirañas would come to know Christ as they heard more and more of the Bible stories of who God is, what He is like, how men have trusted him against all odds, how no opposing force can stand against Him, how those who serve false gods end up corrupted and defeated, and how awful is the penalty for sin, etc.

Our first furlough we spent learning linguistics to begin the long task with one of the more monolingual tribes that had many contacts with some of the other 40 plus tribal people groups within a 30-minute flight from our base in La Pedrera. But this is another story.

The question of how to communicate the gospel to an unreached people groups is of vital importance if understanding biblical truth is the essential basis of faith.[18] This implies that it is our responsibility to learn a number of skills: language learning skill, linguistic techniques to eventually break down the language into writing, and the skill of how to teach the Bible in a way that makes sense to both the oral and eventually the literate people in any group. This is not a game. It is not because we love the problem solving task of cross cultural language learning and communications; rather, it is the only way to fulfill the task of world evangelism. It is our responsibility to communicate the gospel to them, not their responsibility to learn how we understood the gospel. This chapter will discuss the developing trend of communicating the gospel through the skill of Chronological Bible Storying and Teaching (hence CBS and CBT).

Introduction

WHAT is the hope of reaching the four billion persons who are oral learners? What is the hope for getting God's word to the speakers of the four thousand languages still without His word? These people can't, don't and won't take in new information or communicate among themselves by literate means. It is estimated that 90% of the world's Christian workers use highly literate communication styles such as the printed page, expositional, analytical, and logical presentations of God's Word. It must be remembered that it is the messenger's responsibility to communicate the message in terms that are understood, not just heard.

The main solution today is Chronological Bible Teaching (CBT) which involves telling the gospel story as it has been revealed in Scripture from the beginning, intermixed with teaching about what the story means. This method of evangelism was popularized by Trevor McIlwain and used extensively by New Tribes Mission since the mid-1970s.

"The work of Trevor McIlwain in the 1970s is the beginning f what

---

18 "When anyone hears the word about the kingdom and **does not understand it**, the evil one comes and snatches what was sown in his heart; this is the seed sown along the path" (NET Matt 13:19).

became CBS. McIlwain worked with New Tribes Missions (NTM) in the Philippines. He tried a number of approaches with a tribal group that had previously professed faith in Christ but has revealed to many old ways and beliefs. Eventually McIlwain chose to teach chronologically through the Bible starting with Genesis. Each session started with a focus on the biblical story, then shifted to expository teaching. This chronological Bible exposition produced a much stronger understanding of God's nature and the Christian faith within the people and transformed their lives. McIlwain named this approach Chronological Bible Teaching.(Lovejoy 2000:3).

McIlwain influenced John R. Cross to write "The Stranger on the Road to Emmaus," which followed the approach Jesus used with the disciples: "beginning with Moses and all the Prophets, he interpreted to them the things written about himself in all the scriptures" (Luke 24:27). This approach is typically connected with a Bible translation and literacy program that parallels the teachings.

Jim Slack, IMB missionary in the Philippines, invited McIlwain to teach his approach to two large groups of Baptist missionaries and national leaders. "But after hearing McIlwain's presentation, Slack and others in both the IMB [formerly known as FMB] and NTM concluded that McIlwain's approach was too literate. It was not reproducible among most Filipino church leaders. So New Tribes missionaries ... began experimenting with and adapting McIlwain's approach. So did Slack and several SBC missionaries. The five NTM missionaries retained the chronological and biblical emphases, but reduced the amount of expository teaching somewhat and emphasized storytelling. ... This group of approaches is sometimes called Chronological Bible Storytelling because it is more narrative and less expositional than McIlwain's approach. But they retained varying degrees of expositional teaching in the story and the instruction that followed the story (Lovejoy 2000:3).

Chronological Bible Storying (CBS) is similar to CBT but it does not interject Bible teaching, just the Bible story followed by discussion questions. It seeks to present the Bible story as accurately as it is in the Scriptures with a minimum of explanation. CBS holds that theological truths are better understood in oral cultures within the story itself, rather than abstract principles taught in literate teaching styles.

By the late 1980s, Jim Slack concluded that existing approaches to chronological Bible presentation were too literate for use with oral communicators. He began working on a form of chronological Bible presentation that utilized storytelling followed by dialog. He carefully avoided including exposition in either the story or the dialog. ... In an effort to differentiate it from the approaches of McIlwain and the others, Slack and [J.O.] Terry called their approach "storying" (Lovejoy 2000:3-4).

CBS is used for evangelism, discipleship and church planting since it provides the necessary background for pre-literate people with no previous exposure to Christianity and who need to understand the concepts that lead up to the Gospels and the coming of Christ.

Chronological Bible Storying

CBS is designed by selected and prepared Bible stories to evangelize, disciple, plant churches and train leaders. These stories are presented in a session that is introduced by an appropriate pre-story interaction to prepare listeners for the story, which is followed by a post-story dialog to aid the listeners to understand the teaching embedded in the story by encouraging discussion of the stories and applying the teaching that they deduced from the story to their lives.

Grant Lovejoy, IMB director of orality strategies, defines CBS as the presentation of selected biblical stories designed to contradict the worldview of the oral people group so as to lay the foundations to bring people to genuine "faith in Christ, mature discipleship and fruitful Christian service." The presentation typically includes a time of dialog after the story during which the storyteller uses Socratic-type questions "to guide the listeners to discover the meaning and significance of the biblical story."(Lovejoy 2000:2).

Rationale for Chronological Bible Storying

Why is Bible Storying so important for witness & teaching? The fact is that a large percentage of the unreached world is not literate – not being able to read the Bible even if they had one. Many of these people do not have a written language yet so they must be reached orally, at least in the meantime. Others simply prefer learning orally in groups.

At least three and one-half billion (60%) of the world's 6.1 billion people are oral communicators. At least one-fourth of the world's population (1,525,383,804 people) are primary oral communicators - illiterates. Primary oral communicators cannot read or write. And, at least fifty percent (50%) of those who live in the United States are oral communicators and cannot perform literate tasks well enough to function as literates. Oral communicators are likely the largest unevangelized population segment in the USA. ...Over sixty percent (60%) of Islamic women are either illiterate or functionally illiterate, as is Africa south of the Sahara. At least seventy percent (70%) of the worlds least reached and unevangelized peoples are oral communicators(Slack 2003).

A major segment of the unreached world is hostile to traditional Christian teaching or preaching but will listen to stories of any sort. "Most of the world's major religions are both propagated by stories and maintained by stories, reputedly of the founder or other holy personages" (Terry 1999).

It is helpful for literate cross-cultural Christian workers to be aware of different degrees of literacy if they are to communicate with people in appropriate ways. These degrees of literacy reflect a continuum. One categorization of salient points along this continuum is that of James B. Slack, which describes five levels of literacy to be considered in presenting the gospel:

- "Illiterates" cannot read or write. They have never "seen" a word. In fact, the word for illiteracy in the Indonesia language is *buta huruf*, meaning "blind to letters." For oral communicators, words do not exist as letters, but as sounds related to images of events and to situations that they are seeing or experiencing.
- "Functional illiterates" have been to school but do not continue to read and write regularly after dropping out of school. Within two years, even those who have gone to school for eight years often can read only simple sentences and can no longer receive, recall or reproduce concepts, ideas, precepts, and principles through literate means. They prefer to get their information orally. Their functional level of illiteracy (as opposed to published data) determines how they learn, how they develop their values and beliefs, and how they pass along their culture, including their religious beliefs and practices.
- "Semi-literates" function in a gray transitional area between oral communication and literacy. Even though these individuals have normally gone to school up to 10 years and are classified in every country of the world as literates, they learn primarily by means of narrative presentations.
- "Literate" learners understand and handle information such as ideas, precepts, concepts, and principles by literate means. They tend to rely on printed material as an aid to recall.
- "Highly literate" learners usually have attended college and are often professionals in the liberal arts fields. They are thoroughly print-culture individuals.(Wills 2004:3-2).

The objectives of Bible Storying are to *publish* the Bible orally, encourage strategic church planting, disciple believers [that is, make them learners of the stories and their applications from the stories], and train emerging leaders empowering them to teach the Bible in a form that is understandable, memorable and reproducible for their own people. CBS has become an important teaching and witness tool among not only Southern Baptist missionaries but all who share in the Great Commission task.

> Beyond all these are a number of hindrances to the Gospel. One is limited literacy. Some peoples are non-literate, not reading at all. So you can't use a tract or give them a Bible to read. Others have limited literacy but struggle with religious vocabulary which they do not know. Others have a Bible in only the trade language used among their people groups, but not in their heart language (Terry 1999).

After developing a basic understanding of orality, literate missionaries and teachers then need to learn effective oral communication styles which are culturally relevant. Many trained oral teachers can easily tell a hundred or more Bible stories and lead their people to learn from them. "In general, there is a cluster of features that oral learners have in common in processing information. They most readily process information that is concrete and sequential, and which is presented in a highly relational context. Other aspects of an effective communication style for a particular oral culture may be discovered by careful observation and participation in the life of the community"(Wills 2004:3-3).

Jim Slack, one of the founders of the CBS, wrote, "All oral communicators find it very difficult to understand, internalize, and recall messages that do not come through proverbs, prose, or carefully constructed stories compatible with their learning preference and cultural presentation style. Their preferred learning and communication style, or format, is the oral narrative. If they are to 'hear' the Gospel of Christ it must come to them through a narrative format" (Slack 2003).

> When this miss-matched communication between literates and oral communicators occurs, and the oral communicator attempts to embrace the literate message, serious syncretism results between what is being heard and what they already believe. Even if they do understand, and "get the message straight," they are helpless when faced with the need to remember and reproduce what they heard. Oral communicators - illiterate, functionally illiterate, and some semi-literates - use different means of constructing, internalizing, recalling, and reproducing information and beliefs than do literates. An oral

communicator's patterns are the exact opposite of literate, word-culture patterns.(Slack 2003).

The stories provide a broad and memorable way of describing the characteristics of God, those of the natural (carnal) man, stories of Jesus as both man and God, and those of the born again believer, which present what God expects of all believers.

J. O. Terry, IMB missionary in Asia, categorized the stories that deal with the issues of the authority and the sovereignty of God, which show why we are accountable to Him, then the broken relationship as a result of sin beginning with Adam and Eve and continuing through their descendants, our ancestors, resulting in God's judgment of sin, God's promise of an Coming One to suffer for man's sin, and the fulfillment of all prophecy in Jesus who returned to the Father when his ministry on earth was finished.(Terry 1999).

Some are resistant to the Gospel message and attempts to present it. They may have been cautioned against its message as being Western and part of a plan of imperialism. In extreme cases the people may be openly hostile to what they construe as "preaching". So any attempt to witness in a manner that suggests preaching, is quickly and openly opposed. It is not the message so much as the manner of the presentation they are rejecting. The same message in a more compatible and culturally acceptable form such as Bible Storying is both enjoyable and acceptable to listeners.(Terry 1999).

Implications for Chronological Bible Storying

Slack reported that demographers and researchers such as Miles Smith-Morris looked ahead years ago and saw the realities of our century. They had evidence years ago that global literacy levels would not improve appreciably by A.D. 2000. Furthermore, 9,100 language or dialectical variants of those languages have no Scripture or portions available. "Even if literacy were successful among them, there would be no Scripture, or Scripture portions, in their language for them to read. A narrative, chronological-storying approach to the communication of the Gospel is of an even greater necessity" (Slack 2003).

The application of the principles of orality indicates a change in mission strategy. Lovejoy describes the IMB missionaries who plant 75% of their churches among 20% of the population that is literate. "Those were the people we could best communicate with." Had they learned how to evangelize oral people they would not have neglected the 80% who are oral communicators (Lovejoy 2000:10).

Terry suggests that an understanding of the target people's worldview be undertaken to give clues as to which stories are definitely needed and which ones might best be skipped for the time being. How many stories are needed to bring people from where they are in their spiritual condition to have an opportunity to understand who Jesus is and why we must accept by faith what he was sent to do (Terry 1999).

> Well-meaning ministers and missionaries assume that anybody, even a child, can under-stand simple outlines of the Gospel passages they use to present Christ's Gospel. Social, anthropological, and linguistic research reveal that is a misconception. Primary oral communicators do not understand the Gospel when it is presented to them by means of expository outlines, principles, precepts, steps, and logically developed discourses (Slack 2003).

The practice of storying is a long process. It is building the foundations of faith, so that the results are a genuine "conversion" of worldview and beliefs of how to live.

"Once the initial worldview study has been done, storyers select stories to supplement the core list. These additional stories contain biblical teachings that are needed to speak to the aspects of the prevailing worldview that are inconsistent with a biblical worldview. Dealing with these issues before the call for decision is designed to minimize syncretism" (Lovejoy 2000:11). J. O. Terry outlines five options for telling the stories:[19]

1. Tell one story each encounter. This is the best approach if you plan to discuss the stories with your listeners to draw out the truths in the stories by talking about them and the implication for the listeners. This is the normal strategy followed in Chronological Bible Storying. If the story list is short you may have time to go more slowly and deliberately.
2. Tell a cluster of stories each encounter. This approach takes advantage of the fact that stories tend to group together around certain themes or characters which link the stories together. The creation stories (of the spirit world, the natural world and then of man and woman) deal with God's sovereignty. Then follows a cluster of judgment stories (Adam and Eve's sin, Cain's sin, the sinful world in Noah's day). Then follow the promise stories (God's promise to Abraham of a descendant to bless all peoples, the same promise to Isaac and Jacob). The Abraham stories also have the substitute sacrifice which is one of the key stories leading to Christ as the substitute sacrifice for our sin.
   The stories of Jesus also fall into clusters (annunciation and birth, baptism and tempting by Satan, healings, forgiveness of sin stories,

---

[19] More practical suggestions given in Appendix 1

power encounter stories, passion and death stories).
3. Tell as a continuous fast-tracked story. This is the best approach if time is very limited or there is a single opportunity to use the Bible story to evangelize. This approach may be done in a small group publicly, used in a limited group in a home, used bedside in a hospital, or even one-on-one. In this approach there is no attempt to stop the narrative in order to discuss the story. The story continues, usually in a somewhat condensed manner moving smoothly from episode to episode while touching upon all the basic Bible truths leading to salvation. Depending upon the worldview of the listeners more or less attention is given to the Old Testament stories as a preparation for the stories of Jesus. This approach is often done with some kind of picture set to illustrate the stories and to give a focus. Larger flat pictures are needed for the public groups, booklets or even photo-album pictures may be used for smaller more intimate groups of listeners.
4. Tell a single appropriate story or cluster but not a chronological sequence. We often call this situational storying as we choose a story best suited to the situation at hand in which we have an opportunity to witness or minister. This may be a point of encounter opportunity to open up a witness. It may be a ministry situation in which you have opportunity to minister through prayer for a person or family. Before you pray, lift up Jesus with an appropriate story or two. Then pray for the person and, before you go, offer to share more stories if invited back. Then you will have opportunity to tell the chronologically arranged stories leading to salvation.
5. Probing for responsiveness and opening the way for a longer storying strategy to follow. By telling the story in a short form, the volunteer or ISCer may open up a door for an evangelist to come and, over a much longer period of time, begin to tell the stories and lead the people to talk about what God is saying to them through the stories. This could happen as a follow-up to crusades where volunteers take advantage of home visits and other personal opportunities to introduce the Bible story. Special projects like well drilling, construction of houses, disaster and relief aid all provide times of contact and increased interest and curiosity which give opportunity for short track Bible storying. This, too, is a further opportunity for a longer and more thorough Bible storying strategy by a local missionary or Baptist partner.(Terry 1999).

"For evangelizing we identify a core group of stories that are essential to tell God's overarching story of salvation. Typically this list of core stories includes 22-25 stories spanning from creation to the resurrection of Jesus. This group of stories is theologically necessary to set forth the character of God, the reality and seriousness of human sin, the necessity of satisfying God's righteousness, the mercy and grace of God in providing Jesus as the only acceptable substitute for us, the necessity of faith in him alone, and his triumphant resurrection from the dead"(Lovejoy 2000:11).

Criticism of Chronological Bible Storying

This methodology of evangelizing without the necessity of literacy or a written text is not without its critics. This new approach of orality is called a *heresy* by some because it is telling biblical stories based on pictures and images. Orality is said to short-cut Bible translation and language methods of teaching the Word of God to "people groups." The rationale for this is, of course, the "urgency" in fulfilling the Great Commission "mandate." "Orality is by its very nature condescending, treating Third World peoples as 'children' who supposedly do not have the 'ability' or 'desire' to learn to read. It is being touted as an alternative method of evangelism. However, it is very evident that some mission groups have no intention of EVER teaching these people to read, or give them a Bible in their own language" (Discernment Group 2005).

There may be this temptation to rely exclusively on Storying to effect a church planting movement, especially when such evident conversions occur, but it is not the intent of the Orality Network.

> "In the past we have sometimes supposed that Bible translation must precede evangelism, church planting, leadership training, and the like. We will gladly partner with Bible translators because we believe in the value of their work, but we will not let the pace of Bible translation or the pace of literacy training determine with whom we will seek to sow the good seed of the gospel. We will sow it orally in the heart language through chronological Bible storying and seek to encourage those won to Christ to do the same. We support providing literacy training for those who want it but refuse to embrace any ministry approach that is dependent on literacy." Among the Klem tribe in sub-Sahara 75% of the illiterates expressed no interest in learning to read. "We have anecdotal reports, however, that literacy enrollment tripled in the aftermath of the introduction of storying"(Lovejoy 2000:10).

In their classic description of the ministry to oral people, "Making Disciples of Oral Learners," presented to the Lausanne Committee for World Evangelism, Avery Wills and Steve Evans clarified this misconception of the exaggerated value of, and exclusive use of, CBS with this statement:

> This [CBS] does not mean that we discourage literacy or neglect literates. Experience shows that once oral learners accept the gospel, some will have the desire and persistence to become literate in order to read the Bible for themselves. The development of oral strategies is not a deterrent to translating the Bible into every language. In fact, the opposite is true. These burgeoning church planting movements that result from an oral proclamation will need the whole counsel of God. Requiring non-Christians to learn to read just so that they can consider the Christian faith puts unnecessary obstacles in their path (Wills 2004:2-1).

They later add even more clarification in their report through their comprehensive strategy concept that includes storying and translating. After all, the only way to do storying is to learn the unreached people's language through linguistic analysis if previously unwritten, then begin Storying as soon as a Level 4 language proficiency is gained. This is the same proficiency necessary to begin translation. Thus while the translation is beginning, Storying is beginning as well. Language proficiency is imperative or misunderstandings are inevitable which could communicate false ideas unawares.

> We wish all peoples had the written translation of the Scripture in their heart language. But, for the illiterate, written Scripture is not accessible even if it is available in their own language. On the other hand, a Bible translation program that begins with the oral presentation of the Bible through storying and continues with a translation and literacy program is the most comprehensive strategy for communicating the word of God in their heart language. It offers a viable possibility of making disciples of oral learners while at the same time providing the whole counsel of God ... We do not want our call for oral approaches to be seen as setting oral and literate approaches in opposition to one another. It is not a matter of "either or," but "both and"(Wills 2004:2-2).

Conclusion

God's word has transforming impact on people's lives when we present it in ways that they can understand it. For example, missionaries worked for twenty five years with the Tiv tribe in central Nigeria and saw only twenty five baptized believers as a result. That is an average of one believer per year of ministry. Their medium of communication was preaching, which they had learned in Bible school was the proper way to evangelize.

Then some young Tiv Christians set the gospel story to musical chants, the indigenous medium of communication. Almost immediately the gospel began to spread like wildfire and soon a quarter million Tivs were worshipping Jesus. The Tivs were not as resistant as the missionaries had thought. A change in method brought abundant fruit. Prior to this the gospel had been "proclaimed," but it had not been heard! The communication strategy chosen had not spoken to the heart of the people. This story underscores that groups may not be necessarily unresponsive, but have not yet received the gospel in their learning style. Where traditional literate methods have failed to reach people, appropriate oral strategies have succeeded.(Wills 2004:2-2).

Appendix 1: Techniques for Chronological Bible Storying

How to Begin a Bible Storying Encounter

Using a pocket photo album. Some like to begin a casual conversation and then move it toward the family. The photo album is opened to show a picture of the storyer's family. After some comment the storyer mentions having another family he/she is part of. The next picture is that of one's church showing people and not just a building. Discuss what it means to have a family like this. Then mention that we are all part of a larger family which has a problem. Turn now to Adam and Eve and their disobedience and proceed through the selected pictures to the resurrection of Jesus. Then offer an opportunity to be a part of the family of Jesus which we enter through faith in him as God's provision for our "family problem"® sin.

Visiting bedside in a home or hospital. Because of the person's illness or possible short attention span this should be a very brief presentation which hits only the high spots and minimally in the Old Testament with major emphasis upon Jesus. At the conclusion offer to come again and give a more in-depth presentation when the person is stronger or if other family members desire it.

Family presentation in a home. This is a more relaxed presentation often done by women during a home visit. Many times children are present and may need to be accommodated by the choice of stories and by minimizing some of the harshness of the judgment stories. This presentation may be done by prior appointment or invitation of the family. Picture booklets or small flipcharts can be a very helpful way of illustrating the stories as they are told. Flipcharts have a disadvantage of having pictures already selected and locked into an order. Presentation books have an advantage in that picture books can be cut up so that individual pictures may be selected and arranged in the desired order. That way the presentation can be edited by adding pictures or deleting pictures according to the stories being used.

Using a preaching poster. This approach works well for a small public gathering and can be set up in a moment by hanging the chart on some handy projection and beginning the story. It takes advantage of the elements of surprise and curiosity. One such poster is "The Origin & Destiny of Man" which depicts the Bible story in seven pages. (See Visual Resource List at end.)

No visual, just telling the story. The best way to get into such an opportunity is by asking questions related to origins of man and the nature of man. The objective is to raise sensitivity and to create an atmosphere of curiosity and conjecture into which the storyer says there are some stories which speak to those very questions, and then proceeds to begin the Bible story, expanding where necessary, and skipping over parts to keep the narrative lively and moving toward the story of Jesus.

Keep the storying on a win/win basis. Try not to get involved in a debate with the listeners. If you are challenged at some point in the story, tell the listeners that is what God had recorded in the Bible. And you are not free to change the story. In some circumstances you may need to let some with strong objection have an opportunity to tell their story after you finish yours. You will need to trust the power of God's Word over the word and account of man.

If questions do arise and can be answered briefly you may choose to do so. Beware of people with "pet" questions. Others may ask questions in an attempt to demonstrate what they know about the Bible. Try to overlook these or simply thank the person and continue on. Sometime you can answer a sincere question with reference to another story, hopefully one that has already been covered (Terry 1999).

Bringing Closure to Your Bible Storying Strategy

Simple invitation. The simplest invitation at the conclusion of your storying is to invite people to believe on this Jesus and what he has done on their behalf. Whether this is understandable or an acceptable practice will need to be informed by local missionaries or evangelists. Usually foreigners can do things the local leaders cannot easily do or would feel uncomfortable doing. Be careful that any positive response such as a raised hand or verbal acknowledgement is not simply a desire to keep a good relationship with the foreigner. It would be good to have people tell why they are responding that way—to verbalize their sinful condition and desire to believe that Jesus died for their sins.

The one-on-one presentation is the easiest to bring closure as the invitation can be personalized and extended as needed. A tract that summarizes the major points of the story in a narrative form may be helpful if the people are literate. A picture tract can be helpful for non-literates to cue them to remember the stories.

Invitation to talk one-by-one. This is an invitation to a less public time when a more intimate presentation of the invitation to believe is given. Circumstances will dictate when best to do this. The seekers in the group are invited to come to you to express their response to the story of Jesus. Ask if you can go to their home to talk with the family about the story and what they should do after hearing it.

When a public response is not possible or difficult for seekers. This is particularly a problem for women in Muslim lands and common among young people in many places. One possibility for an invitation is for a "silent heart" response in which the women or young people in their own hearts decide what they must do. They can be led to pray a silent prayer to acknowledge their belief on Jesus, to receive forgiveness of sin, and to be filled with assurance of the Spirit, resulting in joy and peace. Signaling their response before others is the problem. Others have invited women to respond by writing on a piece of paper and giving it privately to the storyer, or in whispering to the storyer their response. Prayer is offered for all the women and for God's protection and blessing of those believing on Jesus. Again, be sensitive to local practice and advice of those who live and work there.

Invitation to view Jesus Film. This is a way of preparing a people for the visualized story of Jesus in which the whole group sees the story together and are challenged to believe on Jesus in the story review at the close of the film.

Public invitation by storyer or evangelist. This is the most open way to for a people to acknowledge their belief in Jesus, hopefully as a result of expressing their sinful condition before a righteous God and their helplessness to save themselves from God's wrath. Follow the culturally acceptable pattern.

Your own favorite invitation or closure. You may have your own favorite invitation or closure to a presentation of the gospel. Check with a local pastor or missionary to see if it is culturally acceptable and not likely to be misunderstood by the listeners. Some use the Gospel Bridge picture or a variation of it.

Immediate affirmation of new believers. It is essential to immediately affirm new believers by going back over the key stories:

- mankind's broken relationship with God due to sin,
- God's judgment of sin,
- the substitute sacrifice,
- the covering sacrifice of blood,
- the promise of one who would suffer for our sins, and
- the death and resurrection of Jesus, or
- using affirming scriptures which show they have made the right decision according to God's Word.

Pray with the believers, one-by-one if possible, for the whole group as an alternative. Ask God to strengthen each one and to protect them from Satan's attack (Terry 1999).

Training Storying Workers

Experience has proven that a first time through the stories for training workers will mainly disciple them and clarify many questions they have about their own salvation and why it was necessary. A second and third time through the stories, if done as a continuous training session, may be needed to get them equipped. One of the best training schemes is to have a potential worker with you as a helper. Teach them the story lesson before going to do it with the target group. Gradually increase their participation in the lesson until they are ready to do the story itself. Experience with tribal leaders has found they readily pick up the stories and can retell them. They may not do as well with a guided discussion that has a lot of structure. Periodic refreshing of Bible stories in camps and special sessions is helpful.(Terry 1999).

The integration of audio-visuals and storytelling with literacy can be very motivating in communities traditionally resistant to the written form of their language or indifferent to reading.

The majority of this course has been designed for non-literates, people of cultures where books are not necessarily valued and where important information is passed orally from one person to another. However, this lesson is included in order to give the church planter and church developer an opportunity to promote the written "lord of God and introduce literacy when it is appropriate in the community in which he is working. We must always have a leader who can read the Word to others as we were admonished in 1 Timothy 4:13. " Until I come devote yourself to the public reading of the Scripture, to preaching and to teaching."

In promoting oral strategies we must not overlook those who have a desire to learn to read and those who can already read to some degree but need to build fluency. We attempt here to provide some practical ideas on using media and storytelling to introduce print, provide practice for semi-literates and motivate non-reading cultures toward the printed word.

The integration of audiovisuals and storytelling with literacy can be very motivating in communities traditionally resistant to the written form of their language or indifferent to reading. Even in largely literate societies the use of read -along audiocassettes and video versions of stories have gained great popularity.

We should take advantage of the high interest in pictures, cassettes and video to present the message or story and then introduce the printed form afterwards. This is considerably more motivating and effective than literacy classes based exclusively on written text. Remember that literacy can be taught in classes and workshops or woven into church, Bible Study or Sunday School activities.

Oral and visual media linked to literacy classes have proven effective in different contexts. Here are some examples:

After live storytelling, the story can then be used to develop a literacy lesson.(Terry 1999).

To develop reading fluency for new readers:

1. Present story in oral form.
2. Retell the story or have participants retell the story in their own words.

Use pictures to enhance retelling (if available).
3. Discuss the story. With text in front of students (preferably in large letter format) encourage recall and comprehension through questions or clarification.
4. Discuss the application of the story to our lives or the Biblical principle of the story.
5. Look at text verse by verse. Read verse while students look at text or play the audio tape. Ask students to identify key words or phrases within the verse. Show words or sentences on cardboard strips. Ask them to point to certain words within the text.
6. Read a sentence aloud and have students read the last word in the sentence together aloud. Repeat process reading several verses.
7. Have students read a verse silently and then answer a question about the verse.
8. Have certain students read the parts of one character in the story or the narrator. (Readers' Theater) This will be enhanced if you can use repeating patterns. We should take advantage of the high interest in pictures, cassettes and video to present the message or story and then introduce the printed form afterwards. This is considerably more motivating and effective than literacy classes based exclusively on written text.

We should take advantage of the high interest in pictures, cassettes and video to present the message or story and then introduce the printed form afterwards. This is considerably more motivating and effective than literacy classes based exclusively on written text (Terry 1999).

Steps for Using a Story as an Introduction to Print (pre-literacy)

1. Present story in oral form (audio, video or live storytelling).
2. Retell the story or have participants retell the story in their own words. Use pictures to enhance retelling (if available).
3. Discuss the story. Encourage recall and comprehension through questions or clarification. Enhance interest in the story by bringing the audience's experience somehow into the story.
4. Read the story aloud from the Bible or play it on a tape.
5. Talk about key characters, animals, or objects in the story. Present these nouns on word cards in very large print.
6. Use word cards in conjunction with pictures. Use word cards to introduce letters of the alphabet. Use a different color marker for the letter you wish to emphasize or for the initial letter of the word.
7. Bring meaning to the printed words by going back to the story and text (Terry 1999).

Appendix 2

LIST OF VISUAL RESOURCES

"Telling the Story." Color chronological Bible teaching pictures. 105 picture set includes Acts. 40 Picture set includes basic evangelistic pictures.
    Church Strengthening Ministry
    P.O. Box 2656 Makati Central Post Office
    1266 Makati City
    Metro Manila, PHILIPPINES
    Fax 63-2-512-1499
    e-mail: csm@i-manila.com.ph

"Telling the Story." Color chronological Bible teaching pictures. Same as above but laminated for greater durability. Also CD-ROM of color and b/w teaching pictures. Ask for catalog.
    New Tribes Mission
    1000 E. First Street
    Sanford, FL 322771-1487
    Tel 407-323-3430
    e-mail bookstore_hq@ntm.org

"Look, Listen & Live" Eight chronologically arranged flipcharts of color pictures—five OT story sets, 2 sets of Jesus, 1 Acts
    Language Recordings International
    P.O.Box 40181
    Pasadena, CA 91114
    Tel 250-0207
    Fax 250-0136

"Jim & Jane Meet Jesus" Felt set for evangelistic presentations
    Marie Achill
    Christian Felts Company
    15306 Ashburton
    Houston, TX 77040
    Tel 713-466-0073

Betty Lukens, Bible in Felt (600 piece felt set, manual for 150 stories)
  Mardel Christian Education Office Supply or Chinese Baptist Press
    1444 240 Penn Park Blvd. 322 Prince Edward Road West
    Oklahoma City, OK 73159 Kowloon, HONG KONG
    Tel 405-681-1444 fax 852-2336-4186
    Fax 405-681-7392

"The Origin & Destiny of Man" preaching poster (Bible story in seven pages)
    Kannok (OMF Publishers)
        1694/1 Prachasongkhro Road
        Huay Kwang, Bangkok 10400
        THAILAND
        Fax 662-275-2800

The New "Panorama" Bible Study Course No. 1 "The Plan of the Ages"
(Color timeline chart with 11-page synopsis of Bible story.)
    Fleming H. Revell Company
    Old Tappan
    New Jersey

Retrieved 8/3/07 from
www.chronologicalbiblestorying.com/short cbs_short_11.htm

Appendix 3 Bibliography of Resources

Storytelling

Building on Firm Foundations. Chapters 5 & 6 (NOTE: other chapters of book not to be counted as collateral reading) McIlwain, 1987. (*Chronological approach*).
Handbook for Story Tellers. Bauer, 1977.
How To Read the Bible as Literature. Ryken, 1994.
Look What Happened to the Frog: Storytelling in Education. Cooper and Collins, 1992.
Mission On the Way. Chapter 2. VanEngen, 1996. *(Overview of narrative theology)*
Passing the Baton. Chapter 11. Steffen, 1993. (*Chronological approach*)
Reconnecting God's Story to Ministry, Steffen, 1996. (*textbook used in previous semesters*)
Reconnecting God's Story to Ministry, Steffen, 2005 2nd edition
Religious Education Through Story Telling. Cather, 1925 (*old book but has some relevant material for today*).
Story as a Way of Knowing. Bradt, 1997
Story Telling – It's Easy. Barrett, 1960.
Storytelling in Religious Education. Shaw, 1999 (*this is not written from an evangelical, conservative viewpoint*)
"*The Art of Storytelling: Easy Steps to Presenting an Unforgettable Story.*" J. Walsh, 2003. (class textbook, 2004 & 2005)
The Power of Story, Ford, 1994
The Story Teller in Religious Education: How to Tell Stories to Children and Young People. Brown, 1951. (*another older text but has some good information*).
The Use of the Story in Religious Education. Eggleston, 1920.
The World of Storytelling. Pellowski, 1990.
Understanding Folk Religion: A Christian response to popular beliefs and practices. Chapter 10 "Sacred Myths." Heibert, Shaw & Tienou., 1999.

Article

* "Don't Show the 'Jesus' Film..." Steffen, *EMQ,* July 1993.
* "Place, Movement and Gesture in Biblical Storytelling." D. Dewey (*available from Dewey's website –* **www.angelfire.com**/ny2/DennisDewey/Gesture.txt)
"Telling gospel as story opens Muslim ears." Craig Bird, *PULSE,* July 21, 1995.
"I Am Writing Blindly." Roger Rosenblatt, *TIME,* November 6, 2000 (*one page article based on message found in sunken Russian submarine*)
"Storying the Storybook to Tribals: A Philippines perspective of the chronological teaching model." Steffen, *International Journal of Frontier Missions,* Vol 12:2 April-June 1995, pp 99-104.

Sampling: Books / articles related to Postmodernism & Orality
"Chronological Bible Storying in Light of Post Modern Worldview." Johnson, H. (n.d.). available at Strategy Resources for Effective Communication of the Gospel website (see website listing for address).
"Making disciples by sacred story." (Feb. 2004). *Christianity Today*.
"Ministry to Millennials." (n.d.) available: **www.alliance-youth.com**/pdf/millennials.pdf
"Orality: The next wave of mission advance." (Jan/Feb 2004). *Mission Frontiers*.
"Poetry, Singing, and Context." (Oct. 2001). *Missiology: An international review* (Vol. 24, 4) pp. 475-487.
DAWN Report, December 2003, Issue No. 52 (issue dedicated to storytelling)
Friends: How to Evangelize Generation X. Moore, 1997.
Generating Hope: A Strategy for Reaching The Postmodern Generation. Long, 1997.
GenXers After God: Helping a Generation Pursue Jesus. Hahn & Verhaagen, 1998.
Jesus For a New Generation. K. Ford, 1995.
The Gospel According to Generation X. Lewis, Dodd, and Tippens, 1995.

WEBSITES with Links and Resources
Chronological Bible: **www.ChronologicalBibleStorying.com**
Dennis Dewey (Christian storyteller): **www. dennisdewey.org**
Epic Partners International (Campus Crusade, Southern Baptist, Wycliffe, Seed Company, & YWAM): **www. EpicPartners.org**
Following Jesus – **Making Disciples of Oral Learners**: **www.FJseries.org**
Lausanne Committee on World Evangelization: "Report from the LCWE Issue Group" #IG25, "**Making Disciples of Oral learners**"; this has an annotated resource list; **www.lausanne.org**/Brix?pageID=13890
National Storytelling Network: **www. storynet.org**
Network of Biblical Storytellers: **www. nobs.org**
New Way – (media in missions; articles, links, resources on orality and more): **www.newwway.org**
Oral Bible Network: **www. OralBible.com**
Strategy Resources for Effective Communication of the Gospel: **www.communication-strategy.net**/synapse/documents/Files_public.cfm?website=communication-strategy.net
  Click "World of Orality"; Power point and Workbook
William Wilder (Christian storyteller, has visited TFC): **www. williamwilder.com**